"I must warn you," she said, a wry smile curving her lips, "attempts to intimidate me usually have precisely the opposite effect. You won't frighten me away."

Thorne realized he was beginning to enjoy himself. Certainly he no longer wanted to drive her away. Instead he wondered if he could persuade her to stay. "In that case, you are welcome to join me. But you have on far too many clothes. You would be far more comfortable without your gown."

Her eyes widened at his brazen suggestion. He'd often been accused of having a wicked sense of humor, yet suddenly she was no longer amused. She lifted her chin again, eyeing him coolly.

The directness in her gaze, in her stance, was challenge incarnate. And he could never resist a challenge. Especially not from a woman so alluring as this one.

He took the final step toward her, so their bodies almost touched. It startled him, how badly he wanted her. He couldn't remember ever being this aroused this swiftly. . . .

By Nicole Jordan

Paradise Series:
MASTER OF TEMPTATION
LORD OF SEDUCTION

Notorious Series:
THE SEDUCTION
THE PASSION
DESIRE
ECSTASY
THE PRINCE OF PLEASURE

Other Novels:
THE LOVER

LORD OF SEDUCTION

NICOLE JORDAN

BALLANTINE BOOKS • NEW YORK

A Ballantine Book
Published by The Random House Publishing Group

www.ballantinebooks.com

ISBN 0-345-46785-X

Manufactured in the United States of America

First Edition: December 2004

OPM   9   8   7   6   5   4   3   2   1

To my terrific agent, Karen Solem,
for all you are and all you do.
A million thanks.

Prologue

〜〜ⵣ ⵣ〜

The passion in her kiss caught him off guard. Christopher, Viscount Thorne, braced himself as his mistress clung tightly to him, her fingers twining sensuously in his hair, her mouth trying to devour his.

Moments before, he'd been admitted by a servant to the elegant little house in St. John's Wood and shown upstairs to the parlor that he'd recently refurbished for Rosamond at significant expense. But he barely had time to shed his greatcoat before she threw herself at him with a breathy little sigh.

"At last," she'd exclaimed, pressing her lips hotly against his.

Thorne couldn't quite understand her lust. As kisses went, this one was hungry and eager, tasting of urgent need, almost of desperation. He had significant expertise arousing a woman's body, but he'd done nothing yet to elicit such a fervent response. He'd had only to cup Rosamond's luscious breasts to evoke soft little moans of pleasure from her.

Gingerly pulling her hands from his hair, Thorne drew back to study his mistress of two months. She was a creature of remarkable beauty, with translucent skin, large blue eyes, and a petite but magnificently shaped figure. Her blond tresses, several shades lighter than his own hair's gold hue, spilled over her shoulders in sensual disarray, as if she'd just arisen from her bed and intended to return there as soon as she could lure him to join her. Her careless coiffure and diaphanous dressing gown—open to the waist to expose her ripe, rose-tipped breasts—were clearly calculated to arouse any hot-blooded male.

"Your eagerness is flattering, darling," Thorne admonished, "but there is no need for such haste. We have the entire night."

"I know, but I don't want to waste a moment of it. Come, my lord, please. . . ."

Eagerly Rosamond took his hand and led him into the adjacent perfumed bedchamber. Candlelight filled the room with a golden glow, while a fire blazed in the hearth, illuminating the pale silken sheets of the enormous bed.

Thorne permitted Rosamond to guide him to the bed and press him back so that he was half-sitting, half-leaning against the high mattress. With a graceful shrug then, she slid her dressing gown off her shoulders and down her hips so that the garment pooled on the carpet, baring her voluptuous body to his heated gaze.

Thorne felt his loins throb.

When she knelt before him, he concluded that she meant to attend him while he was still fully clothed. But he let Rosamond have her way with him . . . watching indulgently as she unfastened the front placket of his satin evening breeches, then his drawers, so that his rigid erection sprang free.

Her warm fingers curved around the base of his pulsing arousal, and he felt all the muscles in his body tighten. Then, squeezing his swollen sacs, Rosamond ran her tongue around the engorged tip of his phallus, tracing the sensitive ridge, and a delicious shock flared through Thorne.

His hand moved to her fair hair, and he shut his eyes at the burgeoning pleasure. Eventually she drew him fully into her open mouth, welcoming him gladly, sucking and licking and teasing the thick shaft. Stifling a groan, Thorne gave himself up to her expert ministrations and the ravishing delight she offered.

It was several moments more before he realized that the soft sounds coming from Rosamond's own throat were not moans but quiet little sobs.

She was weeping—and not with passion.

Bewildered, Thorne opened his eyes to stare down at the beauty kneeling between his spread thighs. His lovemaking frequently made women sob with ecstasy, but obviously something else was the matter here.

Catching Rosamond's wrists to stop her, he drew her to her feet. Her pale cheeks were streaked with tears, while her huge blue eyes shimmered with a disturbing sadness.

"Tell me what is wrong, sweetheart," he said gently.

"Forgive me, my lord. I am overwrought." She brushed at her streaming eyes. "The thought of never kissing you again, never making love to you again, makes me weep."

"I beg your pardon?" Thorne murmured, not certain he had heard correctly.

"This will be our last night together," she said sorrowfully.

He felt the heat of passion start to fade. "Pray tell me why you think so."

"Your father says you mean to offer for a bride any day now."

Mention of his illustrious father definitely cooled Thorne's ardor. The Duke of Redcliffe had long tried to rule his life and, in recent years, had schemed and plotted to get him respectably married. Indeed, avoiding his father's machinations had become a game of sorts.

"You never told me you planned to wed," Rosamond added with a pout of her lush lips.

Thorne felt the hardness of his erection fade altogether. "Possibly," he replied, releasing her wrists, "because I have no intention of shackling myself with chains of matrimony."

"Your father says differently."

"I'm certain he does," Thorne said dryly, torn between amusement and exasperation at his noble father.

"I do understand the ways of the quality," Rosamond declared. "You are a duke's only son and heir, and Redcliffe craves seeing you settled with a proper wife and a son of your own to carry on the title. Furthermore, he wants no impediments to your securing a distinguished bride, and the wealthy young lady he has chosen for you has grave objections to you flaunting your mistresses. At least, that is what his grace told me."

"I assure you," Thorne vowed in clipped tones, "I will never marry my father's choice of a bride."

"Even so, this must be farewell between us. . . ." Tears welled in Rosamond's eyes again. "I have agreed to your father's terms."

"Terms?"

"Redcliffe offered me his patronage," she confessed. "He promised to secure me a leading role in the opera if I break off my liaison with you."

"My father *bribed* you?" Thorne's eyebrows shot up as he debated whether to laugh or curse. His father had never gone so far as to interfere directly in his amorous affairs before, but this was a devilish intrusion—bribing his mistress to leave his protection in order to clear the way for his marriage to a wealthy, well-born debutante.

Thorne bit off an oath, promising to deliver a few select words to his sire when next they met.

"It is not precisely a bribe," Rosamond objected. "And it is for your own sake more than mine."

"You may spare me your concern, love," Thorne replied, his drawl languid.

She bit her lip, evidently realizing the hollowness of her argument. "Truly, I will miss you dreadfully, my lord. No one is as magnificent a lover as you."

"I am gratified you think so."

Rosamond peered up at him through her kohl-darkened lashes. "Are you very angry with me?"

Thorne fastened his breeches while he pondered what he felt. Admittedly his pride smarted to have his mistress choose her opera career over him. And unquestionably it stung to be outmaneuvered by his father.

He could offer Rosamond a higher bribe, no doubt, but he didn't want a mistress who was so disloyal that her allegiance could be bought—a sardonic grin touched Thorne's mouth. Rosamond's delectable charms had always been for sale to the highest bidder.

But his father had won this round of their game, he conceded, amused in spite of himself. He would regret losing Rosamond, naturally, since her amorous skills could satisfy even a man of his jaded and discriminating tastes. But he could bear the disappointment.

Summoning a smile, he ran his thumb tenderly over her lower lip. "No, I am not angry with you, love. My heart is wounded, of course, but I understand why you would favor your career over me."

"I shall return the jewelry and carriage, if you wish, since I have been with you barely two months—"

"You may keep them."

"Oh, my lord, you are so generous!" She tried to kiss him again, but Thorne grasped her naked shoulders to hold her away.

"I promise to vacate this house next week," Rosamond offered magnanimously.

"There is no rush. At the moment I have no candidates in mind to replace you."

"But I will need to live closer to the Opera in any case."

"How remiss of me not to perceive your needs," Thorne observed wryly.

"Thank you for being so understanding, my lord. . . . But please, won't you stay the night? I had intended to make this an occasion you would long remember."

With a reluctant glance at her luscious nude body, Thorne shook his head. "I think not, sweetheart."

Reaching for him again, Rosamond gave him one last, clinging kiss, until he gently pried her hands away.

Leaving her sobbing anew, Thorne made his way downstairs and collected his greatcoat, then let himself out the rear door, heading toward the mews behind the house.

Since he'd planned to stay the evening, his horses had already been stabled, and he had to rouse his coachman from a pleasant game of draughts in order to ready his carriage.

Waiting in the frigid night air, Thorne stamped his feet against the cold. This was the harshest winter in memory, and he found himself longing for the golden warmth of Cyrene—the small island in the western Mediterranean where he spent several months of each year. He would have made his home there permanently had not many of his missions required his presence in England.

Oddly enough, he had his father to thank for the drastic change in his fate. Years ago his outrageous behavior so provoked his illustrious sire that Thorne was banished to the Isle of Cyrene, where he was given the chance to redeem himself. He'd joined the secret society of protectors headquartered there—the Guardians of the Sword. The order had been formed centuries ago with the purpose of rooting out evil and tyranny across Europe, its members sworn to uphold the ancient ideals once championed by a legendary leader.

Thorne had not only developed a passion for the golden island, but his recklessness and his love of danger had proved assets in his new career, and he'd become a highly effective Guardian. He had continued, however, to be at odds with his ducal father—despite the affection they bore for each other—since he refused to tame his wild ways.

Watching as his team was harnessed, Thorne recalled the conversation they'd had just last month when the duke called him on the carpet for partaking in a duel.

"Fiend seize it, son, you and your rakehell friends are the scourge of London society. One day you will try my patience too far!"

"I thought I already had," Thorne replied lazily, discretion forbidding him to explain that the duel had been a calculated step in his current covert assignment.

Since the French Revolution, his father had known the secret order existed, for the Guardians had rescued several of his noble relations from *Madame Guillotine*. Redcliffe had been a willing financial contributor ever since, but wasn't privy to any real knowledge about the organization. And Thorne was prevented by his sworn oath of allegiance from divulging any details about his missions, even to his own flesh and blood.

In obvious irritation, the duke narrowed his penetrating hazel eyes. "I suppose you won't be satisfied until you prove the death of me."

His father greatly exaggerated, Thorne knew. Gossip contended that Redcliffe had been just as wild in his own youth. Everyone said father and son were much alike, both in appearance and personality—tall, tawny-haired, with chiseled, square-jawed features and a natural, roguish charm they'd each wielded practically from the cradle. But a lifelong career in politics had sobered the duke to the point of blandness, and since he'd become a member of the Cabinet several years ago, Redcliffe had been doggedly determined to see Thorne wed.

"No, sir," Thorne countered his father's claim honestly. "I would greatly regret your death."

"Then settle down, Christopher. It is long past time for you to take a bride."

Remembering now, Thorne shook his head. He was a man of passion, restless and hot-blooded, and the eligible specimens of brides offered for his consideration thus far were decidedly too tame for him.

His friends claimed he had no nerves, but that wasn't true. He simply loved the thrill of danger. The challenges and risks he faced in his clandestine profession made him feel vital and alive, while pitting his wits and skills against a worthy opponent was more exhilarating even than carnal pleasure.

He enjoyed the chase, not being the prey himself . . . as he was in the game of matrimony. Long before he reached manhood, he'd been pursued for his face and fortune and title—by frivolous young debs and pretty, grasping widows eager to ensnare him in their marriage nets. He'd grown adept at eluding their pursuit over the years, although defying his father's designs took more finesse.

For that, Thorne owed his late mother a debt of gratitude. The duchess had left him her sizable fortune specifically so he wouldn't be obliged to remain beneath the duke's controlling thumb.

Thorne had no desire for a marriage like the one his parents had known—an alliance of social and political convenience—because it had been so completely dull and ordinary. If he ever did marry, it sure as the devil wouldn't be to a milquetoast miss his father chose for him, but to a woman with the courage and passion to be a Guardian's life mate.

A woman who could prove his match.

He would never settle for less.

Nor would he tamely acquiesce simply to satisfy the duke's political ambitions and late-born sense of propriety. Understandably his father worried that he wouldn't live long enough to provide a successor to the dukedom. Yet, Thorne rationalized, it would hardly be fair to offer marriage to an unsuspecting gentlewoman when he might not survive one of his missions.

Someday, in the distant future, he would be obliged to sire an heir to carry on the title. But *he* would be the one to decide when that day came. And who his bride would be.

Meanwhile, he fully intended to enjoy his bachelorhood along with his "rakehell friends," and to continue to pursue his frequently dangerous occupation as a Guardian.

Just then his groom held open the door to his town coach for him.

"Home, my lord?" his coachman queried.

The question reminded Thorne that he had just been rejected by his mistress. Rejection was a novel experience for him. Usually he could have any woman he wanted.

"No, not home. Take me to Madam Venus's club."

Climbing inside, he sank back against the velvet squabs. Venus's sin club on Mount Street was part gaming hell, part high-class brothel. There he could find delectable female companionship if it suited his mood, or a high-stakes game of faro or hazard amid excellent company. A number of his friends regularly patronized Venus's establishment, all wellborn hellraisers—as his father would dub them.

One of his closest friends, Nathaniel Lunsford, was a fellow Guardian. Nathaniel had intended to call at Venus's club later this evening, Thorne recalled. He himself had declined, for he'd expected to spend the entire night in the silken arms of his beautiful—now former—mistress.

Wincing at the memory, Thorne settled in for the half-hour drive, focusing primarily on cooling the savage ache in his loins that the lovely Rosamond had intentionally aroused, curse her.

By the time his carriage came to a halt, Thorne had himself well under control. Soft lights shone from the windows of the large mansion as he mounted the front steps, and he could hear the convivial chatter of contented guests as he was admitted by a hulking brute of a footman.

Venus's nightly soirees were famous for their superb wines, exhilarating games of chance, and titillating sexual indulgences, but she employed several ruffians as bruisers to maintain order should any of her patrons become too inebriated or unruly.

The large, elegant drawing room was the center of the club's activity. One end boasted a low stage for erotic performances and an orchestra that played quietly for the benefit of the patrons who enjoyed dancing. The remainder of the room was decorated with plush brocade sofas and card tables. Additionally, Thorne knew, there were several smaller salons on this same floor for the serious gamesters, and private bedchambers above where guests could retire with their chosen partner—or partners, in many cases.

Now, as at every other soiree, a dozen nubile, barebreasted beauties circulated the drawing room, their lips and nipples rouged provocatively, as they offered both refreshments and themselves to the gentlemen present.

Accepting a brandy but declining the carnal services, Thorne stood a moment surveying the company. There was no immediate sign of Nathaniel, nor did he see the lovely madam of the club—the statuesque, flame-haired Venus.

Hearing his name hailed, he advanced toward one of the card tables.

"Hah! You owe me twenty guineas, Hastings!" a seated gentleman proclaimed. "I told you he would show."

"My dear Boothe," Lord Hastings drawled. "The wager was whether Thorne would concede victory to his illustrious papa. So tell us, Kit, did La Rose refuse you her favors?"

Technically Rosamond had done just the opposite tonight, but Thorne didn't intend to mince words. Instead he flashed a self-mocking grin, admitting his defeat. "Sadly lowering, isn't it?"

"And you did nothing to fight back?"

Evidently word had already gotten around about his father's latest attempt to force his hand. Not only had the duke bribed his mistress, he had also spread the tale about town—and his friends meant to rag him about it.

"I fear not," Thorne replied. "It would have required too much effort."

Drawing up a chair, he joined the table, even though he had no particular desire for cards at present. For the next round, he pretended an interest in the play while conversation flowed around him:

"His grace won't win in the end. Thorne has slipped out of more marriage traps than an eel out of nets."

"Never knew a gentleman so wary of getting leg-shackled as you, Thorne. The married state ain't so bad."

"Might as well give in gracefully. Redcliffe has deep enough pockets to buy off all your mistresses from now to eternity."

"Know what you should do, old trout? Take refuge on your island. Foil your sire's damnable plots. He cannot reach you there."

"I might consider that," Thorne said with all sincerity.

A moment later he felt a light touch on his shoulder. He looked up to find the strikingly beautiful Madam Venus gazing down at him with a sympathetic smile.

Bending low, she murmured in his ear, using the sultry voice that had won her legions of admirers. "How very tiresome of his grace to insist that you take a bride. He should know that you are not a man to find wedlock appealing."

"Indeed," Thorne agreed, although realizing her attempt to soothe his wounded vanity was merely the savvy strategy of a woman who understood how to make men dance to her tune.

Venus drew a finger along his jawline in a caress meant to be arousing, while her voice dropped to a whisper. "I have just the perfect consolation for you, my lord. A sensual experience guaranteed to make you forget Rosamond Dixon."

Feeling the spontaneous response of his body, Thorne had no need to wonder how Venus had made such a great success of her sin club. She made a man feel like a king and a panting slave at the same time.

He supposed she was offering him one or more of her *filles de joie,* since Venus rarely consorted with her clientele. But the beauties she employed would be talented enough to ease his male ache until he settled on another mistress, Thorne reflected.

"I could be persuaded, my lovely Venus," he began. Just then a commotion sounded above the genial din of the drawing room, and he heard someone shout his name.

"Thorne! Are you here? Thorne!"

He glanced beyond Venus to see a young gentleman pushing his way through the crowd, and recognized Laurence Carstairs, one of his longtime acquaintances. Laurence prided himself on being a fashionable buck, but just now his cravat was askew, and he was breathing hard, as if he'd run some distance.

"Thorne, you need to come at once!" Grief shone in his eyes. "It's Nathaniel. . . . He has been . . . He . . ."

"Take a breath, man, and tell me what happened. What about Nathaniel?"

"He is . . . merciful God . . . Nate is dead."

Not comprehending at first, Thorne simply stared. Yet he felt Venus's fingers clench on his shoulder, and a brief upward glance showed that her face had drained of all color.

It must be some mistake, he thought, dazed. His friend could not possibly have been killed.

"Dead?" Thorne repeated in a hoarse voice that sounded nothing like his own.

"Knifed . . . in the ribs. In an alley off St. James Street." Laurence's voice cracked in a sob. "Robbed, most likely. His body lies there still. I summoned the Watch . . . but Thorne, you should come."

"Yes," he muttered, staggering to his feet.

Blood rushed to his head so swiftly that for an instant he feared he might pass out. He felt Venus's fingers clutch his elbow, whether to offer support or to ease her own dizziness, he couldn't say.

In a stupor, he brushed off her grasp and turned blindly to follow Laurence from the club.

The frigid night air instantly pierced the elegant superfine of his cutaway evening coat, yet Thorne scarcely noticed the cold as they hastened along the dim streets toward nearby Mayfair. A half dozen blocks later, Laurence turned off St. James and into a dark, grimy alley.

His heart pounding, Thorne involuntarily slowed his footsteps. The alley reeked of slops and refuse, but his inability to breathe had nothing to do with the stench.

Ahead he could see the flickering glow of an oil lamp held aloft, while several bystanders hovered near a supine figure.

Even as his mind rebelled, he forced himself to move closer, till he stood over the body. He had no difficulty recognizing his friend's features.

Shock buffeting him, Thorne sank to his knees.

Nathaniel's evening cloak was open, as was his black coat and brocade waistcoat. His white shirt-front was dark with blood.

With shaking fingers, Thorne reached down to touch the side of Nate's throat.

" 'Is purse is gone, guv'nor," someone muttered.

His pulse is gone, as well.

God in heaven. Nathaniel looked so damned peaceful, as if he were merely sleeping off a night of too much carousing, as he had so many times in their younger days when they had sown their wild oats together.

Thorne felt anguish rip though him. His hands balled into fists, while a cry welled up in his throat, threatening to choke him. Nathaniel was truly gone.

"Whot should we do with the body, guv'nor?"

Thorne couldn't answer.

He felt Laurence kneel beside him, heard the man's ragged voice. "His family will have to be told. God . . . his sister will be devastated."

Numbly Thorne nodded. Nathaniel had left behind a younger sister and a female cousin, he remembered.

Just now, however, he couldn't contemplate the future or consider the family Nathaniel had left behind. He couldn't think of anyone else's pain, for at the moment, his own grief felt too great to bear.

One

She wished she could paint him. His nude body was beautiful, set against the backdrop of a turquoise sea.

Feeling her pulse leap, Diana Sheridan stared transfixed at the breathtaking sight as Christopher Thorne rose from the gently foaming waves.

The sun-drenched cove below the bluffs was one of many small bays and inlets secreted along the island's rugged, picturesque shoreline. The scene would make a magnificent landscape on canvas, Diana well knew. The golden line of sand dotted with palms . . . the white, rocky promontory stretching to meet the sparkling, endless Mediterranean beyond . . . dazzled in the sunlight. But it was the man's virile form glistening with seawater that most captured her attention.

She wet her dry lips.

She had seen Lord Thorne only once from afar, several years ago. If she'd thought him a beautiful man then, she was even more captivated by his physical attributes now. Unable to help herself, Diana studied his body, admiring him from both artistic and feminine perspectives.

She had never seen a completely nude man, nor had she ever painted one. She'd trained in human anatomy and the techniques of oils by duplicating sketchings and paintings by prominent artists and by studying plaster casts of ancient statues. But canvas was still inanimate, and statues had no color, no life.

Not as this man did.

Even the great masters would have relished so vital a subject.

Admittedly she had a measure of talent, yet she wasn't certain she could do Christopher Thorne justice. If she could capture the vivid feeling of life, the play and ripple of muscle in his lean, lithe body, or the way the sun's glowing warmth caressed his skin like a lover's touch—

He looked almost leonine. His streaming wet hair was dark gold in color, while a sprinkling of hair on his powerful chest arrowed down to his groin to widen in a thicker thatch. He moved with the grace of a lion, as well, as he climbed up the narrow beach and flung himself down on a linen towel spread on the sand.

Diana stood riveted, fascinated by his body—his broad shoulders, strong back, slim hips, tight buttocks, athletic flanks. . . .

Her heart was beating far too rapidly, she realized, and her skin had suddenly flushed. Worse, she felt an unmistakable warmth pool between her thighs at the primal sight of him.

"Don't be a fool," she suddenly muttered, scolding

herself beneath her breath. "You should know better than to allow an attractive man to affect you."

Perhaps she could blame her flush on the unfamiliar climate. It was barely mid-March, but the golden afternoon was warmer than many summer days in England. And her unsteadiness was no doubt caused by spending several weeks at sea navigating a pitching ship's deck. She'd arrived on Cyrene with her younger cousin Amy merely two hours ago, and she still hadn't properly regained her balance.

They'd traveled a great distance in search of Thorne—from London and the cold Atlantic, past the peninsula of Portugal and Spain, around Gibraltar, and another day's sail beyond the Balearic Islands of Ibiza and Mallorca and Menorca, before finally reaching Cyrene's sole harbor and colorful little seaport.

When she'd hired a carriage at the town stables and sought out Thorne's estates, they were taken to a splendid villa perched on the eastern shore of the island. His servants suggested he might be found in the cove beneath the bluffs, at the rear of the villa, so Diana left Amy to enjoy a refreshing tea while she investigated. Upon seeing a man swimming below, Diana had carefully negotiated the steps carved into the rock. But when she reached the beach, she was taken aback to discover him nude.

No doubt she should have expected something so scandalous from Lord Thorne. This was the charmingly wicked nobleman she had heard so much about over the years—both from her cousin Nathaniel and from the scandal sheets. By all reports, Thorne was a rebel: wild and reckless and totally unconventional.

It was no surprise that he was one of England's most eligible and unattainable catches. He bore the title of viscount, as well as being heir to a dukedom. And his fortune was said to be substantial, even without the prospect of one day inheriting his father's vast estates.

After seeing him now, however, Diana could understand better why he was considered a devil with women: because he was so sinfully beautiful. But she'd fallen in love with a beautiful face before, a disastrous mistake that had led to her social ruin.

"Confound him, don't you dare allow his looks to addle your wits," Diana chastised herself.

Trying to regain control of her senses, she remained in the shadow of the bluff as she debated whether to leave or to make herself known to Thorne.

She needed to speak to him alone, the sooner the better, for he had been awarded guardianship of Nathaniel's younger sister, Amy. At nineteen, Amy was now an heiress and, as such, was the target of numerous fortune-hunters and rakes bent on seduction.

Nathaniel's will hadn't surprised Diana, for Thorne was his longtime friend, and women were rarely appointed legal guardians. Besides, in society's eyes, her own single state, as well as the scandal in her past, precluded her from making a proper steward for her flighty young cousin.

But a man like Lord Thorne was hardly a suitable guardian either, even if he *had* made Nathaniel a promise to look after his sister.

Diana was very protective of her spoiled but basically lovable younger cousin. At her uncle's passing several years ago, she'd taken over raising the girl, while her cousin Nathaniel assumed legal guardianship. Yet the responsibility she felt was based as much on affection as on moral duty or the ties of blood. She loved Amy dearly, like a sister or even a daughter.

And now she was the only family Amy had left . . . and Amy was hers.

Since Nathaniel's shocking death, they'd both spent the past year in mourning for him, quietly living in the country. But such a tranquil life had made Amy highly susceptible to male attention and flattery, and now she fancied herself in love with the handsome fortune-hunter who'd begun to pursue her over the Christmas season.

Diana was determined to prevent the girl from making the same ruinous mistake she had once made. To stop Amy from being so badly hurt, the way she had been.

If it meant dealing with the devilish Lord Thorne, Diana would do it.

She certainly wouldn't allow his rakish reputation to intimidate her—for the sake of her own pride if nothing else. She'd vowed she was through hiding herself away. No longer would she voluntarily be held back because of her dubious past. Nor would she willingly suffer any more of society's punishment.

She was starting an entirely new life of independence, Diana reminded herself. Indeed, this was the first test of the first real freedom she'd ever had.

She had never expected to visit such a glorious island as Cyrene. The golden sunlight, the fresh, salty sea breeze, the magnificent vista, all were completely foreign to her. Faith, she'd never been to the seashore before this. Since being orphaned at age seven, she'd spent most of her life at her uncle's country estate in Derbyshire.

Diana squared her shoulders. She didn't intend to let any man, wicked or not, beautiful or not, naked or not, drive her back into her shell.

Summoning her courage, she took a deep breath,

raised her muslin skirts to keep them from dragging in the sand, and stepped forward into the sunlight.

He knew he was being watched.

A sixth sense alerting him to danger, Thorne glanced covertly at his pile of clothing, assuring himself that the dagger he usually carried was close to hand.

Pretending to keep his eyes shut, he stretched languidly and rolled over onto his back, so that he could glimpse the intruder who was now moving toward him.

The watcher wore skirts.

What the devil was a woman doing down here in his private cove? And a lady, by the looks of her attire.

Irritation was Thorne's first automatic response. The last genteel female to unexpectedly see him in the buff had tried to trap him into wedlock.

In fact, that lamentable incident was what had driven him to take refuge on Cyrene for the past two months. At a house party in the English countryside in January, a calculating young debutante had sneaked into his bedchamber while he slept and was caught naked with him by her avaricious mother.

Feigning shock, Mama had immediately petitioned his ducal father, insisting that Thorne be forced to marry the girl. Redcliffe contended that he should do the honorable thing and accept his fate, but innocent of seducing the little schemer, Thorne had refused to be dishonorably trapped in marriage. As soon as he concluded his current assignment for the Guardians, he'd sailed for Cyrene to escape their connivances and his father's hounding.

Highly suspicious now, Thorne peered through his

lowered eyelids at the interloper. She had stopped a short distance away—the moment he'd rolled over, in fact—and was staring at him as if fascinated.

If she was a blasted husband-hunter, he would send her packing. And if not . . .

He couldn't deny that she was a beauty, with her delicate, fine-boned face, flawless ivory skin, and nicely curved body. Her high-waisted muslin gown of dark blue flattered her slender, shapely figure and firm, high breasts, and sent an immediate shaft of awareness lancing through his loins.

She looked, however, to be a bit older than the usual debs who pursued him, perhaps in her mid-twenties. She wore her rich dark hair pinned up in a simple knot, Thorne noted, and her eyes, which were just as dark and lustrous, held awe and curiosity as she surveyed him.

Deliberately he opened his own eyes fully and locked gazes with her.

The impact made him feel an instantaneous heat—an involuntary physical response that came as a sweet, if unwelcome, shock.

She felt the same sweet shock, he was certain. She had stiffened, looking wary and unsettled now, as if all her feminine instincts were on keen alert. Just as all his male instincts had suddenly roared to vibrant life.

To Thorne's further irritation, he could feel himself hardening. It was difficult to remain unmoved, though, when a lovely young woman was contemplating his body so intently.

Cursing his swelling erection, Thorne pushed himself up on one elbow. "Do you realize you are trespassing on private land?"

"Your servants said I might find you here."

Her low, husky voice sent a further charge of heat along his nerve endings. "Did my father send you?" he demanded. "If so, then pray let me inform you that I have no intention of wedding you."

She blinked at that. "I beg your pardon?"

"The last young lady to see me nude claimed I compromised her and insisted that I wed her. If that is your aim, sweeting, you can turn around at once and take yourself away."

He watched as her sensual mouth thinned in a wry smile. "I promise you, my lord, you are safe with me. I have no interest in marriage whatsoever."

Her claim reassured him to a degree, yet Thorne couldn't let himself relax. "You obviously have an interest in my body."

Color rose in her cheeks, and she looked flustered to be caught ogling him. "Forgive me. I was contemplating you with an artist's eye . . . trying to determine how I would paint you."

Thorne's lips curved in a sardonic grin. "Now *that* is a novel tactic no one has ever used on me before."

Her chin lifted with a trace of defiance. "I am perfectly serious. I am an artist."

He regarded her for a long moment. "If that's true, then I suppose I should be flattered by your attention."

"It *is* true. You would make an admirable subject for a portrait."

"Is that all? You see me as one of your subjects?" He arched a taunting eyebrow. "You don't feel the slightest urges beyond the artistic?"

"I regret to disappoint you, but no, my interest in your male anatomy is purely objective."

"How lowering. I am mortally wounded."

Her wry smile held genuine humor this time. "I

should think you would be pleased. By all reports, you have an army of eager females fawning all over you."

"A regiment, at the very least," Thorne drawled, feigning a shudder. "And all with matrimony in mind."

"But you have no desire to be leg-shackled," she said in understanding as she took a step toward him. "Well, you can rest easy, my lord. I have no intention of wedding anyone, most certainly not a man of your rakish reputation."

"I am hardly a rake."

"If you were a gentleman"—she gave his lower body a pointed glance—"you would cover yourself."

Realizing his manhood was fully erect now, Thorne reached for his shirt. "I confess that a beautiful woman staring at my loins has an arousing effect."

The flush in her cheeks fascinated him. In truth, *she* fascinated him. From her bold appraisal, he had to conclude that she was no meek-mannered miss. Nothing like the chaste, featherheaded young innocents who often pursued him. If he hadn't sent her scurrying away in fright by now, she had to have some measure of experience. An enticing thought, Thorne reflected.

Draping the shirt around his hips, he tied the sleeves together and rose to his feet. "Better?"

"Yes . . . I think so."

"I *am* a gentleman, you know—although my father would sometimes dispute it. What of you?" His gaze slid down her body. "Most ladies would think twice before coming to a secluded cove where a strange man was sea-bathing in the nude."

Her eyes kindled a little at that. "Of course I am a lady."

"Yet you come here alone, and you don't shy from the sight of me."

"I wished to speak to you in private. And I must warn you, attempts to intimidate me usually have precisely the opposite effect. You won't frighten me away."

Thorne realized he was beginning to enjoy himself. Certainly he no longer wanted to drive her away. Instead he wondered if he could persuade her to stay. "In that case, you are welcome to join me. But you have on far too many clothes. You would be far more comfortable without your gown."

Her eyes widened at his brazen suggestion.

"Wouldn't you care to take a swim?" he pressed, moving toward her. "The water is a bit cool but invigorating."

"I don't know how to swim."

"I would be delighted to teach you."

With an unwilling smile, she shook her head sadly. "I should have known the tales I've heard about you are true. You are indeed a seasoned rake."

"Oh, no," he murmured, halting before her. "If I were truly a rake, I would take advantage of having a beautiful woman alone and try to steal a kiss from her."

He'd often been accused of having a wicked sense of humor, so he wasn't surprised that his brazenness didn't appear to shock her. Yet suddenly she was no longer amused. She lifted her chin again, eyeing him coolly.

The directness in her gaze, in her stance, was challenge incarnate. And he could never resist a challenge. Especially not from a woman so alluring as this one.

Her lips were temptingly close and perfectly shaped, while all his senses avidly relayed the fact that she was lushly curved in all the right places. He wanted to draw her down into the sand with him and slowly strip her gown from her body, exploring those sweet curves with his hands and mouth. . . .

A jolt of pure desire sizzled through Thorne at the prospect.

He took the final step toward her, so their bodies almost touched. It startled him, how badly he wanted her. He couldn't remember ever being this aroused this swiftly.

Neither could Diana.

Gazing up at Thorne, she once again felt transfixed. His eyes were a stunning hazel—gold dappled with flecks of green—and deep enough to drown in.

She drew a shaky breath at his unsettling nearness. Any well-bred lady would doubtless have fled at the first sight of his nudity. But dismayingly, her strongest urge was to touch him, to see if his skin was as warm and supple as it looked. If the muscle and sinew rippling beneath the surface was as hard as she suspected. If his firm, beautiful mouth would taste as arousing as she imagined it would.

He seemed to understand her dilemma, for a beguiling hint of wickedness glimmered in those gold-green eyes as he studied her in turn. Her heart skipped a beat at the seductive sensuality she saw there.

He was near enough for her to feel his warmth. The fine cambric covering his loins was better than nothing but still was almost sheer, leaving her all too aware of his masculine attributes. She was even more disturbed by the way her body flared in response. She couldn't help feeling the power that had beguiled so many women into his arms.

Then he flashed her a slow, devastating smile that took her breath away.

Merciful heavens, he was dangerous, Diana thought, feeling slightly dazed.

That smile could prove deadly, she had no doubt, for it melted away any thought of resistance . . . as he likely intended.

When he lowered his head toward hers, she realized with a sense of shock that he intended to kiss her. His boldness caught her off guard, but she could not have moved if her life had depended on it. Instead she watched spellbound as he bent the final distance.

His breath fanned warm against her lips . . . then his mouth covered hers. At the first touch, sensation arced between them, making her pulse leap.

He kissed her as if he were sampling some exotic fruit for the first time, savoring her flavor. When unconsciously Diana parted her lips, his tongue slid inside her mouth in a sensual invasion. Another frisson of fiery sensation sparked between them as he tasted her.

His kiss was incredibly arousing, his mouth settling on hers in a more determined caress, creating an irresistible friction. When she gave a little whimper of surprise, his hand rose to cradle her jaw, his long, lean fingers holding her still for his seductive assault.

She had been kissed before—several times—by the man she had once intended to marry. Yet her former betrothed's kisses had been sweet, worshipful, as if she were made of spun glass and fragile enough to break.

This man, on the contrary, treated her like a flesh-and-blood woman. A woman he *wanted*.

Thorne angled his head and deepened his kiss, his mouth suddenly turning more demanding. Diana shivered as his tongue plunged between her lips, hot and silky. Of their own accord, her hands rose to clutch his shoulders. Beneath his golden, sun-warmed skin, she could feel the hardness of his corded muscles.

At the same time his own hands moved to her hips to pull her closer, flush against him . . . making her keenly aware of his huge phallus swelling against her stomach.

She had wondered about that hard ridge of male flesh, and now she knew. At the erotic pressure, she could feel a shameful tingling in her breasts, feel a brazen heat uncoiling between her thighs. The wanton intensity of her body's reaction startled her; the desire he stirred in her was impossible to deny.

Then his hand left her jaw and slid slowly along the column of her throat to cup her breast, and her shock deepened. Her betrothed had never touched her this way . . . exciting her, arousing her. . . .

When instinctively she arched against the alluring pressure, Thorne made a satisfied male sound low in his throat. A moment later his fingers curled over the square neckline of her gown, dipping beneath the fabric of her shift to explore the swell of her breast, finding the taut nipple.

Fire shot through her, making her knees weak.

His knuckles teased the furled bud, startling a raw moan from Diana, yet penetrating her dazed mind at the same time. She had wanted to test the boundaries of her newfound liberation, but this was beyond brazen. Their embrace had turned too passionate. . . .

With a gasp, she pushed at his bare chest and broke away.

Her breasts rose and fell rapidly as she stared at him.

For a long moment, Thorne stared back. His eyes had darkened to forest green fractured with chips of gold, while his expression had become shuttered, as if he didn't trust her or the searing flame that had momentarily kindled between them.

His voice was slightly hoarse when he finally spoke. "I was right. Your lips are every bit as inviting as they look."

No apology, no contrition at all, for his outrageous behavior, Diana realized.

Unsettled, she pressed a hand to her stomach to calm the excited flutter there and retreated a few steps, to a safer distance. It was impossible to recover her dazed senses or to quell her erratic heartbeat, but she made an effort to pretend nonchalance.

"I suppose you simply cannot help yourself, Lord Thorne. Rumor has it that you try to seduce every woman you meet."

"Only the ones who interest me." He smiled—charmingly—which only set her pulse racing harder. "I admit you interest me, sweetheart. And I expect I was driven by the island's enchantment, as well."

"Enchantment?"

"You haven't heard the legend of our island? The sun god Apollo fell in love with the nymph Cyrene, but when she spurned him, he created an island paradise here and held her captive until she came to love him in return. The spell he cast is said to uncontrollably arouse the senses of mere mortals and drive them to passion."

Diana returned a skeptical look. It was certainly true that the island's beauty stirred her blood, but she couldn't quite credit the tale of a mythical spell.

Her gaze pinned Thorne, while her mouth curved with sardonic amusement. "It sounds more as if you are exploiting a myth as a convenient excuse for your dissolute behavior."

"Perhaps so," Thorne allowed, flashing her that provocative, heart-melting grin. "We have never met before, have we, love? You must be new to Cyrene, for I know all the beauties here, and I could never have forgotten you."

"No, we have never actually met," Diana replied.

When Viscount Thorne had come to visit Nathaniel shortly after her disastrous aborted elopement, she was purposely kept out of sight because her uncle deemed Thorne a dangerous rake, and she was considered susceptible to rakes.

She hadn't attended Nathaniel's funeral last year either, since it had been held in London, several days' journey from the Lunsford country estate where she lived. And by the time she received word of her cousin's untimely death, Nathaniel had already been buried. At least Amy had been able to attend her brother's service, for the girl was in London at the time, preparing for her comeout.

Diana suspected, however, that Thorne would at least recognize her name, for she'd written to him on several occasions during the past year—although his solicitors had always handled his return correspondence with her.

"I am Nathaniel's cousin, Diana Sheridan."

At her revelation, he gave her a measuring stare. "You might have said so from the first," he said finally.

Detecting a hint of ruefulness in his tone, Diana couldn't repress a smile. "Why? Would it have prevented you from assaulting me?"

"Very likely. In all honor, I never would have touched you." Turning casually, Thorne bent to pick up the linen towel and draped it over his shoulder, so that it covered much of his bare body in the style of a toga. "My friends' sisters and cousins are off-limits, even to rakes like me."

"I am gratified to know you have *some* scruples," Diana observed dryly.

"A very few." His expression sobering, he regarded her with his penetrating gaze. "Why are you here on Cyrene?"

"Your solicitors in England informed me you could be found here. It wasn't easy persuading them to divulge your location, but I made them see the necessity, since you are Amy's legal guardian."

"And you came all this way just to speak to me?"

"I would not have been forced to such lengths had you been in London as expected. Your sudden disappearance . . . complicated matters. But then I decided to use it to Amy's benefit. Nathaniel seemed convinced you would help her if she was ever in trouble. And she is in trouble now."

"What kind of trouble?"

"It's commonly known that she is a substantial heiress. And recently a certain fortune-hunter has been courting her so earnestly, she believes herself in love. I brought her to Cyrene, primarily to escape his pursuit, in the hopes that the respite will give her a chance to get over her infatuation. I am also hoping that you can persuade her to wait until she has her Season before bestowing her affections again. Perhaps with the delay, Amy will settle on a more respectable suitor. I have had . . . difficulty, however, making her see reason."

"And you think I can?"

"She is very fond of you, at least. She might listen to you. In any event, I needed to discuss the particulars of her comeout with you."

Diana paused to let Thorne digest her disclosures.

As Amy's guardian, he had done his legal duty by the girl, although mainly he'd allowed his solicitors to deal with Amy's fortune. Yet it was time now for him to take a serious interest in his ward's future.

For the past year while Amy mourned her brother, convention required that she postpone all social functions, including her formal presentation. But she was nineteen now, past the age when young ladies usually made their bow to society.

"Her comeout?" Thorne repeated warily.

Diana nodded. "I think it would benefit her greatly if you could convince your Aunt Hennessy to sponsor Amy's Season this spring." Thorne's aunt, Lady Hennessy, was a leader of English society and, as such, stood the greatest chance of giving Amy a successful debut.

Grimacing, Thorne ran a hand roughly through his tawny wet mane. "The thought of being responsible for a girl's comeout makes me shudder. To be perfectly blunt, I never wanted the office of guardian in the first place. In fact, I'm not the best choice Nathaniel could have made."

"I fully agree," Diana said lightly, "but he trusted you to care for his sister. And your aunt could prove a major advantage to Amy's presentation to society."

"I suppose so," Thorne agreed with reluctance.

"There is one other significant reason I wanted to see you," Diana added. "To deliver a letter Nathaniel left for you."

Reaching inside her muslin sleeve, she withdrew a tightly folded sheet of vellum and handed it to Thorne. "Apparently he wrote this shortly before his death, in the event something dire should befall him."

Thorne stood staring down at the letter, at his name,

which had been written in a bold scrawl, and Diana caught the anguish in his gaze. He still grieved for his friend, she had no doubt.

She had been devastated, as well, by Nathaniel's death, for he'd been more a beloved brother than cousin to her.

"Where did you find this?" Thorne asked, his low voice almost hoarse.

"In Nathaniel's personal effects, which he had bequeathed to Amy. I discovered it when I was packing her belongings for our journey to Cyrene. A note accompanied the letter, asking Amy to forward it to you, but with her flighty nature, she must have overlooked it." Diana paused, debating how much more to say. "The letter was sealed, of course, and nearly a year old, but I opened it in case Nathaniel's message contained anything of importance."

Thorne's piercing gaze locked on her again. "And did it?"

"I believe so," Diana said with conviction. "No doubt you will prefer privacy to read it, so I shall return to your house to wait for you."

She hesitated once more, wishing she could erase that grim look from Thorne's eyes. "Perhaps we can discuss this and Amy's situation once you put on some proper clothing."

Her deliberately provoking remark managed to dredge a faint smile from him, but by the time she turned away, Thorne was already unfolding the letter, and she knew she had already been dismissed from his thoughts.

If you are reading this, old friend, then I am most likely dead.

Thorne scanned the contents swiftly, then reread every dismaying word more slowly. He could hear the thudding of his heart over the murmur of the waves as the import of Nathaniel's revelations sank in.

> *I have spent the past several days looking over my shoulder, unable to shake the sensation of being followed.*
>
> *And perhaps I am. Some weeks ago I came to suspect a traitor of attempting to expose our identities to the French, so I set about investigating. I now fear that my lovely Venus may be involved in spying for the enemy, yet I don't wish to accuse her until I have proof of my suspicions.*
>
> *Furthermore—I regret to confess to my own shame—I revealed information to her which I never should have. An egregious error, I know. And it is no excuse or consolation whatsoever that I was duped by her seductive beauty.*
>
> *But I prefer to correct my mistake before telling S. G. Thus I have been making inquiries into V's past.*
>
> *If she is indeed guilty, however, her accomplices will not be pleased by my actions and may seek to stop me. In the event of my untimely death, I want you to have a path to follow, old chap. Thus I shall leave this letter for my sister to deliver, for I know you will carry on if I should fail.*

The letter was signed merely with a scrawling *N*.

Lifting his gaze, Thorne stared unseeingly out at the aquamarine sea, a turmoil of emotion churning inside him like acid: guilt, anger, self-castigation. He hadn't known a thing about Nathaniel's investigation. Not even the slightest hint.

He had no trouble deciphering the cryptic references in the message, of course. "Our identities" meant the sixty-odd Guardians who operated clandestinely in Britain and across Europe. And the initials S. G. referred to their remarkable leader, Sir Gawain Olwen. Nathaniel wouldn't refer to the order by name when anyone, his sister or cousin included, could stumble across his missive. The Guardians of the Sword worked in secret for a reason—because their effectiveness would greatly diminish if they could no longer execute their missions in the shadows.

Yet if Nathaniel had let slip key intelligence to Madam Venus, he would be reluctant to confess his sin to Sir Gawain before trying to rectify it.

A harsh invective escaped Thorne's lips. He understood why Nathaniel would want to keep such a damning miscalculation secret from him. But his own obtuseness was inexcusable—for not suspecting his friend's murder might have been caused for more sinister reasons.

How could he have been so blind? At the time, Nathaniel's death had been ruled a random robbery by the authorities . . . a wealthy mark forced into an alley and knifed for his purse. Thorne hadn't understood how a Guardian of Nathaniel's fighting skills had allowed himself to be taken unaware. But a weeklong exhaustive search of the surrounding district had turned up no witnesses or suspects or leads to his killer, or any alternative theories regarding motive.

Now, however, it seemed far more likely Nathaniel had been murdered to silence his investigation of a traitor.

Thorne bowed his head as guilt washed over him anew. *He* had been the one to recruit Nathaniel into the Guardians in the first place. And now his friend was likely dead as a result.

Involuntarily Thorne clenched his fist around the letter as he silently made a solemn vow.

He would unearth the traitor Nathaniel had been seeking, but more crucially, he would find his friend's killer or die trying.

Two

"So *did* you see Thorne?" Amy demanded when Diana found her in a guest bedchamber upstairs.

Diana had difficulty repressing a smile at the question. She had indeed seen Thorne. In fact, she'd received a significant eyeful of him. "I found him on the beach."

"What did he say? Did he agree to ask his aunt to sponsor my comeout?"

"He didn't refuse outright, but we had little chance to discuss it, since he was engaged in swimming. But I expect he will return to the house shortly."

Amy's mouth turned down in a pout. She was a vivacious, strikingly pretty girl, with lively blue eyes and pert blond curls cut short in the current fashion. But she could be unattractively stubborn when she chose. She made no secret of her eagerness to move to London under the auspices of Thorne's aunt, for she longed to escape Diana's control.

Diana watched, unsurprised, as her cousin began to pace the room restlessly.

"I wish he would come," Amy complained. "I am

going mad after so many weeks at sea with nothing to do."

"Why don't you change into your riding habit? I expect Thorne will readily lend you a mount from his stables."

Amy brightened instantly. She was a bruising rider, having grown up in the country in a family of horse enthusiasts. Diana herself rode more sedately but was just as accomplished, for after being banished from society, she'd spent countless hours in the saddle roaming the environs of the Lunsford estate. For the past six years, riding and her art had been her only real diversions.

"That is a famous idea," Amy exclaimed. "Do you wish to go with me?"

After enduring the confinement of their voyage, Diana would have greatly enjoyed the freedom and exercise of a ride and a chance to explore the beautiful island, but she was more interested in getting Amy's future settled. "I think I will wait for Thorne to return. No doubt he can spare a groom to accompany you."

Amy offered her a smile that held a hint of bitterness. "Are you certain you trust me to go off with a strange man? You aren't concerned I might throw myself into his arms?"

Diana forced herself not to retort. Over the past few months she had become quite adept at weathering Amy's dramatics, and knew that treading lightly was the best way to deal with her cousin's resentment at being thwarted in love.

"I imagine Thorne's servants can be counted on to behave with discretion, even if you cannot," she replied dryly. "Moreover, if you were to throw yourself at one of them, you would only make Thorne think twice about inflicting you on his aunt for an entire season."

Amy scowled much like a frustrated child rather than the grown young lady she was. Admittedly she'd been spoiled more than a little by her doting family and was accustomed to having her way, but Diana was willing to make allowances, especially during the past difficult year. Amy's grief at losing her brother only a few years after losing her father was understandable.

Diana not only shared her cousin's grief, but knew all too well what it was to be an orphan. She also knew what it was to be desperately in love, although she was certain Amy's present ardor was no more than a severe case of infatuation.

She could have predicted the girl's response, though, and wasn't disappointed: Amy's chin rose belligerently. "I won't change my mind about Reggie, you know. No matter how long you keep me incarcerated here on this remote island."

"It is hardly incarceration. We will be returning to London in time for the start of the Season."

"Where I shall hardly be permitted a moment's freedom. You think to marry me off to some wealthy fop so your conscience will be eased."

They'd engaged in this same dispute frequently during the past month or more.

"That isn't true, Amy, and you know it."

"It is! You are afraid I will follow in your footsteps. But just because your heart was once broken by a fortune-hunter doesn't mean every man who courts me is pursuing me for my inheritance."

"No, it doesn't. But the odds are much greater that a penniless suitor is more interested in your fortune than yourself."

"Reginald loves me for myself, I tell you. And I love him!"

"Perhaps you do now. But your feelings for him may not stand the test of time. If you truly love him, delaying your courtship for a single season won't influence your affections in the end. And during your stay in London, you could meet any number of gentlemen whom you might come to love more."

"And in the meantime, I will only be miserable."

"I regret that, Amy. But being miserable now is better than being locked in a wretched marriage for the rest of your days." Diana paused, meeting her cousin's morose gaze. "It is because I want so much for you to be happy that I won't let you throw your life away as I did. I want you to be certain of your heart," she said softly. "I want you to have choices I never had. Choices I lost through my own naïveté."

For a moment Amy looked contrite, but then she tossed her head and turned away to dress.

Repressing a sigh, Diana left her cousin and went to her own adjacent bedchamber to freshen up.

Thorne's servants had been understandably wary when two strange ladies and their maid deposited themselves on his lordship's doorstep. But Thorne's valet had recognized Amy from her visits to London, and he'd ordered their bags taken upstairs to their rooms.

Entering, Diana glanced approvingly around her. The chamber was bright and airy and elegant, with tall French doors leading to an outer gallery that wrapped around much of the house. Thorne's magnificent villa, Diana knew, was built in the Spanish style of a great hacienda, boasting four galleried wings constructed around an open central courtyard.

The Lunsford manor in Derbyshire was grand, but nothing so luxurious as this.

Lured by the splendor of the view, Diana stepped out onto the gallery to watch the sparkling, azure Mediterranean. When hunger pangs finally reminded her that she had missed tea, she reluctantly returned inside to wash and to tidy her hair—a much easier task than usual. Her fingers were normally smeared with paint or ink, but she hadn't picked up a brush or pen since the previous day on board the schooner.

This morning she had simply allowed herself to take in the incredible sights of the island: the rugged coastline protected by jagged cliffs and dangerous reefs; the fortresses and watchtowers overlooking the many small bays and inlets; the gentle hills and forested mountain peaks; the prosperous valleys ripe with orchards and vineyards and olive groves; and finally the secluded cove below Thorne's villa. The jeweled colors of the sea—emerald and sapphire and turquoise—framing a magnificent, golden man.

Her fingers itched now to put all that she had seen on paper or canvas, but her artistic urges would have to wait, Diana thought regretfully.

The moment she descended the sweeping staircase to the grand entrance hall, she encountered Thorne's butler, who offered to serve her tea in the courtyard. At her ready acceptance, he showed her along a corridor to another set of French doors, these opening into the large interior square at the heart of the villa.

The courtyard was a place of beauty, Diana saw, rippling with sunlight yet shaded by feathery palm trees and sweetened by a profusion of flowers and vines—bougainvillea, hibiscus, oleander, geraniums. In the center, a lively marble fountain played a cheerful melody.

A tea table was set up in one corner, and Diana had barely been seated when several liveried footmen brought her tea and scones and finger sandwiches, plus a pitcher of fruit juice, which the butler informed her was a mixture of pomegranate, orange, and peach.

Diana sat back, enjoying the novel taste as much as the blissful moment. It was difficult to remember that snow still covered the ground when they had left England three weeks ago.

She was unaware that she had shut her eyes until she heard an amused masculine voice break the peaceful silence.

"I am gratified to see you making yourself at home, Miss Sheridan."

Steeling herself for another lethal assault on her senses, Diana opened her eyes to find Thorne standing before her. He wore boots and breeches now, and a cambric shirt open at the neck. Below the strong column of his throat, she could see the fine golden hairs of his chest. Involuntarily her gaze swept downward again, following the tapering line of his torso to his loins.

Flushing at the brazen images branded on her memory, Diana tore her gaze away and glanced up at Thorne's face—which was her second mistake.

His fair hair had dried to a tousled mass of gold, and a few errant locks spilled carelessly over his forehead, as if he'd just risen from his bed. His sensual mouth was curved in a lazy smile that instantly set her heart aflutter, while his stunning, long-lashed hazel eyes glimmered with the frank interest that had held her riveted on the beach.

He was gorgeous and fascinating, a lethal combination, Diana warned herself.

When she realized she was staring again, she muttered a silent oath and sat upright. Thorne was studying her in turn, no longer dismissing her as he had when she'd given him Nathaniel's letter.

Unsettled by his blatant assessment, Diana took a sip of juice and cleared her throat. "I apologize for invading your privacy earlier, my lord. I should have waited for a more opportune moment."

"I'm not sorry," Thorne remarked easily as he seated himself across the table from her. "Now that we have become so . . . intimately acquainted, we needn't stand on ceremony. After all, you are cousin to my ward, which I presume makes us some sort of relation."

He poured himself a tall glass of juice, then returned his gaze to Diana. "Nathaniel told me a bit about you, but he didn't say you were a beauty."

Her lips twisted wryly. "Just how am I supposed to respond to such a bold remark? If I demur, then I will seem coy, yet if I agree, I will only appear vain. But perhaps that is your aim—to render me speechless."

His brilliant grin flashed in appreciation. "A pity you are wise to my tactics." Thorne regarded her over the rim of his glass. "I confess I have been curious about you, Miss Sheridan. I've known the Lunsford family since my university days when I developed a friendship with Nathaniel, but I never met you. You lived at Lunsford Hall all that time?"

"Yes. My uncle and aunt took me in when I was a child, after my parents died in a carriage accident."

"But you seem to have hidden yourself away like a hermit. You never accompanied your cousins to London? I believe they came each Season even after Mrs. Lunsford passed away, what, some eight years ago?"

Diana felt herself stiffen at the probing question.

She had always accompanied the family to London, until her fateful Season when she had disgraced herself. Doubtless Thorne had heard about her notorious past, even if he wasn't aware of the details, but she felt a grave reluctance to discuss it further. "I prefer the country to London."

"I believe you were ill the one time I visited the Hall."

That was one deception she had no reason to perpetuate. "I was not ill," Diana replied with exaggerated sweetness. "My uncle simply didn't wish me to meet you. Your reputation preceded you."

Thorne's eyebrow arched. "Yet I was permitted to socialize with Amy."

"At her young age, she wasn't considered vulnerable to rakes."

"Ah, there is that erroneous term again."

"You cannot deny you are renowned for scandal, Lord Thorne."

"I don't intend to," he said, his irreverent smile showing again. "But in my own defense, I'll wager that fully half the tales you hear about me are false."

Diana suspected there was some truth to his denial. Nathaniel, who had been an excellent judge of character, had considered this man to be his closest friend, so Thorne could not be *dreadfully* wicked. And she knew that with her own dubious past, she could hardly throw stones at him. Yet she couldn't exonerate him so easily.

"I doubt you are as innocent as you claim. If your normal conduct is half so outrageous as it was with me on the beach a short while ago, it is no wonder you find yourself the subject of lurid tales."

He refused to take offense, merely regarded her evenly. "Yet you bear some measure of blame in that instance, my sweet. I would never have considered you so ripe for a kiss if not for your fascination with my body."

Having just raised her glass to her lips to drink, Diana choked on her juice. Coughing, she covered her mouth with her hand and sent him a darkling glance.

Thorne's bland look held supreme innocence, yet the wicked sparkle in his eyes suggested he had meant to unbalance her.

Managing to regain her composure, Diana adopted a mild tone. "I think you delight in being provoking."

"Yes," he replied without apology. "However, I *am* aware of the bounds of proper conduct. I don't regret kissing you, but I would have refrained had I known your identity. I was entirely serious when I said I follow a gentleman's code of honor."

Diana tended to believe him, although she was certain it was Thorne's own particular definition of honor that he followed and no one else's.

"As for avoiding scandal," he added, "if you are to remain in my house, I intend to hire a chaperone to live here for the duration of your stay. Two young ladies alone in a notorious bachelor's establishment will provide ready fodder for gossip, and I want no scandal attached to my ward's name."

Without pause then, he changed the subject. "So tell me about this bounder who is pursuing Amy."

"I'm not certain he is a bounder," Diana replied. "Merely that he is most likely a fortune-hunter. His name is Reginald Kneighly. Do you know him?"

She saw Thorne's brows draw together. "We have a slight acquaintance. He's something of a gamester, and his pockets are frequently empty."

Diana nodded. "Mr. Kneighly has distant relatives in Derbyshire and first appeared there at Christmas, apparently to escape his creditors. He began wooing Amy without my knowledge, and they went to great lengths to keep their liaison secret, no doubt because she knew how I would respond." Diana winced at the memory. "I should have suspected sooner, but by the time I discovered their deception, it was too late. Amy already believed herself to be in love."

Thorne grimaced, expressing Diana's sentiments exactly.

"I thought it imperative to get her away from him at once," she went on. "I would have taken her to London, but you had disappeared. And since the Season doesn't start until mid-April, I brought her here."

"But you plan to launch her this spring?"

"She missed her comeout last year because she was in mourning for Nathaniel, so it is beyond time. I thought a Season would both take Amy's mind off her infatuation and give her the opportunity to develop an affection for someone more suitable. My hope is that she will find a husband who will love her for herself, not for her money. If she can make a love match or at least marry a man who will care for her and protect her, then she won't be so vulnerable to fortune-hunters. Or to rakes bent on seduction." This last with a pointed glance at Thorne.

He ignored Diana's gibe and cut straight to the heart of the matter. "What is it specifically you want of me?"

"To persuade your Aunt Hennessy to sponsor her."

"You cannot serve that office?"

Diana shook her head. She not only held no position in society, but a cloud of scandal still lingered over her. And her tarnished reputation would only be a detriment to Amy's chances for a good match. "I have neither the consequence nor the connections your aunt does. And you yourself are hardly the appropriate choice to bring her out. There is already enough question about the propriety of you being Amy's guardian."

A glimmer of humor appeared in his eyes again. "Quite true."

"There is one other advantage to my proposal. You may not be aware of it, but Amy went to boarding school with your cousin Cecily, who will be having her comeout this spring under Lady Hennessy's sponsorship. Sharing a Season with Cecily will provide Amy the companionship of someone closer to her own age, and with more similar interests than mine."

Thorne steepled his fingers thoughtfully. "I admit it would be a relief to get Amy settled. I've always been fond of her, and I want to honor my duty to Nathaniel. Certainly I want to protect her from a fortune-hunter."

"Then you will petition your aunt in her behalf?"

"I wish to speak to Amy first, to judge the situation for myself."

"By all means." Diana smiled ruefully. "You will find her attitude rather . . . rebellious. She is still furious at me for stopping her budding affair."

"I can only imagine," Thorne replied, his tone sardonic. "But you were right to bring her here."

Just then Amy entered the courtyard and exclaimed in delight when she saw him. "Thorne!"

When he rose to his feet to greet her, she launched herself at him, laughing. Thorne allowed her to kiss his cheek but then pried her fingers away from his neck and held her at arm's length.

"Hello, bratling," he said fondly.

Her blue eyes sparkled as she gazed up at him.

"You cannot call me brat any longer, for I am all grown up now."

"Yes, I can see you've become quite a beauty."

"Indeed, I have." She twirled around for him proudly, showing off her velvet riding habit, then flung herself in a chair, not even waiting for Thorne to resume his own seat before continuing.

"I am so glad to see you, Thorne—*and* your beautiful island. I have longed to visit here, ever since you told me about Cyrene and its marvelous legends."

Diana winced inwardly. She had practically had to browbeat Amy to get her on board the packet ship. But she was pleased to see the girl respond so easily to Thorne. They obviously had a teasing, comfortable friendship, and it would do Amy good to have an older male figure to take the place of her late brother.

"So, Diana has spoken to you?" Amy pressed. "Will you ask your aunt?"

"Your cousin spoke to me, yes, and I have agreed to consider the proposal."

"Thorne . . . *please?*" Amy leaned forward, touching his arm and giving him a pleading smile.

Thorne seemed unswayed. "You may bat your eyelashes all you want, minx, but more devious females than you have tried to wrap me around their fingers and failed. I said I will consider it."

"Well, I hope you do it soon. You cannot know how miserable I have been, living in the country this past year, away from London and all of my friends. And Diana has become such a dragon of late. It will be so much more pleasant having my Season with your aunt and your cousin Cecily. I doubt Lady Hennessy will hover over me the way Diana does now, watching my every step."

"If you think that, brat, you don't know my Aunt Hennessy."

Amy started to pout, but then apparently changed her mind. "It is not solely for my benefit that I ask, but Diana's, as well. She won't mind turning me over to your aunt. In truth, Diana is eager to wash her hands of me so she can pursue her art career."

"Amy," Diana said sharply. "I most certainly do not want to wash my hands of you."

Amy turned innocent eyes to her. "But if you are accepted into the academy, you will have no time for me. You know it."

"Academy?" Thorne asked curiously.

Diana was the one to reply. "I may have a chance to train at the British Academy for the Fine Arts."

"That is the rival to the Royal Academy of Art, isn't it?"

"Yes."

"It would be a great honor for her to be accepted," Amy interjected. "They have never before admitted a female artist. But Diana is rightly concerned that the scandal in her past will present too great an obstacle."

When Thorne raised an eyebrow, Diana felt herself flushing. Knowing his penetrating gaze was raking her again, she busied herself pouring a cup of tea, while Amy whispered to him in a confidential undervoice:

"Diana is considered something of a scarlet lady. It is because of the scandal that she cannot sponsor me. And why she is acting so vengeful now. She was once jilted by a fortune-hunter, so she considers all men to be fortune-hunters."

"*Amy,*" Diana said in a quelling tone, "you will give Thorne a disgust of your manners."

Thorne eyed his ward lazily. "Indeed, brat. You've made me realize the grave injustice I did you by not beating you more often during your youth."

His low drawl made Amy laugh. "You never beat me."

"But I might start if you don't stubble your gossiping tongue and apologize to your cousin."

Her smile fading, she eyed him as if wondering whether to take his threat seriously. But then she mumbled a grudging apology. "Pray forgive me, Diana. I didn't mean to be so beastly."

"You're forgiven," Diana replied, amazed that the girl had capitulated so swiftly.

"Why don't you take yourself off, minx," Thorne suggested, "while I speak further with your cousin?"

"Oh, very well . . . if you permit me to ride one of your horses."

"That I can agree to. Go apply to my head groom for a mount. I trust you with my horseflesh, if not the reins of my curricle. On horseback you aren't likely to wind up in a ditch as you did when I attempted to teach you to drive."

"Oh, Thorne, it was not entirely my fault that your fractious team shied at that farm dray. And I have become a much better driver since then—"

"I'm not about to risk my fine steeds to find out. You will have to satisfy yourself with riding. But I purchased several Arab mares recently that will be ideal for you, and they could certainly use the exercise."

"Arabians? Famous!" With a brilliant smile, Amy bounded out of her seat and kissed Thorne soundly on the cheek again before he waved her off. She was humming as she skipped away.

It warmed Diana's heart to see her cousin so carefree. When she caught Thorne watching her, she voiced the thought. "I haven't seen her this lighthearted since Nathaniel died. Bringing her here may be just the thing to divert her from her thwarted romance."

Thorne's mouth pursed in a sour expression. "I see your dilemma. Her beauty combined with her significant fortune would make her prime prey for a fortune-hunter. Her personality, however, isn't quite as sweet as I remember."

"She is merely frustrated."

His gaze skimmed her face. "I hope you will expound on her comment about you, my dear dragon. I knew there was some difficulty in your past, but not the particulars."

Diana made a careless attempt at a smile. She was under no obligation to explain herself to Thorne, yet she found she wanted him to understand.

"Part of Amy's claim is true," she said, keeping her tone light. "I was jilted because I wasn't an heiress. He overestimated the size of my fortune and underestimated my uncle's protectiveness."

"And now you're concerned Amy is making the same mistake you made, falling in love with a fortune-hunter." It was not a question, and Diana knew he didn't expect an answer. "I take it your scandal happened a number of years ago?" Thorne added.

"Yes. During my London Season. I was eighteen, a year younger than Amy is now." Diana glanced down at her clasped hands, remembering. She couldn't look back on that painful time without feeling the devastation of her broken heart. She couldn't deny, either, that Amy's similar love affair had reopened old wounds and made her relive her own past hurts.

"I fell madly in love with a gentleman," she confessed. "An artist like myself. The match would not have been inappropriate, since he was titled, but his pockets were not very deep, so my Uncle Basil refused to consider his suit. That was when I agreed to an elopement."

She laughed softly. "I am ashamed to admit it, but I was totally fooled. He had the soul of an artist and the tongue of a poet, and I was blind to the practical realities of life." Her voice lowered a register, and she averted her gaze, focusing on a nearby blossom of bougainvillea. "I thought we would have a wonderful future together, earning our fame and fortune with our art. I would have lived in a garret attic had he asked. But he had loftier plans for us. He thought he could force my uncle to relent once we were wed."

"So you eloped to Scotland?" Thorne asked.

"We attempted to. But our hired carriage broke down barely a day outside London, which allowed my Uncle Basil to catch up with us. When Uncle vowed he wouldn't release my modest inheritance until I was twenty-one, my suitor abruptly cried off, pleading debts that couldn't wait. I was brought home in disgrace." Her mouth curled with wry bitterness. "As you can imagine, I was considered a fallen woman after that."

Bracing herself, she lifted a defiant gaze to meet Thorne's, intending to reject his scorn or pity if he offered either. But his eyes held neither, only curiosity and perhaps sympathy.

"Well," Diana muttered in a lame tone, "you can see how inappropriate it would be for me to sponsor Amy."

Thorne nodded. "Yet if Nathaniel intended for her to have her comeout last year, he must have planned some kind of suitable arrangement."

"He meant to hire a respectable widow to act as Amy's chaperone—one of our neighbors in Derbyshire, in fact—but she has since passed away."

After another moment, Thorne nodded again. "And this artistic opportunity you spoke of?"

Diana was glad for the change of subject. "I have been invited to interview with the president of the British Academy when I am next in London."

"I try to attend the Royal Academy exhibition each year. And my father is one of their patrons. But I'm not very familiar with this newer academy."

"It was established some years ago as a backlash against the rigid conservatism of the Royal Academy. But neither has yet to accept any women into its classes."

"You must be extremely talented if they are considering your application. Is your expertise in landscapes or portraitures?"

"I enjoy both. And presently I work almost exclusively with oils."

"That is an unusual medium for a female, isn't it?"

Diana smiled. "Indeed. Normally girls are permitted to draw and dabble in watercolors only. But my uncle recognized my odd passion when I was quite young and was kind enough to hire a drawing master who taught me rudimentary oils. And in the past few years, I have trained with an elderly artist who retired near Lunsford Hall."

"And you mean to earn fame and fortune with your art? Somehow you don't strike me as the sort who would paint simply for the income."

"I don't need the income, since my inheritance is adequate for my needs. But of course I would like to sell my work, for it would be a measure of my skills. And while my paintings do very well locally, London is a vastly different market. Training at the academy would gain my work wider acceptance."

"And would allow you to take control of your future," Thorne observed in a thoughtful tone.

Diana felt her eyes widen. It amazed her that he understood the driving force behind her ambition.

After her uncle died when she was twenty-one, she had indeed decided to take control of her future and follow her dream to live her life as an artist. She'd found a mentor who helped mold and polish her talent, but when she outgrew his ability to instruct her, he had advocated her move to London.

The notion had held enormous appeal to Diana. Earning the respect of the art world as a renowned artist would give her the kind of freedom she had never before enjoyed. And for the first time since her aborted elopement, she had a goal that excited her.

She intended to start a new life for herself, where she no longer had to bow to society's dictates.

But she didn't want Thorne to think her dreams were more important to her than Amy's future.

"I assure you," she said finally, "that my career is secondary to Amy's needs. I have no intention of abandoning her—but it would clearly be better for her if I remained in the background."

Thorne was studying her intently, with something akin to admiration in his eyes. "You are very unique in my experience, Miss Sheridan," he said softly.

Diana felt herself flush, certain he intended his remark as a compliment and wasn't merely trying to provoke her again. "Would you care for tea, my lord?"

Without waiting for an answer, she made a show of pouring him a cup and adding sugar and cream.

Thorne watched her distracted movements, admiring the delicate flush on her cheeks. He hadn't lied when he'd termed Diana Sheridan unique. With her passion for art and her fierce protectiveness toward her cousin, she seemed unlike most any other woman of his acquaintance.

He found her immensely intriguing—in part, he realized, because she was something of a black sheep as he was. And because she hadn't tried to deny it or make excuses for herself. Her frank confession had made him like her even more.

The tale of her scarlet past and her subsequent vulnerability had aroused all his protective instincts. It had also made him recognize that their experiences were merely opposite sides of the same coin: She had been jilted because she wasn't an heiress, while he'd had women chasing him most of his life for his title and fortune.

Her beauty was a prime attraction, as well, he willingly admitted. Her lustrous hair was a rich brunette, but not so dark as to be called raven. He was sorely tempted to pull out the pins to see how it would look tangled after lovemaking. And he was incapable of looking at her delicious mouth without thinking of sin and sex.

In the cove earlier, he had wanted to do much more than merely kiss her—and so had she, he was certain. Too many women had arched beneath him in passion for him to mistake her response to his mouth, to his body.

Even now the lady was as aware of him as he was of her.

It was a pity she was off-limits to him, Thorne reflected. Doubtless she would be a pleasure to have in his bed. But there was no reason they couldn't enjoy a game of wits between them. She was just the sort of clever-tongued adversary he appreciated. And he would take sinful delight in testing his skills with such a lovely opponent. He suspected she could hold her own with him.

He didn't anticipate, however, the method she would use to abruptly steer the subject away from herself.

"Did you have a chance to examine Nathaniel's letter?" Diana asked as she handed him his full cup.

Caught off guard, Thorne forced himself to drink the tea he didn't want. "I read it, yes."

"I presume you could make sense of his more cryptic remarks."

"Remarks?"

"It raises suspicions about Nathaniel's death, don't you agree? I think he must have been purposely murdered for more than just his purse."

Thorne deliberately arched an eyebrow, trying to convey skepticism. "My lovely Miss Sheridan, have you perhaps been reading too many Minerva Press novels, as Amy is so fond of doing?"

Her gaze turned cool. "*My dear Lord Thorne*, except in my art I am not given to flights of fancy. Nor am I a fool. Nathaniel was a wonderful man, and I loved him like a brother. I expect you to investigate his death further. If you do not, I assure you that I will."

Her retort made Thorne swiftly reconsider his tactics. Diana Sheridan had a sharp mind, he reflected, feeling a reluctant surge of admiration. And a strong backbone. She wouldn't be placated by some fabricated tale.

He intended to downplay her concerns, of course. He needed to be careful what he told her in order to keep the Guardians' existence a secret. But perhaps she could be trusted with a partial truth. . . .

He offered her a rueful smile. "I, too, loved Nathaniel like a brother. And I meant no insult to you by attempting to conceal his secrets. It wasn't widely known, but Nathaniel occasionally performed tasks for the British Foreign Office."

She stared at him. "Then it *is* possible his death was more than simple robbery."

"It's possible, yes. Perhaps you understand now why I cannot be more forthcoming. But you may trust me to investigate the matter fully. If Nathaniel met with foul play as the result of some sinister plot regarding his work, I promise you justice will be done."

She studied him for a long moment, her gaze troubled. "I suppose I must be satisfied with that."

"I'm afraid you must." Then, to distract her: "You haven't mentioned your suspicions to Amy, I hope."

"No, I never even showed her the contents of the letter," Diana said, still frowning. "I thought it best to wait until I had spoken to you."

"I appreciate your discretion. Now, if you will excuse me"—Thorne rose to his feet and gave her a polite bow—"I believe I will set some inquiries in motion."

He made his escape, aware that her uneasy gaze was following him all the while.

Three

As he rode through the gates of Olwen Castle a short while later, Thorne purposely tried to put Diana Sheridan out of his mind. He needed to focus on the task ahead—unearthing Nathaniel's killer and the traitor who'd sought to expose the Guardians' identities to the French.

Thorne knew he would be expected at the castle, since after reading the staggering contents of the letter, he'd immediately sent a message to Sir Gawain requesting an interview.

He hadn't exactly lied when he'd told Diana that Nathaniel worked for the British Foreign Office. That was the excuse the Guardians often used to protect their identities and to explain their clandestine activities.

Publicly Sir Gawain Olwen was thought to head a small, select branch of the Foreign Office. But few people realized the vast extent of their organization, or how deeply the Guardians permeated present British and other European society. Or knew the remarkable tale of their inception.

The Guardians of the Sword had been formed more

than a thousand years ago by a handful of Britain's most legendary warriors—outcasts who had found exile there. Now the order was run by their descendants and operated mainly across Europe, and it was headquartered at Cyrene because the location offered rapid access to parts of the Continent where crises tended to develop with alarming frequency.

Commanded by Sir Gawain, the Guardians were well connected and well financed, and they functioned something like a modern force of mercenaries—but with a higher calling: protecting the weak, the vulnerable, the deserving. Fighting tyranny. Working for the good of mankind.

For the past three decades, the order had primarily endeavored to meet the grave challenges spawned by the French Revolution and Napoleon's subsequent rush to conquer all the known world, performing missions far too difficult and dangerous for the Foreign Office to undertake.

And throughout all their perilous endeavors, they'd developed into a band of close friends and adventurers who would die for one another and for their cause.

Thorne would lay down his life for the order without hesitation, for he fiercely believed in their noble ideals. The Guardians had been his salvation. Before he'd joined, his wild, self-indulgent existence had taken him down a path of debauchery and destruction. Now the order not only filled his craving for danger and excitement, but gave him a laudable purpose in life.

It enraged him that someone would plot to destroy the Guardians, and it enraged him more that Nathaniel likely had been a target of such treachery.

But if Nathaniel had been murdered by a traitor, Thorne intended to strike back and avenge his friend's death. First, however, he needed to develop a plan of attack.

When he entered the stableyard, he immediately saw his fellow Guardian, Alex Ryder.

Tall and hard, dark haired and dark eyed, Ryder was one of the most dangerous of all their members. He'd once hired out his services as a mercenary and had since developed an unmatched expertise with weapons and explosives. Unlike Thorne, though, Ryder had grown up on Cyrene.

"So what is this about Nate leaving you a letter outlining his suspicions of a conspiracy?" Ryder asked as Thorne dismounted.

"It's true," Thorne replied. "He wrote his message more than a year ago, just before his death, but his sister failed to deliver it to me. That task fell to her cousin, Diana Sheridan."

"The two of them just arrived today?"

"Yes—quite unexpectedly."

Ryder sent him an ironic grin. "You do always seem to have a surfeit of females after you, old sport. It's as if your charm is a magnet for anything in skirts."

Thorne winced. "I would happily exchange my success for a little respite."

Turning his horse over to a groom, he made his way with Ryder through the bailey to the huge wooden entrance doors of the great hall.

Olwen Castle had been in Sir Gawain's family for centuries. Standing at the southern end of the island, where the hills were the lowest and most vulnerable to attack, the impressive stronghold was defended by massive walls and battlements bristling with cannon.

The interior was less warlike, with fine tapestries and carpets and gleaming furnishings gracing the great hall, tempering the cold stone. Numerous artifacts of a bygone era were scattered about, however—armor and weapons, swords and maces and shields, many belonging to the knights who had first settled the island more than a millennium ago.

Thorne and Ryder strode swiftly through the great hall and along a stone corridor to a large, comfortable chamber that served as the baronet's study, where an elderly gentleman sat behind his desk.

Sir Gawain rose at their entrance. Tall and lean and gravely serious, he had shrewd, light blue eyes that seemed to miss nothing. His lined face appeared strained, as if the great responsibility of leading the Guardians for two decades had taken a toll. He also limped slightly—the result of an injury during a mission long ago, Thorne knew.

"Good, you are here," Sir Gawain said, tugging the bellpull behind his desk. "Permit me to summon Yates."

They settled in comfortable chairs while they waited. Barely a moment later, a young man hobbled in on a wooden leg. John Yates was a former cavalry lieutenant who had lost a leg in the Peninsular War and who now worked as Sir Gawain's secretary and chief assistant.

Two years before, Yates had nearly died from his septic wound. Now, beneath his shock of pale blond hair, Yates's face glowed with good health. Yet his brown eyes were serious as he greeted Thorne and Ryder and seated himself.

It took Thorne only a short while to tell them how Diana Sheridan had found the letter in Amy's belongings, and then to recount the major revelations in Nathaniel's message: that Nate had come to suspect a traitor of attempting to expose the Guardians' identities to the French. And his fear that the lovely brothel madam, Venus, was involved in spying for the enemy.

To protect Nathaniel's memory, Thorne had decided to keep private Nate's confession about being duped by the beautiful Venus and his shame at revealing confidential information.

At the conclusion, Alex Ryder was the first to speak. "It seems our unfortunate Nathaniel might indeed have stumbled onto a plot to destroy our order. The French would have been keenly interested in putting an end to our existence then."

Thorne nodded. Before Napoleon's hard-won defeat last spring, the French would have been eager to stop the secret society that had played such havoc with their attempts to rule the world.

Yates's face held a reflective scowl. "That was not the only instance of someone attempting to expose the identities of the Guardians. You'll recall there was another incident last September. You weren't here at the time," he said to Thorne.

Thorne thought back to the previous fall. He and Ryder had both been absent from Cyrene on various missions when two visitors to the island, Danielle and Peter Newham, had been apprehended for stealing a membership roster of the Guardians.

"If I recall," Thorne mused, "when questioned, the Newhams confessed that they had been hired by an Englishman to discover a list of our members."

"Yes," Yates replied. "A man by the name of Thomas Forrester."

"You sent agents to investigate the Newhams' story, but the trail went nowhere?"

"It went completely cold. We discovered that Thomas Forrester did actually exist—he had been living in London—but that he had recently died in a fire."

"I find this highly interesting," Sir Gawain remarked gravely. "Two apparently separate events begin to appear related."

"Perhaps Madam Venus had some connection to this dead Englishman?" Ryder wondered aloud.

"It does seem possible," Sir Gawain replied.

"I intend to find out," Thorne said.

"And how does Nathaniel fit in?" Ryder asked. "Were Nate and Venus lovers, do you think?"

"It wouldn't surprise me," Thorne prevaricated. "Nathaniel was spending an unusual amount of time at her sin club just before his death. And his letter admitted he was investigating Venus and her involvement with French spies. He might have invited himself into her bed in order to learn whatever secrets she was hiding."

Yates was still frowning. "So what do we do now?"

"I plan to return to London very shortly," Thorne answered, "to retrace Nathaniel's steps during his final days. Meanwhile, I want to plant one of our agents in Venus's club. I thought perhaps Macky might be right for the job, since he's a former actor. With his physical attributes and thespian skills, he could play the role of cicisbeo."

Ryder raised an eyebrow. "You want Beau Macklin to get himself hired by Venus to service her wealthy female clientele?"

"Precisely."

"What a torturous assignment," Ryder observed, clearly amused.

"But potentially effective. In Venus's employ, he can keep his ear to the ground and ferret out secrets we couldn't hope to obtain otherwise."

"Agreed," Sir Gawain said, although with evident reluctance.

"Then I have your permission to commission Macky, sir?"

"Yes," Sir Gawain replied. "And you should also attempt to discover if Madam Venus has any connection to the late Thomas Forrester. Moreover, we shall need to reopen the investigation into Forrester's death, to determine why he wished to learn the Guardians' identities."

Thorne had an even broader goal in mind: to prevent any other Guardians from being killed. But he knew there was no need to state the obvious.

He also realized Sir Gawain was scrutinizing him solemnly. "You must take care, Thorne. If Nathaniel Lunsford was killed because he was growing too close to a traitor, then if you start probing, you could make yourself a target, as well. You needn't take any unnecessary risks."

"I won't take any risk that I deem unnecessary," Thorne hedged.

John Yates spoke up then. "I wish to be part of the investigation, sir."

Yates had personal reasons for wanting to be involved in solving the mystery of Nathaniel's murder, Thorne knew, yet the request clearly did not sit well with Sir Gawain.

"It will inconvenience me greatly to have my secretary absent, you know. You are more valuable to me here."

"But, sir, I was the one betrayed by Danielle Newham. I want to set things right."

Sir Gawain's pained expression faded into resignation. "Very well. I will endeavor to carry on without you." He turned to Thorne. "When do you expect to leave for England?"

"A week, perhaps. I'll need time to set up Macky's ruse. And I don't want to arrive in London just when he begins work at the club. It could too easily rouse Venus's suspicions. Also, there are a few other personal arrangements I must make first."

Out of the corner of his eye, he caught Ryder's taunting grin. "I thought," Ryder mused, "that you were rusticating here on Cyrene to escape your father's machinations. Won't he present complications if you return to London so soon?"

"Fortuitously I've thought of a plan to deal with my father."

"Oh? Would you care to elaborate?"

Thorne hooded his gaze. "Not just yet. Give me a day or two to see if I can make it work."

He first had to ascertain if Diana Sheridan would be amenable to his proposition.

His plan was not entirely selfish, for it would also benefit her. And surprisingly, Thorne found himself wanting to aid her. Perhaps his usual defenses had been weakened by the tale of her rejection by a fickle suitor, but Thorne found himself instinctively wanting to protect her. Which shouldn't amaze him. After all, he had taken a sworn oath as a protector.

At the thought of confronting the spirited Miss Sheridan with his proposal, Thorne felt the stirring of a familiar excitement. What he was considering would no doubt challenge all his powers of persuasion.

But he thrived on challenges.

And he couldn't help but reflect how damned boring his life had been of late.

*   *   *

"You wish me to do *what*?" Diana Sheridan exclaimed, staring at him as if he had lost his senses.

Thorne couldn't repress a smile. He obviously had shocked her with his proposal. Upon returning home, he'd summoned Miss Sheridan directly to the drawing room, where he poured them both a glass of sherry before making his proposition.

"I wish you to do me the honor of becoming my betrothed," he repeated quite seriously.

Her brows narrowing in a frown, she sank down distractedly onto the settee. "I did not think I could possibly have heard you correctly. Barely a few hours ago you told me in no uncertain terms that you refused to be leg-shackled."

"I still do. It would be a betrothal in name only."

She pinned him with her darkly brilliant gaze. "If you think to make me one of your conquests, Lord Thorne, simply because you learned of my notoriety, pray let me disabuse you of the notion at once."

I would very much like to make you one of my conquests, Thorne reflected silently. Diana had already dressed for dinner in a flattering, rose-colored silk gown that showed her figure to advantage, and he would like nothing more than to slowly peel it from her body and explore her charms. . . .

But he quelled the lustful urge and shook his head. "That could not be further from my intent, Miss Sheridan. On the contrary, I am throwing myself on your good graces. You would be doing me an immense service—saving me from a fate worse than death."

"Which is?"

"Wedding my father's choice of a bride."

"I think you had best explain."

Thorne settled himself in a chair opposite her,

where he could watch every nuance of her expression. "I plan to return to London very soon to look into Nathaniel's murder, just as I promised you. But to properly focus on an investigation, I need to first free myself from a distracting entanglement."

"Entanglement?"

"I believe I mentioned that the last young lady to see me nude claimed I compromised her? It was a scheme to ensnare me in wedlock, and her mother is still plaguing me, demanding that I wed the girl. And my illustrious father has taken their side."

Diana's mouth curled dryly, as if she understood his dilemma. "That would account for your sudden and unexpected disappearance from England, I suppose."

"Precisely," Thorne agreed. "My case is not quite desperate, but I anticipate difficulties if I show my face in London without some sort of defense. A betrothal would offer me shelter from their machinations. And it would put an end to my father's badgering."

Humor lit her eyes before she shook her head, whether in disbelief or exasperation, Thorne couldn't tell. "I always heard you were daring and reckless, my lord, but I think you must be a trifle mad. And I would have to be mad to accept."

He adopted a lazy smile. "In some circles, you might be considered mad to refuse. Most single ladies of my acquaintance would jump at an offer of matrimony from me. Evidently I was right. You *are* very unique, Miss Sheridan."

"Why? Because I have the good taste to prefer spinsterhood above allying myself with a rogue like you?"

"Now you wound my feelings."

"I doubt that is possible," she retorted lightly. She

shook her head again. "So you wish me to pretend to be your betrothed?"

"Yes. It would only be a temporary arrangement, of course. Once Amy is safely settled, you may cry off. That is the usual etiquette—for the lady to withdraw from the betrothal. You simply have to announce that you and I don't suit."

"That would be no falsehood," Diana muttered. "We wouldn't suit in the slightest. It strains the imagination to think I would ever accept a proposal of marriage from you."

Understanding her instinctive resistance, Thorne held up a hand. "Please, hear me out before you refuse."

Skeptically, she crossed her arms over her chest. "Very well, I am willing to listen."

"There are several advantages to both you and Amy. Not the least of which is the prestige of my family name. You intimated that your reputation is somewhat tarnished by your past elopement. I doubt I'm misjudging to suggest that a betrothal to me would make you more acceptable to society."

He could tell by the flush on her cheeks that he had struck a sensitive nerve, but even so, Diana eyed him coolly. "I have lived comfortably with the tarnish for the past six years. Why should I care if you can add a little polish?"

"Because you could keep a closer eye on Amy during her Season. You told me you intend to remain in the background for her comeout, but if you are engaged to me—and have my aunt's backing—you could both participate in social events and use your powers of persuasion to help Amy get over her infatuation. You are obviously a good influence on her, despite her current pique with you."

That gave Diana pause, he could see. "There is also the matter of your own protection," Thorne continued. "If we're to be thrown together while working in Amy's behalf, your reputation may only suffer further from your association with me. But our betrothal should stem much of the gossip and shield you from the worst suppositions."

"Possibly," she murmured, deep in thought.

"And in any case, I feel an obligation toward you. Amy is my ward. As I see it, your being her cousin makes me in some way responsible for you."

A spark of defiance lit Diana's dark eyes. "I assure you, it does *not* make you responsible, my lord. I don't require your protection. And I am perfectly capable of taking care of myself."

"I'll warrant you are," he said soothingly. "But you can't deny the benefit to Amy."

When she made no reply other than pressing her lips together, Thorne added his final argument. "I believe I could also help your chances of being accepted into the British Academy to train. I know several of the Academy's patrons and can use my connections to your benefit. By the time our betrothal ends, you will likely have established yourself in the art world."

He had expected her to be pleased by the offer, but unexpectedly, it seemed only to trouble her. Any hint of amusement left her expression. In fact, she actually grimaced.

"You realize that if I accept, I may be seen as a fortune-hunter myself. Society will assume that I trapped you into offering for me. Frankly, I can think of few things more odious than being accused of throwing myself at your head."

"But we would know the truth, wouldn't we?"

He had kept his tone light, meaning to tease her a little, but she only regarded him solemnly.

"I'm certain you have reservations, Miss Sheridan, so perhaps you would like some time to consider my proposal," Thorne offered. He glanced down at his legs, reminded that he still wore boots and breeches. "I must dress for dinner. You can give me your answer when I return."

When he stood and took his leave, Diana mutely watched him go. She sat there for a long moment, a little stunned by his proposal. Christopher Thorne had asked for her hand, not in marriage, but in a pretend betrothal.

Leaving her glass of sherry untouched, Diana rose to her feet and restlessly crossed the elegant drawing room to the French doors, which opened onto the terraced gardens. The beautiful gardens offered a magnificent view of the Mediterranean, and the setting sun had turned the sea a shimmering golden red, but Diana scarcely noticed as she stepped outside.

Of course she had reservations. Grave, numerous ones.

She cast a dark glare behind her, in the direction she had last seen Thorne. It irked her that he'd treated his offer so casually. He had thought nothing of making such an explosive proposition and then walking away, leaving her to stew.

A betrothal would scarcely affect him, after all. He was a nobleman born to privilege and power, accustomed to having his own way. He was the rakish darling of society who would forever be excused for his outrageous misdeeds.

For her, however, a betrothal would be an event of enormous magnitude.

From the countless tales she'd heard about Thorne,

she had always presumed him to be a charming rogue who viewed women as a challenge and life as a lark. Clearly he had more substance than she'd given him credit for, but his brazenness in the cove today only confirmed how dangerous he was to her.

He was sinfully beautiful, heart-stoppingly seductive, and without a doubt, she was highly vulnerable to beautiful, seductive men. She'd proved that profoundly at the tender age of eighteen with her former suitor.

Wincing at the memory, Diana found herself pacing the gardens, hardly aware of her surroundings as she pondered her dilemma. After her aunt had died, she'd been put under the lax care of a female governess-chaperone, whose negligence had made it possible for her to make the greatest mistake of her life.

She'd been heartbroken by her betrothed's betrayal, both because his pretense of loving her was false and because her dreams of living the wonderful, creative world of the artist had been so callously ended.

Certainly she had never planned to accept another proposal of marriage after that.

As for love, she was determined never to give her heart so foolishly again. After being so badly hurt, she was wary of any man who tried to woo her because she couldn't trust their motives. She refused to be any man's prey ever again. Or to be deceived and shamed so thoroughly. Spinsterhood was far preferable to risking such vulnerability.

With her modest fortune, she could doubtless find a husband, even despite her ruined reputation, but she had no desire to imprison herself in a loveless marriage simply to give herself respectability.

She had strong maternal instincts, however, and regretted that she would likely never have children of her own.

Perhaps that was why she was so protective of Amy, Diana reflected. Amy was her charge. Perhaps not legally, but in every way that counted. She loved her cousin sincerely and would do almost anything for her sake.

She had a moral duty, too. Except for her, Amy had no close family left. The Lunsfords had taken *her* in when she had been orphaned. She would never abandon Amy at this crucial time in her life.

She couldn't deny, either, wanting to be a part of Amy's comeout so she could try to provide guidance and counsel. Nor could she deny seeing the advantages Thorne had pointed out—to herself as well as to her cousin.

A betrothal would give her instant respectability. In the last year, without Nathaniel to lend her countenance and protection, more than one gentleman had considered her fair game because of her scandalous past and had made her an indecent offer.

It didn't matter that she was still a virgin and practically an innocent when it came to carnal matters. She was still considered ruined in the eyes of society.

Respectability would also benefit her artistic career, Diana knew. And she did long to be admitted into the academy, although she wanted it to be because of her talent rather than through Thorne's connections.

She had worked fiercely to become worthy of admittance. Snubbed by the local gentry since her aborted elopement, she'd lived a quiet, retiring existence, channeling her restlessness into her art, teaching herself to express her feelings in works with emotional power and beauty.

For years that had been enough. She had been fairly

content with her life. But since Nathaniel's death, she had come to know a growing dissatisfaction. The burning desire to do more. To *be* more. In the past months she had renewed her fragile dreams of becoming a renowned artist.

Yet it was the possibility of freedom that held an even greater allure. An unwed lady of doubtful reputation had few choices; a female artist seldom had opportunities to exhibit her work.

Surprisingly, Thorne had understood the unfairness of her situation, although Diana doubted he could truly know the depths of her resentment. Surely no man could comprehend what it was like for her to spend a life shackled by convention, forced to obscure her artistic skill because of her gender.

The prejudice against her would be even worse in London. Alone, she would be subjected to the numerous small cruelties that only polite society could contrive. But as Thorne's betrothed . . .

His consequence could indeed shelter her from the gossip and intolerance she would face when she returned.

Perhaps she *should* consider accepting his proposal, Diana reflected.

She pressed a hand to her stomach, trying to quell the butterflies rioting there. She really wanted nothing to do with a man of Thorne's rakish stamp. Yet as he'd said, they would be thrown together simply by virtue of their connection to Amy. And her reputation would only suffer because of it. More critically, Amy could benefit greatly. . . .

Diana gave a start when Thorne suddenly materialized on the terrace behind her.

Dusk had begun to fall without her even noticing, and the glow from beyond the French doors of the drawing room told her that the lamps had been lit for the evening.

In the dimming light, Thorne moved toward her with a muscular grace that reminded her vividly of their encounter in the cove earlier, when he'd been entirely nude. She had a lustful vision of his body, recalling how hard and lithe it had felt pressed against her, how his fingers had aroused her nipple. . . .

Stop remembering, you shameless goose!

He had dressed for dinner in a superbly fitting, dark green coat and white cravat that accentuated the masculine appeal of his chiseled features and golden hair.

Deplorably, the sight of him made Diana warm and breathless.

It was alarming how vividly his mere nearness affected her senses. When Thorne came to a halt before her, she had to force herself not to turn and flee.

"I met Amy in the corridor," he remarked. "She just returned from her ride and is changing her gown." His gaze raked over her. "I failed to comment earlier, but you look ravishing."

She was becoming accustomed to his outrageous frankness and so paid his compliment no mind, although she couldn't possibly ignore the admiring heat that had kindled in his eyes. His hot gaze burned through the silk of her dress to the pulsing skin beneath.

"So have you considered my offer, sweeting?"

Diana dragged in a deep breath, wondering if she was making a huge mistake. "Yes. I have considered it."

"And?"

"And yes, I will agree to a betrothal. But it will only

be temporary. Only until Amy's future is successfully settled."

"Of course." A faint smile curved Thorne's mouth as he gave her an elaborate bow. "You do me great honor."

"There is no need for such pretense, my lord," Diana said wryly.

"If we're officially betrothed, you must call me Thorne. Or Christopher."

"Thorne will do. I don't wish us to become overly familiar for the brief duration of our arrangement."

He grinned more broadly at that. "I fear some measure of familiarity is inevitable, love."

"I disagree. And such endearments are not necessary to our charade, either."

"Ah, but they *are* if we expect to convince the ton we are actually engaged. My reservations against wedlock are well known. The only credible reason I would willingly give up my bachelorhood is if I were ensnared by love. So the pretense that you stole my heart is one we should cultivate."

Diana felt herself grimace, dismayed by the prospect of having to feign love between them. It would be difficult enough to deny the searing attraction she already felt for Thorne, without the additional complication of pretending an emotional entanglement. But he did have a point. "I suppose you are right."

"I am. And we should begin to prepare our audience as soon as possible. Tomorrow a ship will be sailing from Cyrene, so I'll use it to send notices to the London papers of our betrothal, and to inform my father also. And I will write my Aunt Hennessy. I must give her some advance notice if she's to sponsor Amy's comeout, as well as warn her about my unexpected betrothal. Doubtless she will be astonished."

"Will we be leaving for London shortly?" Diana asked. "If so, I should tell Amy to keep her trunks packed."

"A week should give me time to arrange matters in England satisfactorily. I thought to depart next Wednesday or Thursday."

"But that will put our arrival in London very close to the start of the Season."

"My ship is much faster than the packet that brought you here. Our voyage should take two weeks rather than three or more, barring any major storms at sea. And we have several tasks to accomplish before we leave. During the next sennight I'll have a dressmaker make up wardrobes for both you and Amy."

Diana frowned. "It won't be necessary for me to have more than a new gown or two. I am not the one making my comeout."

"It will, love. I want my betrothed to be dressed in the height of fashion, especially if you plan to squire Amy about London. The French modiste I have in mind recently hails from Paris, where she once designed gowns for the nobility."

"How is it that you are so aware of ladies' fashions?" she asked with a sardonic note in her voice, but her attempt to provoke Thorne only succeeded in rousing a hint of wicked humor in his eyes.

"I make it my business to know what pleases a woman. And most women of my acquaintance are keenly interested in adorning their plumage. Cyrene isn't so different from England in that respect. Or in the way society is ruled, either. Our island society is led by some three dozen British families who have their own little ton and can be quite as ruthless as

London's beau monde. Which reminds me . . . I've arranged for a respectable widow, Señora Padillo, to act as chaperone for the duration of your stay."

"Thank you," Diana said with all sincerity.

"And I have a friend whom I mean to introduce to Amy tomorrow. John Yates will be traveling to England with us, and I intend for him to help keep her occupied until our departure."

"To divert her mind from her infatuation?"

"Precisely. Her fortune-hunter requires *some* competition." There was a glint in Thorne's eye that suggested he would enjoy creating an element of subterfuge.

"And I suppose you don't mean to tell Amy that you are scheming against her? Rather devious, is it not?"

"Merely shrewd. I've been playing these amorous games since before Amy cut her eyeteeth, so I know what is most likely to be effective. Moreover, I have the distinct impression that simple logic and sage advice won't work with her."

"No, they won't," Diana agreed.

"I also think a measure of secrecy is in order where Amy is concerned. When we tell her of our betrothal, we need only say it's a temporary arrangement to improve the odds of your being admitted to the Academy. I don't want her knowing anything of our suspicions regarding her brother's murder."

"That indeed would be wise." Diana hesitated, searching Thorne's face. "What do you intend to do about Nathaniel's murder?"

"I am devising a plan, I promise you."

"I want his killer found and punished."

"So do I, sweeting."

"I also wish I could help obtain justice for him. I would be pleased to contribute in any way I can."

Thorne shook his head. He didn't want Diana involved in the slightest. He didn't want her learning about the Guardians, and if his investigation turned dangerous, he didn't want to put her at risk. Nor did he want the distraction of her interference, no matter how courageous or well intentioned. "I applaud your convictions, but I believe I can handle it."

She gave him a penetrating look. "Do *you* work for the Foreign Office?"

If he lied, Thorne decided, he not only wouldn't satisfy her curiosity, but would open himself up to further questions later.

"Yes," he replied honestly. "I do. As does John Yates." He met her gaze levelly. "Discretion prevents me from revealing more. I'm afraid I must ask you to trust me on this, Diana."

Her brows drawing together in a frown, she studied him for a long moment. "I think you must be less of a rogue than you appear."

"Didn't I try to tell you so?" he replied lightly.

"Yes, but I didn't believe you."

"What must I do to persuade you, my lovely lady?" he murmured.

Reaching for her hand, he brought her fingers to his lips and brushed her knuckles in a provocative kiss.

Abruptly Diana snatched her hand away, as if she'd been seared by the contact. "I promise you, seducing me is not the way."

Thorne bit back a self-deprecating laugh. He, too, had felt the scorching heat between them, and he couldn't seem to help himself. He had needed to touch her, and kissing her hand was the only acceptable means if he intended to remain a gentleman.

"I thought we agreed that I must be seen to fawn over you if we're to make our pretense of a love match seem believable."

"Not in private, we don't," Diana replied firmly.

"I beg to differ. We will have to diligently practice small intimacies if we're to make our ruse second nature."

He took a step toward her, expecting her to retreat, but she froze, staring up at him as if unable to act on her own powers of reasoning.

Thorne likewise went still. Her sweet scent rose to wreathe his senses; her womanly warmth teased him. He found himself staring at Diana's tempting lips . . . and silently cursing under his breath.

He couldn't fathom the unreasonable attraction he felt for her. Nor could he fathom her determined resistance. Few women had proved so impervious to his charm.

Admittedly he was piqued. Which was amusing in itself. How often had he politely discarded a woman for becoming overly amorous and making him feel like prey?

But perhaps Diana was only feigning disinterest?

He raised his hand to her mouth, gliding his thumb slowly over her lower lip, and was gratified when she gave a breathy little gasp.

"Do you realize," he murmured, "that indifference is irresistible to most men? It only makes them yearn to prove your interest can be aroused."

She drew in a shaky breath and stepped back, putting a safer distance between them. "Loath as I am to spoil your conceit, sir rogue," she said sweetly, "my indifference is not intended to challenge your virility. And I should warn you, if you wish me to continue this fraudulent betrothal, it will behoove you to attempt to control your lustful urges."

Thorne's mouth curved in a rueful smile. "If I must . . . Very well, then, if you won't permit me to kiss you, my love"—he offered his arm—"may I escort you in to dinner?"

Four

To Diana's dismay, their charade proved difficult from the very start, since Thorne insisted on playing her affianced husband to the hilt, even in private.

When together they entertained callers who came to meet her and offer well-wishes on their sudden betrothal, she found maintaining the deception a greater strain than she'd ever expected. Worse, Thorne spent the better part of each day and evening in her company, even offering advice when she and Amy pored over fashion plates and decided on styles and fabrics for their new wardrobes.

The enforced proximity was unnerving.

Diana was extremely glad for the respite when, three afternoons later, Thorne chose to show them some of the island.

It *was* glorious to be out of doors on such a day, in such enchanting surroundings, Diana reflected as they rode up a sun-splashed mountain slope wooded with Allepo pine and holm oak. She was still too aware of the charismatic man riding beside her, but at least Amy and John Yates had accompanied them.

Up ahead, Amy was barely speaking to the former

cavalry lieutenant. Confidentially Yates had agreed to help divert the girl from her thwarted romance, but they'd taken an instant and dismaying dislike to each other.

"Your plan to have Mr. Yates entertain Amy doesn't seem to be working," Diana observed to Thorne, wondering if she should perhaps intervene.

"He is distracting her, isn't he?" Thorne said with apparent unconcern.

"I suppose so," Diana conceded. "But they have spent most of their time together squabbling. They seem to have little in common but a mutual respect for each other's horsemanship."

"Fortunately they needn't have anything in common for our purposes. We only want to give Amy something to fret about other than her fortune-hunter."

That we have surely done, Diana thought wryly. The news of their betrothal had surprised but delighted Amy, since it improved the odds that Thorne's aunt could be persuaded to sponsor her. She'd also sweetly expressed relief that Diana would have the protection of Thorne's name for her return to London.

Diana shook herself, determined to forget her temporary betrothal for the moment and simply enjoy the scenery. Thorne was taking them to view the ruins that had once been a Roman bath, which centuries later was still fed by the same hot spring.

Eventually the forest trail opened onto a clearing and a vista that made Diana suddenly halt her horse and stare transfixed. The scenic splendor took her breath away.

On her right, dramatic cliffs plunged precipitously to the rocky coves below, the drop protected only by a crumbling stone wall and ending in a swirl of emerald and sapphire water.

In front of her stood an ancient, once-majestic edifice, now chiefly collapsed into piles of rubble. The half dozen rectangular pools terraced into the hillside must have been the heated baths, but growing in every crevice was a treasure of delicate flora—orchids and ferns, rock roses and cyclamen and honeysuckle.

"Oh, my God," she murmured in awe.

Thorne had stopped beside her, letting her drink in the sight. "Spectacular, isn't it?"

Diana merely nodded in mute appreciation. *Spectacular* was too tame a word. From this vantage, it seemed as if the whole Isle of Cyrene sat like a glowing jewel in the vast Mediterranean, remote yet imbued with a beguiling power.

Her throat tightened with an unaccustomed ache. She suddenly felt a sense of profound elation. Of pure, unadulterated freedom.

"You claimed," she said, "that Apollo cast a spell over this island, and just now I could almost believe it."

Thorne's voice held a similar reverence when he replied. "Cyrene does have an uncanny beauty."

Yet he was watching *her*, Diana realized, not the setting.

When she looked away uncomfortably, he asked, "Would you like to explore?"

"Yes, very much."

They rode closer, coming to a halt at the base of the ruins, before an arched portal.

Above, Amy was already scrambling up the wide steps of the baths. Directly behind her, John Yates managed to climb the terrace on his wooden leg with

surprising alacrity. Yet he stopped and stared in dis-
approval when Amy bent to pluck a pale pink orchid
and tuck it in her blond curls.

"I should have known you would desecrate an
ancient site of the gods, Miss Lunsford," Yates muttered.

"Oh, pooh! Pray don't be a spoilsport," Amy retorted. "There are hundreds of flowers here. The gods
won't miss one little orchid."

Ignoring their bickering, Thorne dismounted and,
before Diana could protest, reached up to lift her
down from her horse.

The press of his fingers at her waist stirred a now-
familiar warmth in her, and when she met his gaze,
she felt her heartbeat falter.

Suddenly breathless, her pulse far too unsteady,
Diana stepped away from his too-intimate nearness.
Cyrene might truly be a paradise with an uncanny
beauty, yet there was danger here, too—in the person
of Lord Thorne.

She followed the ascending path her cousin had already taken, and for the next half hour, explored the
ruins and the sea cliffs. Yet deplorably, her mind kept
focusing on Thorne's image. His golden hair, his
beautiful, masculine features, his sensual mouth, his
incredibly virile body . . . Adonis in the flesh. And instead of pure landscapes, she kept imagining which
views of Thorne she would paint if she had her oils
and canvas with her.

When eventually they had to leave the ruins to return home, Diana tore herself away with relief. As
they rode down through the wooded mountain slopes,
however, she was still making mental paintings of
Thorne.

They had just reached a meadow blazing with wild-flowers when she became aware that he was speaking beside her.

"Sweeting, as soon as we return, I plan to lock you in my bedchamber and make mad, passionate love to you."

Turning her head, Diana gave him a startled look. "*What* did you say?"

"At least that gained your attention." His smile was amused. "I'm not accustomed to being ignored so blatantly, you know. I asked you a question three different times, but you never heard a word."

He was mistaken, Diana knew. She couldn't possibly ignore this man.

"I was thinking about the ruins," she lied, "trying to determine the composition of the scenes I might paint."

"As you were doing when you first saw me nude."

She averted her gaze from his provocative one. "I think we should forget that unfortunate encounter."

"Impossible," Thorne said emphatically.

Diana agreed entirely, but she was grateful when an exclamation from up ahead precluded her thinking of a reply. Her cousin, it seemed, had just challenged Mr. Yates to a horse race.

"First one across the meadow wins!" Amy cried, spurring her mount into a gallop.

John Yates muttered an oath about irritating hoydens, but he, too, dug in his heels and urged his horse after her.

Diana immediately gathered her reins, delighted to participate, knowing a race would provide a much-needed distraction from the all-too-distracting man riding beside her.

*   *   *

Thorne woke suddenly, his heart racing, his erection throbbing. When he recognized his darkened bedchamber, a low curse spilled from his lips, breaking the silence of the night.

He had been dreaming of Diana Sheridan again. Vivid, erotic images that left him burning with a fierce ache. He was still feverish, a sheen of sweat covering his nude body.

Irritated, Thorne threw off the bedcovers and strode to the window to open it. Ever since Diana's arrival, he'd had difficulty sleeping, knowing she was in his house, in a bed he owned. Even though he had purposely moved to another wing so he wouldn't be tempted.

She was forbidden fruit for him.

He doubted she was still a virgin, for most likely her fortune-hunter had seduced her. And a woman that beautiful was bound to have taken lovers over the years, albeit discreetly. Yet he would be a cad to take advantage of her while she was living under his roof. And as her betrothed, he was responsible for her now.

Despite his rational mind, though, despite the demands of honor, he kept having fantasies of Diana, lovely illusions where she willingly gave him her luscious body.

And when he was near her in the flesh, his craving for her was even more powerful. At the ruins this afternoon he'd had difficulty keeping his hands off her. It was fortunate they weren't alone, or he would have found a way to make use of the hot baths.

For a long moment Thorne stood at the open window, letting the breeze wash over his overheated body and chase away the remnants of his erotic dream. The spring nights on Cyrene were still cool enough to be bracing, and he was grateful for the therapeutic effect. Yet he knew he wouldn't be able to sleep any time soon.

When his erection finally receded, Thorne turned away and threw on a dressing gown, then left his bedchamber, intending to go down to his study and pour himself a stiff brandy.

Diana bit her lower lip in fierce concentration as her pencil flew over her sketch pad. She'd been unable to sleep with her mind overflowing with ideas for paintings. After tossing and turning for hours, she finally rose, driven by the need to capture her ideas on paper.

The household appeared to be asleep as she descended the stairs to the library. Thorne's villa seemed to offer every possible comfort, but the library with its vast array of leather-bound volumes held a hushed reverence conducive to creativity and enough well-placed lamps to provide good lighting. And if she needed inspiration, the French doors opened onto the terraced gardens and the vista of the magnificent Mediterranean.

She had been so busy the past three days, she hadn't yet had time to paint at all. Moreover, she hadn't wanted to impose on Thorne by asking him to donate one of the rooms in his house. She needed a space to set up her easel where she could create a mess without fear of ruining the elegant furnishings. Besides, she would only be here a handful of days longer. Until then she would make do with pencil or charcoal sketches and store up memories for the long voyage to England.

The trouble was, her mind stubbornly continued conjuring images of a certain wicked rogue.

Thorne swimming in the cove below, as she'd first seen him.

Thorne bathing naked in one of the heated pools of the ruins.

Thorne standing on the rock wall, staring out at the shimmering blue sea, his fair hair ruffled by the breeze.

It was this last subject she was working on now, striving to capture the vitality that was so much a part of him. The boldness and daring she sensed in him.

Her pencil moved almost of its own accord, the quiet rasp the only sound in the hushed silence of the room.

She had no notion how much time had passed before she suddenly realized she wasn't alone. With a start, Diana looked up to see Thorne standing at the library door.

"I saw the lamplight," he said, taking a step into the room.

He wore a brocade dressing gown of black and crimson, she realized, and his feet and legs were bare.

Her own dishevelment was not much better. She wore a white satin wrapper over her nightdress, and her unbound hair flowed down her back in disarray. Worse, she was curled up on a stuffed leather couch, her legs tucked beneath her.

There was no impropriety, really, for she was fully clothed, but the look in Thorne's eyes made her supremely aware that the hour was late and she was alone with him.

He seemed intrigued most with her hair, for he studied it for a long moment. When finally he locked gazes with her, a frisson of heat ran down Diana's spine.

Abruptly uncurling her legs, she sat up straighter

and smoothed the skirts of her wrapper over her knees.

All her nerves were on full alert when Thorne strolled across the room to stand before her. It was when he glanced down at the sketch she'd made that she realized her mistake of failing to close her sketch pad. His eyes sparked with interest when he saw that he was her subject.

Without waiting for permission, he settled on the couch beside her and reached for the sketchbook in her hands. "May I?"

For a moment, Diana clutched at the pad, refusing to relinquish the embarrassing proof that she was obsessed with this man. But really she had nothing to hide. She was, after all, an artist. Artists chose fascinating subjects like Viscount Thorne all the time.

Even so, color flooded her cheeks when she reluctantly loosened her grip.

Taking the book from her, he studied the drawing for another long moment. "This is stunning," he said finally, his earnestness unmistakable.

Diana knew it was one of her better executions. In the sketch, Thorne looked almost alive, with an excitement expressed not only in his face, but in every line of his body as he stared out to sea, a man ripe for passion and adventure.

"You claimed you had skill," Thorne added, "but I didn't realize your talent was this remarkable."

His praise warmed her, but she tried to make light of it. "I am fortunate to have a natural flair for capturing a likeness and putting it down."

Tearing his gaze away from her sketch, he glanced up at her. "You are far too modest, love. You said you also enjoy painting landscapes. Are they as good as this?"

"Perhaps a bit better," Diana answered honestly. "I find painting landscapes even more satisfying than painting people, but I intend to focus on portraits because they command more respect. The Royal Academy is the arbiter of artistic taste and holds to a rigid hierarchy, where there is little esteem for landscapes."

"Oh?" His eyebrow rose with curiosity.

"Historical works hold the loftiest importance, portraitures are next, then landscapes, and finally genre paintings—depictions of domestic life."

"Thus your desire to become a portraitist."

"Yes," she admitted softly.

"It must be frustrating for you to be forced to repress your great gift because of your sex."

Diana winced as the familiar resentment rose in her. "As a man, you likely can't begin to imagine my frustrations. There are so many restrictions placed on a woman, it is difficult to compete for notice, let alone for respect."

Thorne flashed a sympathetic smile. "I can empathize with the frustration at least. I've been battling the constraints of society since the day I was born."

That won a smile from Diana. "I don't doubt it."

Shifting his attention back to her sketchbook, he flipped to the previous page. His gaze riveted on the drawing of him, bathing at the ruins. His torso was naked, although the pool concealed his lower body to his waist. There was a wicked gleam in his eyes, a come-hither look that was sinful and daring and full of charm.

"I am very flattered," Thorne remarked, his voice warm with satisfaction.

Diana felt her cheeks burn, but she strove for nonchalance. "You needn't be. If one wants to be a successful portrait painter, it is wise to flatter the subject—that, according to Sir Thomas Lawrence, who commands four hundred guineas for a full-length view. I hope to be a fraction as successful someday, so I am striving to work on my technique."

"If you say so," he murmured blandly, although she could tell by the gleam in his eye that he didn't believe her.

He flipped backward again, this time to see himself rising from the water of the cove, his entire body bare, his loins fully exposed, his erection long and swollen. "I see you have endowed me with ample physical attributes."

Scandalized to be caught making such an erotic rendering, Diana snatched the sketchbook from him and firmly closed it.

A smile played across Thorne's lips as he viewed the flush on her face. "You needn't rely only on memory, sweeting. You are welcome to paint me in the flesh. I will be more than happy to sit for you any time you wish."

"Thank you, but I *don't* wish you to sit for me. My memory is more than adequate for my work."

"A pity." His gaze turned speculative. "In those last two drawings you made me appear highly seductive. I'm curious what else you see in me."

"You don't need me to pay you compliments, Lord Thorne. You know full well how beautiful you are."

He frowned a little at her description. "Should I consider that an insult? Men aren't supposed to be beautiful."

"You are. Sinfully so. And I think you know it."

"Is that why you've made me look like a rake? Because my appearance is somehow sinful?"

She tried to keep her answer dispassionate and

objective. "In part. It's more the intangible quality to your countenance. Not simply your classic bone structure, but something in your expression . . . a wickedness, a recklessness, a wildness—"

"A wickedness, hmmm?" His gaze skimmed her face.

She froze when he raised a finger to her lips. "Would you care to know what I see in you, love?"

Diana didn't want to admit her intense curiosity, but her reply seemed dredged from her throat. "Yes."

"I see a beauty with an alluring combination of vulnerability and strength. A woman with an unmistakable sensuality. Your eyes are so dark and expressive. . . . A man could lose himself in your eyes, I think." His voice lowered another level. "There's a hint of mystery there that makes me want to discover what secrets you are concealing."

The tenderness in his husky murmur made Diana's breath catch, while the look in his eyes held her spellbound.

His gaze dropped to her lips. "Your lush mouth invites sin. And the satin fall of your hair. . . ." His hand lifted to touch the shining mass. "I wondered how it would look unpinned, but it's even more lovely than I imagined it."

"Thorne . . ." She knew it was madness to listen to his sweet blandishments, yet she couldn't seem to complete her protest.

"You are pure temptation, Diana." The flecks of gold in his hazel eyes had warmed to a heated shimmer, rousing a disquieting desire deep within her. "You've even begun haunting my dreams."

"You dream of me?" Her voice had dropped to a whisper.

His eyes swept over her face in a way that made her

pulse tremble. "Yes, I dream of you. I can't help myself. I want very much to make love to you, Diana. I want to watch your beautiful eyes turn even darker with passion."

He had leaned forward as he spoke, and now his beautiful face was very near, his lips nearly touching hers, making her recall vividly the searing heat of his kiss on the beach. Yet if he kissed her now, Diana knew she would be lost. They were alone here together, with this raging attraction between them.

In the hushed silence of the room, she could hear her rapid heartbeat as she struggled for the will to end this brazen encounter. It took all the resolve she possessed, but she drew back and brought her sketch pad up between them, holding it defensively over her breasts. "Thorne, stop. . . . I thought we agreed . . . you wouldn't try to seduce me."

Thorne shook himself, as if coming out of a daze. "You're right," he muttered. "This is too damned dangerous." His voice was low and hoarse and filled with discernible frustration. "I had best leave."

"No, I should be the one to leave."

Clutching her pad, she rose and fled the library, shutting the door behind her. In the sudden darkness, Diana leaned back against the panel and let out the shaky breath she'd been holding. For a long moment she remained exactly where she stood, still trembling, her pulse far too rapid as she contemplated her deplorable dilemma.

There was no question that she was fiercely attracted to Thorne. Against her will, she found him more appealing than any man she had ever known. And more beguiling.

His wicked, sensual charm seemed as effortless and natural as breathing—no doubt because it was. He could no more stop himself from seducing a woman than change the color of his eyes.

And he could rouse a woman's desire for him just as effortlessly.

Yet somehow she had to resist her fascination. She didn't want to be another one of Thorne's many conquests. It would be the height of idiocy to succumb.

Squeezing her eyes shut, Diana shook her head in dismay. Thorne had called her a temptation, but *he* was the one who was pure temptation.

He was right in one respect, however.

Their being alone together was too damned dangerous.

After their late-night encounter in the library, Diana did her utmost to avoid being alone with Thorne, yet she was still required to share more of his company than she knew was wise.

For both Diana and Amy, the remainder of the week proved just as busy as the beginning, with their evenings spent attending suppers and soirees among island society, and their daylight hours devoted to wardrobe fittings.

They would wait to shop in London for accessories such as shoes, bonnets, reticules, fans, and handkerchiefs. But the French modiste was designing them gowns for every other occasion—morning, afternoon, dinner, ball, carriage, walking, riding—as well as cloaks and spencers and pelisses.

When Diana protested that so many garments would never be ready in time for them to sail, Thorne informed her that the dressmaker would be accompanying them to England, and that two weeks at sea should be ample to complete most of their wardrobes. Diana could scarcely believe he had hired the undivided services of an expensive modiste for an entire month, but she supposed a man as wealthy as Thorne could waste his fortune any way he chose.

Thorne could have told her he was taking the Frenchwoman along for an entirely different purpose: added protection for Diana. The more passengers on board his schooner, he rationalized, the greater the likelihood he would be able to keep his hands off her.

He was convinced now that Diana needed protection from him. He couldn't remember reacting so explosively to a woman in his life. It was ludicrous, actually. He'd first met her barely a few days ago.

And encountering her in the library had seriously increased the fever he felt for her. That night he'd wanted nothing more than to press Diana back upon the sofa and slide between her slender thighs to give them both the ecstasy they craved. He'd wanted her to leave, knowing that had she remained, he would never have been able to resist taking her.

Thorne could scarcely believe the intensity of his attraction for Diana, or how urgently his body responded to her. He suffered an unshakable case of lust every time he looked at her. And he still found himself dreaming erotic dreams of her each night. He still woke each morning with a throbbing erection.

Diana Sheridan did something unnatural to him.

Part of his attraction, no doubt, was because she resisted him so vigorously. He couldn't recall the last time a woman had actively sought to escape his attention. And her adamant aversion to marriage increased his level of comfort while decreasing his need to maintain such strict defenses. Moreover, he'd had no sexual release since returning to Cyrene, and celibacy was not a state he relished.

Yet there was more to Diana Sheridan than her

beautiful face and body; something complex and enticing about her called to him. Each time he learned more about her, he became more intrigued. Her fortitude in the face of adversity, in particular, had earned his respect and admiration.

Regardless of the cause of his attraction, however, the simple truth was that she was a greater temptation than any he'd ever dealt with.

It was perhaps too far-fetched to blame the island's mythical spell and the infamous seductive effect on a mortal's senses. But he might have made a mistake by delaying their departure for quite so long. It had been imperative to set plans in place for infiltrating Venus's sin club, and to gain his aunt's support before arriving, but Thorne regretted now not embarking sooner. Yet he had to control himself for only a few more days. Surely he could quell his desire for Diana for that long.

Even so, he would be very glad to put Cyrene behind him and get on with executing his mission in London—finding Nathaniel's killer.

He knew he was making another mistake two nights later, the final evening before their scheduled departure. They had no social engagements planned for tonight but would dine at home since their ship would set sail early the next morning.

When Thorne arrived in the drawing room, it was approaching sunset, but there was no sign of Diana or his ward. Through the French doors, however, he could see the distant figure of a woman beyond the terraced gardens.

She stood near the edge of the bluff, gazing up at a carob tree silhouetted against the red-gold sky. When he made out the shape of an easel, he knew it had to be Diana.

The view no doubt was what had lured her, Thorne reflected. At this time of evening it would be spectacular. The bluffs faced east, but as sometimes happened, the clouds on the horizon would form a roiling collage of incredible colors.

Without allowing himself to think, he followed Diana's path out to the bluffs.

The vista was indeed magnificent, he saw as he drew closer. The smoldering fire of the setting sun reflected on the sea, turning the surface to flame, while the hovering clouds made a brilliant canopy at the horizon's edge.

When he reached Diana, he saw that she stood with a palette in one hand, a brush in the other, and was swiftly blocking out a landscape on the canvas, using clean, sure strokes.

She seemed so immersed in her work that Thorne didn't think she even noticed his presence.

When she finally spoke, her quiet murmur was filled with reverence. "This entire week I have watched the sunset sky from my bedchamber window, and I couldn't resist coming here on my last evening."

I couldn't resist coming here either, Thorne thought, although the sunset was not what had drawn him.

Remaining silent, he watched Diana at work. Now and then she bent to the wooden box at her feet—which was filled with brushes and jars of turpentine and bladders of paint—and chose another brush, but otherwise she kept her gaze wholly focused on the breathtaking vista and the canvas before her.

What she was doing seemed magical; right before his eyes, a scene was taking shape on the canvas.

In the foreground of her composition stood the sharp outline of what would be the carob tree. Below the bluff's edge was the white rock promontory that sheltered the cove. And beyond that, the sea stretched to the distant horizon and melted into a churning turmoil of flaming clouds.

It wasn't the painting being born, however, that captured Thorne's fascinated attention; it was the painter.

Diana had drawn her lower lip between her teeth, and the intensity of her concentration revealed her ardor for her work; he could actually feel her fierce passion. And the loving care she took with each brushstroke was almost . . . sensual.

Her own vibrancy was just as sensual. The setting sun at her back turned her hair to dark fire, while the crimson-gold light of the sky bathed her beautiful features with enchanting radiance.

Seeing her this way aroused a fierce yearning within Thorne to share her passion. He suddenly had no doubt that she would make love with the same sensual intensity.

He couldn't have said how long he stood there watching her, but eventually he realized the sunset had faded and the evening light had dimmed to dusk.

A moment later the sky turned charcoal gray with only a few pale streaks of pink remaining at the edge.

"I wish it would last longer," Diana murmured with obvious frustration. "But at least I memorized enough to complete this scene."

Thorne tried to shake himself from his daze. She was speaking of art, while all he could think about was making love to her. Devil take it, he had to regain control of his lustful thoughts.

"It is so difficult to capture a sunset," she added softly, her tone regretful.

A sudden image struck Thorne, making him see a vivid parallel: Winning this woman would be like capturing a sunset. Diana was much like a sunset, with her captivating vibrancy, and grasping that elusive magic would be complex and arduous. Even so, he felt desire fill him at the possibility.

Unsuspecting of Thorne's reflections, Diana gave a wistful sigh. She could do no more this evening, for it was too dark to see, despite the quarter moon that had slowly materialized in the inky sky overhead.

Bending, she set down her palette and stowed her brush, yet she couldn't bring herself to gather her materials to return to the villa. Instead, she kept her gaze on the vista beyond the bluffs. She could hear the quiet whisper of the waves in the cove below, could feel the fresh caress of the breeze on her face.

She didn't want to leave this place, this moment. This was the last night she would ever spend on this beautiful isle, and she didn't want it to end.

As if dazed, she moved a few steps closer to the bluff. There was such freedom here. She had never felt so free. And there was an enchantment to the evening that touched her soul with a strange mingling of peace and excitement.

She understood the excitement, though. She might have been absorbed in her work, but never for a moment had she been unaware of the man who had followed her here.

Just now her awareness of Thorne returned with a vengeance. When he moved to stand directly behind her, she felt his presence like a tangible caress.

Diana tensed, knowing she should resist the traitorous warmth rising within her at his nearness. "I suppose we should return," she said in a breathy voice. "Amy will be missing us."

"I expect so," he agreed.

Yet he made no move to go.

Around them full night descended. The gentle silence of darkness enveloped them, as soft as the sea breeze, while the rising moon sent a wash of silvery light over the rippling water. From somewhere in the distance, a nightingale drifted into ethereal song.

Diana thought she must be dreaming, and yet she felt vividly alive. Her pulse was reckless, her skin oversensitive, her breasts tight and feverish.

Then Thorne touched her. His hand reached up to caress her hair, stroking slowly over the smooth chignon she wore above her nape.

Feeling her breath falter, Diana wondered if he meant to unpin her hair. But his hand moved on, his fingertips tracing the shell of her ear, leaving a trail of heat in their wake.

When his thumb grazed along her jawline to brush her parted lips, her breath fled altogether, but she made no protest, merely stood mutely, unable to make a sound.

Both his hands rose then, to the bare skin of her shoulders. The neckline of her silk dinner gown was low enough to expose the beginning swells of her bosom, so when he slid his arms around her, gliding his palms down over her bare flesh, he met with no resistance. When his fingers found the peaks beneath the thin silk of her bodice and chemise, Diana's heart lurched painfully.

"Thorne . . ."

"Hush, love."

He caught her nipples between his fingers and exerted gentle pressure, sending fire lancing through her. At the same time his lips pressed briefly to the curve of her neck, the touch hot and tender, making a heavy ache form deep in her lower body.

The magic was seducing her senses, Diana knew, and she was helpless to fight it.

No, that was a lie. She didn't want to fight it. If Thorne wished to make love to her in the moonlit darkness, she feared she might not have the will to stop him. It would be so easy to let herself be swept away. She had never experienced real passion before. Never known the kind of ecstasy that poets lauded. And now, wrapped in Thorne's erotic embrace, she wanted desperately for him to show her the kind of carnal bliss she had only dreamed of until now.

She felt her limbs growing liquid and weak. He was kneading her breasts so slowly and exquisitely that the pleasure nearly melted her, setting up hot, churning sensations deep in her body.

"You tantalize me," he whispered, his voice hoarse.

He tantalized her in turn. He filled her with a hungry longing. A longing she had harbored inside herself for years. She'd simply never realized it until just this moment.

She was scarcely aware when Thorne pulled at the bodice of her gown and the fabric of her chemise, drawing both down over the top edge of her corset, exposing her aching breasts to the cool night air. Without pause, his thumbs moved in a maddeningly light caress over their tips, making her shudder with longing.

Her entire body was aroused now, yet he seemed content merely to torment her . . . stroking the swollen globes, flicking the throbbing crests, cupping and teasing the buds with expert skill.

Involuntarily Diana arched her back, thrusting her breasts against his magical hands. An almost unbearable ache was rising down at the pit of her stomach and between her thighs. At her movement, though, she felt the rigid blade of Thorne's arousal against her buttocks, proof of his urgent desire.

A tremor knifed through her.

That seemed to be the signal he was waiting for, for one hand left her breast and moved downward, his palm stroking over her rib cage, and lower . . . over her stomach . . . and lower still, to the juncture of her thighs, his fingers probing through the silk of her skirts.

Whimpering, Diana arched helplessly against him.

The sultry, pleading sound clouded Thorne's senses, while the feel of her buttocks pressing so tauntingly against him drove his throbbing manhood tight against his satin breeches. Not allowing himself to think, he pulled Diana even closer, into the hard heat of his body.

He had the fiercest urge to turn her around and lower his head to her breasts, suckling each of her nipples, savoring her with his mouth. He had an even fiercer urge to explore her silken mysteries.

He could picture her naked, her ivory skin shimmering in the moonlight, her pale, silken thighs opening for him. *Why are you waiting?* a dark voice whispered. *She's hot and willing, yours for the taking.*

He could feel her tremors burn through him with an exquisite torture. He wanted her as badly as he'd ever wanted any woman in his life. He wanted Diana moaning beneath him, sheathing him in her wet heat.

He wanted to hear her cries of passion when he exploded inside her. . . .

Thorne drew a sharp breath, fighting against the hot tide of his desire. He was close, within a hairsbreadth, of breaking his vow not to seduce her.

Hell and damnation. He had gone too far.

Pressing his forehead against her fragrant hair, he held her sweet body against him in an agony of want, cursing himself for his damnable weakness. He had vowed he wouldn't touch Diana, but here he was, nearly seducing her again.

Why was it that every encounter with this woman shot his control to hell? Never had a sworn oath seemed so fragile a barrier.

He had to regain his control, though. Only sheer strength of will allowed him to step back from the dark grip of passion.

Drawing a labored breath, Thorne forced himself to release her. Instantly he felt her stillness; even in the darkness he could sense her bewilderment at his sudden abandonment. But he clenched his teeth to ignore it and the burning in his loins.

One thing was imminently clear. He had to get this bewitching siren off the island before he did something irrevocable.

Five

It was with a vast sense of relief that Diana boarded Thorne's schooner the next morning. The Isle of Cyrene was enchanting and incredibly beautiful, but the sooner they departed, the sooner she could regain command of her senses.

At dinner the previous evening, following her scandalous tryst with Thorne on the bluffs, she had scarcely known where to look. Whenever she met his gaze across the table, she remembered his arousing fingers stroking her breasts, and her entire body flushed. Thankfully Thorne had been able to summon the kind of control she had not and had drawn back at the last moment.

Yet she could sense the war he was still fighting with himself. His eyes darkened whenever they rested on her, while his jaw tightened, as if he was fiercely repressing his primitive urges.

Their mutual tension, however, was unexpectedly broken as they finished the dessert course of cheese and fruit. A visitor called at Thorne's villa, bearing news that completely took Diana's mind off her own personal dilemma.

Sir Gawain Olwen was a tall, lean, elderly gentleman whose manners were courteous and stately. Diana had met the baronet at a soiree earlier in the week and been gratified by his kind welcome.

Apologizing for the interruption, Sir Gawain requested a private interview with Thorne and remained closeted with him for nearly a half hour. Before Sir Gawain took his leave, however, he paused at the drawing room door to wish Miss Sheridan and Miss Lunsford a safe voyage to England.

When the baronet had gone, Thorne went to the sideboard to pour himself a generous snifter of brandy.

"Is something amiss?" Diana asked, seeing his grim expression.

"You might say so," Thorne replied darkly. "Sir Gawain received a dispatch late last night. Napoleon Bonaparte recently escaped from Elba and landed in France, but it's just been confirmed he is marching on Paris. In fact, he may have arrived by now. The fear is that Boney means to raise an army and retake control of his empire."

Diana felt her stomach tense with dread. The Corsican Tyrant who had sought to conquer the civilized world and had waged a decades-long war in Europe and Africa had abdicated the previous year and been safely incarcerated on the island of Elba. But now apparently he was threatening again.

"And if he regains his empire?" Diana wondered.

"The Allies will have to try to stop him, of course."

The alarming news cast a pall over their final evening on Cyrene, a pall that continued when they boarded the ship the next morning.

Even Amy realized the possible peril of the Monster unleashed, for she appeared unusually somber, Diana noted. The two cousins were standing with John Yates at the railing as the schooner sailed from the harbor.

Beside them, Yates looked quietly angry, not speaking a word until Amy asked a question to which Diana herself wanted to know the answer. "Can Napoleon be defeated again?"

"I have no doubt," Yates replied grimly, "but it will likely be bloody, damn him. The Allied armies will be recalled, and countless good men will lose their lives."

Amy glanced down at his wooden leg. "Will you have to fight?" she asked in a curiously quiet voice.

His mouth curled with bitterness. "I would gladly go, but the British cavalry won't have much use for a cripple."

"Don't call yourself that!" Amy exclaimed.

When Yates stared at her, her chin rose. "I think it outrageous that anyone would think you less of a man because you lost a limb in the service of your country."

Diana could see Yates's surprise at such a fervent declaration. He was clearly taken aback that a girl of Amy's flighty nature not only wasn't repulsed by his missing leg, but thought of it as a badge of courage.

"I think you brave and honorable for being wounded in battle," Amy added indignantly. "And I refuse to let you disparage yourself that way."

Diana had to hide a gratified smile. Her cousin occasionally made her proud. From Amy's complaints over the past week, she didn't appear even to *like* John Yates, for she considered him far too stern and managing, while he plainly thought her a spoiled brat. They had fought frequently since their first meeting, but he had gritted his teeth and endured, doubtless because he had promised Thorne.

The ship dipped just then as it left the sheltered harbor and encountered the open sea, forcing them all to grasp the railing for balance.

A moment later, Amy put a hand to her stomach, looking a little green around the mouth. "If you will excuse me, I think I will retire to my cabin. Sailing disagrees with me—"

She turned and fled, leaving John Yates to stare after her.

"I never would have taken her for a patriot," he finally said.

Diana repressed another smile. "Amy can be quite surprising. She has been pampered and indulged most of her life, but she has a generous heart. I have high hopes she will grow up some day soon—perhaps during her Season."

Yates nodded thoughtfully, although his expression held skepticism.

Before he could reply, a movement overhead caught Diana's attention—the crew raising another sail. Then across the deck, she spied Thorne speaking to his captain. When Thorne suddenly looked up and met her gaze, she had a momentary flash of strong bronzed fingers cupping her pale breasts.

Quickly Diana turned back to watch the receding island. This would likely be her last view of Cyrene, but she couldn't regret leaving.

It seemed they were all glad to get away from the island and eager to reach England. She, for her art career, Amy for her comeout, and Thorne and Yates to unearth the mystery of Nathaniel's death.

Diana felt her tension ease a measure as she regarded the magnificent coastline of Cyrene for the final time. She would have to endure a two-week voyage in close quarters with Thorne, but she hoped the threat wouldn't be so great without the magical, mythical influence of the island to cloud her senses.

For the next week Diana managed to avoid any intimate encounters with Thorne, much to her relief. They took meals together in the stateroom along with the captain and the other civilian passengers, including her maid and the French modiste, but Diana made a point of never being alone with Thorne.

For occupation, she set up her easel in her cabin and applied herself to painting for the majority of each day. She also stood for wardrobe fittings, and for exercise, she strolled the deck with Amy.

Fortunately, Amy's tendency toward seasickness quickly subsided. The weather remained fair much of the first week, so the seas were relatively calm, but the girl's cure was due more to John Yates. Sympathetic to Amy's malady that first morning, Yates had given her a concoction that settled her stomach—which put him in Amy's good graces for the time being.

As for Thorne, he seemed to keep busy aiding the crew. It surprised Diana that a nobleman would engage in such humble manual activity, but when Amy quizzed him about it, Thorne claimed he craved physical exertion and a means to work off his restlessness.

Diana supposed that climbing the rigging of a three-masted schooner *was* a cure for restlessness, but admittedly the danger to Thorne alarmed her a little. The sight of him in his shirtsleeves as he labored on the deck disturbed her even more.

Thus Diana shocked herself when she allowed him

to pose for her *without* his shirt the very next afternoon.

It occurred at the beginning of their second week. The temperature had grown decidedly cooler as soon as the ship rounded Gibraltar and entered the choppy gray waters of the Atlantic, so Diana was grateful for the coal brazier that warmed her small cabin as she worked. That afternoon, however, she left her door open to allow the cloying fumes of turpentine and linseed oil to escape.

She realized her mistake the instant Thorne appeared in the doorway.

"So this is where you've been hiding yourself." Without asking permission, he sauntered inside her cabin. His gaze first lit on the paint-splattered smock she wore, then roamed around the half of the cabin that she had converted into a studio.

She had finished the sunset seascape she'd begun her last evening on Cyrene and propped the wet canvas against the bulkhead to dry, along with several other landscapes, including the Roman ruins, the quaint little town perched above the harbor, and the island itself with its rugged slopes and golden valleys.

But it was the sunset painting that held Thorne's gaze riveted. He moved past her, as if drawn by some unseen force, and stood staring down at her rendering.

Diana considered this one of her better works. With vividness and luminosity, she had captured the dramatic shifting light on the clouds and the sea, immortalizing the scene in crimson and gold. But she held her breath, waiting to hear Thorne's opinion.

He was silent for quite a long moment. "I admit I have only an amateur's eye, but to me this seems quite brilliant. I'm reminded of a landscape by Turner I saw last summer at the Royal Academy exhibition, although this is less turbulent."

Warmth filled Diana at his praise. Turner was renowned for his dramatic portrayals of mist and sea and sky, and in particular, his battles at sea. He was one of the youngest artists ever to be elected a full member of the Royal Academy, and he now served as Professor of Perspective.

"Thank you," she murmured. "That is high praise indeed."

"I gather you have deliberately striven for this softer look."

"Yes. My favorite landscape artist is John Constable. He creates a glowing serenity in his nature scenes that brings peace to the soul—an effect that is almost magical. I've aspired to master his technique."

"I would say the effect of this painting is almost magical."

Tearing his gaze from the sunset, Thorne studied the three other landscapes.

"These really are remarkable," he said finally. "You clearly have a gift." When he looked up to meet Diana's gaze, she could see genuine admiration and respect in the depths of his eyes. "It seems you were born to paint."

Diana felt herself flushing, yet she couldn't dispute him. For as long as she could remember, she had always wanted to paint. After the deaths of her parents, when she'd gone to live with her Lunsford cousins, she had poured her heart into her watercolor paintings. And when she had discovered oils, her entire life had changed; her art had truly become a passion.

"I don't see any portraits here," Thorne commented.

"Because I have not painted any recently. Since

leaving England, I've found too many wonderful scenes that cried out for attention."

"Yet if you're to make your reputation as a portraitist, shouldn't you practice?"

"I suppose so," Diana conceded. "Finding subjects to sit for me is a problem, however. I've employed Amy once too often, and she refuses to accommodate me any longer, claiming the boredom drives her mad."

"As I said, you are welcome to employ me."

Diana hesitated, seeing that Thorne was entirely serious. She did indeed need practice, particularly with men. She had painted her own male servants at home, but never a nobleman like Thorne. Capturing that elusive air of aristocracy would be a challenge. And so would depicting his uncommon masculine beauty, or more specifically, his potent virility.

She'd never had the chance to scrutinize the male form. By convention, women artists were prevented from studying nude models, and Diana's mentor had been quite strict in that regard. It was difficult to duplicate flesh tones or the virile ripple of muscle if one had never seen them before.

To his surprise, as well as her own, Diana found herself accepting his offer.

"Very well, I would be grateful if you would sit for me."

She could tell she had taken Thorne off guard, for he'd obviously expected her to decline. His reaction pleased Diana. If she was to hold her own against him, she would have to remain on the offensive, staying one step ahead of him.

Yet she had an even more basic rationale in mind. If she could become accustomed to Thorne's physical perfection, she reasoned, viewing him merely as an artistic subject, she would be better able to resist him. For her own self-preservation, it would behoove her to become inured to his charms.

Quickly Diana glanced around the cabin, searching for a location to pose him. She would have liked to paint him on the deck of the ship, using masts and sails for a backdrop, but this canvas would be for practice only, and if she was successful, she could always add the masts in afterward. For now she merely needed the light coming over her shoulder, with enough brightness to illuminate his chiseled features. The sunlight streaming in the porthole window would do now, allowing her to decide on shadowing later.

Her imagination leaping ahead, she pictured Thorne leaning casually against a timber mast, a sea wind ruffling his golden hair. Frowning thoughtfully, Diana pointed to the bulkhead opposite the porthole, near the sleeping bunks.

"Stand there, if you will?" When he obliged, she nodded. "Now prop your shoulder against the bulkhead, and cross one foot over the other."

"Like this?" He slouched against the paneling, crossing his right boot over his left.

"That should work." Her gaze scrutinized his attire. In addition to boots and leather breeches, he wore a rough, short-waisted seaman's jacket with no cravat—not what she had in mind, which was a nobleman indulging in sport on his yacht. "Now, if you will kindly remove your jacket and shirt."

When he arched an eyebrow, Diana felt color rise in her cheeks. "I have studied male anatomy before, but always from drawings or plaster casts of Hellenic statues. I could use the experience painting a torso of a live man."

Thorne flashed her that quick, enchanting smile.

"Just my torso? I will be delighted to remove all my clothes."

Diana sent him a quelling look. "That would only invite scandal, and I have enough of that in my past, thank you. For propriety's sake, I mean to leave the cabin door open while I work. In truth, I should probably call my maid to chaperone us right now."

"Surely such drastic measures aren't necessary. We're betrothed, remember? And as such, we're permitted greater license."

"Perhaps so. And my maid is busy helping to sew our new gowns. But in the future I will make certain we are not alone."

"If you must," Thorne replied with an exaggerated sigh.

While he was undressing, Diana occupied herself by gathering the materials she would need. She had already prepared a canvas, stretching linen over a wooden frame and applying sizing to fill in the fabric's porous weave and then allowing it to dry thoroughly. Now she prepared a palette with the appropriate colors of oil paint, and chose several brushes.

"Will this do?" her subject queried, breaking into her concentration.

When she looked up to see Thorne had complied in baring his torso, her breath faltered. He was golden and glorious, she thought, admiring his strong, elegantly muscled body. She wondered if his flesh would be as hard and firm as it looked.

Alarmed by how badly she wanted to touch him to find out, Diana gave a curt nod. "Will you resume your pose, please?"

Casually he leaned against the bulkhead again and crossed his booted feet.

A long moment of silence followed while she deliberated how she would block out his portrait. Staring at the blank white canvas, she tried to visualize the image she wanted, the composition, the exact lines. . . .

"I fail to comprehend why I cannot pose nude for you," Thorne remarked at last. "You have already seen me in the buff when I was swimming."

Diana's gaze flew back to him. A wicked smile lit his eyes. He was teasing her, trying to provoke her again, she realized, feeling a flutter in her stomach.

She squared her shoulders. This Thorne was totally disarming and highly dangerous, yet she wouldn't allow herself to be intimidated. "I am interested in painting you for the sole purpose of training, nothing more."

"But a torso is hardly adequate for your training, is it?"

She didn't reply.

"I think you would find the rest of my body quite interesting."

Instinctively Diana's lips curved, but she repressed her amusement. "You obviously have an elevated opinion of your attributes, Lord Thorne."

Thorne glanced down at his loins. "My attributes are not elevated at the moment."

It took her several beats to understand his double entendre. "You are shameless," she scolded, her tone exasperated.

"No doubt."

"And highly provoking."

"Most definitely." A sultry smile spread across his mouth. "What must I do to persuade you to let me undress for you?"

His audacity knew no bounds. "Nothing," Diana

retorted firmly. "You could not possibly persuade me."

"I'll wager I could if I applied all my charm."

She summoned a deliberate frown. "Do you know what your trouble is, Thorne?"

"What?"

"You have been thoroughly spoiled from the cradle. As a wealthy nobleman, you have been permitted to have your way much too often."

"My father could dispute you."

When mutely she returned her attention to the canvas, Thorne queried in a provoking tone, "Do you know what *your* trouble is, my sweet dragon?"

"No, but I expect you will enlighten me."

"You're afraid I will succeed in seducing you."

"Will you turn your head a bit more to the left so that you look toward the porthole? I want the light to strike your face at a certain angle."

"Is that all you mean to say? You are supposed to return my banter, perhaps a flirtatious smile."

"I fear I must disappoint you. Flirting is not in my nature. And even if it were, I would know better than to encourage your outrageous remarks."

Thorne shook his head sadly. "You are truly a challenge, love."

"And you are truly a vexation." She made her first brushstroke. "Perhaps we could debate the issue at some future point. For now, will you please keep quiet and let me concentrate?"

Obligingly Thorne fell silent. From that point on Diana was all business. She focused on her canvas, glanced up to scrutinize his body, then returned her bemused gaze to the canvas.

Pausing once, she crossed the small space between them and placed her fingers on Thorne's jaw, positioning his head, then his right arm. Then without speaking, she went back to her work.

Thorne watched her with a sense of mingled pleasure and pain. His body had reacted instantly to her touch, but it was the sensual intensity on Diana's face that had aroused him and made him hard. He'd never realized that painting could be such an erotic act.

He found himself cursing silently. Perhaps posing for her had been a mistake. He hadn't anticipated that being her artistic subject would prove such temptation, that remaining so still while her gaze roamed over his body would only stoke his lust further.

She bit her lower lip as she applied each careful stroke of the brush, while her dark eyes had grown almost slumberous. Thorne had no difficulty picturing her in the throes of passion, just as he saw her in his dreams.

The minutes ticked by and became a torment. Standing in one pose for so long cramped different muscles in his body, but the ache in his loins was more excruciating. Even so, he didn't want to interrupt Diana's concentration, so he endured.

"Would you permit me a moment to stretch?" he said finally. "We have been at this for an hour or more."

She glanced up, dismay on her beautiful features. "Oh, heavens, forgive me. I tend to lose track of time. Yes, please take a moment to stretch."

Pushing away from his slouching position, Thorne shrugged his shoulders, circling them to ease the stiffness, then rubbed his arms to bring back the circulation.

"If I could have another half hour of your time," Diana was saying, "I should have the main outline—

Are you cold?" she asked, as if recognizing one source of his discomfort.

"My chest is a bit chilled," Thorne admitted wryly, not admitting that his loins were still on fire. He threw her a provocative glance. "You could warm me if you wanted to."

Her eyes widened at his suggestive remark before her mouth curled in exasperation. "But I don't want to. Take one of the blankets from a bunk and wrap it around your shoulders. And go warm yourself at the brazier."

"You are no fun."

He did as she suggested, retrieving a blanket to drape around his shoulders, but then he moved toward her easel rather than the brazier. "May I see what you've done?"

"No! Certainly not." Diana shifted to block the canvas from view, stepping in front of him. "I don't like anyone looking at my work before it is completed."

"Self-conscious, are you?"

"No, I just don't want subjects advising me how to paint them."

"Very well, I will wait. But I think I deserve a reward for posing there so obediently."

He was standing very close to her now, and his gaze moved instinctively to her luscious mouth.

Diana gave a start, as if suddenly realizing the proximity of his bare chest, and she stepped back a pace. "I won't kiss you again, Thorne, so you can just erase that thought from your lecherous mind."

He feigned a wounded look, even though his mind had very much been focused on stealing a kiss from her. "You malign me. I wasn't thinking of a kiss as my reward. More along the lines of a glass of wine."

"Oh. Very well, help yourself."

Thorne picked his way through various frames and bolts of linen on the cabin floor to the desk, where a decanter of wine rested. His ship was equipped with a number of little luxuries for its passengers, and he poured himself an ample portion of a fine Madeira.

"Would you care for a glass, love?"

"Hmmm?"

She had returned to her easel and forgotten him already. It would have been insulting had not Thorne become accustomed to the novelty by now.

Taking the opportunity for a respite, he pulled out the desk chair and sat down, watching Diana again as he sipped his wine. Her concentration was not quite so fierce just now, but instead was thoughtful and pondering as she applied a judicious brushstroke here and there.

Silence descended over the cabin once more. Other than the normal creaks of the swaying ship and the distant snap of canvas overhead, there was nothing to take Thorne's mind off his painful physical condition. Eventually he asked a question merely to divert his lustful thoughts.

"Have you really never studied nudes? I thought artists learned to draw from nude models."

"Most do," she answered, her tone distracted. "But the Royal Academy has strict rules that serve as the standard for the artistic community. Only men are permitted to view nude models."

"That policy puts female artists at a disadvantage, doesn't it?"

"Yes. Before that day in the cove when I discovered you swimming, I had never seen a naked man."

"Not even your former suitor?"

There was a brief hesitation, as if Diana suddenly

realized where the conversation had taken them. "No, not even him."

"What was he, a prude? Did he make love with his nightshirt on?"

She fixed Thorne with a cool frown. "We never made love, if you must know."

"Never?"

"Not ever."

His eyebrow arched. "Do you mean to tell me you are still a virgin?"

"Well . . . yes."

The delicate color that suffused her face told him she was embarrassed by her confession, or perhaps by the intimacy of his question, but he couldn't regret asking.

She was still a virgin.

Thorne marveled at the revelation. For some unknown reason, it pleased him that she was still untouched.

His gratification was tempered, however, when another thought struck him: Diana knew nothing of the pleasures her body was made for.

In fact, it was possible she'd never had much pleasure in her life, sexually or otherwise. She herself had admitted that since the scandal of her elopement, she had hidden herself away in the country. Other than her art, her life might well have been monotonous and barren.

Thorne frowned. He was beginning to see more clearly what Diana had been up against. She had been branded a social outcast while the bounder who had betrayed her had gotten off scot-free. It was damned unfair.

"It seems rather inequitable that you alone suffered the consequences of your elopement," he said softly.

Diana glanced down at the brush in her hand, unable to explain the sudden ache in her throat. She didn't want Thorne's pity, yet she was touched by his understanding. Society's punishment had been reserved strictly for her.

And he had hit on a prime source of her resentment—being disgraced with none of the benefits. She had never made love, never known passion; in fact, she didn't really know how to kiss well. It didn't seem fair that she should be considered a fallen woman when she was really a virginal innocent. She had made one horrendous mistake—falling in love with the wrong man—and had paid for it ever since. Living her life alone, with no prospect of marriage or children. No husband, no lover, no real companionship.

Although she had refused to let herself admit it, she *had* been lonely, even before losing most of her remaining family. She had only Amy left, and Amy really was too young to offer much emotional support or sympathy.

She looked up to find Thorne watching her, his eyes soft with understanding. His expression made her throat tighten even further. He knew her darkest secret and yet didn't condemn her for it. More touching still, he didn't believe she had deserved the punishment that society had meted out to her. Even Nathaniel hadn't defended her so unequivocally.

Swallowing hard, Diana averted her gaze. "I brought the scandal on myself," she replied, trying to make light of Thorne's sympathy.

"Did you?"

She managed a smile. "I am not a helpless, languishing female, Thorne. I take full responsibility for what I did."

"No, helpless you are not. And you have my complete admiration. I could never have borne being imprisoned by society's dictates, as you've been. Essentially being locked in a convent with no hope for redemption."

When she fell mute, Thorne spoke quietly into the silence. "I've been called an expert at lovemaking. I could show you what you have missed."

Diana's gaze flew to his. He was entirely serious, she realized, seeing his somber expression. He wasn't trying to provoke her or even seduce her.

For a wild, brief moment she even considered accepting his offer. The truth was, she hated being a spinster. Hated being at the mercy of rigid convention. Hated being alone.

She would indeed like to know what physical pleasure she had missed. She wanted to know passion.

Thorne could show her, Diana had no doubt. She remembered the incredible pleasure he had given her when he merely caressed her breasts that night.

He had made his desire for her perfectly clear. Even now there was something warm and exciting and flattering in the way he was looking at her.

His offer was so very tempting. She had never known a man like Thorne. His daring boldness was exciting. He seemed to take joy from life, to drink it in—a quality that was irresistible to a woman who had led the sheltered life she had. She'd never met anyone who was so vibrant and magnetic, so arousing to be near. She felt intoxicatingly alive in his presence; the dangerous edge of his sensual appeal was a potent elixir.

Diana squeezed her eyes shut. During her first betrothal, she had let herself dream of the kind of ecstasy Thorne promised. Longed for the shared passion between a man and a woman that could make them one entity.

She still longed for it, if she was honest with herself.

Yet she realized the total impossibility of indulging in an affair with Thorne. She had vowed to take control of her life, to embark on a new path, where she could savor the freedom that she'd been denied since her scandalous elopement. But she wasn't wanton enough to throw aside all her ingrained morals.

Moreover, she had obligations. Certainly she had to think of Amy. She had to avoid any further scandal to keep from damaging her cousin's chances for a successful comeout.

And if she took her intimacy with Thorne any further, she would no doubt suffer for it.

No, Diana reflected regretfully, no matter how tempting, the promise of fleeting pleasure was not worth the risk.

Reluctantly she shook her head. "Thank you—" Hearing the huskiness of her voice, Diana stopped and tried to compose herself. Forcing a careless smile, she began again. "I appreciate your kindness, Thorne, but I think I prefer to keep my virginity intact."

He cocked his head, regarding her soberly. "I can bring you pleasure and still leave your virginity intact."

She felt her eyes widen at that. "Truly? Is that possible?"

With a glance at the open cabin door, Thorne lowered his voice, as if to keep from being overheard by anyone who might be passing by in the corridor. "I needn't penetrate your body with my flesh. Do you remember when I touched you that night on the bluffs? When I aroused you?"

How could she possibly forget? She paused before saying, "Yes."

"That was only the beginning. If I had wanted to go further, I would have stimulated you by stroking between your thighs with my hands and mouth."

"Your *mouth*?"

He smiled at her faintly shocked tone. "There is a tiny bud hidden by your woman's cleft that is the heart of your sexual pleasure. Caressing it can bring you to intense arousal. If I were to kiss you there, if I used my tongue to stroke you, you would find the experience especially pleasurable."

Diana felt warmth ripple through her. Just the thought of Thorne's tongue caressing between her thighs aroused her.

"I never realized." She glanced down at his loins, seeing the unmistakable bulge in his breeches. She knew her cheeks were scarlet, and yet she was profoundly curious. "I have seen paintings of lovers coupling, but a man's sexual arousal is a mystery to me. You grew quite . . . large that day at the cove."

His smile was tender. "Many women appreciate a man's large size."

"But why?"

"Reportedly because a prominent erection fills them more deeply. They find it more arousing."

"But how could it . . . possibly fit?"

"Easily. The center of your woman's body grows warm and moist as you prepare to receive a man. When your softness sheathes my hardness, your tissues flow around me."

"Oh."

Thorne watched Diana with mingled tenderness and understanding. She looked ruffled, deliciously so, and obviously flustered by her ignorance and the intimacy of their discussion. But she deserved to have her curiosity satisfied.

"Do you feel moisture gathering between your thighs just now? If I touched you, would I find you hot and wet?"

She shut her eyes, not replying, but he had his answer when she shivered.

"You have a similar arousing effect on me, love," Thorne said, his voice husky with desire. "You have made me hugely swollen."

"Thorne . . ." As if recalling the brazenness of their conversation, Diana suddenly shook herself and turned away. "This conversation has become much too improper."

Setting down his glass, Thorne rose from his chair and went to her. When Diana wouldn't meet his eyes, he brought his fingers up to cup her chin.

She drew back from him as if burned.

Shrugging then, she gave an embarrassed laugh and pretended nonchalance. "I don't need you to show me what I have missed, Thorne. Despite my tarnished reputation, I am not abandoned enough to let you seduce me."

Thorne allowed the heat of his gaze to travel slowly from her lush mouth to her dark eyes, and back to her mouth. In all truth, her seduction was not his intent. He wanted Diana to know pleasure. Wanted to be the one to *initiate* her into pleasure. He wanted her passionate and wild, her limbs entwined and clinging to his while she shattered beneath him.

Yet contrarily, her utter carnal innocence aroused his protective instincts. Even more than his fierce desire to make love to her, he wanted to protect her from himself.

He could show her how to climax, but he didn't

dare. He didn't trust himself to be able to stop at just that.

Thorne roughly cleared his throat. "Don't worry," he assured her, "I won't press you. I only want you to understand and enjoy your own body. But you can learn how to pleasure yourself without me. Tonight as you fall asleep, you can caress yourself, just as I would."

When she stared at him, he pictured Diana lying in her bed with her thighs parted, her fingers roaming over her sex. . . . The erotic image sent a streak of heat stabbing through Thorne and made him even harder. His erection ached so brutally, he thought he might burst.

He clenched his jaw, knowing he had to leave her before his control snapped altogether. "I think perhaps we should continue this sitting another time," he grated.

"Perhaps so," Diana agreed with obvious relief.

Turning away, he quickly pulled on his shirt and jacket. Without glancing at her again, he made his way painfully along the ship's corridor to his own cabin and shut the door firmly behind him.

He was so hot and aroused, he was sweating. In sweet agony, Thorne pressed his damp forehead against the door panel. What he wouldn't give to be free of this savage, restless hunger that had plagued him since laying eyes on that bewitching woman.

Somehow he had to quell the reckless fantasy he'd built up about Diana over the past two weeks. Had to expunge any thoughts of her seduction from his mind.

With a curse, he unbuttoned his breeches and drawers and closed his fist around his straining shaft, imagining Diana's tight, hot sheath enveloping him, her hips jerking with ecstasy as he thrust hard into her. . . .

It took only three quick strokes of his hand before he exploded.

Shuddering, Thorne groaned through gritted teeth and sagged against the wooden panel, while his seed spurted wildly between his fingers.

It was a long moment before his heart stopped pounding, longer still before his senses returned, before his heated flesh cooled.

He had temporarily sated his body, bringing a measure of sexual relief. Yet he knew his desperate ministrations wouldn't provide anywhere near the satisfaction of making love to Diana Sheridan for real.

Nor would it quell the raging fever she had aroused in him without even trying.

Six

LONDON

After the golden climate of Cyrene, Diana found the chill April fog of London vastly unappealing. But the impending call on Thorne's aunt discomfited her more. As the carriage drew up before Lady Hennessy's elegant mansion in Berkeley Square, Diana's stomach felt tied in knots.

Upon docking this morning, Thorne had insisted on coming directly here, intent on settling the issue of Amy's comeout. Amy had fidgeted the entire way, and Diana's nerves were not much calmer.

Her reception, she suspected, would be less than welcoming, simply because of her scandalous reputation. And now that she was betrothed to Thorne—however temporarily or falsely—the prospect of facing his august family was intimidating enough to make her regret ever agreeing to his mad proposal.

Thorne alone seemed unconcerned by the forthcoming interview, Diana noted. On the other hand, he'd kept his expression enigmatic in her company ever since the afternoon of his portrait sitting, when she had painted him without his shirt.

By tacit agreement, they hadn't repeated any further private encounters for the remainder of the sea voyage. Strangely, although their brazen conversation that day had brought about a new, disturbing level of intimacy between them, Diana felt *more* comfortable with Thorne rather than less. Now that he knew all her secrets, she could attempt to view him simply as a friend instead of as a potential lover, treating him as she had treated her cousin Nathaniel.

Thorne seemed just as intent on keeping their relationship impersonal, for which Diana was grateful. She was also grateful that he seemed to understand her trepidation just now.

He gave her a bracing smile as he handed her down from the carriage. "Cheer up, love. My aunt is not the terror you're obviously expecting."

When he ushered the two cousins up the front steps, they were admitted by a stately butler, who promptly sent a footman to announce their arrival to her ladyship.

No sooner had the door closed than a fashionably dressed young lady came rushing down the grand staircase, exclaiming in delight, "Oh, famous, you are here at last!"

Amy laughed with glee and hurried forward, embracing the high-spirited newcomer fervently. Then evidently remembering her manners, she turned back to Diana and introduced Miss Cecily Barnes, Thorne's cousin on his mother's side.

Cecily was several inches taller than Amy, and her hair was a vivid shade of red, but the two young ladies seemed to be bosom friends, despite their differences.

After murmuring a polite greeting, Cecily clutched Amy's hands, barely containing her excitement. "It is so famous—Aunt Hennessy says you may have your comeout with me."

"Truly?" Amy looked relieved enough to swoon, but she refrained when an elegant, portly, silver-haired woman appeared in the entrance hall.

Diana instinctively stiffened as a pair of bright hazel eyes very much like Thorne's swept over her.

Then to her amazement, Lady Hennessy smiled warmly at her before offering her cheek to Thorne. "You are full of surprises, aren't you, dear boy?"

Diana suspected that few people called Thorne "dear boy" these days, but there was obviously great affection between them.

"As always, love," he replied unrepentantly as he kissed his aunt's cheek.

The countess drew back. "Now, pray present me to your betrothed before I expire from curiosity."

Thorne put a possessive hand at the small of Diana's back, rousing her instant awareness as he introduced her.

Before he was halfway done, Lady Hennessy took Diana's gloved hand in both of hers. "Welcome to the family, my dear. You must be very special indeed to have landed my scapegrace nephew."

Diana admittedly was taken aback by the warmth of her reception, but before she could do more than murmur a reply, Amy broke in.

"Oh, Lady Hennessy, is it true? Do you mean to sponsor my Season?"

The elder lady sent an exasperated look at the girl. "If you promise to behave yourself, I will bring you out, and gladly. It will be good for Cecily to have a boon companion to bear her company. And it should be no more trouble to launch two girls than one."

Amy made a graceful curtsey. "You are too kind, my lady."

"Pah, kindness has little to do with it. Simply put, I could use the diversion. An aging widow like myself finds little pleasure in her waning years."

Thorne chuckled at that. "What drivel. You are hardly aging, darling aunt. Your beauty would put this season's crop of debs to shame."

"Well, I admit I was a beauty in my day, but that was long ago." Lady Hennessy glanced at the two girls. "Run along, now, and allow us some privacy. Cecily, you may show Amy to her rooms."

Grinning, both girls curtsied again and rushed off, already chattering about the delights that awaited them.

Thorne's aunt arched a quizzical eyebrow at her nephew. "I trust you mean to tell me how your betrothal came about. It is a nine days' wonder here in London, as I'm sure you realize."

His arm slipping around his betrothed's waist, Thorne gave Diana an intimate smile reserved for lovers. "It was simple. I took one look at her and fell head over heels."

"I was certain that must be the case. Your father was rattled by the news, of course. In truth, he doesn't quite believe it—he claims you are up to some trick. Redcliffe is my younger brother," she confided to Diana, "and he has long feared he would never have a grandson to carry on the title."

Her attention returned to Thorne. "I am gratified that you have finally decided to quit opposing Ivan, so there will finally be peace in the family. Come, join me in my sitting room and tell me all about it."

"I am afraid we cannot stay, Aunt. Diana is eager to visit her studio. She is an artist, you know."

"So your letter said." She murmured this last gingerly, as if she intended to reserve judgment about Diana's unconventional career, but at least her tone held no overt condemnation, as Diana certainly had expected. "But you cannot run off so soon. You only just arrived."

Scarcely having been given the chance to say a word, Diana decided it was time to enter the conversation. Smiling politely, she offered her carefully prepared speech. "I do so appreciate your kindness in taking Amy under your wing. I will miss her, but I know I am leaving her in excellent hands. With your permission, I would like to visit her from time to time to make certain she is behaving."

"But you are staying here with me, of course?" Lady Hennessy glanced in surprise at Thorne, who said, "That is up to Diana."

Diana felt her own eyes widen at the mistaken assumption. "No, my lady, I have already hired a house where I plan to live. I must have a studio where I can work."

"I see no reason you cannot *work* there, but you will reside here."

"But I wouldn't dream of imposing."

"Nonsense. You would not be imposing in the least. I have opened this huge house for the Season, and there is more than ample room. And if you mean to stifle the gossipmongers, then you had better do so from under my roof. You can live here with Amy and Cecily and visit your studio daily, where you can paint to your heart's content."

Diana hesitated, gratified by the extremely generous offer. Lady Hennessy undoubtedly had a shrewd understanding of polite society, and since she was a fixture in the ton, with her blessing, Diana's acceptance would be far more likely.

"Well, then . . . I thank you, my lady."

"Pah, don't thank me yet. I shall be thanking *you* soon enough, I expect, for I mean you to spell me occasionally from my custodial duties. Supervising two rambunctious girls will no doubt be exhausting."

"I would be happy to spell you," Diana said with a genuine smile.

"Excellent. I will have Jives fetch your baggage along with Amy's." A mischievous twinkle lit the countess's hazel eyes as she added, "You may visit your studio now, Miss Sheridan, but when you return, I will expect a full accounting of your betrothal."

Diana winced inwardly, but managed to reply with a gracious, "Of course."

Accompanied by Thorne, she returned to the street, where his carriage waited, along with an entire dray loaded with trunks.

Diana had to sort out which ones contained their new wardrobes, and which contained her art supplies and the paintings she'd made, to have them delivered to her studio.

When she was finally settled in the carriage again with Thorne, she gave him a quelling frown. "You could have warned me. You asked your aunt to invite me to stay with her, didn't you?"

"I might have suggested the arrangement, but I left it to her to make the offer. You don't want to live there?"

"It isn't that." Still frowning, Diana turned to gaze out the carriage window.

She had been eager to set up her own residence in a

quiet street, yet not simply to have a studio where she could work. For the first time in all her twenty-four years, she wanted to live in her own home. A place that belonged solely to her, where she would no longer be the dependent orphaned relation, living on the goodwill of relatives, no matter how dear. Where she would have the freedom of not being judged. Where finally her life would be her own.

But mostly it was her pride that was smarting. She disliked suffering anyone's charity, and Lady Hennessy's offer was extremely charitable. But then, Diana reminded herself, she was in no position to refuse. Indeed, she should appreciate such kindness.

"It will be better," Thorne observed, "for both you and Amy if you're quartered with my aunt. Her sponsorship will cloak you in a positive fog of respectability."

"I know, and I am grateful to her." Diana shrugged off her frustration. "And truly, I didn't want to leave Amy behind in someone else's hands. I felt like a mother hen forsaking my chick. But I consoled myself that she would have to leave the nest sometime, and that I could rely on your aunt to manage her. And John Yates promised to look in on Amy from time to time."

"Now you won't have to forsake her. It also seems fortuitous that your studio is not too distant from my aunt's house—less than a mile, I believe. Still, you will need your own carriage to travel back and forth."

"I had planned to hire my own carriage, thank you."

"I can handle hiring one for you."

Diana gave him a cool glance. "I see the wisdom of accepting your aunt's charity, Thorne, but I do not require yours."

His green-gold eyes considered her for a moment. "You needn't be so prickly, my dear dragon," he finally said. "Charity has nothing to do with my offer. Even if I didn't feel obliged to Nathaniel to see you safely settled, as your betrothed, I have a duty to ensure your protection. We're pretending to have a love match, remember? My aunt was entirely correct. The gossip rags will be full of on-dits about us just now, so keeping up appearances is imperative. The harpies will tear you to shreds if they see a chink in our story."

Diana's gaze slid uncomfortably away from his. She had read compassion there, as if he understood her wounded pride. "You are right, of course," she conceded.

After that they maintained a mutual silence until they drew up before a modest, three-story house on Hawlings Street. The residence belonged to a friend of her drawing master, a man who was also an artist but who had recently retired to the country. It was equipped with a spacious studio on the upper floor, and Diana had hired it this past February, within minutes of laying eyes on it.

When she was escorted up the front steps by Thorne, she was greeted by the cheerful housekeeper, who headed the small staff of servants that had already settled in.

The main floor held a pleasant parlor, dining room, servants' quarters, and kitchens; the second floor, bedchambers and a sizable drawing room for entertaining guests.

After viewing the lower floors, Thorne asked to see the studio, so Diana led him up another flight of stairs. The studio was actually two rooms: The main one was huge, with tall, north-facing windows to provide ample light and filled with various kinds of furniture and props—to serve as backdrops, Diana explained. The other smaller room was used as a storeroom for more props and supplies and finished paintings.

When Thorne asked about all the paper-wrapped bundles he saw in the storeroom, Diana answered, "I had a number of my paintings shipped to London, so that I might show them during my interview with the British Academy for the Fine Arts."

"Will you allow me to see those?"

"Someday, if you wish."

"I do wish."

She led him back to the main studio, then shut the door behind her. Since Thorne had stopped to study the odd assortment of props, Diana nearly ran into him.

When he turned instinctively and grasped her upper arms to steady her, her breath faltered. This was the closest they had come to intimacy since their fateful hour when she had painted him half-nude.

Suddenly the air between them was rife with sensual tension; they both felt it.

Diana went still, afraid to move. Thorne was gazing down at her with an intent look in his eyes that made her wonder if he meant to kiss her. She shivered, keenly aware of the rich, disturbing promise of his mouth.

His beautiful mouth.

She stared at it, vividly recalling their last intimate conversation. Thorne had described in sensual detail how his mouth could arouse her if he kissed her between her thighs. How she could arouse herself by pretending *his* hands were caressing her rather than her own.

She hadn't dared entertain his scandalous suggestion of arousing herself, for fear that such a wanton act would only increase her longing for him. But just now the image filled her mind, of them lying nude together as lovers while Thorne initiated her to the pleasures he had depicted.

She suspected he was picturing the same titillating images as she, yet he was the first to break the silence—by roughly clearing his throat. "Well then, I will take my leave. I'll have a hired carriage sent round to return you to my aunt's house when you are ready."

"Thank you. Thorne?" she added when he turned to go. "What will you do about Nathaniel?"

"I told you, I mean to investigate his death."

"I know, but what precisely do you mean to *do*? Venus is a Cyprian, I gathered from his letter."

She thought at first Thorne didn't intend to answer. But then he replied with evident reluctance. "A rather successful Cyprian, actually. She owns a fashionable sin club near Mayfair."

"A sin club?"

"Where gentlemen go to indulge in various carnal delights. Not the sort of establishment to be discussed with a lady like yourself."

"Oh." His explanation brought a flush of color to Diana's cheeks, and an instant stab of jealousy to her breast, as she pictured Thorne indulging in the delights he spoke of.

But then she knew he was a highly physical man. And it was really none of her concern what members of the demimonde he chose to consort with. No doubt he had his pick of "fashionable impures," as they were termed. He might even keep a mistress here in London, Diana realized with another pang of distress.

As for sin clubs, ladies did not acknowledge that such places even existed. Very likely Thorne had mentioned it purposely to put her off, so he wouldn't have to answer the probing questions she was longing to ask. He obviously didn't want her to know anything about his plans to investigate.

She was no longer even certain she wanted to know, since she suspected he would begin by visiting Venus's sin club. Yet she did have one concern that she couldn't repress.

"Will you please be careful?" Diana murmured, gazing up at him. "If Nathaniel was murdered, it is possible that you could be also."

His mouth curled in his familiar reckless grin. "I could almost believe you care about me, love."

"Of course I care."

"Don't worry, I am difficult to kill."

He left her gazing solemnly after him and made his way out to his waiting carriage, relieved to have escaped. He didn't want Diana questioning his plans, for fear of her learning about the Guardians. He didn't want to be alone with her, either, for fear of losing his control.

His mind persisted in harboring fantasies of her. He'd experienced another erotic one just now, where he had savagely covered her kissable lips while he pinned her up against the wall and drove his aching flesh into the hot slick depths of her.

Fiend seize it! That woman was supremely dangerous to him, in more ways than one.

Unfortunately, Thorne acknowledged sardonically as he settled back against the leather seat cushions, he had always craved danger.

Perhaps that was why he craved Diana Sheridan like a starving man hungered for sustenance.

Thorne took the time to visit his house in Cavendish Square, arranged to hire a town carriage for Diana, perused some correspondence that had accumulated in his two-month absence, then changed his clothes for something less elegant, and rode out again, hunting a certain set of lodgings in Mayfair.

Since he was well known there, he was readily admitted by the servants. Finding Macky's bedchamber dark even though the afternoon was well advanced, Thorne forcibly curbed his impatience and settled in a wing chair to wait for the slumbering man to become aware of his visitor.

It did not take long. One moment Macky was snoring softly, his head buried under a pillow. The next he was sitting bolt upright in bed, a dagger clutched in his fist while his bloodshot blue eyes intently scanned the chamber, searching for danger.

When they lit on Thorne, Macky fell back among the pillows with a relieved chuckle and shut his eyes again.

"Rough night?" Thorne asked.

Grimacing, Macky rubbed his stubbled jaw and returned a slow grin, as if remembering fondly. "Devil a bit."

"I gather you managed to secure a position at Venus's club?"

"Surely you didn't think I would fail? Where is your faith, m'lord?"

Thorne had had every faith Macky would succeed in his mission. Beau Macklin was a former provincial actor turned Guardian. Born in the stews of London, he'd spent the early years of his youth as a pickpocket, miraculously escaping a life of crime when he was taken up by a traveling theater company after trying to steal the manager's pocket watch.

A few years older than Thorne's age of thirty-one, Macky was tall and muscular, with curling chestnut hair and a handsome visage. With his flair for accents, he was capable of playing numerous characters, anything from ruffian to bruiser to nobleman. The role of "gallant" was his favorite, for even ladies far above his class fell for his roguish charm with laughable ease.

His most usual guise these days was that of a gentleman about town. Thus, in order to be hired as an employee of Venus's sin club, his social status had to have been lowered several notches.

Macky, however, didn't seem to mind the demotion, Thorne judged from the man's crooked grin.

"I confess I was surprised to get your orders," Macky admitted as he sat up again respectfully, "but it has turned out to be a most pleasurable assignment, if I do say so."

"So Venus accepted you without suspicion?"

"Entirely. You know the design of the club. The male attendants are not the prime attraction—present more for show than for sport. But I've worked there five nights now, and four of those nights, my services were solicited by a female patron. If this assignment continues, it may well put me in an early grave, but I vow I could die a happy man."

Thorne gave a slow chuckle. "You cannot expire just yet, my friend. Not until you have some results to show for your efforts. Have you made any progress becoming acquainted with Venus's regular employees?"

"A very little. Madam Venus was quite clear when

she hired me. Her male attendants are not allowed to fraternize with her girls. But I've made a friend of one particular beauty by the name of Kitty. She's a bit on the shy side, but she has worked there longer than most. If anyone knows Venus's secrets, it might be Kitty."

"What about the men?"

"Most of them are relative newcomers. It seems common practice for them to attract the eye of a patron and move on to a more private arrangement, possibly even marriage. I approached the club's two bruisers, all friendly-like, but I doubt I can inspire them to confide in me, since they seem very dedicated to the madam."

"Well, do your best," Thorne urged. "I'm most interested in discovering if Venus had any connection to the late Thomas Forrester."

"So your orders said. Do you think it likely?"

"My gut tells me so. It's just too much of a coincidence that Forrester was seeking a list of Guardians barely a few months after Nathaniel began suspecting Venus of trying to expose our identities to the French."

Frowning, Macky eyed Thorne with curiosity. "You didn't ask me to pursue Forrester's trail this time."

"No. I'm leaving that for John Yates to handle. He accompanied me from Cyrene."

Macky nodded. "Since Yates became Sir Gawain's secretary, I regularly get dispatches from him, but I've only met him once, and that was before he lost a leg, poor bastard. I suppose he wants to make up for being duped by Forrester's spies last fall?"

"In part. And he wants justice for Nathaniel," Thorne added grimly, "as I do. Yates will be a better executor, though, for this particular task. He isn't well known in London, as I am. It would seem highly odd if I started asking questions in that part of town."

"After half a year, Forrester's trail will be damned cold. I already investigated every lead I could find. When he died in that fire last fall, he took his secrets with him."

"But once you learned of his death, you didn't look much further. I want Yates to dig deeper this time, try to find anything you might have missed. He's to start by interviewing Forrester's neighbors—making up a tale about Forrester being a long-lost relative who's come into a fortune. The scent of riches may bring a few rats scurrying out of the woodwork."

"Well, let me know if I can help in any way."

"You can. Yates will be paying you a visit shortly so that you can tell him everything you remember about Forrester from your inquiry last fall. But otherwise, I want you to keep your focus on Venus's club. She is the more likely route for unearthing any information of value. I intend to ply Venus directly myself during the next week or so."

"The task of seducing her won't be a hardship for you, I'll wager."

Thorne shook his head. "I will have to be more subtle than that. If she is guilty of treason, as Nathaniel suspected, then she would be instantly suspicious of any behavior out of the ordinary. And for me to suddenly pursue her after my return from Cyrene would be extraordinary, since I've never shown any specific interest in her before now. Besides, I am recently betrothed, and it would hardly be respectful of my future bride to show a notorious madam such marked attention."

"Aye, your betrothal." Macky's raised eyebrows

expressed his rabid curiosity. "A rather surprising turn of events, that was, if I may say so, your lordship."

"You may. I surprised myself as much as anyone else," Thorne said cryptically. Not intending to explain further, he rose to his feet. "I will leave you to your beauty sleep."

Macky grinned again. "Aye, I'll need as much rest as possible before I have to report in for my duties this evening."

"Pray don't enjoy your duties too much. You have a job to do."

"I'll try, m'lord," Macky said cheekily before rolling over and burying his face in the pillows.

Thorne let himself out and returned to the street, his sense of frustration only slightly eased after his conversation with Macky. At last they were taking steps to find Nathaniel's killer, but their progress would doubtless be slow.

In the three weeks since reading Nathaniel's letter, Thorne had felt an increasing urgency to get on with the task. The delay, however, wasn't the sole cause of his restlessness, he knew. A certain virginal, sable-haired temptress was just as much to blame.

Schooling himself to patience, Thorne mounted his horse and turned in the direction of his home. He should be grateful to have this mystery to occupy his mind, he reminded himself, for it forced him to focus—at least temporarily—on something other than his bewitching betrothed.

He returned home to change his attire for evening clothes and then paid a duty call on his father. As expected, he found the Duke of Redcliffe out, and so proceeded to Brooks Gentleman's Club, where he settled in for a long evening of dinner and gaming—with the more calculated purpose of establishing the story of his betrothal and promoting the pretense of a love match.

Also as expected, he was roasted unmercifully by his friends. Word soon spread that Thorne was at Brooks, which attracted a large gathering of acquaintances. He spent hours answering inquiries and pleasantly lying through his teeth, but he bore the torment with apparent good-humored grace, all the while hoping that Diana was faring better.

Diana was just as uncomfortable, for her conscience was pricking her for telling such blatant falsehoods to Thorne's kindly aunt.

It distressed her even more to be the subject of such distasteful speculation among the ton. Lady Hennessy had saved every rag and publication since the cataclysmic betrothal announcement and had given them to Diana, expressing the belief that forewarned was forearmed.

If the papers were any indication, all London had taken notice of Thorne's shocking engagement. Indeed, one might have supposed the event was nearly as monumental as Napoleon's escape from Elba. And not only because no one expected Thorne to become ensnared by matrimony, but also because whispers of Diana's scandalous past still followed her.

Forcing herself to read each and every word, Diana felt the same sinking, sickening feeling of mortification that had hounded her after her aborted elopement six years earlier. The gossip was rife that Thorne had chosen her specifically in order to flout his esteemed father. And fresh speculation had begun once she was shockingly revealed to be an artist. Incredibly, the morning following her arrival in London, the society columns were devoted almost solely to her.

Directly after breakfast, Diana retreated to the morning parlor to read the latest slander in private. No sooner had she finished, however, than Lady Hennessy's butler informed her that she had a caller—the Duke of Redcliffe.

Her heart suddenly thudding at the prospect of facing Thorne's noble father, Diana asked for his grace to be shown in. Rising nervously, she smoothed her skirts, glad to have worn one of her new, exquisitely fashionable morning gowns, and stood waiting.

Her first impression of the aristocratic gentleman who strode into the parlor was one of awe. The duke was perhaps not quite so tall as his son, but he possessed the same athletic grace, the same striking, square-jawed features, the same virility. With his fair hair silvering at the temples, however, combined with his stately bearing, he seemed somehow even more imposing than Thorne.

Redcliffe executed a curt bow, saying, "My compliments, Miss Sheridan. I am pleased to make your acquaintance." His deep voice was languid with aristocratic hauteur, his tone barely civil despite the polite salutation. He did not seem pleased to meet her in the least.

He was here to inspect her, Diana knew.

Determined not to be intimidated, she forced a courteous smile and responded with her most charming manner. "As I am you, your grace. Would you care to be seated? Perhaps take some refreshment?"

"I cannot stay. I am expected at Whitehall. I merely wished to offer you my felicitations on your surprising engagement."

"Thank you."

The duke's glance fell on the table, where copies of the *Morning Post* and the *Morning Chronicle* were opened to the society pages.

Seeing his chiseled mouth curl with distaste, Diana preempted whatever remark he might have made. "No doubt you find the gossip about me alarming. I certainly would, were I in your shoes."

Arching a quizzical eyebrow, he shifted his keen gaze back to her. "Would you indeed?"

"Yet surely," Diana continued, "you of all people know that you cannot believe everything you read in the papers. I am certain you have been the subject of countless reports that bore little resemblance to truth."

"To be sure, I have, Miss Sheridan." He studied her with a speculative look, like a sleepy panther mildly intrigued by a mouse. "Are you saying the reports about your previous elopement and your current profession are false?"

"No, your grace. I am saying that tales are often embellished to titillate and shock. I also harbor the belief that if your son is not offended by my background, then I cannot permit his family's objections to matter."

"Did I say I object?" Redcliffe inquired in a deceptively lazy voice.

Diana was taken aback by the question. "Do you not?"

"I confess my first reaction was dismay that my son had entered into a mésalliance merely to spite me. But I soon realized I should be relieved by any betrothal at all. I have long wanted to see Thorne put an end to his wild ways and become . . . respectably settled, and my hope is that his marriage will accomplish that."

His emphasis on *respectably* was deliberate, Diana knew. And she suspected Redcliffe was not relieved at all, that his appearance of unruffled calm was merely an act.

She understood his reservations, of course. A woman with her past—or her present, for that matter—wasn't worthy to be the wife of a future duke. And she could not dispute him.

Still, she had promised Thorne to maintain the pretense that their betrothal was real, even though it would require all her acting skills to convince his father.

"Your concern is only natural, your grace," Diana said sweetly, "but I am very much in love with your son, and he professes to love me."

"You are to be applauded, Miss Sheridan," he said dryly. "My son has never before claimed to be in love. But I should like to offer you a warning. Thorne has always had a reckless nature, and it extends to his amorous affairs. He plays with hearts like they were so many draughts. Women are merely sport to him."

To her surprise, Thorne's cool voice sounded from the doorway. "That might once have been the case, Father," he drawled as he sauntered into the parlor, "but it was before I met Diana."

Moving across the room to join her, he raised her fingers to his lips and offered her a brilliant smile. "Good morning, my love."

Diana felt her heartbeat quicken, both at his romantic gesture and at the tender expression in his eyes. Even if his show of adoration was merely a sham for his father's sake, it was extremely beguiling. And so was Thorne's appearance. He looked particularly striking this morning, his tall, elegantly athletic form flattered by the burgundy coat and buff pantaloons he wore.

Protectively placing a hand at her back, Thorne turned to confront his father. "I see you have met my lovely bride-to-be."

The duke didn't seem at all disconcerted to be caught discussing his son's affairs; rather just the opposite. For a moment the two men stood regarding each other, an unspoken challenge crackling between them.

Redcliffe was the first to break the silence. "I understand Miss Sheridan is quite an exceptional talent."

Thorne's mouth twisted. "My congratulations to your network of spies, sir. You must have employed them to learn of Diana's remarkable skill, since the gossip columns have said nothing about it. You sent your minions to Derbyshire to inquire about her, did you not?"

"Did you expect otherwise? When my only son and heir becomes betrothed, I think I have a right—even the obligation—to be concerned. But you wrong me in one respect. Miss Sheridan's reputation in the artistic community precedes her to London, and it is a very favorable one." The duke addressed Diana then. "I am a patron of the Royal Academy, Miss Sheridan."

"So Thorne tells me, your grace."

"I should like to view your work. Perhaps I might be able to endorse you. My opinion carries some weight in artistic circles."

"Thank you, but I hope to have the endorsement of the British Academy very soon," Diana said coolly.

"I can vouch that her work truly is exceptional,"

Thorne interjected sincerely. "Diana's talent is part of what led me to fall in love with her."

Redcliffe's mouth thinned with skepticism, while his tone turned wry. "I would think less of you, Christopher, if you had chosen a hack." His expression sobered then as he regarded his son. "At least you are wise enough to bring her here to your aunt. Once society learns of Judith's sponsorship, Miss Sheridan's acceptance should be assured."

"I am well aware of that, sir. And I have no doubt you will also come to accept Diana, once you know her. Meanwhile, I would be obliged if you could manage to conceal your displeasure at my betrothal."

"I cannot say I am displeased. On the contrary, I have high hopes that your betrothal will finally cure you of scandal."

Thorne's eyes narrowed. "I have similar hopes that you will no longer insist on involving yourself in my affairs."

"If you are wed, then I should no longer have reason to involve myself. But perhaps you will endeavor to cool the gossips' tongue-wagging, for your bride's sake, if not for the obligation you owe your family name."

"I will make every effort to do your bidding, Father," Thorne replied ironically. "You know I exist only to please you."

"The devil you do," his father retorted, his lips curving with unwilling amusement.

Turning, Redcliffe gave Diana another bow, this one more respectful than his first had been. "I bid you good day, Miss Sheridan. If you insist upon wedding this wild son of mine, you may count on my support. But I hope you don't come to regret it."

When the duke had departed, Diana drew a long breath, relieved to have survived the interview.

"You handled that well," Thorne commented.

"Then why is there still an army of butterflies doing battle in my stomach?"

He regarded her with sympathetic amusement. "I regret I wasn't here to intercept him. I should have known he would call here so he could scrutinize you."

"He was rightly disturbed about your unsuitable choice of bride."

"But you didn't allow him to intimidate you. Not that I expected it. You are no doubt a match for my father."

Diana felt herself smile. "I consider that high praise." Surprisingly, however, she'd found herself liking Thorne's father, possibly because she had glimpsed the affection they bore for each other, despite the obvious contention between them. "He was plainly troubled by my notoriety, but the betrothal itself appears to gratify him."

"My matrimonial prospects have long been a game between us," Thorne said dryly. "My father claims unjustly that I am the bane of his existence and tries to rule my life, to turn me into a staid, respectable member of society like he has become."

"He has not had much success, I suspect."

"Not a bit."

Diana could well believe the duke had had difficulty in molding his son to conform. Thorne was a rebel at heart and had no qualms about defying his father, or the whole of society, for that matter. No doubt it was disgraceful of her, but Thorne's daring was one of the things she admired about him. She herself had never had the courage to dare defy society after her elopement. At least not until now.

"Don't concern yourself with my father," Thorne advised. "Whether or not he approves of you, he would never publicly oppose our betrothal. Instead he'll close ranks around you and pretend to accept you into the family."

Diana suddenly recalled that she was alone with Thorne in his aunt's parlor. "Did you come here this morning for some specific reason?"

"I thought perhaps you and Amy might enjoy a ride in the park after being confined aboard ship for so long. And it will be helpful for us to be seen together."

She returned a rueful smile. "Nothing would delight me more than a ride, but I promised Amy to accompany her shopping, and I expect that will take the better part of the day."

"Then I should take you for a drive in the park this afternoon at five."

Diana nodded. At that hour, Hyde Park was the fashionable place to see and be seen. "I should enjoy that."

"We will need to arrange some evening outings, in addition. Do you like the theater? Or opera?"

"Very much. Although I have had little opportunity to attend either, living in the country."

He raised a finger to touch her cheek. "We will have to remedy that," he said softly. "You shouldn't be required to spend all your time working or supervising Amy. You deserve a bit of pleasure in your life."

I can bring you pleasure.

A tremor of heat thrummed through Diana's body as she recalled the offer Thorne had made her on board his ship. He had not been speaking of the theater then, though.

He must have felt the same heat, for his jaw suddenly tightened and he stepped back. "I will call for you at five."

When she was alone once more, Diana released a pent-up sigh of relief. It was deplorable, how Thorne managed to arouse her with merely a look. She could still feel her budded nipples pressing against the fabric of her bodice, still feel a treacherous warmth between her thighs.

The warmth inside her faded, however, when, sinking onto the settee, she glimpsed the newspapers.

Diana winced. She was a scandal-glossed novelty for the moment, but with the support of Thorne's illustrious family, she might very well succeed in weathering the storm. Even so, she was conscious of a vague despondency descending over her.

As a bride, she was completely unsuitable for Thorne, and her unworthiness depressed her.

Yet her dejection had more to do with Thorne himself, and the memory of his father's warning: *He plays with hearts like they were so many draughts. Women are merely sport to him.*

Diana felt an arrow of pain stab through her.

It was safest to think of Thorne as a rogue and treat him with disdain, but she could no longer lie to herself. He was not the rake she had always thought him. His genuine kindness toward her, his employment by the Foreign Office, his restraint when he could so easily have seduced her, all had increased her fascination for him, even more than his arousing physical beauty.

Yet Thorne wasn't the kind of man ever to give his heart. Passion certainly, but not love. A man of his reckless nature was unlikely to ever settle down in matrimony, as his father wished.

Diana gave a despairing sigh. She would do well to remember that their betrothal was completely false, as was their claim of a love match.

And somehow she would have to erect better defenses against Thorne if she didn't want her heart broken, as it had been once before.

Seven

Thorne paused in the doorway of Venus's sin club two nights later, forcibly repressing his more violent emotions.

The elegant drawing room glittered under the crystal chandeliers and pulsed with the gaiety of satisfied guests and orchestra music—much as it had the unforgettable night of Nathaniel's death more than a year ago.

Thorne had visited Venus's club on numerous occasions since then, but this was the first time since realizing that the notorious madam might be implicated in his friend's murder.

Just now he found it difficult to calm his basest urges. All his primal instincts were clamoring for him to seek out the lovely Venus and throttle her until she confessed her part in Nathaniel's slaying.

As Thorne stood watching, he couldn't help recalling the image of Nathaniel's laughing face. Nate was much like his younger sister Amy, with high spirits and a lust for life that was infectious. He'd enjoyed Venus's club more than any other London hell, relishing the gaming and the male camaraderie and the female companionship.

He and Thorne had often patronized the club together, ever since its opening four years ago. In fact Thorne could still vividly recall their first visit, when Nathaniel had become happily sotted, not only on the excellent wine, but on the corporeal delights that could be found here.

In the days immediately preceding his death, he had seemed especially eager to return. Was that because he'd been ensnared in Venus's silken clutches even then?

For a moment, all the grief Thorne had felt that terrible night came rushing back, tightening his throat and curling his hands into fists. But he couldn't let grief dull his reflexes. Instead, he had to keep his craving for revenge tightly leashed. Had to focus, to keep his wits sharp, his emotions cool and logical.

Setting his jaw, Thorne strolled into the room, with John Yates a step behind him. He'd brought Yates primarily to give him a glimpse of Venus, but also to introduce the younger man to some of his tamer gaming acquaintances.

Almost immediately Yates spied the evening's prime entertainment. When he stumbled to a startled halt, Thorne's gaze was drawn to the dais at the far end of the room, where three nude beauties were onstage, lustily cavorting with a Roman senator. One "slave" was feeding the senator grapes and alternately offering her nipples to suck on. A second was lapping at his huge cock with her long, talented tongue. The third was dribbling red wine over her ripe breasts and even riper mound, stroking the lips of her sex, not merely to arouse her "master" but to tempt the avidly watching gentlemen in the audience.

His face flushing, Yates averted his gaze, apparently trying to hide his shock. Quite possibly he'd never attended a club like this, Thorne suspected.

Which was a far cry from his own experience. In his wilder days, he would have joined the beauties onstage. But scenes like this one had begun to lose their appeal long ago and now roused little more than a feeling of boredom in him. Once he'd joined the Guardians, he had found a purpose for his life that had relegated mindless sexual gratification to the mere trivial.

Nowadays, if he were to indulge in a fantasy such as the one being enacted onstage, he would replace the three beauties with one specific woman.

The image of Diana down on her knees before him, his hands buried in her hair, guiding her as his swollen cock slid in and out of her lush mouth, was arousing enough to make Thorne instantly hard.

"The gaming here will be more to your taste than the entertainment," he said to Yates. "Let me introduce you to some friends of mine, who are congregated at that table over there."

He led Yates toward a seated group of gentlemen who were playing a convivial game of vingt-et-un, and made the introductions. Some of these same men, Thorne recalled, had been present the night Nathaniel died, including the Earl of Hastings and Baron Boothe. Mr. Laurence Carstairs, who had discovered Nathaniel's body in the alley, was also here. And Carstairs was precisely the man Thorne wanted most to question.

John Yates was heartily welcomed and invited to enter the game. Thorne, seating himself next to Carstairs, also joined the play, mainly to distract himself from his fantasy about Diana.

It unnerved him a little that he couldn't prevent his erotic musings at even the most inappropriate times. But then Diana Sheridan was unlike any woman he'd ever known.

Most certainly she wasn't the kind of grasping, shallow beauty who normally pursued him, only after his title and fortune. He couldn't recall any woman who was so unimpressed by his prime attributes. Nor could he remember one who actually dealt with him without trying to impress him.

Perhaps that was why he felt so much at ease with her. He didn't have to fear that she would try to trap him into marriage. Diana had dreams of her own, dreams that didn't hinge on capturing a husband. Aspirations of independence where she could boldly indulge her deepest passion.

But that didn't explain why he wanted her so badly. Why he lusted after her almost to the point of obsession. More likely it was her unique combination of qualities that attracted him so strongly. She was not only beautiful, but intelligent and spirited and challenging. Undeniably, he found her company delightful.

If he had been in the market for a mistress, he would have chosen a candidate like Diana. But Diana herself was forbidden to him, and strangely, he had little desire for any other woman just now.

None of the demireps in Venus's employ, for example, could hold a candle to Diana. Nor could Venus herself.

The thought of trying to seduce Venus was actually distasteful to him. When Macky had suggested that course the other day, Thorne had found himself recoiling.

Which was faintly amusing. Before meeting Diana,

he would have had no qualms about pursuing Venus sexually in order to discover her secrets. He would have sought to become her lover, playing the game of seduction that he excelled at. It was partly because of Nathaniel's alleged relationship with Venus that he was reluctant now. But he knew Diana was more to blame. He was resolved to find another way to expose Venus's role in his friend's death.

"Welcome back, my lord," Venus's husky feminine voice whispered in his ear just then. "We have missed you."

The muscles in his body instinctively stiffened, but with effort, Thorne relaxed and smiled up at the tall, flame-haired madam. "I have missed you and your club, darling. I can never find such delightful pleasures anywhere else in the world."

"We strive to please. Allow me to replenish your glass."

Venus snapped her fingers at a server, who hurriedly appeared with a bottle of vintage port. As if tiring of the card game, Thorne took the opportunity to withdraw and rose to his feet, so he might have a word in private with Venus.

"My compliments, love, on your exquisite taste in wines. I don't believe I ever asked where you procure such quality stock for your cellars. I could only wish my majordomo were half so successful."

She returned a coy smile. "I have my secrets, my lord. As you do yours. Your betrothal took all of London quite by surprise. I trust it won't diminish your attendance here after you are wed."

"I hardly think so. I'm not the kind of man to be bear-led by a wife," Thorne replied. "Nor is my betrothed the type to object to my seeking pleasures outside the marriage bed. She happens to be more worldly than most ladies."

"How fortuitous for you," Venus purred. "I confess I found it amusing to watch his grace's efforts to turn you into a docile lapdog. I doubt any woman alive can tame you."

"I trust not, since I have no desire to be tamed." His smile was lavish. "I much prefer to have my women wild."

"I can help in that respect. You need only say the word."

Thorne shook his head, feigning regret. "For the moment, I intend to remain faithful to my impending vows. After the nuptials will be another question entirely."

"If your betrothed is so broad-minded, then perhaps she might enjoy the pleasures we offer here. I can assure her of an enjoyable experience."

The thought of Diana enjoying the sinful pleasures offered by this den of iniquity brought a fierce stab of disquiet to Thorne's breast. But he merely smiled and said, "Perhaps. I will consider it, Madam Venus. But jealousy may very well prevent me from accepting your most kind offer. I'm certain you can understand why I wouldn't want another man touching my bride."

"Of course, my lord. But the excitement can be all the more sweet if emotions such as jealousy and possessiveness are engaged."

Gallantly, Thorne brought Venus's fingers to his lips. "No doubt you are right."

Thorne remained standing as Venus left him to continue her rounds and to see to the satisfaction of her other guests. But a burning anger made his vision blur with a red haze.

An anger, he knew, that was due in large part to his unreasonably fierce possessiveness of Diana. And also because of Venus's unruffled pretense of delight when addressing him. Quite possibly the beautiful madam thought she had gotten away with murder. But if she had killed Nathaniel, Thorne vowed silently, he would make her pay dearly.

With that muttered vow he recognized yet another change he had undergone in the past few years. Normally the challenge of searching out a killer was the kind of thrill he lived for. He had discovered, however, that there was no thrill when the victim was a cherished friend, as Nathaniel had been.

And he knew he would have to tread carefully with Venus. Women in her profession seldom succeeded because of beauty or carnal talents alone. They prospered because they were clever and adaptable.

Venus had cleverly established her club on Compton Street, near enough to Mayfair to be accessible to the wealthy gentry, and close to the theater district, where most of her demireps came from.

The club catered solely to an elite clientele and employed high-stakes gaming and imaginative sexual experiences to draw large numbers of adventuresome patrons nightly. Upon tiring of the gaming or the erotic entertainment provided, guests could indulge in various fantasies of their own, including multiple partners, and make use of spirits or opium or instruments of pleasure to heighten sexual arousal. Brutality or bestiality, however, were not permitted here, unlike some sin clubs, where a patron could buy whatever pleasure he fancied.

Just then Thorne saw Macky across the room, smiling down at a masked lady. Venus's female clients usually came here masked, so as not to be recognized.

Most often they were members of the nobility, ladies who were trapped in marriages of convenience to husbands who ignored them or were too old to care about infidelity. And sometimes they were older beauties who had done their duty by birthing an heir and so now were allowed to go their own way.

Macky must have been waiting to catch his attention, for with the slightest nod, the actor indicated the pretty, half-nude blonde standing a few yards behind him.

That would be Kitty Wathen, one of Venus's long-time *filles de joie,* Thorne surmised, recognizing her from the description in Macky's reports. Kitty was fairly petite, with luscious breasts that were firm and round as melons.

Macky claimed he hadn't yet become intimate enough with the girl to probe about her employer's past, but their friendship was developing at a steady pace. And Kitty might know if Venus had taken Nathaniel for her lover during the last weeks of his life. Meanwhile, Thorne meant to question his own sources in depth.

Reseating himself at the gaming table beside Laurence Carstairs, Thorne settled in for a long night. Before he was through, he intended to discover everything Carstairs knew about Nathaniel's relationship with Venus, and what Nathaniel might have done during his final days that had gotten him killed.

The president of the British Academy for the Fine Arts, Sir George Enderly, appeared surprised to see Thorne when he escorted Diana to her interview the following morning. But Sir George quickly expressed delight, no doubt because he saw in Thorne a potential new patron.

Diana had previously sent several of her best portraits and landscapes here to be judged, and they were currently on display in the president's office. Thorne had no difficulty recognizing her work, one of which was the vivid seascape she had begun on the island bluffs. But all her paintings held a unique luminosity and character that were both compelling and fresh.

He would have liked the chance to study them in depth, but he left Diana to be interviewed in private and toured the exhibition room while he waited, with the primary goal of viewing her competition. To his admittedly inexperienced eye, the quality of her work was far superior to that of all but a few artists, whose names he recognized.

When the interview was concluded and Sir George and Diana joined him, Thorne took the opportunity to express his opinion. "I am certain you recognize what a superb talent Miss Sheridan is, Sir George."

"Indeed I do, my lord. But there are various considerations to take into account when deliberating whom to accept into the academy."

"Chiefly an applicant's sex, I would imagine?"

"Regrettably, yes. We must concern ourselves with how our major patrons would feel about allowing a female into our ranks. We are funded by private sources, you understand."

"And yet you provide lively competition for the Royal Academy by supporting the more innovative artists. I should think having a woman would be an advantage you could exploit."

"How so, my lord?"

"Just think what a stir it could cause. Miss Sheridan's uniqueness could be a draw for your exhibitions. . . . I understand you operate similarly to the Royal Academy, holding periodic exhibitions."

"We do, indeed. We both sponsor showings and award prizes. And our school offers classes in drawing, painting, sculpture, and er . . . anatomy. Of course, Miss Sheridan would not attend *those,* my lord."

Despite his liberal views regarding female artists, Thorne found himself quite glad Diana would not be painting other nude males.

He smiled cordially at Sir George. "My father, the Duke of Redcliffe, was an intimate of the late Sir Joshua." Sir Joshua Reynolds, a superb portraitist himself, had been president of the Royal Academy of Art for years, and thus a chief arbiter of artistic standards in Britain. "But even my father was wont to complain that Sir Joshua's strict interpretation of merit was stifling creativity."

"Sadly, that is true, Lord Thorne."

"I'm certain that under your stewardship, this academy will be more open-minded than your rival, and that you will make the right decision regarding Miss Sheridan's admittance."

Sir George actually preened. "Thank you, my lord. And I promise you, we will consider Miss Sheridan's acceptance with all due speed." He turned to Diana to shake her hand. "I hope we may keep possession of your paintings for a while longer."

"Yes, of course," she agreed, before leaving the building with Thorne.

"Thank you for accompanying me," she said once they were settled in his town coach. "Sir George was obviously impressed by your interest. Your show of support will at least encourage them to take my application seriously."

"I can better understand your frustration after

hearing him excuse their biases with so little regard for your talent."

Diana bit her lower lip. "I swore I would not allow my hopes to get too high, but it is hard."

"I could always become a patron and insist on your acceptance. A large donation to grease the right palms would likely ensure your entrance."

Her smile was amused but soft with gratitude. "I am touched by your offer, Thorne, but I would prefer to be accepted on my own merits rather than have you purchase admittance for me. It would defeat the whole purpose of my studying there if the art community believed the only way I could gain entrance was through bribery."

"Very well," Thorne conceded before his mouth curved wryly. "But I may still consider becoming a patron, just out of contrariness. I suspect it would put my father's nose out of joint to see me support his rivals."

She eyed Thorne curiously. "Did you make up that tale of your father advising Sir Joshua Reynolds about artistic standards?"

"I might have embellished it a bit."

Diana shook her head in exasperation. "You are completely outrageous."

"I have never tried to deny it, love," Thorne responded lightly, although his thoughts were far from light. He was still smoldering with resentment in Diana's behalf.

It would be a monumental shame if she was refused the chance to develop her exceptional gift by training at the academy. But her concern was a valid one; it would likely prove a detriment if she was thought to have bought her admittance.

Therefore, Thorne resolved silently, if her application was refused, he would simply have to devise a private way to secure her admittance.

He changed the subject, however, so as not to rouse her misgivings.

They had nearly reached his aunt's house in Berkeley Square when Diana suddenly gave a start. She had been gazing out the carriage window, and now she uttered an unladylike oath. "I don't believe it—"

"Believe what?"

Diana shifted her incredulous gaze to Thorne. "That was Amy! With the fortune-hunter I told you about—Reginald Kneighly. She was descending from his curricle!"

Leaning forward, Diana pulled the check string, and the coach immediately slowed. "She must have stolen away to meet him in secret. The nerve of her!"

She was almost out the door when Thorne forestalled her. "Just a moment, sweeting. What do you intend to do?"

"I shall confine her to her rooms with nothing but bread and water—if I don't throttle her first."

The small panel behind the driver's box opened just then. "Milord?" his coachman asked. "You wish a new destination?"

"No, drive on," Thorne ordered.

"Aye, milord," he said, snapping the panel shut once more.

When Diana protested, Thorne shook his head. "Confronting Amy just now may not be the wisest course. You need to consider the consequences first."

"What consequences?" she demanded, obviously smoldering.

"I know you want to protect Amy, but forbidding her to see her beau is not the way to handle her. It will only make her rebel. I should know. I've been rebelling against authority for most of my life, my own father particularly."

"Then what do you suggest? I *must* keep him away from her, Thorne, or she will ruin herself, just as I did." Diana's voice broke on a sob, and she covered her face with her hands.

Thorne felt his heart contract at her obvious distress. Not confident, however, that he could console her as a friend would, he forcibly resisted the urge to take Diana in his arms. He understood her emotional turmoil. She was highly protective of the people she loved, and with Amy she was like a lioness with her cub. Her own past, as well, would make her overly sensitive regarding fortune-hunters, to the point where she couldn't even think rationally.

"Don't allow yourself to become so upset," Thorne said soothingly. "I assure you, I'm not about to let Amy be harmed."

"Then you should do something to stop their lovers' trysts!"

"I intend to. But becoming a watering pot won't benefit our cause."

Stiffening her spine, Diana shot Thorne a fierce glare. A moment later, however, she sat back and dashed away her tears. "You are right." Her hands clenched into fists. "If only I could make Amy see that Kneighly is pursuing her solely for her fortune. If only I could expose his true motives somehow."

Thorne frowned, thinking hard. "There might be a way."

And if he could creatively involve Venus, he might be able to address two problems at once—to end Amy's infatuation with her fortune-hunter and to use her fortune-hunter as an excuse to get close to Venus.

He preferred not to reveal his impulsive plan to

Diana, but he knew she wouldn't acquiesce quietly otherwise. She was looking at him expectantly, her anxiety palpable as she waited for his explanation.

"I have an idea to lure Kneighly away from Amy, or at least to scotch her infatuation with him."

"What idea? How could you possibly scotch her infatuation?"

Thorne drew a slow breath as he debated how much to disclose. In the end, he decided to tell Diana the truth, for she would be less likely to interfere if he took her into his confidence.

"I need a means of getting close to Venus without rousing her suspicions. This could be my excuse."

Diana's eyes widened, and he could see her sharp mind working out questions. But all she said was, "I am listening."

"I want to hire Venus to seduce Kneighly away from Amy."

"Seduce him? Do you think she could manage it?"

"I have no doubt. Enticing men is Venus's business, and she is very good at it."

"So you expect her to captivate Kneighly?" Diana asked thoughtfully. "Then you'll make Amy aware of her suitor's transgressions in hopes she will be so angry at him, she'll no longer desire to marry him? A woman scorned, so to speak?"

"Something like that. Venus is unlikely to become involved in a seduction herself, but will send one of her employees in her stead. Even so, utilizing her services will give me the opportunity to probe her relationship with Nathaniel. I expect Venus will see my request as perfectly reasonable, since Amy is my ward, and I would naturally be concerned and eager to pry her from a fortune-hunter's clutches."

"I see." Diana hesitated. "It is rather devious."

"Perhaps."

"And immoral."

"No doubt. But as the saying goes, all's fair in love and war. And you want me to succeed in uncovering Nathaniel's killer, don't you?"

"Of course."

When Diana fell silent, Thorne allowed her a moment to deliberate. He did indeed need a good excuse to approach Venus. Last night upon questioning Carstairs, he'd learned that Nathaniel had likely been Venus's lover for a short time, since he'd been seen exiting the madam's rooms. But Carstairs had never heard of Thomas Forrester—the late Englishman who'd hired spies to learn the Guardians' identities.

If Thorne hoped to discover much more about Venus, he knew it would require more intimacy with her than he currently commanded.

Convinced this was the right course, he reached for Diana's gloved hand. "My beautiful dragon, do you trust me?"

She looked searchingly at him. "I suppose so."

His mouth twisted. "I am gratified by your confidence. But pray, allow me to handle Kneighly my way. I promise you, I will wean him away from Amy."

"Very well," Diana said with grave reluctance.

"You will have to pretend you never saw Amy in his company just now. If you rant at her for trysting with Kneighly behind your back, you will only strengthen her illusions of being in love. Nothing is more capable of rousing young ardor than the forbidden."

Diana pressed her lips together and gave a stubborn sniff, but after a moment she capitulated. "Very well, I won't take her to task just now. But your plan had better work."

"It will. Now dry your eyes, love, or Amy will suspect something is amiss."

Taking the linen handkerchief he offered, Diana dabbed at her eyes, looking a trifle embarrassed by her outburst. "How is it," she muttered, "that you know so much about the way young girls think?"

Thorne grinned, unabashed. "Because I've made it a point to study girls all my life. Trust me, when it comes to the game of love, Amy doesn't stand a chance against me."

Eight

"*But of* course, my lord," Venus said in her husky voice. "I understand perfectly why you would wish to free your ward of this danger. And I will certainly use every means at my disposal to assist you."

Venus was half-reclining on a brocade settee, sipping her morning chocolate and looking the picture of sinful decadence in a lacy peignoir that did little to conceal her ample charms. Surprisingly, when Thorne had called upon her late this morning, she'd received him in her private boudoir rather than the small salon where she normally conducted business.

His unusual request had clearly surprised Venus, as well.

"I am curious, however," she mused, "why you thought to apply to me. Could you not challenge Mr. Kneighly to a duel and frighten him away? You have the reputation of being a deadly shot."

Sitting at ease in an adjacent chair, Thorne returned a charming smile. "Threatening to kill him would be the surest way to earn my ward's wrath, I'm afraid. And it would have no effect in diminishing her affections for him. Amy has a deep romantic streak. If she considers herself thwarted in love by her evil guardian, she is likely to do something foolish, such as elope with the bounder."

"Ah, I see. You could perhaps send an emissary in your stead to persuade him to terminate his suit."

"To break his bones, you mean?"

It was Venus's turn to smile. "Precisely. Surely you have grooms or footmen or such who could intimidate him and use physical coercion if need be. If not, then I can oblige you. I employ two footmen primarily for their brawn, in the event I need assistance with difficult patrons."

Macky had mentioned two muscular bruisers, Thorne remembered. In fact, one of them had admitted him into the club this morning.

He shook his head. "Certainly I could have the job done. But I fear if Amy's true love is wounded, he would only present an even more sympathetic figure in her eyes. I also considered bribing Kneighly to leave town, or finding some means of leverage against him. A man with his gaming debts would doubtless have vulnerabilities I could exploit. But the end result would be the same. No, Venus, my ward needs to be shown decisive proof that Kneighly has a passion for some other woman. That will be the surest way to convince Amy that he doesn't love her and is interested only in her fortune."

"I have indeed heard of Mr. Kneighly's gaming debts," Venus said thoughtfully.

"Then you know him?"

"We have met, although he has never attended my club. I make it my business to know all the gentlemen in London who could be potential patrons."

"I suspected as much."

"So you wish one of my girls to lure him away from your ward, my lord?"

"Yes. I would imagine several of your lovely doves might appeal to him. What about the petite blonde—Kitty, I believe her name is? Her coloring is even a bit like Amy's, although she is much better endowed than my ward."

"Kitty might do very well. You have a good eye."

Thorne smiled. "Thank you, my sweet. I am willing to pay handsomely for your services, of course."

"Then I can promise you will be satisfied with the outcome. By the time we are through, your ward will clearly be convinced that Mr. Kneighly's passions lie elsewhere."

"Excellent."

Thorne hesitated. He couldn't question Venus about her relationship to the late Thomas Forrester, but there should be no harm in mentioning Nathaniel. "I know Nathaniel would be grateful to you for helping to protect his sister."

Venus's green eyes immediately darkened, and she lowered her eyelashes, as if to hide her sorrow. "I am pleased to assist."

"Nathaniel was quite fond of you, Venus. He spoke highly of you."

At that, she glanced up at Thorne. "What did he say?"

Thorne let his lips form a secretive half-smile. "Nathaniel was a gentleman, of course, not the type to boast of his amorous conquests."

Frowning, she averted her gaze.

"He was also very fond of your club. In fact, this was his destination the night he was killed, did you know?"

"I suspected as much." Her voice was a bit hoarse.

"His death was a great shock . . . and a terrible shame."

"Indeed," Thorne agreed, his tone grim. Noting that Venus wouldn't meet his eyes, he resisted the urge to wrap his fingers around her lovely throat and shake her. Instead, he rose languidly from his chair.

"Well, then, madam," Thorne said, bending to kiss the hand she offered him, "since you have agreed to address the problem of my ward's fortune-hunter, I will take my leave."

"Are you certain I cannot tempt you to remain awhile longer?" With a provocative gesture, Venus rearranged her peignoir over her lush breasts, clearly issuing him a sexual invitation. To distract him from thoughts of Nathaniel, perhaps?

"I am flattered, love, but regrettably, I have other business to attend to."

Shutting the boudoir door behind him, he descended the stairs to the front entrance, where the same hulking footman opened the door for him.

He didn't think it was his imagination when he felt the bruiser's gaze boring into his back, but he controlled the urge to look behind him, instead making a mental reminder to ask Macky more about Venus's hired ruffians.

Curiously, Thorne realized, the scowling footman was still watching him when he settled into his coach once more. Perhaps because his visit here this morning had struck a nerve? If so, he was even more glad to have involved Venus, for it might lead him to clues regarding Nathaniel's death. And if not, he would soon have the problem of Amy's fortune-hunter solved.

He didn't regret his course, even if it relied on rather underhanded means. Diana had accused him of being devious, Thorne remembered, but he wouldn't hesitate to set honor aside for a good reason. And to his mind, safeguarding the dependents under his protection was the best reason in the world.

He learned the names of the bruisers when he met Macky in a smoke-filled tavern near Covent Garden two afternoons later.

"Sam Birkin is the larger one," Macky said over a pint of ale. "Billy Finch is the ugliest—scowls all the time. Kitty says they both have been in Venus's employ since she opened her club."

"And did Kitty have anything to say about Venus and Nathaniel's relationship?" Thorne asked.

Macky nodded. "Aye, they were lovers, all right. Kitty said it shocked her a bit, since Venus rarely invites any man into her bed. But Nate was sharing it for at least a week or two before he died."

Thorne gave a grim frown. "I wonder that I never noticed."

"He likely didn't want you to know. Kitty said it seemed they were attempting to keep their affair a secret, or at least Nathaniel always entered the back way." Macky suddenly brightened. "But I learned one bit of information that will please you."

"What?" Thorne asked, trying to control his impatience.

"Madam Venus once worked as a lightskirt at another club—Mme Fouchet's. Do you know it?"

Thorne's eyebrow rose thoughtfully. "Yes, I know it."

Mme Fouchet's was the most elite sin club in London, catering purely to patrons of sexual fantasies. The madam herself was a Frenchwoman who, with her noble protector, had fled the Terror in France, and then opened her own business when he'd died.

Thorne raised his pint in salute. "My compliments, friend. You've just unearthed the first promising clue in our case."

Macky raised his own pint in acknowledgment. "Let's hope it leads to some fruitful answers."

Mme Fouchet did not appear surprised to see Lord Thorne when he called early that evening at her sin club, several hours before her fantasy entertainment normally began. But she did seem highly curious with his choice of topics.

"I am interested in one of your present rivals," Thorne began once he was seated in the Frenchwoman's elegant salon. "Madam Venus. I understand you once employed her here?"

Mme Fouchet eyed him keenly, but she answered his question without hesitation. "I did indeed, my lord."

"I hoped you could tell me about Venus."

"She performed here for two years, with great success. Her services were highly sought after by my patrons. I regretted to see her go."

"Why did she leave?"

Fouchet's smile was wry. "Because she was clever enough to realize the profit in running an establishment such as this instead of working in one. It was an amicable parting, and I have occasionally encountered her since. But she is busy with her own club. As you said, we are rivals."

"Venus is not her real name, is it?"

"*Mais non.* My girls usually adopt a fictitious appellation to make them seem more mysterious. I believe her true name was Madeline. I recall it because I once had a cousin by the same name, although with a French spelling."

"And Madeline's surname?"

"Forgive me, my lord, but it escapes me—if indeed I ever knew it. The girls who come to me are not eager to share their pasts with me, you comprehend?"

Thorne presumed it was because their pasts must have been difficult ones for them to end up at a brothel, even a high-class one such as this. "So when she first applied here, you readily accepted her?"

"Immediately, my lord. Venus was unique. Not only a beauty, but very tall with brilliant red hair and green eyes. That combination is very appealing to many gentlemen."

"Was there anything else you remember about her, Mme Fouchet?"

The Frenchwoman pursed her lips thoughtfully. "Now that you ask . . . Once she mentioned that she had lost her parents tragically. I seem to recall that they were killed violently many years ago. Venus was still angry about their deaths. *Pardonez-moi,* but that is all that I remember."

Thorne smiled easily as he mentally tucked away the discovery that Venus was an orphan. "One last question, madam, if I may. Are you acquainted with an Englishman by the name of Thomas Forrester?"

Her frown deepened. "I don't believe so. But I see many gentlemen here who do not reveal to me their true names. They are too . . . how do you say . . . bashful?"

"I expect bashful is an eloquent description," Thorne said, smiling as he rose. "You have been extremely helpful. If you think of anything further about Venus, will you send me word?"

"*Oui, monseigneur,* I will be most happy to accommodate you."

With a gracious smile, she accepted the sheaf of banknotes Thorne handed her.

"For your trouble thus far, madam. I trust I may rely upon your discretion?"

"But of course, my lord. I would not remain in business long if I shared my clients' secrets."

Thorne had hoped Mme Fouchet's recollections would lead to more revelations about Venus. Several days later, however, he could claim no more progress on that front. Kitty had no clue what Venus's last name might be. And the search for Thomas Forrester's past was proving just as elusive.

John Yates had interviewed neighbors of the late Forrester, with little results. The man apparently had kept to himself, and when his lodging house burned down with him in it, no one had even claimed his charred body for burial. The other residents of the house had sought new lodgings elsewhere in London, so Yates was now attempting to track them down on the chance someone might shed some light on the late Englishman's past.

For his own next steps, Thorne intended to question the other Guardians currently working in London— some half-dozen of them—to see if they'd ever run across Forrester during any of their missions. He also meant to brief the Foreign Office about events thus far. Yet the lack of any concrete evidence was beginning to frustrate him.

No doubt, Thorne reflected, the stalemate was at the heart of his disquiet since returning to London. But in truth, ever since Nathaniel's death last spring, he'd experienced a vague dissatisfaction with his life that he had never openly acknowledged.

Until now. Only now was he willing to admit that he felt a discontent that was palpable.

The feeling was caused by more than an impasse in the investigation, Thorne suspected. He couldn't blame his personal affairs, though. His father had ceased to plague him with matrimonial prospects, and the gossip about his betrothal had died down to mere curiosity. Under his aunt's auspices, Diana was gradually being accepted by the ton, and he had confidence that she would eventually be admitted into the academy to train.

It was possible, however, that the reason for his discontent was Diana herself. Quite unexpectedly Thorne found himself missing her. Perhaps because in the past week since her interview, he'd had little chance for private conversation with her. He'd managed to see Diana every day by arranging at least one social engagement with her, but even then, they always seemed to be surrounded by crowds.

Chiefly she was busy preparing Amy for the start of the Season with shopping expeditions and imperative morning calls on the arbiters of the beau monde. And when Thorne rode or drove with Diana in the park, they were accosted by friends and acquaintances and inquisitive social climbers. On three separate evenings he had escorted the ladies out: to Drury Lane Theatre for a play, to a private music concert given by one of Lady Hennessy's cronies, and to a small rout party to officially introduce Amy and his cousin Cecily into polite company. But he rarely had a chance to be alone with Diana.

He should have been satisfied with the tepid state of their relationship. His attraction for her was like an addiction, and the greater the distance he kept between them, the better chance he had of conquering his craving.

Late that afternoon, however, Thorne couldn't stop himself from calling at her studio in the hope of catching Diana there. She'd told him she wanted to work for a few hours before their evening engagements. He could use the valid excuse of reporting progress on their plan to best Amy's fortune-hunter. And also to confirm that Diana, along with Amy and Cecily, had been granted vouchers to attend this evening's subscription ball at Almack's—the exclusive assembly hall where only the cream of society was admitted.

He might be making a mistake, Thorne knew, but he wanted to see Diana alone. It had been too long since he had sparred with her, since he had won her smile, since he had touched her.

When he was shown up to her studio by her housekeeper, Thorne found Diana standing before her easel, wearing a paint-spattered smock and holding a palette in one hand and a brush in the other.

His heart quickened at her smile of greeting. She seemed genuinely glad to see him, but she asked for a few more moments to finish a difficult shadow and requested her housekeeper to send up tea and wine for Lord Thorne.

While he waited, Thorne inspected the various canvases that lined the walls of the huge room. There were dozens he hadn't seen before, ranging from breathtaking to powerful to quietly poignant. He spent a good ten minutes marveling.

The academy had evidently returned some of Diana's paintings to her, for he recognized two of them, but he didn't know if that was a good sign or bad.

"No further word from Sir George about your admittance?" Thorne asked when Diana finally declared the shadow vanquished and gave him her attention.

"No, none," she replied as she put up her instruments. "I am trying not to dwell on it."

He indicated a portrait of an old man, stooped and bent. The luminous glow of his age-lined face held an inner strength that brought to mind a work by Rembrandt.

"You simply amaze me," Thorne said with genuine awe in his tone.

"Thank you. He was one of my uncle's tenant farmers."

"Did you ever finish my portrait?"

"No, I haven't had time."

Her swift answer made him glance across the room at Diana. She seemed a bit flustered by his question, he noted as she removed her smock to reveal an afternoon gown of jonquil muslin.

When she moved closer, he also noticed the streak of crimson paint on her cheek, but refrained from reaching up to wipe it away, deciding not to test his fortitude by touching her.

"To what do I owe the honor of your call, Thorne? I expected to see you in a few hours." They were to attend a dinner this evening, with cards and dancing afterward, since Lady Hennessy wished Amy and Cecily to practice their dance steps as much as possible before the ball soon to be held in their honor.

"I came to inform you of our change in plans for this evening. We'll be attending Almack's instead. And I thought you might like to hear how our scheme to defeat Reginald Kneighly is progressing."

Diana's eyes widened at both his revelations—but just then the housekeeper returned with a footman, both bearing trays laden with a hearty tea, including scones and crumpets with butter and jam.

With a warning glance at Thorne, Diana waited until the trays were deposited on the table near the hearth before inviting him to join her. It was mid-April, but the vast studio was chill enough to require a fire. Arranged in front of the cheerful blaze was a pleasant sitting area with two armchairs and a chaise longue—for the comfort of Diana's subjects, Thorne suspected.

They were alone and settled in the two armchairs before Diana spoke again. Most any other lady he knew would have quizzed him eagerly about Almack's, but she went straight to the subject of Kneighly.

"So tell me what happened," she said as she poured. "Did you speak to Venus, and did she agree?"

"Yes to both questions." He gave her an abbreviated account of his conversation with Venus, and the madam's promise to have one of her Cyprians seduce Kneighly with the goal of dividing him from Amy.

"It seems to be working," Thorne remarked, taking a bite of a warm crumpet.

"How do you know?"

"Because I am having Kneighly followed. I know every move he's made during the past week. He has become quite enamored of the lovely Kitty in the short time since she contrived an introduction. In fact, he spent the last two nights at her apartments, no doubt in her bed."

Diana stared, before shaking her head in exasperated amusement. "I was wrong. You are *beyond* devious. You truly set your minions to spy on him?"

"And on Amy, as well. For her own protection, of course."

"Of course." Diana's smile faded. "Have there been any more clandestine meetings between her and Kneighly?"

"Not a one. Kitty is keeping him too well occupied."

"Good. I have tried to keep Amy busy every waking hour. And I've attempted to keep a close watch on her without appearing to. She doesn't seem to have noticed her suitor's defection yet, if indeed he is defecting. I suppose because she is swept up in the excitement of her comeout, with the Season having officially started this week, and the ball Lady Hennessy is holding for both girls in less than a fortnight."

"Let us hope Amy remains distracted until our plan succeeds," Thorne replied.

"Speaking of success . . . are you making any headway in your investigation into Nathaniel's death?"

Thorne's good humor faded. "Some," he prevaricated.

"Then you have managed to question Venus?"

"Why do you ask?"

"You told me you needed a means of getting close to her without rousing her suspicions, so you could probe her relationship with Nathaniel."

"So?"

"So, if you haven't yet succeeded, I have an idea I wish to discuss with you."

The uncustomary hesitancy in Diana's tone sent warning bells off in his mind. "Why do I have the feeling I won't like what you have to say?"

"Probably because you won't like it. I have been thinking about how I could help your investigation."

"I don't require your help—" Thorne began before Diana held up a hand.

"Hear me out, will you? I attended you when you made your outrageous proposal for our betrothal, didn't I?"

Thorne crossed his arms over his chest. "Very well, I'm listening."

"I want to offer to paint your Madam Venus."

His eyebrow shot up sharply, but with effort he refrained from automatically rejecting her idea. "Why the devil would you want to paint her?"

"Because it could be the perfect way to get close to her without arousing her suspicions."

"If you alight on Venus's doorstep with an outlandish proposition like that, you will do nothing *but* arouse her suspicions."

Diana shook her head. "I don't believe so. I can use any number of reasons for approaching her. I can thank her for luring Kneighly away from my cousin Amy, for one. Or I could say I need a new model for a portrait to impress the British Academy. . . . I'm certain we could devise some excuse that Venus would accept. And if she has an ounce of vanity, she will be flattered by my request."

"But what aim would it serve?"

"If I become her portraitist, she is likely to tell me things she would never tell another soul. It is a strange phenomenon, Thorne. People tend to lose their inhibitions when they sit for an artist, and they often divulge intimate confidences, much as they would to their confessor. And even if Venus proves to be less garrulous than usual, I would have the opportunity to ask her questions that would seem impertinent under any other circumstance."

She did have a point, Thorne reflected. What better way to delve into Venus's secrets and learn about her past than to inveigle her into a setting that naturally fostered conversation? Diana could perhaps even discover Venus's last name, or where she had been raised before she suddenly appeared at Mme Fouchet's sin club. . . .

But he didn't want Diana involved. She could be putting herself in danger if Venus was truly a traitor in league with French spies.

"It's out of the question," Thorne said, snatching at the first excuse that came to him. "We have taken care to present you to the ton as a picture of propriety. Painting the portrait of a notorious madam will only belie our efforts and could further damage your reputation."

"My reputation is hardly lily white, true, but for once that can work to my advantage. Just think of it, Thorne. Venus is more likely to accept my offer simply *because* of the scandal in my past. And I could get by with attending her sin club when most other ladies could not."

"You are not attending any sin club," Thorne said emphatically. "Most especially Venus's."

Diana narrowed her gaze at his proprietary tone. "It can be accomplished in secret then, at my studio. No one even need know she is posing for me. Thorne, please. I could help you—I'm certain of it."

He tried again. "I am accustomed to working alone."

Her glance showed her skepticism even before she said dryly, "I very much doubt that that is true. You just told me you rely on spies to keep you informed. I'm sure in your work with the Foreign Office, you call upon quite a number of sources."

Thorne remained mute, which only increased Diana's frustration. "I don't see why you won't let me assist you."

"It could be too dangerous for you," he answered honestly. "I'm not about to put you at risk."

"You could set your spies to watch us, so that I am not in any danger."

Again she had a point. He wanted to keep Diana safe. But there was such a thing as going too far in his desire to shelter her. He could be allowing his very protectiveness to get in the way of his investigation. If Diana were anyone else, he would allow her to help; no, he would *welcome* her help. Diana was clever enough to be a match even for the sharp-witted Venus.

She was also feisty and brave enough to put herself in harm's way for her late cousin's sake. He admired that about her, Thorne reflected. Not that he would tell her so.

"You are treating me as if I am a fragile, incompetent female," she protested when he didn't answer.

He smiled unwillingly, knowing he was guilty as charged, but he turned aside her complaint. "No, I am treating you as if you were a nosy, interfering female, which you are."

She met his gaze with muted belligerence, obviously determined not to be bullied. "Thorne, I want to feel as if I'm helping to achieve justice for Nathaniel." Setting down her teacup, she rose to her feet. "If you refuse me, I may have to take matters into my own hands."

He stood also. "What do you mean?"

"I can always approach Venus without your permission."

"I wouldn't advise it."

When Diana started to turn away, Thorne reached out to grasp her arm, intent on stopping her. Instantly she stiffened, tilting her chin up and staring at him in defiance.

Even that brief contact set off a spark of heat between them. The heat, combined with the challenge in her gaze, was too much for Thorne to resist. He knew he was going to kiss her; he couldn't help himself.

He also knew the moment Diana realized his intention, for her eyes instinctively widened.

The air around them shimmered with sudden sexual awareness as he stepped closer.

Nine

Alarm flooded Diana as he fitted his palm to her nape.

"Thorne . . ." she managed to say in a breathless rasp.

"Hush, sweetheart."

She watched him, unable to move. Doubtless he was attempting to distract her from her goal, and yet desire had darkened his eyes. The same desire that was suddenly flooding her. She couldn't make herself draw away, even though she knew how dangerous it would be to let him kiss her.

His head was bending, his sensual mouth descending, and then it was too late. Thorne claimed her lips, cutting off any further protest. Sensation flashed through her with enough force to leave her knees weak.

She wanted to resist, but his hand reached up behind her head, grasping the knot of her chignon, his fingers twisting in her hair possessively, holding her immobile.

When Diana whimpered at the scalding pressure of

his mouth, his kiss softened the slightest degree and became more beguiling. Her body jolted with the erotic touch of his tongue against hers.

Thorne must have felt her reaction, for he made a sound deep in his throat like a growl. "God, I want you."

The hunger in his voice made her limbs even weaker. And when he tightened his arms about her and pulled her hard against him, her head spun at the passionate intensity of his assault. Diana found herself clinging to him, melting.

For a long moment, his lips devoured hers. Then suddenly he bent and scooped her up in his arms. He kept on kissing her, ruthlessly, deliberately, as he turned and sank down with her onto the chaise longue, so that she was cradled on his lap, his arm supporting her back.

With the last vestiges of her sanity, Diana pushed at his chest. "Thorne, stop! You are only trying to distract me."

"Not entirely," he rasped, his lips still hotly savoring hers. "I've wanted to do this for days . . . to drive you mad the way you have done to me."

Unerringly his hand found the apex of her thighs beneath her gown. Through her muslin skirts, his fingers pressed against her mound, creating a delicious friction across her most sensitive flesh. Diana gasped at the incredible sensation.

At her response, Thorne raised his head a few inches and smiled down at her. "Did you do as I told you and learn to touch yourself?"

"N-no . . ." she exclaimed shakily.

"Then I intend to take this opportunity to show you how." He reached for the hem of her gown.

Panicking, Diana grasped his arm to forestall him. "You can't."

"Why not?"

"Because . . . it would be scandalous."

"As you said, your reputation gives you more license than the typical unmarried lady. And no one will know. We'll hear any of your servants coming, and we can't be seen over the chaise."

It was true, Diana realized. The back of the chaise was to the door, giving them a measure of privacy, even if one of her servants should happen to enter without being summoned—which wasn't likely, since they knew better than to disturb her when she was working in her studio.

"I know you are curious," Thorne murmured while she debated. "So I will take the choice from you. I intend to arouse you, love, to show you what pleasure is. You don't have to do a thing but remain still. Now, just relax."

She couldn't possibly obey, though. Every nerve in her body had come to tingling life, sharp as a razor's edge. She felt the hem of her gown being raised, felt the warmth of the hearth fire against her naked skin. But it was Thorne's hand trailing up her inner thigh that made shivers race across her skin.

Her heart began thudding as he bared her lower body completely to his gaze. He was looking at her sex, she realized.

"Lovely," he said. His voice, male and sensual, washed over her. "I have fantasized about this for weeks."

When his fingers tangled in the nest of dark curls between her thighs, Diana went rigid, her own fingers clutching at his arm.

"Close your eyes," he commanded as he bent to kiss her again.

She wanted to resist, but Thorne's mouth kept caressing hers, long drugging kisses that clouded her senses. Gently urging her thighs apart then, he cupped her sex. Her nerves leapt in response. Then he ran one fingertip through the curls there, pressing against her cleft. Diana sucked in a breath but held herself completely still as his touch played over her feminine softness.

All her awareness centered on his caressing hand, on his fingertips sliding over her heated flesh that was already swollen and slick with moisture. Her body tightened unbearably as he stroked, and when he parted her feminine folds, she froze, not daring to breathe.

She could feel him probing the entrance to her body. Then he boldly slid one long finger inside her, and her breath fled altogether.

He paused, letting her grow accustomed to his unexpected invasion. The flush of heat inside her spread like wildfire, making her quiver. Then his finger withdrew, only to glide back inside her and press even deeper.

Diana arched and gave a little moan.

"Easy," he murmured, his voice soft, husky, stroking her as his hand was doing.

Easy? How could she be easy when his first touch had triggered a tumult inside her? She felt dazed and utterly wanton.

"You're extremely responsive," Thorne breathed with satisfaction. "I knew you would be."

Deliberately he slipped a second finger inside her to join the first, opening her further.

"You're very tight but wet enough to accept more."

His thumb found the small nub of her sex and rolled it back and forth, gliding languidly while his fingers fully penetrated her slickness.

Diana dragged in another breath and her thighs fell apart. Thorne seemed pleased with her response, for he gave a murmur of approval.

"Your nipples are hard, delicious points, aren't they?" he whispered against her lips.

They were indeed, she thought, dazed; the peaks of her breasts throbbed. But the ache low in her body was now an exquisite agony. Thorne had ignited a fire inside her.

"I could make it even more enjoyable for you if I sucked your nipples," he mused. "I could draw down your bodice and increase the pleasure for you. But for now, I want to arouse you with just my hand."

His tone was so confident that it surprised Diana when he stopped caressing her.

Easing her away from him a little, he unfastened the buttons of his pantaloons and drawers, so that his erection sprang free. Then he grasped her hand and guided her fingers to his rigid length.

"Now it's your turn to touch me."

Diana drew a gasping breath at the feel of him. He was scalding hot and hard as granite, but the skin covering his arousal was soft as velvet, and the sacs beneath were firm as melons ready to burst.

While she was still holding him, he slid two fingers inside her again.

"Now imagine my cock inside you, like my fingers."

At the same time he slid his tongue deep into her mouth, mimicking the teasing thrusts he was making with his fingers.

Diana could envision the image he'd described: Thorne's thighs spreading hers wider . . . his huge, jutting arousal slowly penetrating inside her. . . . Each languid plunge of his fingers was in rhythm with his tongue and soon had her flushed and panting.

Helplessly, she arched against his hand, her hips moving, asking for something she couldn't even identify. Yet he held her securely, his fingers probing still more insistently, his slick thumb caressing her ruthlessly.

Flames fanned out over her body. Desperate for something to anchor her, Diana reached up and twined her hands in Thorne's tawny hair, clutching fiercely. Her body shuddered with wanting.

It frightened her, the fire Thorne had unleashed inside her. Her hips were writhing now, straining against his magical hand, seeking release from the terrible, exquisite tension, from the vibrant, burning heat.

"I am so hot . . ." she whimpered.

"Don't fight it," Thorne murmured in a hoarse, approving tone against her trembling mouth. "Just let it come."

Her fingernails sank into his hair as he drove her higher. Soft cries came from her throat as a wild frenzy took possession of her body. She shook and shuddered as hot bursts of pleasure jerked through her repeatedly, jagged and intense. She was caught in a storm of fire, of sensations too keen to be borne. She was bursting with the inferno, shattering. Thorne kissed her again, his mouth capturing hers to mute her hoarse scream of pleasure. . . .

A red-black haze still enveloped her when Diana finally regained her senses. Thorne was feathering soft kisses over her cheeks, her forehead, her lips. The tremors faded slowly, leaving a hot glow in her limp body.

She felt fractured. She had never known sensation like that existed; where everything else in the world fell away and nothing mattered but Thorne's wonderful touch.

Dazed, Diana opened her eyes to find him gazing down at her. His soft smile was tender, satisfied.

She licked her dry lips. "I never knew. . . ."

"Never knew what, love?"

"What it would feel like. It was like . . . an explosion. Like fireworks exploding inside me."

"That is an apt description. But lovemaking can be even hotter."

Her mouth curved ruefully. "I don't think I could bear any hotter."

"Oh, you can, I promise you."

Withdrawing a handkerchief from his jacket pocket, Thorne gently rubbed her cheek, removing a smudge of paint. "It can be even better with a man's flesh deep inside you . . . for both of us."

At his statement, Thorne made a sound low in his throat and shut his eyes, pressing his forehead against hers, as if striving for control. "I would like nothing more than to bury myself between your sweet thighs, but I vowed to remain a gentleman. And I mean for you to remain a virgin. Next time I'll use my mouth. For now, let me show you how you can bring yourself to climax."

Reaching for her hand, he guided her fingers to her sex, making Diana touch herself.

It was the sudden realization of her wantonness that finally brought her to her senses. "No . . . this has gone far enough."

Weakly pushing down her skirts, she swung her legs to the floor and levered herself off Thorne's lap. Standing on shaken limbs, she retreated a few steps, putting a safer distance between them before finding the courage to meet his eyes. "I can't let you distract me this way."

His hot gaze raked her face, his expression intent, as if he was trying to judge her sincerity.

Diana was completely sincere, though. She scowled at Thorne, eyeing him with mistrust. "You tried to divert my attention by seducing me witless, didn't you?"

"That isn't entirely true. I couldn't help myself. You have a damnably painful effect on me, vixen."

"What do you mean, painful?"

"I've been in a constant state of arousal since I met you. It is extremely painful for a man to become aroused with no relief."

At his statement, her attention shifted to Thorne's loins. The front placket of his pantaloons was still open, with the thick, swollen length of his erection rising nearly to his abdomen. She stared, fascinated by his male anatomy.

"Yes, behold your effect," he said dryly.

Diana's gaze narrowed doubtfully. "I certainly didn't mean to arouse you. I'm sorry."

Thorne laughed, wincing at the same time. "You can't help it, sweetheart. You're beautiful and intriguing and incredibly stimulating to a man like me."

"I don't want you to be in pain, Thorne. Is there . . . something I should do?"

He shook his head. "I can satisfy myself if the pain gets too great. I've managed that way these past few weeks. I have taken to pleasuring myself so I can control the temptation to carry you off and ravish you."

"Then you don't want me to . . . caress you?"

His smile was pained but infinitely sensual as he fastened the buttons of his trousers. "You're not experienced enough yet. If you knew the images going through my mind, they would shock you. Even so, I will be happy to show you how to pleasure yourself."

"I think not," Diana replied, trying to regain control of their conversation.

"If you change your mind, let me know. Now that you've felt the ecstasy of sexual release, you'll want more. It can become a sweet craving—"

"Thorne, stop this! You won't make me forget our argument. I want to paint Madam Venus."

Every ounce of levity faded from his expression. He returned her gaze for a long moment. "You aren't going to give up, are you?"

"No. And I know you don't expect me to. You realize I am right. I can help you."

"Perhaps, but I sure as hell don't like it. I don't want you near Venus."

"I will be careful. You can instruct me on what to say to Venus, how to uncover her secrets."

Thorne ran a hand raggedly through his fair hair, not replying.

"Please," Diana pleaded, "you must allow me to paint her. It will work, I promise you."

Setting his teeth, he gave her a measuring stare. "I don't share your confidence in the least. But I would rather have you working under my direction than risk you going off on your own—devil take you."

"I hoped you would see reason."

Her relieved smile brought a scowl to Thorne's face. "This is deadly serious, Diana. Nathaniel was killed, quite possibly by Venus. If you find yourself i difficulty with her, I may not be able to rescue yo

You will have to use your wits and remain constantly on your guard."

She was drawn in by the sheer intensity of Thorne's eyes. "I understand," she said solemnly.

"And I mean to put you through grueling rehearsals, covering every feasible topic that might come up before I let you go near her."

"I will do everything exactly as you tell me to."

He nodded reluctantly. "Very well, then. You may paint Venus. But I want to decide how best to approach her. There are several ways to gain her cooperation, as you said. Let me think about it, and I will let you know when I escort you to Almack's this evening. Meanwhile, don't you dare do a thing."

"I won't. And you won't regret this, Thorne."

"I hope to God I don't."

With that muttered utterance, he rose to his feet. As he smoothed out the front placket of his trousers, an ironic smile twisted the corner of his mouth.

Diana retreated another step, concerned that Thorne might try to kiss her farewell—or more. But to her surprise, he turned away and left the studio without another word, shutting the door firmly behind him.

He wasn't happy with her, she knew. Not only had she defied him, but he was still in physical pain, if the bulge in his trousers was any indication. She wondered if Thorne had been telling the truth, that he now pleasured himself so he could control the urge to ravish her.

It amazed her that with all the beautiful women he could have, he considered her a temptation. But she felt the same way about him.

That was why she hadn't finished his portrait. She'd lied to Thorne about her reason. She hadn't dared focus so much of her attention on his beautiful body. He already took up too much of her thoughts, day and night.

And now he had set her in turmoil again. He'd given her an irresistible taste of passion and left her hungering for more.

Shakily, Diana crossed the studio to the cheval glass that she kept for the benefit of her clients. Her limbs were still weak from the ecstasy he had shown her. And she was acutely conscious of the heat that lingered in the feminine core of her body, of the way her tight nipples rubbed against the fabric of her bodice. Thorne had said he wanted to suckle her nipples to increase her enjoyment. . . .

Remembering, she felt her cheeks flood with fiery warmth, a mingling of shame and excitement. His brazen declarations weren't the only thing she recalled, either. She remembered the way his rigid phallus felt to her touch, the way his stroking fingers had aroused her so expertly as he showed her the secret to sexual pleasure.

Diana muttered an oath beneath her breath. How had she let it happen when she'd been so determined to resist him? How could she be so eager to experience that incredible fire again?

Feeling outrageously wanton, she raised her skirts to bare her lower body, studying the downy curls between her thighs. She hadn't dared take Thorne's advice to pleasure herself when he'd suggested it on the ship several weeks ago, but now . . .

Watching in the glass, she cupped her mound tentatively, finding the delicate bud of her sex. It was only a short step from there to imagine Thorne standing behind her, his arms wrapped around her hips, his fingers caressing her feminine cleft, driving her to rapture.

A sizzling heat spiraled upward through her body, nearly burning her.

Dropping her skirts swiftly, Diana let out another low curse and turned away. She wished to high heaven that Thorne hadn't shown her the physical side of passion, for now he would only be that much harder to resist.

Since her chief concerns had centered on painting Venus and thwarting Reginald Kneighly—even before being distracted by Thorne's shocking intimacies—Diana had failed to ask him how, with her dubious past, she could possibly be permitted inside Almack's elite assembly rooms.

Suddenly recalling his pronouncement, she took extreme care to eliminate all traces of paint from her face and hands and then rushed home to Berkeley Square to bathe and dress in an exquisite gown of ivory silk. The patronesses reportedly were sticklers for proper appearance.

Amy and Cecily were beside themselves at being admitted to the hallowed halls of Almack's, and lamentably, Diana found herself just as eager to attend. She fully understood the honor being granted her, even if she still could scarcely believe it. Gaining entrance to Almack's was the highest distinction of social success achievable, even more coveted than a presentation to the Queen.

Thorne must have worked miracles to obtain a voucher for her from one of the patronesses—seven ladies who ruled the ton by controlling who received the cherished vouchers.

When Thorne arrived to escort his aunt and her charges, Diana took advantage of the girls' excited chatter to ask him how he'd managed to have her included.

"Lady Jersey is rather fond of me," was his wry reply.

Which meant, Diana suspected, that he'd employed his vaunted powers of seduction to charm the reigning sovereign of London society, Sally Jersey.

"She also," Thorne added blandly, "has a soft spot in her heart for eloping lovers, since she herself married Jersey at Gretna Green."

That helped to explain Lady Jersey's benevolence, Diana conceded. But an hour later as they ascended the staircase to Almack's ballroom, she felt an attack of nerves bordering on panic at having to face such haughty company. It would be mortifying to be cut dead by the denizens of this exclusive assembly—

She was absurdly grateful when Thorne's hand pressed into the small of her back, his touch reassuring as he guided her through the sacred portals. When Diana glanced up at him, his grin was bracing, as if he understood her fears.

"Buck up, love," he commanded softly. "You've done your penance, and you can hold your own with the best of them."

She flashed Thorne a brilliant smile of gratitude. Perhaps her youthful transgression finally would be forgiven, or at least relegated to the past. But if not, then she would brazen it out. Thorne was right; she had nothing to be ashamed of now. Lifting her chin, Diana allowed him to usher her into the vast ballroom after the rest of their party.

Her newfound fortitude came just in time, since from the moment they entered, they were the focus of all eyes. The room was suddenly abuzz with polite whispers. Yet Diana soon realized Thorne's presence was even more of a novelty than her own.

Lady Hennessy was the first to comment on it. "What did I tell you, dear boy? Everyone is atwitter at your appearance here. My nephew," the countess confided in an amused undertone to Diana, "has attended Almack's only once before this, and that was purely to oblige me. Until your betrothal, he always avoided respectable society as much as possible."

"Certainly I avoided Almack's," Thorne acknowledged with a feigned shudder. "Possibly because it is considered London's Marriage Mart. But now that Diana is to be my bride, I no longer need fear falling victim to the matrimonial nets cast here."

As he spoke, he gave Diana a warm look that anyone watching would interpret as loving. He was showing the world that she had captured his heart, Diana knew, making their sham engagement appear real. Even so, her stomach fluttered with awareness as she met his hazel eyes, helpless to stop remembering the scandalous things he had done to her barely a few short hours ago.

Just then a lively, elegantly dressed woman glided up to them. Diana recognized Lady Jersey from the sketches in the newspapers.

The patroness air-kissed Lady Hennessy's cheeks, welcomed Diana more coolly, greeted Cecily and Amy with gracious condescension, and admonished Thorne for letting years go by since he'd last graced their halls. "La, I thought we would never manage to lure the infamous Viscount Thorne here again."

He bowed and kissed Lady Jersey's hand. "With such charming inducement as you, Sally, how could I resist?"

Laughing flirtatiously, she rapped his knuckles with

her fan. "Well, pray remember, I expect you to fulfill your promise."

"I shall. Directly after my lovely Diana honors me with her hand for a set."

When the patroness had left, Diana glanced up at Thorne. "What promise?"

"I agreed to dance with the wallflowers."

In exchange for her voucher, no doubt. "How noble of you," Diana said lightly.

Thorne's acknowledging grin was odiously smug. "Indeed."

Yet it *was* noble of him, she reflected, caught by the laughter dancing in his eyes. Thorne was here solely for her sake, because he knew how important the evening was to her social success; her attendance here would likely assure her acceptance by the ton.

It was during the next quarter hour, however, that Diana began to comprehend the full extent of his sacrifice. From the first, Thorne attracted considerable attention, with countless people coming up to greet him and fawn over him. Yet he took their obsequiousness in good stride, even when they begged to introduce their daughters. Flushed and smiling, the young ladies seemed dazzled by his virile, golden elegance, but not by a flicker of an eyelash did he display his desire to be elsewhere. Instead he wielded his irresistible charm in equal measure.

Until, that is, a tall, dark-haired gentleman approached.

"Present me to this delectable creature, Thorne," he demanded, eyeing Diana with his quizzing glass.

With obvious reluctance, Thorne made her known to his friend, Baron Boothe.

Bowing low over her hand, Lord Boothe barely

contained a lecherous grin as he measured her bosom beneath the modest cut of her gown.

Then he spoke to Thorne as if Diana weren't even present. "Quite nice, old trout. I was shocked by the announcement of your betrothal, but I can now see the appeal. I should have known you would choose a beauty." He finally lifted his gaze to Diana's, but there was a smirk on his lips that made her want to shudder. "Pray, do me the honor of dancing with me, Miss Sheridan."

Thorne's smile was cool as he preempted her response. "I'm afraid Miss Sheridan's card is full."

Boothe frowned. "I see your problem. You are jealous as a hound."

"I commend your acumen," Thorne replied. "But I'll warrant you understand why I don't want to share my intended bride."

The baron gave a wicked chuckle. "You fear I will steal her away from you." He shook his head. "Wouldn't dream of poaching, you know. You are far too good a shot."

Boothe bowed again to Diana, drawling, "Your servant, Miss Sheridan," before wandering off.

Diana was heartily glad to see him go, but curious about Thorne's motives. "Why did you claim my dance card was full when you knew it wasn't?"

"Because Boothe is a rake of the first order, and it will do your reputation no good to be seen dancing with him."

Her eyes widening, Diana stared up at him with droll amusement.

At her pointed look, Thorne broke into another grin. "I do grasp the irony. I, pretending to be the arbiter of what is proper. But you'll forgive me if I don't want him touching you. Now, come, dance with me before I must immolate myself on the altar of Sally Jersey's dictates."

As Thorne led her onto the ballroom floor for the minuet, Diana found her tension easing for the first time this evening. His show of jealousy was perhaps an act to reinforce their pretense of a love match, but it was still extremely pleasant to be under his protection when confronting society's roués and rulers.

By the time the set ended and Thorne returned her to his aunt's side, Diana felt fully able to face the rest of the evening on her own. When he didn't immediately leave her, she assured him that she had found her courage. "You needn't remain here and play chaperone. I can manage from here."

"Yes," Lady Hennessy added, amused. "Go fulfill your obligation and dance with the wallflowers, Thorne. I will see that Diana has proper partners, just as I will for Cecily and Amy."

Thorne grimaced but turned away, prepared to do his duty.

The rest of the evening passed in an agreeable blur for Diana. She never lacked for respectable dance partners, and was even made to feel welcome by the countess's cronies and several ladies nearer her own age, all of whom expressed surprise and admiration that she'd captured the elusive Lord Thorne.

Diana took greater pleasure in watching Thorne. He not only danced with the young wallflowers, but he did so with a purposeful display of enjoyment, with the intention, Diana suspected, of bringing them into fashion. If so, he was highly successful.

His tactics were the same with each young lady: flashing his most charming smile, focusing his sole attention on his partner, bending low to hear whatever she was saying, appearing to hang on her every word, and being delighted by what he heard. And the results were always the same: By the end of the dance, the awestruck girl was chattering happily to him, her blushing features so animated that she looked almost pretty. Thus when Thorne relinquished her, more than one gentleman instantly approached her to request a dance.

Diana shook her head mentally at the phenomenon. It was a foible of society that being singled out by a nobleman of Viscount Thorne's consequence would virtually assure those young ladies of acceptance—just as Thorne had done for her. But she was still touched by his kindness, her heart warmed by tenderness.

"My nephew," Lady Hennessy murmured beside her, "may be a wicked scapegrace, but occasionally he surprises me. I think perhaps he might make an admirable husband after all."

Suddenly realizing Thorne's aunt had been watching *her* watch *him,* Diana felt her own cheeks blushing. She couldn't refute that Thorne would make some fortunate woman a remarkable husband . . . except that he saw matrimony as a fate worse than death.

For a moment Diana felt a pang of something very much like regret that their betrothal would never be real. But then she ruthlessly reined in her wayward thoughts.

She wouldn't let herself dwell on Thorne's virtues or lack of them. In truth, she was determined to stop thinking of him entirely, unless it concerned how to achieve her goal of painting Venus. He had promised he would decide how best to gain the madam's cooperation in sitting for a portrait.

And that was all she cared about, Diana assured herself, ignoring the niggling notion that she was fabricating another deception to match their fraudulent betrothal.

Ten

Diana's first impression, when she received Venus in the parlor of her studio house several mornings later, was one of awe. With her flame-red hair and statuesque figure, the madam was not only beautiful, but utterly compelling. She was also unexpectedly young, perhaps no more than thirty years of age.

Following Thorne's instructions, Diana had written Venus requesting the privilege of painting her, using the excuse of needing a model for a new portrait to impress the academy. Diana was fairly certain Venus would respond to her invitation to call, if only out of curiosity.

After exchanging polite greetings, Madam Venus seated herself gracefully, her green eyes coolly surveying Diana. "I am flattered to be asked to sit for you, Miss Sheridan," she said in a low, husky voice that bore a genteel accent, "but I confess surprise that you have chosen me."

"I heard of your remarkable beauty," Diana prevaricated. "And now that I see you in person, I realize how perfect you are for my needs. You are just the sort of model that the renowned Venetian artist, Ti-

tian, delighted in painting. The British Academy will doubtless take notice of so striking a subject."

"I wonder that Lord Thorne approves of you associating with a woman of my profession."

Diana returned a rueful smile. "Fortunately, I do not require Thorne's approval. I was quite clear when I accepted his proposal. He is not to interfere with my art in any manner. And I am not to interfere in whatever pursuits he indulges in."

"A very permissive arrangement," Venus observed.

"Indeed it is. We have a mutual understanding and mean to have quite a liberal marriage. But in fact, Thorne himself told me about you, Madam Venus."

That admission succeeded in eliciting a raised eyebrow from Venus. "Is that so?"

"Yes," Diana said easily. "Thorne informed me of the assistance you are providing for my troubling cousin Amy. I owe you a debt of gratitude, madam. Amy is very dear to me, and I was at my wits' end, not knowing how I could possibly shake her infatuation for her fortune-hunter. But Thorne tells me your plan is proceeding exceedingly well—that Mr. Kneighly's interest has definitely been ensnared by your employee."

"Kitty is succeeding admirably thus far," the madam agreed. "Her orders are to keep Kneighly so occupied, he won't have a free moment to pursue your cousin. Or the desire, either. And I was happy to help."

"You would be doing me another enormous favor if you would agree to sit for me," Diana continued. "As I said in my letter, the academy is considering me for admission, but they are still wavering because of my sex. A new work could sway their opinion. And if I am privileged enough to be accepted before your portrait is finished, I will have a new painting to enter in their spring exhibition. They hold it in the spring, so as not to compete directly with the Royal Academy's summer exhibition."

Venus pursed her lips, apparently unpersuaded. "I find it hard to believe I could make any difference to the Academy's decision, Miss Sheridan."

"I have little doubt you would. A woman of your extraordinary features and form will hold great appeal with the judges. And I promise to do you justice. I am quite a good artist, actually. I can show you some of my paintings if you wish, so you can judge my skill for yourself."

Diana pretended to study her visitor's features with a dispassionate eye. "I would like to paint you in a classical style, perhaps as an allegorical figure. The Greek goddess Aphrodite would be my first instinct. Your name, Venus, is the Roman equivalent, I'm sure you are aware."

A hint of mocking amusement played on Venus's sensual mouth. The first hint of real emotion she had shown since her arrival. "Oh, yes. The goddess of Love and Beauty. She beguiled all she saw, gods and men alike, and stole away the wits of even the wise."

"Exactly," Diana agreed, not adding that Aphrodite was said to have a dark, malicious side as she conquered with her wiles, exerting a deadly and destructive power over her victims.

Wondering if Venus bore the same treacherous traits, Diana found herself thinking sadly of Nathaniel. But then she gave herself a fierce mental shake. Thorne had warned her to remain on her guard with Venus at all times. She had to follow the script that she and Thorne had worked out, and to improvise if need be.

"Of course I will pay you generously for your time," she added. "And when the portrait has served its purpose, you may keep it."

"I think that is a fair enough bargain."

"Then you will sit for me?"

"How much time will it require?" Venus asked. "I have a business to run, you understand."

"Five or six sittings of several hours each, to be held over the course of a week or two, or longer if you prefer. I must have time for the paint to dry after each session. I will need two or three hours for the first sitting, to make preliminary sketches in oils so I can determine the right composition and colors and so forth. I am prepared to start whenever you are ready."

"I have the time now, Miss Sheridan. Since I have come all this way, I would like to make good use of the morning."

Relief filled Diana upon clearing the most significant hurdle—securing Venus's agreement to pose for her. She smiled warmly. "Of course. I'm certain you must be extremely busy. My studio is upstairs. If you will accompany me, we can begin at once. What kind of refreshment do you prefer? Coffee, chocolate, wine? I like to make my models comfortable," Diana added truthfully when Venus looked surprised.

"I am partial to chocolate. And some biscuits, if you have any. I have not breakfasted."

"I will have them brought up straight away."

Rising, Diana pulled the bell cord for her housekeeper and ordered a tray sent up to her studio. Then she led her guest from the parlor.

She came to an abrupt halt, however, when to her startlement, she encountered a very large, hulking figure of a man in the small entrance hall.

"My footman, Birkin," Venus explained. "He usually accompanies me whenever I go out."

Diana smiled to cover her discomposure. "He may wait in the kitchen if he likes, where he will be more comfortable. Doubtless my cook has baked plenty of ginger biscuits."

Birkin's scowling face lit up at the mention of the sweets. Venus, with a regal nod of her head at the servant, said he could be excused once he told her coachman to return for her in three hours.

Diana preceded Venus up the stairs then and gave her a brief tour of the studio. She could tell by the madam's reaction that Venus was impressed with her work.

"You were not exaggerating, I see," Venus announced with a degree of surprise that both amused and pleased Diana.

She already had everything in order for the session. Earlier her own footman had moved the chaise longue from the sitting area to one side of the studio, so that it faced the north windows. She was certain now that the pose she had in mind for Venus would work: the goddess Aphrodite reclining on the chaise, classically draped in gauzy Grecian robes, surrounded by a few appropriate props.

Diana told Venus what she wanted and then asked if she would mind taking down her hair. "In the portrait I will give you a proper classical hairstyle with a wreath of laurel leaves, but seeing it down will give me a better idea of the effect I should strive for."

When the madam had no objections, Diana indicated the cheval glass and dressing table in one corner where she could arrange her hair, and the high screen where she could change into the costume.

Diana herself made ready to begin painting. She

had already prepared a canvas and set up an easel and arranged her special cabinet designed with drawers for vials and brushes and bladders of paint. Now she made up her palette with the different pigments she would use for the first stage of the portrait.

When they were both ready, she settled Venus on the chaise and experimented with slightly different poses.

"Your hair is amazingly lovely," Diana said as she curled one long tress over the madam's breast.

"It is my pride, I admit. The color is natural," she said a bit defiantly.

"I could tell. Henna couldn't possibly achieve that rich, deep fire."

Venus looked pleased by the compliment and readily obeyed the requests to shift the position of her legs and arms and head. As soon as the refreshments arrived, Diana left her model to enjoy the hot chocolate and biscuits, while she went to work roughing in the outline of a full-length portrait, sketching in silence for a short while. Then she posed Venus again and returned to her easel, chatting politely about innocuous subjects such as London's dreary weather and the best shops on Bond Street. Thorne had coached her on what topics to discuss, but she first needed to establish a rapport with her client before she could attempt any more intimate queries.

The next time Venus addressed her as Miss Sheridan, Diana responded with a smile. "I would be pleased if you would call me Diana."

"And I am Venus."

Venus was not the madam's real name, Thorne had told her. Diana was to try to discover that, as well as any other information about the woman's murky past.

Turning her attention to the large canvas, she painted in the dark areas with burnt umber, using a beeswax medium to thin the pigment. Then she switched brushes and began the light areas of the flesh using a gray tone made of black, ivory, and white. After another quarter of an hour, Diana steered the conversation back to more personal matters.

"I can't begin to express my appreciation for your help with Amy. Since Nathaniel died, raising her has been chiefly my responsibility." Diana casually glanced up from the canvas. "Did you know my cousin Nathaniel?"

Venus's expression remained enigmatic. "We were briefly acquainted."

"He was like a brother to me, and I miss him dreadfully."

When that leading remark elicited no further comment from Venus, Diana changed tacks. "I suppose you know Thorne quite well."

The madam raised an eyebrow, studying Diana for a moment. "I have known Lord Thorne for a number of years," she finally said, "but we have never been intimate, if that will put your mind at ease."

Diana felt herself flushing. She had feared just the opposite. "I admit that does relieve me. It would be foolish to be jealous of his former . . . lovers, but I cannot help myself sometimes."

There was a hint of wistfulness in her tone that Venus must have heard. "I don't think you need worry. You succeeded in doing what no other woman has ever done—gain his offer of marriage."

A false offer, Diana thought wryly.

When she didn't reply, Venus continued. "To be truthful, I was glad for the chance to meet Lord Thorne's betrothed. He has proved so elusive, I never thought any lady could persuade him to give up his bachelorhood. He once vowed that no woman could tame him, and I couldn't imagine him ever reneging on that vow."

Diana smiled at that. "I suspect he was right. I certainly wouldn't want to try to tame him."

"Perhaps that is the basis for your appeal."

"My appeal?"

"I can see why he is attracted to you. You would be highly intriguing to a man like Thorne."

Extremely curious, Diana stopped painting. "Why would you think so?"

"Because you are quite different from the usual women who pursue him. Your interest in art, for one thing. And you have a special quality that is lacking in so many others, both in your maturity and beauty."

Diana's eyes widened. "Coming from you, Venus, I consider that quite a compliment."

She wasn't exaggerating, either. She felt dowdy and plain compared with the compelling madam. She couldn't possibly compete with a woman of that stamp. Men through the years had sold their souls for the favors of courtesans like this one, Diana reflected with a pang of dejection.

She fell silent for a time and began the next steps of the portrait—the white of the robes, the shadow areas, restating the facial features, and painting in the hair. All the while she racked her brain for another topic of conversation that could lead Venus to feel more at ease.

Finally she hit on one.

"I wonder if perhaps . . . that is . . . Thorne has quite a rakish reputation. Of course he professes to love me. And for the moment, he vows he has no interest in any other woman—"

"But you are worried he might stray from the marriage bed," Venus said frankly.

It wasn't difficult for Diana to pretend embarrassment. "Gentlemen have been known to take mistresses once they are wed. I wish I knew how to prevent it. But I am out of my league when dealing with a man like Thorne. I wondered if perhaps . . . Do you think you could advise me about the secrets of holding a man's interest after marriage?"

The amusement in Venus's green eyes was genuine this time. "I should be happy to. Lord Thorne has a reputation as a marvelous lover, which will no doubt be a disadvantage. Such men become easily bored. But I can teach you a trick or two to keep him satisfied. After marriage—and before, as well, if you wish."

It was a probing remark, Diana realized, perhaps designed to discover how far her relationship with Thorne had already gone.

Feeling her cheeks turn warm, she ducked her head, as if too shy to respond. "*After* will be good enough."

She had no intention of admitting she now had firsthand knowledge that Thorne was a marvelous lover or that she was still very inexperienced.

Thorne would be happy to oblige her curiosity, Diana knew, if she asked him to take their physical relationship to greater intimacy while still maintaining her virginity. It was even possible that she could indulge in a discreet affair with him. . . .

That delicious, scandalous thought sent a flood of regret spearing through Diana. She didn't dare allow herself to become so licentious. She had Amy to consider. And her artistic career. And now Venus.

Shaking herself, she returned to her painting.

After a while, Diana stepped back from the canvas.

"There, we should take an intermission. I'm certain you would like to stretch, and I will order another pot of chocolate. It shouldn't take much longer this morning, perhaps an hour or so. And I would be pleased if you could stay for luncheon."

"Thank you, but no. I must watch my figure, you see." Her tone was ironic when she added, "Gentlemen relish curves, but too much plumpness can be a detriment to my business."

They retreated to the sitting area near the fire, and once the chocolate arrived, Diana began to tell Venus how she had become an artist, purposely including a few comments about her childhood and the devastation of losing her parents at so young an age. Thorne had said Venus was an orphan, and to try to make Venus talk about her own childhood.

Venus showed only a polite interest in the path of Diana's art career, but when she mentioned her grief at her parents' death, the dark emotions that flickered across the madam's expression were unmistakable. Diana at least was satisfied that she'd planted the seed for further conversation.

When they returned to work, she began the highlights on the face and robes and rendering the arms and hands more fully. Later, once Venus was gone, she would finish today's session by painting the dark shadows of the robe, adding a preliminary background, and finally refining the features of the face to be ready for the next stage.

Venus's next remark caught her off guard, however. "Have you visited the Isle of Cyrene yet?"

For a moment Diana debated what to reply. She and Thorne hadn't discussed the possibility of this topic being introduced. But she decided she would do best by sticking with the truth.

"I visited Thorne there just recently. Actually, I took Amy to get her away from her suitor."

"I have heard it is very lovely," Venus mused aloud.

"It is. Unlike anywhere I've ever been."

She told Venus some of her impressions of the island, of its golden beauty and enchanting aura.

Venus apparently already knew of the mythical legend regarding the island's creation by Apollo, and of the isle's reputed ability to seduce the senses of mere mortals, but she seemed less interested in the past than the present.

"What do you know of Sir Gawain Olwen? Did you meet him?"

"Briefly," Diana replied. "He seemed a charming, chivalrous gentleman." She looked up from the canvas at Venus. "Are you acquainted with Sir Gawain?"

The madam's jaw seemed to harden for an instant. "Yes, I am acquainted with him," she said, her tone strangely grim. Then suddenly appearing to collect herself, Venus flashed Diana a sensual smile. "But I won't say in what capacity. A woman in my position must conceal her secrets, you know."

Diana suspected Venus was hiding any number of secrets, yet she couldn't shake the feeling that the madam's acquaintance with Sir Gawain had nothing to do with any past amorous affairs.

Thoughtfully, Diana returned to her painting, eager for the sitting to be over so she could relate her impressions to Thorne.

She reported to him that afternoon as they drove to Hyde Park in his curricle. When she described Venus's inquisitiveness about Cyrene and Sir Gawain Olwen, Thorne frowned.

"It's as I feared. She's trying to pry information out of you," he theorized.

"What kind of information?"

Thorne's hesitation was noticeable as he expertly maneuvered his pair of spirited chestnuts through heavy traffic, but finally he sighed. "Matters relating to the Foreign Office. We have a small department headquartered on Cyrene."

Diana's eyes widened. "Why there? Cyrene is so far from England."

"But its proximity to certain European countries is an advantage. In those cases, we can respond much more swiftly to trouble and requests to our government for help than if we relied solely on our agents in London."

"But why did Venus ask about Sir Gawain?"

"Because he heads our department on Cyrene."

"Oh," Diana said dubiously. She waited, wondering if Thorne would be more forthcoming, but he volunteered nothing further. And Diana doubted he wanted to field any more probing questions about his work.

She settled for a bland statement of fact. "I don't know anything about the Foreign Office, or what you do on Cyrene."

"Venus can't be sure what you know, and I suspect she'll try to discover it. It will be interesting to hear what future questions she has for you."

"Shouldn't you tell me something about your work so I can be prepared?"

Thorne shook his head. "The less you know, the less you will have to prevaricate when she questions you." His mouth tightened. "Venus could very well be a traitor as well as a murderer. I still don't like having you involved."

"Well, I am involved now," Diana replied, "and I am not backing out."

She was glad finally to be doing something useful. And admittedly it was a bit exciting to be required to pit her wits against a possible traitor, although she doubted Thorne would wish to hear that.

"In any event," she added, "I think I have enough other topics to discuss with Venus to set her mind at ease and encourage her to open up to me." Diana couldn't refrain from smiling wryly when she recalled one specific topic. "The most promising thus far was when I pretended to be concerned about your fidelity after we are wed. I asked Venus for her advice on how to keep your attention so you don't stray."

Thorne glanced at Diana sharply before his mouth curved in a grin. "You needn't worry about my fidelity just now. I have enough trouble dealing with you and our betrothal. I'm not about to complicate matters further."

Deplorably, Diana felt a strong sense of relief. Thorne seemed to be telling her that he currently didn't have a mistress.

Not that it should matter to her in the least whether he had ten mistresses, except as it affected the public perception of their betrothal, of course.

Besides, she should cease worrying about Thorne, Diana scolded herself, and concentrate on the task at hand—prying secrets from the notorious Madam Venus while she herself played ignorant of any of the important matters that Venus might try to pry out of her.

The following week proved both intriguing and discouraging for Diana. The Season had begun in earnest, with invitations pouring in for balls and routs, dinners and fetes and Venetian breakfasts. And into this madly busy schedule she fit three more sittings with Madam Venus.

During the course of their sessions, Diana tried to conduct a subtle interrogation—and felt as if she was playing a game of cat and mouse. Venus was extremely reticent to talk about her past, and Diana couldn't see that her own purposeful loquaciousness was having much result.

She also began to worry about Amy. The girl was having visible success charming the ton, but one afternoon Diana returned from the studio to find Amy flung facedown on her bed, weeping forlornly. When pressed, Amy muttered that one of her beaux had unexpectedly begged off an engagement for the third time in the past week.

Since there was likely only one beau who could affect her emotions that strongly, Diana deduced that her young cousin was distressed because Reginald Kneighly was seriously neglecting her.

On the one hand, Diana could only be relieved that their clandestine romance had sustained a blow, and hopeful that this apparent trouble would lead to an irrevocable parting between the young lovers. But it was all she could do not to gather Amy in a motherly embrace and try to console her. She didn't honestly believe Amy's affections were deeply engaged yet still hated to see her suffer.

And observing such misery, Diana couldn't help but remember her own desperate love so many years ago, her own bitter despair when her life had been shattered by her betrothed's defection. When she'd embarked on this devious course to separate Amy from her fortune-hunter, she hadn't realized it would make her relive her own past hurts, her own heartache.

With effort, Diana quelled her despondent reflections and focused her attention on her other chief problem—Madam Venus.

After the second sitting, she no longer had any doubt that Venus was conducting a probing interrogation of her own. In fact, it seemed their conversations had become a delicate duel of wits, with each trying to learn information from the other. It was their fourth sitting, however, before she managed to persuade Venus to discuss her childhood—by asking about her weakness for chocolate.

"When I was a young girl," Venus wistfully explained, "my governess brought me hot chocolate in bed each morning. It was my fondest memory." She sighed. "For years afterward I dreamed about enormous, steaming cups of creamy cocoa. In fact, I missed it so much that I vowed when I grew up, I would be wealthy enough to afford to drink hot chocolate every day. I always start my mornings with chocolate in bed now."

Instantly Diana felt her curiosity piqued. Venus must have come from a wealthy family to have had a governess and enjoyed the luxury of chocolate in bed each morning. And if she missed it during later years, she must have fallen on hard times.

"Did something happen to your governess?" Diana asked, trying to keep her eagerness from her tone.

Venus's eyes grew distant, as if she was remembering. "I lost my parents at an early age, as you did. The years that followed were . . . difficult."

"I'm very sorry," Diana replied, feeling an immediate tug of sympathy. "I can only imagine the grief you felt—"

"No, you cannot imagine! Your parents were killed in a carriage accident. Mine were murdered right before my eyes."

Diana couldn't stifle a gasp. "*Murdered?*"

A rasp of dark laughter sounded from Venus's throat. "You may well be shocked. They died a violent death. To this day I still have nightmares about it."

"How horrible!"

"Indeed. But perhaps the worst part was losing my brother at the same time."

Diana felt her stomach lurch. "He was killed, too?"

"No, we both survived. But he might as well have been dead to me. We were separated and put in different charity homes. I was sent to an orphanage for girls, he to a workhouse for boys. It was almost ten years before I saw him again."

"You must have experienced a harsh life," Diana said lamely, unable to think of any more adequate response.

Venus shrugged. "Mine wasn't as unbearable as my brother's. At our home we were made to work as seamstresses, mostly sewing sails for fishing vessels. They treated us humanely enough, yet I couldn't wait to leave."

Not unreasonably Diana found herself thinking about her own situation, and an ache rose in her throat.

"I was very fortunate," she said softly, "that I had my uncle and aunt to take me in. I've always felt grateful that I was spared life in an orphanage. And perhaps a bit guilty," she added with all honesty. She paused, suddenly struck with an idea. "More than once I've thought about making a donation to a deserving home, but I never made the time to search on out, I'm ashamed to say. I know there are few orphanages in existence, and I hear they are always short of funds."

Venus's humorless smile held bitterness. "There is never any money to spend on chocolate, certainly."

"Perhaps I could contribute to the home where you were raised," Diana said innocently. "Was it private or parish?"

"Parish. The Home for Indigent Girls in Rye."

Rye was in Sussex. Despite her sympathy for Venus, Diana felt a tremor of euphoria at having elicited this first genuine fact in her investigation. She knew Thorne would be pleased when she reported to him—

Her elation dimmed when she recalled that she wouldn't see him at all today. But they would both be attending Amy's comeout ball tomorrow evening, she remembered. She would tell Thorne then.

She considered asking the name of the orphanage that Venus's brother had attended, but decided that might raise too many suspicions in her quarry's mind.

Instead Diana steered the conversation safely away from the subject of orphanages by asking her model to lift her chin and turn her head a bit to the right. But she couldn't help feeling a measure of excitement, knowing that at last Thorne would have a clue to follow in the sinister matter of Nathaniel's death.

Eleven

~∽∾ ∾∽~

For their comeout ball, both Amy and Cecily looked remarkably pretty in their finery, Diana thought with pride. Amy was dressed in pink and white to complement her blond looks, Cecily in pale blue so as not to clash with her red hair. Both girls were nearly giddy with excitement, since this event would mark their formal presentation to society.

Lady Hennessy had planned an elegant dinner beforehand for two dozen couples, with the bulk of the guests to arrive afterward at half past nine. The Duke of Redcliffe had been invited as a dinner guest, by dint of being Lady Hennessy's brother as well as Thorne's father.

John Yates was among the first to arrive for the dinner, and the first to compliment Diana on her own gown—a pale gold satin slip with an exquisite overskirt of shimmering gold net.

Thorne was announced shortly afterward, looking carelessly elegant and breathtakingly handsome in his formal evening attire, a black cutaway coat, silver embroidered waistcoat, and white satin knee smalls.

The pristine white of his cravat and shirt points contrasted with his strong, richly tanned features and made Diana's heartbeat quicken alarmingly.

She seemed to have a similar effect on him, for Thorne stopped short when he saw her, his hazel eyes sparking with male admiration.

"I see our talented modiste did you justice, but that gown could be considered a hazard," he said, eyeing the fashionably low décolletage. "That revealing cut is likely to make a man trip over his own jaw." Bending over her hand, he raised her fingers to his lips, adding in a husky undertone, "And make him long to strip it from your beautiful body to uncover the provocative secrets beneath."

Diana felt her cheeks flushing, but she was indeed pleased with her appearance and glad to be wearing the stunning gown when she would again be on display for all of society to see.

She was also eager to request a private word with Thorne later, murmuring that she had some information about Madam Venus to impart—a request that immediately generated Thorne's keen interest.

Her pleasure was short-lived, however. Moments before they went into dinner, Lady Hennessy drew Diana aside, looking uneasy and a bit guilty.

"I have a confession to make, my dear," the elder lady said in an apologetic tone. "I have invited Lord Ackland to the ball."

Diana felt her facial features stiffen. Francis, Baron Ackland, was the nobleman she had loved so many years ago—the titled artist who had jilted her upon being denied access to her modest fortune.

With her wits so scattered, she barely heard what Lady Hennessy was saying. ". . . his wife's mother was a friend of mine, and since Lord and Lady Ackland just returned to town, it would look odd to exclude them when I have invited half of London. . . . I didn't want to tell you, Diana, in the event they didn't plan to attend, but I received Lady Ackland's acceptance just this afternoon. And it probably will be for the best—for everyone to see you in his company, you know, and to show that the past scandal is completely over." Lady Hennessy grimaced. "Oh, heavens, I am babbling. I feared it might upset you, but I had to warn you so you would not be totally caught off guard upon seeing him."

With effort Diana managed a smile; she had indeed been caught off guard. "You did right to warn me, Judith, and to invite them to the ball tonight. I will have to encounter Ackland at some point, and it is doubtless better to get it over with now, and in the public eye."

And yet Diana didn't believe her own reassurances, for she knew that facing Francis would only bring back all the painful memories she had striven so hard to forget.

During the whole of dinner, she tasted little of what she ate. She felt Thorne looking at her oddly, and saw him lift a quizzical eyebrow when she sent back her plate for the fish course practically untouched.

Realizing she appeared distracted, she made a fierce effort to compose herself and managed to give a reasonable pretense of enjoying the remainder of the dinner, including conversing politely with Thorne's illustrious father on her left.

By ten o'clock, however, Diana's nerves were strained with tension. She stood in the receiving lir just inside the ballroom's entrance doors, along w

Lady Hennessy, Cecily, Amy, and Thorne, to welcome the guests. Judging by the throng already filling the room, the ball promised to be the most crowded fete of the Season thus far. If so, it would be a triumph for Amy and Cecily—and for Diana, as well.

Amy, who stood on Diana's right, seemed very cognizant of tonight's importance and was on her best behavior, except when it came to John Yates. Apparently at odds with Yates again, Amy refused his request to sign her dance card.

"It has nothing to do with your missing leg," she muttered. "It is solely because you are rude and overbearing." Leaving Yates red-faced and chagrined, Amy turned and offered a brilliant smile to the next guest in line.

On Diana's left, Thorne assumed a proprietary air as he introduced her to numerous of his acquaintances. But only one incident managed to divert her troubled thoughts—when a pretty young debutante came through the line in the wake of her mother.

"Mrs. Marling and Miss Emma Marling," Thorne said dryly, performing the introductions.

The girl looked daggers at Diana and positively gushed at Thorne, her effusiveness so blatant that he was obviously hard-pressed to keep his temper under control. When the Marlings had moved on, Diana gave him a questioning look.

"I believe I told you," Thorne murmured in a pained undervoice, "that the last young lady to see me nude claimed I compromised her? Miss Marling was the miscreant. In an attempt to trap me into marriage, she stole into my bedchamber when I was asleep and prearranged for her mother to find us together. I, however, declined to do the honorable thing and save the girl's reputation."

Diana's eyebrows rose. "I am astonished that she could get away with such outrageous conduct and still be received by polite society."

"The chit's transgressions are tolerated more than most because her father is an intimate of Prinny's. In fact, Marling is expected to make an appearance with His Royal Highness this evening. And Mrs. Marling was wise enough to keep her daughter's ploy hushed up when they couldn't reel me in like a floundering fish."

Diana knew Lady Hennessy was hoping for a visit by the Prince Regent, for it would set the crowning jewel on Cecily's and Amy's ball. But she hadn't known the identity of the marriage-minded schemer Thorne had been running from.

Diana would have been amused if not for the butterflies rioting in her stomach at the prospect of seeing her former suitor.

Even though she was expecting Lord Ackland, it was still an unwelcome shock when he finally appeared in the line, preceded by his wife. A plump, haughty matron, the baroness seemed quite plain and dumpy next to the tall, fair-haired gentleman whom Diana had once idolized.

Francis looked, she realized, nearly as beautiful and dreamy-eyed as he had six years ago, and for the briefest instant, the sight of him made her heart flutter painfully. For a moment she was a young girl again, feeling the ache of longing, of tenderness, of love.

It was all Diana could do not to stare at him w. he took her hand and pressed it solemnly while g. deeply into her eyes.

But then memory descended mercilessly—th

shame of her jilting and the scandal that followed. The pain of being branded an outcast, so devastatingly alone.

Seeing Lady Ackland's tight, jealous smile, however, Diana crushed the tangled emotions knotting her insides and somehow managed a civil welcome. Then she introduced Lord and Lady Ackland to her current betrothed.

She could tell at once that Thorne recognized the title, for his gaze sharpened and his tone turned cool as he greeted the baron and baroness.

As soon as the couple had moved away, Thorne bent to murmur grimly in Diana's ear. "So he was the bastard who broke your heart. That explains why you've been so quiet all evening. Why you've had that troubled frown between your eyes."

Still a little unsteady, Diana refrained from replying, although she wasn't surprised by Thorne's perceptiveness, since he missed little.

Fortunately, the next guests in line commanded their attention. Shortly afterward, the receiving line was disbanded and the ball opened with the first dance, a cotillion.

Thorne led Diana out, yet it was hardly the opportune moment for private conversation. Halfway through, Diana recalled she had meant to speak to him about Venus. She had to wait for more than a half hour, though, when Thorne whisked her into a waltz, before she could mention her discovery.

When she told him the name and location of the orphanage where Venus had been raised, Thorne promised to follow up on the new lead promptly. Yet he seemed surprisingly uninterested in her achievement. It was just then that she spied Francis waltzing with his wife. Quite without meaning to, Diana found herself studying her former suitor, asking herself how she could have fallen so ardently in love with him.

Certainly she understood why, as a girl, she would have thought him devastatingly handsome. And why she would have been attracted to his artist's soul. No doubt also, she had been too naïve then to recognize the shallowness of his character.

But only now could she comprehend the deeper forces that had driven her: how vulnerable she had been then, how *needy*.

She'd been an orphan much of her life. Even though she had a dear family—her aunt and uncle and cousins—she'd felt an undeniable sense of aloneness. Francis had somehow filled that aching void inside her, had fulfilled her yearning for love.

Diana shook her head sadly, letting out a deep sigh.

She wasn't aware her gaze was still riveted on Francis until she felt Thorne's arm tighten about her waist.

"You should keep your attention focused on me," he said in a biting tone as he whirled her away. When Diana glanced up at him, she saw his jaw was set in a hard line.

Feeling herself flush, she wished the dance would end. Thorne was an expert at waltzing, but the press of bodies and the heat from the myriad chandeliers seemed suddenly oppressive, while the exertion left her feeling a bit dizzy.

Perhaps Thorne noticed her discomfort, for at th conclusion, he wordlessly urged her out the op French doors and onto the terrace.

The late April evening was pleasantly tempe the gardens below, enchantingly lit with C lanterns. The tone of Thorne's voice, howev an unmistakable chill. "You evidently need a moment to recover your composure."

Grateful for the dim light of the terrace that hid her flush, Diana moved over to the stone balustrade, where she stood gazing out over the gardens.

"I should have been better prepared," she said in a low tone, compelled to give Thorne some sort of explanation. "I knew I would have to face him someday if I came to London."

"Do you still love the bastard?" Thorne demanded, joining her at the rail.

She wasn't certain what she still felt for Francis, but it was not love. She'd had six years to get over him, to mourn his defection.

Diana managed a shrug. "I don't believe so, but seeing him was still a shock. It brought back memories I would rather have forgotten. Being jilted is never a pleasant experience." She forced a self-deprecating smile and glanced up at Thorne. "For my own pride's sake, I am glad to be betrothed to you."

Thorne's snort expressed his disgust. "You would prefer to be betrothed to me than that bastard? Am I supposed to take that as a compliment?"

Glancing at him, she made a face, striving for lightness. "Lord Ackland is not a bastard, Thorne. I don't blame him for needing to marry a wealthy wife."

"He left you to deal with the scandal alone. That makes him one in my book."

It was true that Francis had been weak. And she was still disappointed in him. But not bitter. Not any longer.

If anything, she was angry at herself. All those wasted years because she had pined for the elusive promise of love . . .

But she was older and wiser now. Stronger. And she had a bright new future ahead of her. Her imposed seclusion from society was at an end, thanks in large part to Thorne. She had control of her life again.

Yet the memories were still too painful to dwell on.

"I don't wish to speak of it, if you don't mind."

"Very well, we won't speak of it. Come with me," Thorne said brusquely. Grasping her hand, he led her down the wide flight of stone steps to the gardens below.

"Where are you taking me?" Diana protested.

"The orangery. My aunt has a fondness for citrus fruits, so Hennessy had a forcing-house built for her. They often took tea there together."

His long-legged stride ate up the garden path, so that Diana had to hurry to keep up. She found herself somewhat breathless when they arrived at the door.

She had never been inside Lady Hennessy's orangery, although she knew it was used to force out-of-season produce such as strawberries and to grow tropical plants that couldn't withstand London's cool climate.

Just inside the doorway, a lantern had been left burning, she saw when she entered behind Thorne. Like the larger conservatory at her uncle's country estate, this orangery was essentially a greenhouse, with the sides made of wood and mortar, the roof of small glass panes to allow in sunlight. She suspected the structure was kept warm by a coal stove and humid by a fountain; instantly she could feel the warm, moist air on her face and arms, and she could hear trickle of water somewhere beyond the lush vege tion that greeted them.

Shutting the door, Thorne led Diana along

three aisleways into the dimmer interior, which was fragrant with the scents of blossoms and damp earth. Flanking either side of the aisles were large, porcelain cache-pots containing ornamental trees of lime, lemon, and orange, as well as small palms and other exotic plants she didn't even recognize. At the center of the building, a comfortable sitting area complete with tea table and sideboard was grouped against the far wall, in front of a marble fountain.

Diana did recognize the statue of a maiden with a lion sprawled at her feet. "This resembles the fountain in the courtyard of your villa," she said curiously.

"It is the same design. I had it shipped here as a gift to my aunt several years ago. The female figure is supposed to be the nymph, Cyrene."

At the reminder of the island myth, Diana felt her melancholy fade a little. Moving to stand by the flowing fountain, she traced the smooth curves of the wet marble. "What does the lion signify?"

"According to legend, Cyrene was said to wrestle lions," Thorne replied, his tone still brusque. "That's why Apollo fell in love with her."

Diana couldn't help being amused. "Lions? Truly?"

"Truly. He admired her unique courage."

"I wouldn't call it courage," Diana replied with a dubious glance at Thorne. "It seems rather reckless and foolhardy to battle lions."

Thorne felt his heart turn over at the unconscious sensuality in her smile. He was glad to have taken Diana's mind off her damned fortune-hunter. It made own angry tension easier to bear.

ll through dinner he'd realized she was upset something, and discovering the cause of her s had only roused his anger. He had wanted to throttle Ackland with his bare hands—even before he saw Diana gazing after the bastard with that quiet yearning in her eyes.

The savagery that had ripped through him then was pure, primal male jealousy, Thorne admitted with grudging honesty. He'd felt a fierce surge of possessiveness, as well, which was wholly abnormal for him. He couldn't remember a time when he'd felt true possessiveness toward any woman. But he felt it toward Diana.

Thorne muttered a silent oath. He shouldn't care if she was still in love with her blasted suitor, but he sure as hell did. He wanted more than anything to shield her from heartache.

That urgent need, even more than his anger, had driven him to sweep her away from the ball and practically drag her here, where he could have her alone. His one goal now was to make her forget that bastard and her heartbreak.

Thorne drew a slow breath, trying to calm his anger.

Deliberately, he reached up and touched her mouth with his thumb. Diana gave a start at the contact, her lips parting wordlessly, while her gaze flew to his.

The tension Thorne was feeling turned suddenly from dark emotion to raw sexual awareness. Diana felt the same tension, he knew, for her breath had faltered and she was staring at him, as if unable to move.

Thorne felt another rush of tenderness flow through him, even as he realized another truth. Along with the need to soothe her distress and comfort her was a more selfish desire: he wanted her thinking solely of him. And he knew exactly how to manage it.

His thumb glided over her lower lip, then slowly

trailed downward, over her throat to the swell of her bosom. Diana remained rigid as he curled his fingers over her bodice and drew it down a fraction, enough to expose the rose-hued crests of her breasts.

He heard her sharp intake of breath, but when he caught one nipple between the backs of two fingers and exerted gentle pressure, she made a soft, strangled sound and grasped his hand to halt him.

"You can't, Thorne. . . . We must return to the ball or we will be missed."

"Not for a while. And I have no intention of returning just yet. I have something I want to show you first."

"What?"

"Pleasure, love. The next step in your sensual instruction."

He drew down her bodice farther, so that the fragile skin of her shoulders and breasts were free to the night's kiss and to his own. Diana didn't fight him, but she shut her eyes, as if striving for control.

Her nipples had hardened at his first touch, and when his fingers traced a circle around the jutting tips, she stirred restlessly, obviously aroused by the sensation.

"Such lovely breasts," Thorne murmured, cupping the sweet mounds in his palms. He bent to taste one peak, his tongue finding the bud, drawing it against his teeth.

Diana's gasp shivered throughout the hushed room. When he plied the quivering nipple with his lips, she swayed weakly and clutched his arms for support.

It was only a few heartbeats later that Diana felt herself being guided backward, toward the sideboard. Thorne broke off momentarily and, with a sweep of his arm, cleared the center of a silver tea tray. Then he lifted her up and set her on the polished wooden surface, facing him. Before she could protest, he set his lips to her breast again.

The resulting sensations were so intoxicating that she involuntarily quieted. He laved her breasts, nipping gently, making a banquet of the swollen peaks. Diana closed her eyes in a daze of passion.

Still savoring her, he pushed up her delicate skirts, baring all her secrets to him, then slowly smoothed his palms up the insides of her naked thighs. Diana tensed at the delicious heat his erotic caresses were kindling in her.

When he parted the nest of silken curls, she could feel the muscles of her thighs clench. And when he slid his fingers over her pulsing warmth, she whimpered.

"Lie back, love," Thorne ordered, his own voice a husky, sensual rasp.

One hand still caressing between her parted legs, the other pressed her shoulder so that she leaned back helplessly to brace her weight on her elbows.

"I've been longing to put my mouth on you."

Excitement pierced Diana as she realized his brazen intent.

Bending, he brushed a probing kiss over her feminine cleft, and her body tightened unbearably at the touch of his hot mouth.

Then his tongue probed the silky crevice between her thighs, touching the swollen bud of her sex, lightly gliding over its distended surface.

A delicious shock flared through her body.

Gasping, she pushed against his shoulders to no avail. "No—Oh, Thorne—"

"*Yes,*" he said against her hot flesh, punctuating his reply with soft, wicked kisses.

Diana desperately tried to shift her hips, seeking to escape his ravishing mouth, but his hands closed over her hips, holding her captive.

As a wave of delight swept over her, her protest wafted away on a soft moan, and she fell back in wanton surrender.

With a satisfied murmur, Thorne spread her legs wider and held her to him even more firmly, his face pressed hard against her as he explored the yielding, warm folds with his mouth.

Again running his tongue over her throbbing center, he found the swollen tip of her most sensitive flesh, that point of hot pleasure that could leave her sobbing with ecstasy.

Diana responded with a surge of excitement and arched against his mouth as sensation jolted through her.

His lips closed over the taut, erectile nub then, and gently suckled. Diana gave a strangled moan at the intimate caress.

"Good . . . I like to hear you moan for me," Thorne muttered hoarsely.

Incapable of defense against her longing, she let her head fall back and gave herself up to the fierce heat inflaming her senses. Her hips rose involuntarily at the scalding lap and probe of his tongue.

He was savoring her with exquisite skill, deliberately tormenting the quivering, throbbing bud that was the heart of her pleasure, leaving her feverish and frantic, holding her there on the cusp of completion and not allowing her release.

"That's right, tremble for me, sweeting. . . . I want know I am pleasing you."

She couldn't help but comply, he was pleasing her so gloriously. Her body was aching shamelessly for him. "Thorne, I can't bear it—"

He made a raw, satisfied sound deep in his throat and hooked his arms under her thighs, draping her legs over his shoulders to give himself even better access to her secrets.

Fire leapt from his mouth into her flesh, dragging a wrenching shudder from her. His hot, rasping tongue moved in heated pulses over her, tracing and stroking and caressing. And every touch sent her nerves careening. Her breath grew rapid and harsh; her hands rose to his hair, desperately clutching.

Thorne himself was breathing hard, as if touching her excited him beyond bearing. Then, incredibly, he increased her excitement.

When Diana felt the hot wetness of his tongue thrust slowly inside her, the pleasure was so acute, she nearly screamed.

His fingers left her hips then, and came up to cup her breasts. It was the most erotic experience of her life. His face between her burning thighs, his hands moving over her bare breasts, provocatively kneading, while his tongue plunged rhythmically into her, ravishing her ruthlessly.

Her soft, eager whimpers turned to sobs.

She was shuddering uncontrollably now, awash with passion, her skin flaming, her body melting as he plundered her depths with tender savagery. Her breath was burning in and out of her lungs.

Helplessly Diana tossed her head back and forth in frantic pleasure, until suddenly, finally, heat exploded in her like a sunburst, wild sparks of fire that fountained upward.

The sounds of frenzy in her throat filled the hush of the orangery as she climaxed, dissolving into throbbing, impassioned release.

A shudder of primal triumph rocked Thorne. A long moment passed, however, before he rose above Diana to gather her trembling body against him, wrapping her in his arms as if she were something precious he needed to shield and protect.

He *did* need to shield and protect her, he knew—from himself. He lay half-sprawled between her parted thighs, fighting his fiercest desires, clinging to the shreds of his noble intentions.

This was the crucial moment for decision. He knew he could seduce Diana and bring her to the point where she begged for him to go inside her. She was moist and hot and insanely inviting; he was so aroused, he thought he might explode.

But she was also technically a virgin. And taking her would be an irrevocable step. He forced himself to breathe over the burning ache in his loins as desire warred with his conscience.

He would forever wonder what his decision would have been, for just then he heard a whisper of sound behind him, like the orangery door opening.

An instant later a female voice called softly, "Lord Thorne, are you here?"

Thorne froze, while beneath him, Diana gave a frantic start.

"Lord Thorne, I saw you come in here."

He thought he recognized the voice, and it was definitely moving closer through the concealing vegetation.

Not wanting to be discovered in such a dissolute pose, he put his fingers to Diana's lips, hushing her, then quietly helped her straighten her bodice to cover her breasts and pulled down her skirts.

Even in the dim light, her gown looked disheveled, her swollen mouth lush and wet, her hair mussed, as if she'd been thoroughly ravished.

He had just lifted her from the sideboard and set her down on shaking limbs when the voice spoke again from a few yards behind him.

"So you *are* here. I thought so."

Keeping his body close to Diana's in order to conceal her, Thorne turned to face the intruder. His guess was right; it was Miss Emma Marling, the irritating little schemer who had deviously tried to ensnare him in her clutches earlier this year.

Miss Marling gave him a sly smile as she eyed his tousled hair. "For shame, Lord Thorne, taking advantage of a lady this way. Or perhaps not a *lady* . . ."

She let the words trail off suggestively, clearly implying that any female who would let herself be caught in such a secluded place with a rake like Thorne didn't deserve the title of lady.

Swearing a pithy expletive under his breath, Thorne took a step forward, wanting to close his fingers around the malicious chit's neck. He felt certain she knew Diana's identity—

Feeling Diana's warning touch on his arm, though, he flexed his fists, forcing himself to reply calmly. "You do have the most deplorable tendency to appear where you are unwanted, Miss Marling."

"And you, my lord, have a deplorable tendency to be caught seducing virtuous maidens. But then Miss Sheridan is hardly virtuous, is she?"

Behind Thorne, Diana felt her heart thudding, her dismay rising with each snide remark the girl made.

Refusing to cower any longer, she raised her chin and stepped out from his protection.

"Lord Thorne did not seduce me, Miss Marling. And in any case, we are betrothed."

"But you are not yet wed. Just think of the delicious scandal you will cause. You haven't even recovered from the last scandal yet."

It was true, Diana thought, her heart sinking. Society would never forgive her this time. She had little doubt Emma Marling was spiteful enough to reveal this new transgression to anyone who would listen, and no doubt whatsoever that the resultant gossip would spread like wildfire. Her ruination would be complete.

But she forced a smile and answered evenly. "I know you envy me, Miss Marling, but green is not a becoming color for you."

The girl glared, looking as if she longed to scratch Diana's eyes out. "You will regret making game of me, see if you don't!" Spinning on her heel then, she stalked away.

The slamming of the orangery door reverberated through the entire building. In the aftermath, the trickling fountain was the only sound Diana could hear.

She was uncomfortably aware that Thorne had turned and was eyeing her with a morose, hooded gaze.

Diana shut her own eyes, bowing her head as a turmoil of emotions roiled through her dazed mind—dismay, mortification, anger. . . . But the strongest was regret for her reckless idiocy. She had no excuse for her shameful behavior. Thorne had been accused of seducing her, but she was as much to blame as he was.

More so, in fact, since she had known where her surrender could lead—

Thorne's next harshly murmured words, however, took her breath away: "That settles it," he said into the silence. "Our betrothal is no longer a pretense. We will wed for real."

Twelve

Diana stiffened, wondering if she had misheard—or worse, if Thorne's wits had suddenly gone begging. "What do you mean, wed for real?"

"It's simple. Our betrothal was conceived as a ruse, merely for show. But this changes things. You will marry me—the sooner, the better."

"I certainly will not marry you! You promised that our betrothal would only be temporary—"

"That was before this latest contretemps. A scandal will be unavoidable now. The only way to quiet it will be for us to wed."

Diana stared at Thorne in disbelief, realizing he was entirely serious. "You can't possibly want to marry me. You have no desire to wed anyone."

He smiled with sardonic amusement. "Perhaps not, but I intend to give you the protection of my name. That wretched little schemer was right—your reputation won't withstand a fresh uproar."

"That doubtless is true, but I won't let you sacrifice yourself on the altar of matrimony out of guilt, Thorne. I could never look you in the eye again, knowing I had trapped you."

"You hardly trapped me, love. I'm totally at fault for bringing you here."

Diana shook her head adamantly. "I don't hold you to blame. I came here willingly and fully participated."

"I would dispute that." Turning, he leaned lazily back against the sideboard and regarded her silently, cocking one eyebrow, as if trying to understand her. "I am making you a perfectly legitimate offer of marriage this time, Diana. I find it hard to credit that you would refuse."

At that comment, she shrugged in frustration. "Your noble intentions are laudable, but nobility is a terrible basis for marriage."

"Other than that, what objections do you have to marrying me?"

"What objections do I *not* have?" She couldn't believe he was even asking such a question. She didn't want a marriage of convenience with a rakish husband who didn't love her. Certainly not a marriage with Thorne, for if any man could break her heart again, it would be he.

"There are dozens, but the biggest is that you don't love me," she stated flatly. "And I don't love you."

"Love is beside the point at this juncture."

Exasperated, Diana raised her eyes to the glass-paned roof. "This conversation is wholly absurd. I can manage on my own, without you rushing to my rescue. I have lived with scandal before, and I can do it again."

"I think you are forgetting Amy."

She winced then, her heart plummeting. Having tarnish rub off on Amy was precisely what she had to avoid. But Amy was becoming established in so now, Diana reminded herself, so if she could di herself from her cousin, perhaps Amy wouldn't suffer too badly from a fresh scandal. In any event, she would not wed Thorne simply to protect herself.

Stubbornly Diana set her jaw. "Thank you for your kind offer, Lord Thorne, but I must decline. We will maintain our betrothal purely for appearance sake, but I have every intention of crying off once Amy's future is safely settled. For now I intend to return to the ball. I had best find Amy before she hears the lurid gossip from someone else."

When he straightened, as if meaning to accompany her, she held up a hand. "We should return separately. There is no point in pouring fuel on the fire by us being seen together."

Peering down at herself, Diana straightened her disheveled gown. When Thorne took a step closer, she froze, but he only reached up to tuck a stray tendril behind her ear.

"You can't return looking like you've just been ravished."

"No, that would definitely be unwise." Diana managed an uneven smile. "I assure you, I will be fine, Thorne. I've had a great deal of practice facing scandal. Although I suppose I should don my hair shirt first. It goes against the grain to cow down before society, but for Amy's sake, I will have to show remorse and proper humility."

Taking a deep breath to bolster her courage, she turned and made her way through the tropical jungle without once looking back.

Thorne watched her go, his own emotions in turmoil.

Diana's bravery was unexpectedly endearing, especially in light of his own culpability. He wasn't at all accustomed to feeling guilt, but it was pummeling him now with a vengeance. He should have considered the potentially damning consequences before bringing her here and seducing her where they might be discovered.

He hadn't argued further with Diana, but marrying her was the only honorable course after he had compromised her so thoroughly. Her virginity might still be intact, but he'd been within a heartbeat of taking her. If not for the untimely interruption, he very likely would have.

Thorne shook his head, amazed that the prospect of shackling himself in the bonds of matrimony wasn't quite so terrifying or loathsome as he would have found it barely two months ago. When he'd first proposed a betrothal to Diana, he hadn't truly considered going through with a marriage. He'd been too long conditioned to avoid commitment. Too reluctant to give up his freedom.

But now he had no choice. He didn't want Diana hurt by another scandal, especially one that *he* had caused. Marriage would protect her name in a way nothing else could.

Having to wed her wouldn't wholly be a sacrifice, either, Thorne mused with a thoughtful frown. Admittedly he was drawn to her intelligence and spirit. And she had never once bored him. Quite the contrary, Diana was one of the most intriguing women of his acquaintance. She was independent enough that she wouldn't try to control him, so that he could continue to live his life much as he pleased. Furthermore, his marriage would prevent any more of his father' haranguing, which was a significant benefit in itse Thorne acknowledged with a sardonic smile.

In any event, at some point he would need to m and sire an heir to carry on the title, just as his had wanted all along. And compared with all the marital candidates the duke had pressed on him, Diana was a far, far better match.

Thorne felt his eyes glinting as he tallied her attributes. He had little doubt they would be sexually compatible, or that she would prove a match for him. He'd met few women of her genteel station who could make a suitable wife for a Guardian, but Diana could possibly fit that bill. His growing trust in her and respect for her abilities and judgment were arguments in her favor, at least.

Of course, Diana had several arguments of her own against their marriage. Thorne found himself frowning again as he remembered.

Her adamant refusal of his proposal had taken him aback. He'd expected her to be resigned to the inevitability, if not grateful to him for proposing a solution. Her chief reason was that there was no love between them, yet love was certainly not a prerequisite for marriage.

Straightening his clothing, Thorne turned and headed toward the orangery door.

Her refusal notwithstanding, he meant to wed Diana Sheridan. She would simply have to accept that unalterable fact.

When Diana returned to the ballroom, she was grateful to find the Prince Regent in attendance, since the spectacle His Highness presented took inquisitive eyes off her, while ensuring that the ball would be a victory for Amy and Cecily.

For the time being, Diana held off seeking out her cousin, not wanting to spoil Amy's moment of glory, she had little doubt her reprieve would be short-
For the next hour she felt as if she had swallowed

an entire packet of pins as she waited anxiously for the scandal to break.

When she caught sight of Miss Marling gleefully chattering to a gaggle of her friends—and saw the malicious smile the scheming young beauty shot her across the crowded room—Diana knew the moment of her downfall had come.

As soon as Prinny left the ball with his fawning entourage in tow, Diana pulled Amy away from her cluster of admiring beaux and took her down the hall to the library, so they might have some privacy. There, Diana made her confession, revealing that she had been discovered in a compromising position with Thorne and that she suspected a scandal was about to ensue.

Amy heard the tale in silence, her face growing more pale by the second, her distress obvious at the conclusion.

"Oh, Diana," she murmured in a hoarse whisper. "This could ruin all our chances—mine and Cecily's. You *know* how crucial this ball is to our successful debut. And now"—her blue eyes filled with tears—"this may very well bring disgrace down on all our heads."

Feeling a large measure of shame and chagrin, Diana kept her voice low. "I am sorry, Amy. I should have considered the ramifications before letting myself go off alone with Thorne."

The girl's lower lip trembled, while fat tears rolled down her cheeks. "It does seem the slightest bit hypocritical. You have scolded me often enough for my lack of decorum, and now you have behaved like a wanton yourself."

Amy was lashing out in bitter disappointme Diana knew, yet she had no defense against the a sation. But then she took a deep breath. It had been her duty to protect and guide her vulnerable young cousin, and she had nothing to apologize for in being restrictive.

"My behavior, hypocritical or not," Diana said quietly, "is beside the point. My chief intent has been to prevent you from making the same wretched mistake I made, Amy. To keep you from throwing your life away on a fortune-hunter. If I tried to restrain your excesses, it was only for your own good."

Surprisingly, that declaration seemed to bolster Amy's spirits. Gulping back a sob, she dashed furiously at her streaming eyes and raised her chin. "Well, you needn't fear that I am still infatuated with Reginald Kneighly. I have told him we are finished. He neglected me once too often."

Comprehending that Amy had broken off her lamentable romance with Kneighly, Diana felt a fierce wave of relief that was almost enough to compensate for the self-castigation she was feeling.

She was furious at herself for putting her cousin's reputation at risk. But now at least she had another option. If she no longer needed to keep such a close watch over the girl, then she could distance herself from Amy as she'd meant to do all along, before her pretend betrothal to Thorne.

"You cannot be any more upset with me than I am with myself," Diana said finally. "But I hope to prevent any taint of scandal from rubbing off on you. First thing tomorrow, I will move out of Lady Hennessy's house and go to live in my studio."

"Perhaps that would be best," Amy agreed in a ivering voice, her misery apparent. "It cannot ke up for betraying her ladyship's kindness, of course, but . . ." Shaking her head, Amy turned abruptly and hurried from the library.

Alone, Diana winced at the bitter truth of the accusation; she had indeed betrayed the countess in addition to jeopardizing the girls' chances for a successful Season.

She swallowed the sudden ache in her throat, yet she couldn't manage to shrug off her own misery as she slowly followed Amy back to the ballroom.

For the rest of the night, Diana avoided any further intimacy with Thorne, refusing to be seen in his company. But she could tell by the numerous looks flung her way that the damage was already done; in a matter of hours, she had become a social leper.

One haughty dowager gave her a direct cut, while the Duke of Redcliffe's expression held a hint of scorn and perhaps even disappointment.

It was four in the morning before the last guests departed in their carriages. Diana had forced herself to remain in the ballroom until the bitter end, determined not to cower, but also in order to have a private word with Lady Hennessy before she retired to bed.

They left the bleary-eyed servants extinguishing candle flames of myriad chandeliers and mounted the stairs together.

"I fancy the ball went 'famously,' as the girls are wont to say," the elder lady proclaimed as they reached the first landing. "Better than I could even have wished for. Prinny's attendance sealed it, don't you think?"

"It was a major success," Diana agreed. "But Judith, I fear there was one horrendous problem—"

Lady Hennessy had evidently heard about the uproar, for she gave Diana a sympathetic smile and patted her hand. "Thorne told me about it, my dear. I know it distresses you, but I daresay it will all look better in the morning after a good night's sleep."

Not wishing to wait until then to deal with her disgrace, Diana tried again. "Judith, you know I cannot remain here any longer—"

"We shall discuss it in the morning," Lady Hennessy said firmly. "I am so weary, I could swoon right here."

Chagrined to have been so inconsiderate of the elder lady's needs, Diana turned the countess over to her maid and sought her own bed.

Despite her own weariness, however, Diana spent a sleepless night and dragged herself down to the breakfast room at around ten o'clock, feeling utterly wretched. To her surprise, Lady Hennessy joined her a short while later, announcing that her two charges were still abed.

She allowed a footman to serve her coffee and soft-boiled eggs with toast before giving the servant a polite dismissal.

"Now then, my dear," she said kindly when they were alone, "what is all this dustup about?"

Once more Diana found herself confessing an abbreviated version of the events last evening, when she had been discovered in the orangery with Thorne.

Lady Hennessy made a face, as if she had swallowed a lemon. "That outrageous Marling minx should be given a good strapping by her mother. The girl has been after Thorne for a donkey's age. But it is ludicrous to think of her wedded to my nephew. She is merely green with jealousy, my dear, and thus is determined to ruin you."

"I realize that, but I still should have made certain my conduct was above reproach."

"Well, that milk is spilt now. What you must do immediately is announce the date for your wedding. The sooner you wed Thorne, the sooner this contretemps will all blow over."

Diana bit back her instinctive reply. She had no intention of going through with her betrothal to Thorne, either sooner *or* later, but she could scarcely tell Lady Hennessy that. She was still obliged to keep up their pretense of a love match.

"I don't wish to put any undue pressure on Thorne, Judith," she said merely. "I am still not convinced he truly wants to wed anyone, despite his claim to love me. And I think it is a terrible mistake to marry where love isn't certain."

"If you are speaking of Thorne's long-held aversion to marriage, you needn't worry. He simply has never met the right woman before now. All the ladies he knows are far too tame for him. And of course he could never wed one of his opera dancers. Despite his rebellious tendencies, Thorne knows what is due his family name."

Before Diana could reply, Lady Hennessy went on blithely as she spread jam on her toast. "Furthermore, men of his stamp don't like being chased. Females have been casting out lures for Thorne since he left off short coats. And if you only knew of all the encroaching mamas who have flung their daughters at his head."

The countess harrumphed in disgust. "And to make matters worse, my brother has made a huge mistake with Thorne for years, demanding that he wed for convenience. Ivan married strictly for convenience—a political alliance, as well as the union of two very large fortunes—and Thorne wants nothing of the sort for himself. I can perfectly understand why. He is a rebel and a daredevil with a lust for life, Diana, and a cold-blooded marriage would be like steel shackles to him."

"I also can understand, Judith. Which is why I want to make absolutely certain of Thorne's heart before we enter into an irrevocable union."

Lady Hennessy smiled. "I tell you, his reluctance to wed stems from the candidates he has been offered thus far. He simply doesn't want a milksop bride. He needs a woman who can prove his match. A woman he can love." The countess gazed evenly at Diana. "I believe you could be that woman, my dear. Even if Thorne originally proposed to you merely to defy his father."

"So you know?" Diana asked in dismay.

"I had my suspicions. I see through my scapegrace nephew very well."

Diana forced a smile. "I am touched by your faith in me, Judith. You are very kind—and very wise. But you can see why it would never work out between Thorne and myself."

"I am not so certain of that. Marriage could lead to love. Thorne admires you; that much is obvious. And you clearly have a mutual fondness and attraction."

Diana couldn't deny her attraction for Thorne. And she certainly admired him. She yearned for everything he represented: adventure, freedom, living life on one's own terms. She had spent the last six years of her life longing to be free of society's strictures.

For a moment she even let herself fantasize about a true marriage with Thorne, where love and passion were the cornerstones. She had once dreamed of passionately loving a man who loved her passionately in return.

But Diana quickly shook her head, banishing that

impossible notion. Her chances for a marriage like that were hopeless now.

Thorne wasn't the kind of man to give his heart. And she couldn't afford to risk hers again. She had vowed never to let herself become that vulnerable to any man again.

A real marriage to Thorne would leave her too defenseless. She couldn't wed him, knowing he didn't love her. Nor could she look into his eyes, knowing she had trapped him.

No, she couldn't accept his proposal of marriage, despite how adamant he was about doing the honorable thing.

As for the fresh storm of scandal hanging over her head, she would manage somehow. Since Nathaniel's death, she'd had only herself to rely on. But she was strong enough to weather the tempest.

She had to be.

Her confidence, however, was sent reeling that very afternoon. She was in her studio, working on Venus's portrait, when she received a letter from the British Academy's president.

Holding her breath, Diana broke open the seal. The message was curt and devastating:

Madam,

I regret to inform you that your application for study at the British Academy for the Fine Arts has been denied. Doubtless you understand that our distinguished institution cannot afford any taint of scandal.

Sir George Ender

Her knees weakening suddenly, Diana stumbled over to the chaise longue and sank down. For a long while, she simply sat there, clutching the letter to her breast and staring blindly at nothing.

Her lifelong ambition, finished.

The fragile dreams she had cherished over the years, shattered.

That was how Thorne found her a short time later—looking white-faced and anguished, as if she had lost a loved one.

Thorne felt his gut knot. "What's amiss?" he demanded, crossing the studio to her in three strides.

Not replying, Diana silently handed him the letter.

Thorne perused the message swiftly, then crushed the parchment in his fist. The academy had denied her entrance, giving the brewing scandal as their excuse.

Thorne clenched his jaw. Fury was his first reaction. And when Diana's gaze lifted to his, the pain he saw there wrenched at him. She had indeed lost a loved one. Her art meant more to her than a beloved spouse or child or parent meant to almost anyone else. And to be denied admittance for such a reason . . .

Thorne cursed long and vividly, knowing he had caused this bloody mess for Diana. Last night before leaving the ball, his father had taken him to task for his licentiousness, but the scolding was entirely deserved, Thorne was well aware.

His temper just now, however, left him feeling like tearing a strip off someone—and he knew just whose hide would be his target.

"Wait here," Thorne said abruptly to Diana, not giving her the opportunity to say a word. Turning, he stalked out of the studio, taking the letter with him.

It was nearly two hours later before he returned.

Diana had tried to focus on her painting, but her shock and despair had prevented her from making much headway with the final stage of Venus's portrait.

She regarded Thorne's entrance numbly, barely reacting when he handed her a new letter. "What is this?"

"A retraction. Sir George has reconsidered and accepted your application to study at the academy."

Not understanding, Diana broke the seal and read with total disbelief. Yet Thorne was right; the letter contained an apology from Sir George, as well as an effusive acceptance.

"What could possibly have made him change his mind?" she asked, lifting her gaze to Thorne's in bewilderment.

"I offered the academy a large endowment on the condition that you be allowed to train there."

Diana's jaw dropped. "You *bribed* them?"

Thorne's mouth twisted with ironic amusement. "Bribery, threats, a little coercion here and there. Actually I took a page from my father's book and used my wealth to influence their decision." When she simply stared at him, Thorne tapped the underside of her chin. "Close your mouth, love. Openmouthed ladies look so very witless."

The teasing glimmer in his eyes invited her to share his humor, but Diana *did* feel witless. She also didn't know whether to be more embarrassed or vexed. "Thorne, you cannot just interfere like that!"

"Why not?" he asked unrepentantly. "You clearly deserve admittance, and I damned sure won't be the cause of your rejection."

He shifted his gaze, seeing Venus's portrait for the first time. His eyes flared, turned stormy. "Just look at this." He stood back an arm's length from the life-size painting. "This is utterly remarkable." Thorne shook his head in disgust. "I can't believe they were moronic enough to refuse you in the first place. You have more talent than any ten of their professors combined."

Diana raised a hand to her temple, shaking her dazed head. She wanted to scold Thorne and to laugh at the same time. Two hours ago, her future had lain in ruins. Now, thanks to Thorne, she had a fresh chance to fulfill her lifelong dream.

Still, she couldn't just countenance his outrageous generosity. "It won't do, Thorne," Diana began. "I couldn't possibly permit you to bribe my way in. I could never show my face there—"

"Of course you can, and you will. You won't start classes for another month, but your paintings will be displayed at the Academy's exhibit, which opens week after next."

"But I can't allow you to throw away your fortune on me."

Grasping the letter from her paint-stained fingers, he set it down and took both her hands in his. "I don't give a damn how much it costs. I was responsible for what happened last night, and I'm obliged to rectify matters."

"But I was a willing participant—"

"Only because I coerced you." When her frown remained troubled, Thorne lowered his voice. "Diana, let me do this for you. I couldn't live with myself, knowing you were suffering because of me."

The protectiveness in his plea felt strangely wonderful. She'd missed having someone be protective of her. Ever since Nathaniel's death, she had felt even more alone. Especially since her relationship with Amy had become so strained.

She should be grateful to Thorne for caring about her, Diana reminded herself.

She had yet another reason to be grateful to him, Diana recalled, remembering her cousin's admission during their last conversation. He had saved Amy from a fortune-hunter.

Still feeling dazed, Diana shook her head. "Very well. . . . Thank you."

"Good."

He bent his head, obviously intent on kissing her, but Diana suddenly came to her senses and pulled her hands from his.

Drawing back to a safer distance, she eyed him with a suspicious frown. "But if you think this changes anything about our betrothal, you are much mistaken. I have no intention of wedding you."

"We shall see about that," Thorne retorted in a determined undervoice, an ominous glint of amusement in his eyes.

Thirteen

If Diana thought she could persuade Thorne to abandon his notions of a real marriage, she quickly learned she had underestimated his determination.

He was relentless.

He refused to cancel any of their social engagements and insisted they continue to appear in public together, just as if nothing had happened. Worse, he turned the full force of his formidable charm on her.

Since she had moved from Lady Hennessy's Berkeley Square mansion to her own studio house, Diana was breakfasting alone the following morning when Thorne appeared unannounced on her doorstep with a riding mount for her, intent on enjoying a gallop in the park. When she protested that she had work to do, he threatened to abduct her on the spot if she didn't repair upstairs immediately and don her riding habit.

He waited patiently for Diana to change. Then as soon as they were mounted, he dismissed his groom with orders to wait there until they returned.

Diana had never before encountered a Thorne seriously bent on seduction, but as they rode along the

London thoroughfares to Hyde Park, she found herself subjected to an outrageous flirtation.

After Thorne's second flattering comment about her looks in as many moments, Diana eyed him suspiciously. "I still won't marry you," she repeated once again.

He only evinced a regretful smile and shook his head. "There is no hope for it, love. I consider myself quite compromised. But I do agree that our situation has changed." His gaze locked on hers. "What is the saying? You might as well be hanged for a sheep as a lamb? If you're to be condemned for a shameless jade, you may as well enjoy the benefits."

"What do you mean?"

"I think you should accept my offer to show you pleasure. I'm certain you will enjoy yourself far more if I arouse you with my body rather than just my hands and mouth."

Diana nearly choked. "I won't make love to you, Thorne!"

"You're heartless."

He interrupted their conversation to lead her across a busy street filled with carts and drays, then returned to the same subject. "I already warned you, sweeting, that resistance only intrigues and arouses a man more. You should surrender now and save us both the trouble of a chase."

"I have no intention of surrendering to you."

"You know you want to."

Deplorably, she did want to, Diana admitted to herself. Thorne was such a charming devil this morning, with his angel face and laughing gold-green eyes, that it was nearly impossible to resist him.

"I want very much to make love to you," Thorne

admitted, his eyes glinting as he surveyed her. "And now there is no longer any reason to defer."

Diana couldn't quell the traitorous warmth that filled her at his look, or at the thought of his love-making, but she wasn't about to let him know it. "Of course there is reason. I intend to guard what precious little reputation I have left."

A smile played across his lips. "Do you lie in bed at night and wonder how you would move beneath me? How incredible it would feel to have me deep inside you?"

"No, I do *not*." A lie, she knew very well.

"I do. Awake or asleep, I can't get you out of my mind."

It was Diana's turn to shake her head as she gazed at him in exasperation. "You are every bit the rake I first took you for. If only Amy could see you now. It would teach her to beware of libertines."

Diana was grateful when they finally reached the park, for it temporarily put an end to Thorne's blandishments. She also enjoyed their brisk gallop and the momentary feeling of freedom it gave her. By the time they returned to her house, her spirits were higher than at any time in the past two days.

As soon as Thorne reached up to help her dismount, however, her wariness returned.

Grasping her waist, he gazed challengingly into her eyes as he slid her suggestively down his body. Then possessively he cupped his hand at the nape of her neck.

"Thorne, don't you dare think of—"

His head dipped down even before Diana had finished her sentence. When his lips captured hers for a long, lingering kiss, sensation struck her with the force of a summer storm and left her dazed.

Finally recalling they had an audience—his groom was a dozen yards away, pretending disinterest— Diana felt herself flush with embarrassment as she stepped back. Thorne obviously understood how greatly he had unsettled her, for she saw wicked laughter flare in his eyes.

She wanted to box his ears.

"I know," he murmured in a provoking undervoice, "how could I have been such a cad? But I had something to prove to both of us: You want me."

"I do not want you, you conceited oaf!" Diana hissed, trying to keep her own voice low.

His smile held a knowing smugness that was still infuriatingly attractive. Even more infuriating was his hushed command as he tapped her on the nose with a forefinger. "Dream of me, love, when you are alone in your chaste bed tonight."

He sent her another wicked smile before turning to his horse.

To Diana's dismay, that was only the first of numerous incidents during the following week where Thorne won their private battle of wills. It soon became clear to her that he was publicly wooing her while maintaining the pretense that he was besotted with her.

At least the latest blot on her reputation had been mitigated a small measure by her acceptance by the academy. It also helped that her disgrace was overshadowed by world events, so that she was no longer the primary topic of concern.

Instead, the talk was all about Napoleon Bonaparte. In March, the Corsican Tyrant had reentered Paris to begin the reconstruction of his army and empire. And just last week he had been restored power in France with a new constitution. The British papers were filled with impassioned speculation about how the Allies should and would respond to the grave new threat.

Diana's more immediate concern at the moment, however, was dealing with the threat Thorne presented. In public, he was all attentive charm. In private, he kissed and caressed her every chance he got.

It was a mistake to have moved into her house, she realized, for it gave him more opportunities to be alone with her. He continued to show up unannounced, any time he wished, even when she was working, and blithely dismissed her threats to have him thrown out.

Diana found it nearly impossible to defend herself against his outrageous charm, or her own instinctive inclinations. Every time he touched her, her body turned traitor. Which was why, simply out of self-preservation, she began requiring one of her servants—a footman or maid—to remain with her in her studio in case Thorne should drop in.

He even made an appearance during Venus's final sitting, when Diana was trying to complete the madam's portrait. He stayed to flirt with them both, and when Diana finally managed to be rid of him, she apologized profusely for Thorne's brazen behavior.

Venus's indulgent smile was rather amused, and she dismissed Thorne's antics as typical of his reckless nature. The madam, however, had evidently heard about the cloud of scandal that dogged Diana, and she seemed sympathetic and even angry in her behalf.

"It is scarcely fair," Venus muttered, "that women ust bear the sole brunt of censure in these situa-
ns. But at least Lord Thorne intends to wed you.
rriage is the only possible course open to you

now." She gave Diana a long, speculative glance. "Unless you join the demimonde, as I did. You could be highly successful in the flesh trade, you know."

Diana's eyes widened uncertainly. "I suppose I should be flattered by such praise?"

Venus laughed. "Indeed you should. There are few ladies of quality with your beauty and sensual appeal, and many gentlemen find that combination irresistible. If you ever consider changing careers, I would willingly take you on . . . although I imagine Lord Thorne would raise major objections," Venus added dryly. "It is quite apparent that he is enamored of you."

Diana refrained from replying, knowing Thorne's ardor was all an act, even as she wondered how much longer she could hold out against him.

Thorne knew he was breaking numerous social rules in his open pursuit of Diana. Knew he wasn't playing fair. Yet he didn't give a damn. He had no qualms about using every advantage at his command. He was determined to overcome Diana's resistance to their marriage. In fact, he intended to make it impossible for her to refuse.

He himself had become resigned to the inevitability, but he hadn't expected to have to work so hard at convincing her. It had been years since he'd exerted himself to captivate a woman. Longer still since one had actively resisted him the way Diana continued doing. This sensual game with her, however, was one he knew how to win. One he *would* win.

Even so, it was driving him mad. Once they were wed, he would have to spend at least a week in with that bewitching, elusive woman in order to to slake his craving for her. Perhaps after he had love to her a few dozen times, the gnawing want would lessen.

He might not want a bride, but he wanted Diana in his bed. Wanted to feel her warm and soft in his hands. Wanted to watch her dark eyes turn languid with sensuality. Wanted her hot and wild and burning with desire for him.

And sooner or later, Thorne resolutely promised himself, he would have her there.

Only once did he allow her a reprieve from his attentions—when midway through the week he went to Rye to investigate the orphanage where Venus had been raised. With frequent changes of horses for his traveling chaise, Rye was a half-day's drive from London, so Thorne left early in the morning and took John Yates with him.

He had already written the administrator, requesting an appointment. Therefore they were received at once and shown into a cramped office, where Mr. Gough greeted them pleasantly.

Gough was a tall, lanky, elderly man who seemed puzzled by Thorne's visit but professed himself willing to answer any of his lordship's questions.

"I am interested," Thorne said, "in learning about one of your orphans who went by the name of Madeline. She would have come to you as a young girl some twenty years ago."

Gough steepled his fingers in thought. "We have had several girls by that name, my lord."

"This girl had vivid red hair."

"Ah, yes, I know the one you mean. Madeline For-
..."

At the familiar name, Thorne felt the muscles in his

stomach clench, while out of the corner of his eye, he saw John Yates give a start.

He'd suspected a connection between Venus and the late Thomas Forrester, but if they shared the same surname as children, they were more likely sister and brother, not lovers. In her revelations to Diana, Venus had said she had a brother, and that they'd been separated when he was sent to a different workhouse.

"You see, Mr. Gough," Thorne continued, offering a fabricated story, "I am here on a commission for my aunt. Many years ago her ladyship was staying at an inn on the road to London when a young woman named Madeline performed a service for her. My aunt couldn't recall her benefactor's name, only that she had been raised in an orphanage in Rye. She wishes to bequeath this Madeline a modest sum in repayment for her kindness. Whatever you could tell me might help me to locate her."

Evidently believing the story, Gough nodded. "Madeline left here when she was sixteen, I recall. Her brother came for her."

"She had a brother?"

"Yes, my lord, but I don't recall his name."

"Do you know where they went from here?"

"I believe I heard that Madeline went to London, but I'm afraid I don't know where."

"What of her family? How did she come to be here in the first place?"

"I remember she was of genteel birth. Not from Rye, but somewhere in the vicinity. Her parents had been murdered, a very shocking incident, to be sure. Perhaps my wife could tell you more. She was in charge of the dormitories back then."

The two gentlemen had a short wait while Gough went to fetch his wife. In the silence, Thorne met

Yates's eyes and could tell they shared the same thought: It was unwise to leap to any conclusions, but they might have found an explanation for the Forresters' interest in the Guardians. If their parents' violent deaths had been linked to the Guardians somehow, it would give both Madeline and Thomas strong reason to want revenge.

A few moments later, Mrs. Gough came bustling in, but she could add little to her husband's recollections about Madeline Forrester.

"When she first came to us, she was a bitter, silent child, but she was a little beauty even then. I always feared her looks would lead her to a bad end."

Perhaps they had, Thorne reflected. Young Madeline wound up selling her body in a high-class brothel, and eventually became a madam herself. Had her parents not died, she likely would have had an entirely different life. Another strong reason to want vengeance.

"Do you recall anything about her brother, Mrs. Gough?"

"Not much, my lord. Only that he was also sent to a workhouse. Likely it was a parish close to where he lived. There must have been no homes for girls there if Madeline was sent here."

Thorne thanked both Goughs and made a donation to the home's charity fund. Once he and Yates were settled in the traveling chaise on their way back to London, they discussed the possibilities and agreed that their next step was to determine what possible connection the Guardians might have to the murder of Madeline and Thomas Forresters' parents.

"I want you to send a report to Sir Gawain at once," Thorne told Yates. "Request that his records be searched for any missions twenty or so years ago that might have involved the senior Forresters. You're his secretary, so you can best direct him where to begin looking."

"Very well, my lord. But a reply from Cyrene will take a month or so to return to us."

"Too long, I know. Which is why I also want you to write every retired or active Guardian in England who could have participated back then. I've already questioned all our current London agents about Thomas Forrester, to no avail. I also asked the Foreign Office to examine their files for reports of him— although with Boney threatening a new war, I suspect their priorities lie elsewhere. But perhaps one of our older agents can recall something about the Forresters' deaths."

Yates nodded thoughtfully. "An excellent notion. Hopefully we will get lucky, since I discovered nothing from the tenants who lived in that burned-down lodging house where Thomas died." Yates paused. "It was fortunate Miss Sheridan was able to lure the clue about the orphanage from Madam Venus. Otherwise we would still be at a standstill in our investigation."

"Yes, it was fortunate," Thorne agreed grudgingly. "But that will be the last of Miss Sheridan's involvement. Venus's portrait should be finished shortly, and I don't want to risk exposing Miss Sheridan to any potential danger."

"Do you mean to tell her about our discovery regarding Thomas Forrester?"

"No. If she asks, I'll say only that we visited Rye, and that the visit might result in some new leads. I want her well out of it."

Thorne was determined to end her participation in his investigation. If there was any benefit from the scandal, he realized, it was that the emotional turmoil provided Diana a distraction and kept her mind off Nathaniel's death. Thorne also thought it advantageous that four weeks from now, she would have her art classes to occupy her time.

Now he just had to ensure that Diana terminated her relationship with the notorious Madam Venus as soon as possible.

Separating her from Venus, however, wasn't as easy as he had expected, for again he'd underestimated Diana's independent-mindedness. He should have known that once that genie was let out of the bottle, it couldn't easily be stuffed back in.

At week's end when he called at her studio, Diana informed him that she had shown Venus the completed portrait yesterday for the first time. "She seemed to be extremely pleased with the result."

"Of course she was," Thorne replied, studying the stunning portrait with its luminous highlights and shadings. "I suspect this may be some of your best work."

"Venus believes I should have no trouble finding art patrons to support my career."

Thorne looked up at that, meeting Diana's gaze with narrowed brows. "I have no doubt I could find patrons for you."

She cast a swift glance across the vast studio, at the chambermaid who was busily cleaning. "You have done quite enough, Thorne," Diana muttered. "I want my work to be respected on its merits, not as the result of bribes or coercion."

"Of course you do," he said soothingly. "But it won't benefit your reputation any to rely on Venus's clientele for patronage."

Her eyes sparking equally with defiance and wry

amusement, Diana put her hands on her hips. "I don't believe it! The wicked Lord Thorne spouting advice about following the stuffy rules of propriety."

He grinned. "It does strain the imagination, doesn't it? But be that as it may, you should end your connection with Venus now."

"It would be shameful of me to cut her simply to protect my reputation. Venus has been very kind to me. And frankly, I *like* her."

Thorne gave Diana a penetrating look. "I think you're forgetting her possible implication in Nathaniel's death."

She frowned, the sudden flash of guilt and pain in her eyes telling him that he'd struck a nerve. "I suppose I had forgotten," she said lamely. "She seems so congenial."

Deciding he had pressed the issue enough for the moment, Thorne took her arm and led her toward the studio door. "We needn't discuss this now. Go change your gown. I'm abducting you for the day."

Shaking herself, Diana frowned. "Why?"

"There is a garden party in Richmond where we must be seen. Enough elderly dowagers will be attending to make an appearance worth our while. I intend to put you back into their good graces by charming the stockings off them."

Thus, Diana shortly found herself accompanying Thorne to Richmond, an hour's drive southwest of London. Despite the anxiety gnawing at her stomach, she enjoyed the journey. The scenic stretch of countryside along the Thames River boasted numerous magnificent estates with splendid gardens and lush woodlands, so Diana spent most of the time gazing out the windows of Thorne's town coach, admiring the view.

When they arrived, he remained by her side for the entire afternoon as they mingled with an elite company consisting mainly of noble and genteel elderly ladies.

Thorne made good his promise to figuratively relieve them of their stockings. His outrageous charm made Diana smile, while his powers of seduction awed her.

There was only one difficult moment, when a viscountess made a cutting remark in Thorne's hearing about riffraff artists. With a lethal smile, he leapt to Diana's defense, offering a few choice words of his own, commenting that the British Academy did not admit riffraff into their hallowed halls as they had Miss Sheridan, and how it was a pity that snobbery and ignorance kept even members of the quality with claims to taste and refinement from perceiving the benefits of artistic culture.

The sun was setting by the time he handed Diana into his town coach to return to London. Feeling a surge of relief and weariness, Diana lay her head back on the squabs, glad the ordeal was over.

"Tired?" he asked solicitously.

"Mmmmm," she replied, shutting her eyes. "Being on display like that is absurdly exhausting, especially when I'm far from certain all this effort to redeem my reputation will have any effect."

Yet when Thorne tried to gather her against him, Diana sat bolt upright and retreated to the opposing coach seat. "I'll thank you to keep your grasping hands to yourself, my lord. I might see the wisdom in attending these functions with you, but that doesn't permit you to use them as an excuse to molest me."

Thorne gave a low chuckle and left her alone to rest unmolested.

It was perhaps a quarter hour later, when dusk had started to settle, that the coach unexpectedly began to slow. Puzzled, Thorne lowered the window to look out.

On the deserted road up ahead, a rider waited, masked and armed with pistols. In fact, there were two riders flanking the road, Thorne realized grimly. Both brandishing weapons at his coachman and the liveried footman, who stood perched on the rear boot. Evidently the coach was being held up by highwaymen.

Irritation gripping him, Thorne started to draw his head back inside, intent on fetching the loaded pistols he always carried for precisely this purpose. But without warning, a shot rang out. A cry from his coachman told Thorne the servant had been hit—a theory instantly confirmed when the man fell from the box and rolled to the side of the road.

Just as suddenly, the coach lurched violently forward, causing the footman to lose his grip and tumble off to land near the prostrate coachman. With no one driving, the four-horse team bolted.

Gathering speed, the vehicle rushed past the mounted highwaymen. Thorne had only a split second to realize the brigand on the right was aiming a second pistol directly at him. Cursing, he ducked inside and shoved Diana sideways, just as a bullet whizzed past his head.

He heard her give a sharp gasp as she sprawled on the cushions, and fear clenched his chest. Dear God, had she been hit?

Clumsy with panic, he reached for her, but then Diana struggled to sit up, and fierce relief flooded him. She was white-faced, but with a grim look of determination fixed on her features.

Just then the jolting sway of the carriage nearly knocked Thorne to the floorboard and reminded him of the danger they were in, caught inside the speeding vehicle.

He fumbled for the case beneath the seat and managed to open it, revealing a brace of pistols. Grabbing one, he lunged for the window.

"How can I help?" Diana demanded.

"Get the other pistol!" He didn't know if she knew how to shoot, but he wanted her armed.

As she dropped to her knees on the floor, he thrust his head out the window, looking toward the rear for the two masked riders—only to see them galloping after his runaway carriage.

Taking aim, Thorne got off a shot and thought he might have wounded one man, but he had no time to waste. The coach had picked up more speed as the panicked horses began to race wildly.

Bracing himself against the jarring rock, Thorne eased his shoulders all the way out the window and turned to sit on the frame.

"What will you do?" Diana shouted from inside.

"Try to stop the team before we wreck!"

He would have to climb from the window onto the coachman's box so that he could take the reins himself.

Clutching precariously at the roof for balance, Thorne raised himself up to stand on the window frame. By straining, he could just grasp the edge of the coachman's box. Another sickening jolt almost caused him to lose his grip, but he clung tightly. If he was thrown to the ground at this speed, he risked breaking a limb or worse.

The wind roared in his ears along with his pounding heartbeat as he inched forward. He hooked one leg over the box rail, then pulled his chest even with the front of the roof. Then feetfirst, he heaved himself over the rail and into the box, and landed half-kneeling, half-sprawling on the driver's seat, on his stomach.

Swiftly righting himself, Thorne searched in the gathering dusk for the reins. There they were, dangling down past the center pole between the two pairs of galloping horses, flapping on the ground beneath the churning hooves.

And the clattering, bumping coach was close to careening out of control. If it turned over at this speed, Thorne knew it would likely shatter on impact. He might be able to jump free, but Diana was trapped inside, which could mean her death.

Fear momentarily knotted all his muscles, but he couldn't afford the luxury of emotion. Without letting himself think, he carefully climbed onto the dash of the box, then lowered one foot to the splinter bar. From that, he sprang forward, making a wild leap for the flexing hindquarters of the off wheeler.

His chest landed hard on the animal's muscular rump. When it squealed in fright, Thorne grabbed for the bulky leather surcingle that wrapped the horse's belly.

The ground was a blur beneath him as he pulled himself up and forward, till he could grasp the neck collar and make a desperate grab at the near rein.

At the sudden jerking pressure of the bit, the off leader stumbled, nearly going to its knees, while the horse Thorne rode gave a responsive lurch as it struggled for balance.

He hung on for another instant, the rein still clutched in his hand, but then felt himself falling sideways, between the racing horses, so that his left kr ground against the center pole while his left foot dragged the ground.

Thorne grimaced, then clenched his teeth at the sharp pain when his inner ankle was struck by a churning hoof, but he clung frantically with his right arm to the surcingle, while his left pulled with all his might on the rein. He felt another searing pain, this time in his left palm, but miraculously the lead horse responded the barest measure. Eventually the team slowed enough for Thorne to regain his perch, where, despite the pain, he kept giving repeated, rhythmic yanks on the rein.

After what seemed an eternity, he managed to bring the panting, lathered horses down to a trot, then to a walk, and finally to a quivering halt.

The moment the coach rolled to a stop behind him, Thorne slid to the ground, but he failed to account for his weakened limbs or his injured left ankle. His left leg gave way beneath him, so that he slumped to one knee.

For several heartbeats he stayed that way, all his muscles quivering after his struggle with the horses, his blood pumping with rage and pain. Yet he had to see to Diana. . . . He climbed to his feet with an effort just as he heard the carriage door swing open.

Diana stumbled out, still holding the second pistol. She was pale and trembling and disheveled, he saw, and the upper left sleeve of her pelisse was drenched with blood—

Thorne's heart lurched. "Damnation, you *were* hit—"

"I'm all right," she murmured, moving unsteadily ɔward him. "The ball just grazed the top of my ɔoulder. What about you—? You're limping!" she exclaimed as he rapidly closed the distance between them.

Without replying, he roughly pulled her against his body and wrapped his arms around her, his breathing ragged.

Sagging against him, Diana buried her face in his shoulder. "I can't believe you managed to stop the team. . . . You saved our lives, Thorne."

Behind him, the panting, heaving horses simply stood, too weary to rebel any longer. Thorne felt himself shudder when he realized how close they had come to catastrophe, and he felt Diana's similar reflexive shudder.

She was badly shaken after the ordeal, and he wanted nothing more than to hold her until her shivers ceased. But belatedly he recalled that the highwaymen could still be after them. And his missing servants could be in danger, as well.

Drawing back, he took Diana's pistol from her and kept it aimed at the gloomy road behind the coach while, with his left hand, he withdrew a handkerchief from his coat pocket to press it against her shoulder wound.

She winced, but her sharp gasp was not for herself. "Thorne, you *are* hurt!"

Still watching the road, he took stock of his injuries. His left palm was bleeding where the skin had ripped open. His coat was torn, and the left leg of his pantaloons was bloody near the ankle. He had a gash on his right cheek where he'd scraped it against a harness buckle, and he ached in every bone. But none the injuries was serious.

"I'll live," he assured Diana in a hushed "Now keep quiet. We may still be targets."

He waited for a moment in the gathering da

listening for hoofbeats, until finally he was satisfied the highwaymen hadn't followed them.

Clenching the pistol in his teeth then, he started to tie his handkerchief around Diana's upper arm, but she would have none of it. With trembling hands she took the handkerchief from him and gently looped the cambric around his savaged palm, murmuring her sorrow at his pain while tears slipped unheeded down her face.

Thorne felt a surge of tenderness lance through him. Diana had been struck by a bullet, yet *she* was worried for *him*.

A fresh wave of fear and anger washed over him. Diana could so easily have died. And even now his coachman might be lying dead on the side of the road.

What was more, Thorne thought grimly, his jaw hardening, he had no doubt the murderous assault had been deliberate.

Fourteen

Nearly two more hours passed before Thorne had time to reflect on the attack and the possible motives of the perpetrators. His first priority was seeing to his fallen coachman.

After lighting the carriage lamps, Thorne turned the coach around and climbed into the box to drive. Diana sat beside him, since she refused to remain alone inside. Moreover, he needed her help in searching for his missing servants.

He found them more than a mile back. The coachman was clearly not dead, indicated by his alternating curses and groans. The footman was supporting the injured man's head, trying to keep him comfortable. Both men asserted that the highwaymen had fled back in the direction of Richmond, with the coachman terming the brigands "bloody cowards" and lamenting that he'd had no chance even to draw his blunderbuss before they shot him.

The coachman had been struck in the shou Thorne saw when he knelt to inspect the damage wound was unlikely to be fatal, but the ball have to be removed as soon as possible.

"He needs a surgeon," Diana said, voicing Thorne's thoughts.

He nodded, deciding it best to head directly for his own mansion in Mayfair, where his surgeon could be quickly fetched. He considered taking Diana to her studio house first, but he disliked delaying when his servant was so severely injured. He also wanted her shoulder professionally examined, to satisfy himself that her flesh wound wasn't serious. Even more crucially, he didn't want Diana going home until he could install some of his own servants there to protect her. If he was a target for murder, then she could be, as well.

In any case, Diana wouldn't hear of putting her own welfare before that of his coachman. Thus, in a few more moments, the vehicle was conveying them all to Cavendish Square.

The footman drove the now-spent team, while Diana and Thorne rode inside the coach, bracing the injured man against the worst of the jolting while trying to stop the bleeding. He was in obvious pain, even though he tempered his expletives in Diana's presence and settled for mumbled groans. So Thorne gave him a flask of well-aged Scotch whisky to dull his senses.

The coachman was thoroughly sotted by the time they arrived home, where Thorne's capable staff leapt into action, fetching the surgeon and making preparations for the operation—the speed of which made Diana suspect his household had dealt with bullet wounds before. The surgeon, too, showed no surprise he type of injury, but went straight to work on his ent.

ey dug out the ball in the kitchen, with Thorne f helping to hold down the wounded man.

ing to be sent away, Diana waited quietly in

one corner of the vast kitchen. Thorne had given her a brandy to settle her nerves, but her tension didn't ease until the surgeon finally pronounced himself satisfied and said that nothing more could be done tonight.

Once the now unconscious coachman had been carried upstairs to sleep in his own bed in the servant's quarters, the surgeon looked at Diana's shoulder wound and confirmed that it was not much more than a graze but needed to be washed and bandaged. The injury to Thorne's palm, however, was a bit more serious, and so the surgeon proceeded to attend to it right there in the kitchen.

When he poured brandy on the raw flesh, Diana winced at the pain she knew Thorne must be feeling, but when she met his eyes, he only winked at her and brought the brandy bottle to his lips. He kept drinking as the surgeon cleaned and wrapped his left ankle, which to her dismay was not only severely bruised and swollen, but lacerated down to the bone.

Thorne favored that leg when he escorted her and the surgeon upstairs to a guest bedchamber, along with his housekeeper and a maid to attend her. Diana had never been inside his mansion before, and she had a vague impression of elegant decor and excellent taste.

The bedchamber had obviously been prepared for her, for basins of hot water awaited her, a cheery fire blazed in the hearth, and several lamps had been lit to illuminate the green and gold furnishings and be hangings.

Thorne remained outside the room while Di was stripped of her ruined pelisse and gown modesty's sake, she kept on her shift and wra quilt around herself before sitting in a chair be washstand. The surgeon washed away the dried, crusted blood, dusted the wound with basilicum powder, and fashioned a bandage beneath her armpit and over her shoulder.

"This will likely be tender for a few days, Miss Sheridan, but it should heal without too noticeable a scar. You should refrain from overexertion of the musculature, of course, else you could start the gash bleeding again."

He made no comment about how a lady had come by a bullet wound, but merely smiled professionally and took his leave.

When the surgeon had gone, the housekeeper bustled around the room, turning out all but one of the lamps. "I shall bring you some dinner shortly, Miss Sheridan," the elderly woman told her as the chambermaid picked up Diana's discarded, bloodstained clothing.

"Thank you, Mrs. Leale, but I am not at all hungry."

"I can only imagine, after your ordeal," the housekeeper said kindly. "What you need is rest. I've laid a flannel nightdress of mine on the bed for you to wear. The size should fit, although I'm sure the quality is not what you're accustomed to."

"What I need is to borrow a gown and cloak to go home—"

"Lord Thorne informed me you would be staying the night."

Just then Thorne himself knocked and entered the room, followed by another maid carrying a tray laden with covered dishes, which she set on the small table in the sitting area before the hearth.

When he abruptly dismissed his female servants, she noted his high-handedness but waited until the door had shut before protesting. "I shouldn't stay the night at your house, Thorne. It would provide too much fodder for scandal."

"I don't give a damn what the gossips say," he retorted mildly, removing the covers from the dishes. "I'm not letting you out of my sight until I can ensure your safety. And you need to rest. My servants are completely discreet, I promise you."

After turning out the final lamp to leave the room cloaked only in firelight, he gestured at the two armchairs flanking the table. "Now, come and eat. We both need sustenance. Too much brandy on an empty stomach can confound your senses."

She did feel woozy, whether from the spirits she'd consumed or the nerve-racking tension of the past two hours, Diana couldn't say. Either way, she was too weary to argue with Thorne about propriety just now. More crucially, she didn't think she could bear to be alone tonight.

Keeping the quilt wrapped around her, she crossed the room and sat in one of the chairs, waiting while Thorne settled in the other. After a moment he handed her a plate of succulent roasted chicken, tiny new potatoes in cream sauce, and fruit compote spiced with cinnamon. There was wine for her, too, but Thorne poured himself another brandy.

Diana was hungrier than she had thought, and the meal was delicious, yet she mostly picked at her food. Her thoughts kept straying back to the shooting, the wild ride in the coach, and Thorne's desperate gamble to save them. He could so easily have been killed, trampled beneath the galloping hooves and crushed by the carriage wheels. Or shot. The ball that had been deliberately fired at his head had barely missed him.

"It wasn't simple robbery, was it?" she said finally into the silence. "They tried to kill us."

It was the question Thorne had been expecting—and the main reason he had joined Diana for a quiet supper. He suspected her nerves would need soothing after the traumatic events she'd suffered. She doubtless had never been exposed to such danger in her life, and now that it was over, he knew the shock would set in.

He also knew she needed to regain her sense of safety and security, or the suspense and fear would fester inside her like a putrid wound.

As for her question about the holdup, he'd debated for the past half hour what answer he would give her. He was certain the attack hadn't been motivated by robbery. His town coach was well known and provided no anonymity with his crest emblazoned on the door panel. And the highwaymen hadn't demanded money or jewels before they began firing.

What particularly galled Thorne was that he'd been caught unprepared and failed to anticipate their murderous actions. Yet he tried to keep the fury out of his voice as he answered Diana. "No, in all likelihood robbery was not their intent."

"So someone tried to . . . murder us?"

"Me, love. You were not the target. I was."

Diana searched his face for a long moment. "You said Venus may have killed Nathaniel. Do you suspect her of seeking your death, as well?"

She had leapt to the same conclusion he had, and there was no use denying it. Diana was no fool, and would certainly see through any reassuring lies he tried to offer. Besides, she deserved some measure of honesty, and the truth would serve him better in this instance. At least a partial truth.

"I think Venus may hold a grudge against certain members of the Foreign Office, over something that happened many years ago. We're continuing to investigate, but at the moment, her desire for revenge seems the most feasible explanation for why Nathaniel was killed. Venus may wish me dead for the same reason. Regardless, I want you to have nothing more to do with her. Now that her portrait sittings are over, I don't want you to see her ever again."

Diana nodded slowly, concern still darkening her eyes. "But what about you? What will prevent her from attempting to kill you a second time?"

Let her just try, Thorne thought darkly. He needed proof that Venus had been behind the assault before he acted, but he would get it, even if he had to resort to violence with her. He would have no qualms about locking Venus away in chains if necessary and forcing the truth from her with his bare hands. She had threatened him and his, and he wasn't going to stand for it.

To Diana, however, Thorne offered a reassuring smile. "I will take better precautions from now on, of course. And I'll find some means of forcing Venus to show her hand. When she dares make her next attempt, I plan to gain the evidence to expose her."

"But that seems so dangerous," Diana said in dismay. "Is there nothing you can do now to stop her?"

Thorne nodded. "Venus employs two bruisers who might have been our highwaymen. I'll have them watched carefully now. And I mean to install armed footmen and grooms in your house and that of my aunt's. You'll go nowhere without protection, do you understand me?"

Diana's chin rose at his commanding tone. "Yes, if

you promise me that you'll afford yourself the same protection."

"You may be sure I will," he said chiefly to ease her mind.

He wasn't worried about himself. He had no real fear at being a killer's target. The thrill of danger had always excited him, giving him a heady rush that told him he was alive. He had skated close to danger's edge countless times, and never had any regrets before now.

But this time he had made Diana a potential target, as well as himself. It filled him with guilt and dread to realize he had risked her life today, not just his own.

Thorne shuddered at the memory of how close that bullet had come to her head. The incident had succeeded in rousing his protective instincts to a fever pitch. He would keep her safe if it took his last breath.

Now, however, what he wanted most was to hold her. Yet he didn't dare touch her, for fear of losing control.

Involuntarily his gaze traveled over Diana where she sat. She looked so pale and vulnerable and achingly beautiful, with the firelight caressing her face, glinting off the wild tendrils that wisped around her face. The quilt had slipped a little from around her shoulders, allowing him to catch sight of the fresh white bandage and the bloodstained strap of her chemise.

A renewed surge of anger flooded Thorne, while his jaw tightened. "You needn't worry about me," he said more grimly than he intended.

Swiftly draining the last of his brandy, he set down the glass and stood. "You should get some sleep."

At his abrupt and unexpected action, Diana felt a

sudden stab of panic. She couldn't bear for him to leave her.

Quickly setting down her plate, she reached out a hand to him. "Thorne, please . . . don't go just yet."

His jaw hardened even more, if that was possible. He looked supremely dangerous at this moment, with his expression so dark and brooding.

He was capable of violence, she had no doubt; she had met few men more formidable than Thorne. Yet she also sensed his fierce need to keep her safe. Thorne was a protector at heart. He had proved that unquestionably a few short hours ago.

She owed him an immense debt of gratitude, Diana knew. He had saved her life. Yet she was even more grateful that he'd emerged safely. She'd seen most of his valiant endeavors from the coach window, watching desperately as Thorne struggled to stop the panicked team. Fear had risen up to choke her, but it was fear for him, not for herself.

Thorne himself had been fearless, risking injury and even death without hesitation—while even now she was still shaking with the memory and with the sudden realization of how precious life was.

The quilt dropped to the floor as Diana rose, trembling, and slowly moved toward him.

She heard him draw a sharp breath, but she wavered only a moment. Reaching up, she wrapped her uninjured arm around his strong neck and buried her face in his shoulder. "I was so afraid for you," she whispered.

He gave a harsh laugh and held himself stiffly in her embrace, as if tightly leashing his emotions. When she raised her face to his, his breath fanned warm against her mouth. "Diana . . . I can't trust myself if I stay."

"I don't care. I want you to stay."

He was fighting himself, she could tell. He refused to accept her kiss—yet against his will, he tilted her head back, baring the vulnerable arch of her throat, and pressed his lips there. His hot mouth raised chills wherever it touched, at the same time his hands braced against her waist, as if he intended to set her away from him.

"Thorne, make love to me . . ." Diana entreated.

Thorne filled his lungs with an uneven breath as his entire body reacted to her quiet plea. The need that had gripped him in its talons for weeks now tightened its hold ruthlessly, bursting the bonds of what little self-control he had left.

He didn't even remember moving, but the next moment his arms were wrapped tightly around her body and he was kissing her fiercely, slanting his mouth hard over hers, thrusting his tongue deep to meet hers, making her feel his urgent desire. He was on fire, aching with the need to be inside her, with the sheer, overpowering need to mate, to be one with her.

And she responded just as wildly, making soft, pleading sounds as her fingers clutched his hair to draw him even closer.

Their mouths still fused together, he tugged the pins from her dark tresses, so that the silken mass tumbled freely around her shoulders. Still kissing her, Thorne forced himself to slow his urgency long enough to lift Diana in his arms and carry her to the bed. Laying her down, he pulled off her slippers and stockings. Then taking care with her injured shoulder, he drew her chemise over her head to bare her naked beauty to his gaze.

The sight of her kindled a tender ache in his chest, while his body had already hardened with desire.

Swiftly, he tore off his own clothes and joined her on the bed.

The simple contact of their heated flesh had a stunning effect: The erotic intimacy made Diana whimper and press full-length against him while she offered her mouth to him once more. But after an intense moment, Thorne left off. He wanted her fully, utterly aroused when he took her for the first time. He wanted to feel the softness of her breasts in his hands, to feel her nipples harden in his mouth while she wrapped her slender legs around him.

Moving lower, he kissed the ivory column of her throat, her delicate collarbone, her sweet, ripe breasts.

She arched her back when his tongue traced burning kisses around her fullness, and gave a soft cry of surrender when his lips closed wetly over her nipple, tugging and stroking fiercely.

She was trembling with desire by the time he reached down between her thighs, brushing the soft, swollen flesh at the apex. Her feminine cleft was sleek with wetness, and she moaned and twisted beneath him as he stroked the soaked bud.

At her eager response, the heat inside Thorne became flame, hot and searing. He was filled with a wild need to mark Diana as his.

His mouth returning to devour hers, he settled himself between her thighs, his erection stiff against her pulsing flesh. But it was with infinite care that he slowly eased himself inside her.

She tensed momentarily, her breath faltering while she grew accustomed to his impalement. After the span of several heartbeats, she instinctively raised her hips, taking his thick shaft even more deeply until she was filled up with him, welcoming him fully.

Thorne shuddered convulsively as her hot, moist flesh sheathed him, for the added tightness only intensified his unbearable arousal. Then Diana began to move against him, as if she shared the urgent hunger clambering inside him, and the spiraling, searing tension ignited in a firestorm.

Fire. Torment. Purest drugging bliss.

Diana felt the same fire, he was certain. Like a woman too long denied, she whimpered feverishly, her nails digging into his shoulders as helplessly she matched the rhythm of his possession.

Moments later, he felt the wild ripple that shook her body, felt the cry that vibrated through her. She gasped his name in a raw, shaking plea, but he never relented. Instead he ground his teeth to hold back the deep, primal sound rumbling in his chest and held her quaking body still for his careful thrusts, using all his skill to prolong the devastating pleasure for her.

She bucked and writhed beneath him as wave after wave of rapture convulsed her slender form. He captured her wild moans with his mouth . . . until finally he could bear no more. Shaking violently, Thorne gave up the fight and let his own body erupt in frenzied, explosive passion.

In the aftermath, their harsh breaths sounded loud in the silence while the tremors of pleasure softly faded.

Still dazed, Thorne carefully eased his weight from her. Wary of her bandaged shoulder, he gathered Diana's limp body against his, pressing his lips tenderly against her damp temple. Her dark, fragrant hair spilled over his chest as he simply held her, his chest aching with the maze of emotions that tangled within him.

It had been an irrevocable step, taking her virginity.

But since he had every intention of wedding her, her loss of innocence didn't matter a whit. In truth, their coupling had made it all the more certain she would eventually give in to him.

Their lovemaking had also seemed inevitable tonight. After their brush with death, it was only natural for a consoling embrace to lead to such intense passion. He had offered Diana comfort in the most primal way possible.

His own fierce reaction had been unexpected, though. Her passion had shaken him to his core, the wrenching, tearing, exquisite release more powerful than any he'd ever felt.

But then, from the very first, Diana had filled him with a burning need. His desire for her was something that had been building inside him since the moment they'd met.

Thorne stared into the firelit darkness, his mind a restless jumble of reflections. He had won a victory tonight. Or was the victory hers? What was it about this woman that touched him in a way no one ever had before?

Shifting uneasily at the thought, Thorne slipped out from beneath Diana and went to the washstand to retrieve a wet cloth. Returning to the bed, he proceeded to wash the traces of his seed and her virginal blood from her body. He tried to remain impassive, clinical, as he worked, but this was the first time he had seen her fully naked, and her loveliness was everything he had anticipated, alluring enough to take his breath away.

When he forced himself to look up, he found Diana watching him, her eyes dark and solemn. Her hair was a wild cloud around her face, her mouth moist and passion-bruised.

Heat filled Thorne anew when he remembered the way her mouth had softened and shaped itself hungrily to his.

"So, was lovemaking what you expected?" he asked to lighten the somber mood.

"Even better." Her soft smile was half-shy, half-wry. "But I never expected to become so carried away."

"I'm flattered, sweeting."

He brushed back a tendril of hair from her face, trying to ignore the nameless emotion flooding his heart. Instead he deliberately noted her injured shoulder and let anger surge through him again.

He touched the bandage tenderly. "Does it hurt?" he asked.

"No. Does your hand?"

"No, but my ankle throbs like the bloody devil."

She laughed softly and didn't protest when he made her shift her weight so he could turn down the bedcovers.

Thorne lay down beside her, facing her, before pulling the sheets up over them both. This time, however, his intention was not merely to comfort her, but to soften her defenses.

Diana had been so badly wounded with her first betrothal, it was only reasonable for her to fear being hurt again. Thorne knew he would have to show her that he would never hurt her. He would never abandon her the way her cursed fortune-hunter had done.

But if he hoped to overcome her resistance, he would have to change tactics. He was determined to wed her, but pressing his suit was clearly not working, so he meant to do everything he could to bind Diana to him with passion. Perhaps then she would willingly concede to their marriage.

Deliberately Thorne shrugged off the whispering voice that warned him of the danger in his new course. He refused to give up now.

He wanted Diana as his lover. She'd been hot and abandoned, passionate, everything he could desire in a bed partner, but he hungered for even more. He wanted to show her every pleasure ever felt between a man and a woman. He wanted her vibrant and alive with need for him.

Capturing her gaze, Thorne pressed his full length against hers, letting her feel the heat of his body.

"You win, love," he declared softly. "I won't insist that you accept my marriage proposal, if that's what you really want. If I can't have you for my wife, then I'll settle for having you for my lover."

Her brows drawing together, she studied him as if trying to judge his sincerity. "Truly? You will stop demanding that I wed you for real?"

"I will if we become lovers."

The uncertainty in her beautiful eyes told him of the battle that she was waging with herself, but he was prepared to give her a little time. He raised a forefinger to softly stroke her lips, waiting.

At his gentle touch, Diana squeezed her eyes shut so she wouldn't have to endure Thorne's seductive gaze. With her emotions so battered and her senses in such turmoil, it would be too easy to surrender to him without rationally considering the consequences. He was proposing an affair without benefit of marriage. And heaven help her, she wanted to accept. After the incredible passion he had just shown her, she found it difficult to heed her previous arguments about guarding her heart. Thorne's lovemaking had been mo overwhelming than she'd ever imagined possible.

She could scarcely believe she had gone so far a

relinquish her virginity, yet it had been a simple decision, really—driven by a basic need for comfort and an even more fundamental realization of her own mortality.

She could have died today never knowing what it was like to make love, to experience the full measure of her womanhood.

And now that she had tasted Thorne's passion, she found herself craving more.

She didn't want to fight him any longer. For years she had ruthlessly repressed every feminine desire, every emotional need, in an effort to avoid scandal. But her efforts had been futile. She'd endured the loneliness, the barrenness of her austere existence for no reason.

She was through enduring, Diana swore silently to herself, allowing herself to meet Thorne's gaze. For once in her life she wanted to experience true passion.

The strength of her longing shook her.

Thorne seemed to be able to read her mind, for a tender smile touched his mouth.

His flesh was smooth and hot as he pressed his lithe body against hers. Then he bent his head to her breasts in a new assault on her senses, kissing one nipple and gently fondling the other with his fingers, making her feel hot and shivery and dazed all over again.

Diana drew a sharp breath as fire played over her skin and along her nerve endings.

"So, you will be my lover, my beautiful Diana?" he murmured, his voice stroking her like velvet, the same way his lips and fingers were stroking her.

"Yes," she whispered, finally surrendering to the ᴗarning Thorne had aroused in her from their very ᴛ encounter.

Fifteen

Diana's surrender marked the beginning of a searing new intimacy between them, for Thorne taught her the meaning of pleasure.

His first order of business, however, was seeing to her protection. The next morning when he allowed Diana to return to her own home, he insisted that she be accompanied by three of his male servants, who were to be assimilated into her household staff.

Thorne's next step was to pay a call on Madam Venus, where he extended a veiled warning to keep away from Diana.

Venus received him in her boudoir, where she was sipping chocolate on her chaise longue, her lush body swathed in a velvet wrapper to ward off the chill of the rainy day. She frowned when she saw Thorne was using a cane to support his injured left ankle, and frowned again when he took her fingers with his bandaged left hand and bent to kiss her knuckles.

"Did you suffer an accident, my lord?"

"My town coach was held up by highwaymen evening," Thorne said lazily, taking a chair and l aside the cane he'd brought more for effect than from necessity.

"How harrowing."

Yet she didn't seem surprised, he noted, studying Venus closely. However, he didn't expect to wring any confessions from her this morning. Merely to subtly threaten her.

Thorne went on to relate the details of the highway incident of the previous day, including that both his coachman and Miss Sheridan had been shot.

Venus seemed genuinely alarmed at this last revelation. "Diana was shot?" she exclaimed in dismay, sitting up and nearly spilling her chocolate. "Was she badly hurt?"

"Not badly. The bandits were aiming at me, but the bullet missed me and grazed the top of her shoulder."

"That is dreadful!"

Thorne offered Venus a chilling smile. "It was fortunate they didn't seriously injure her, for their lives would have been forfeit. Indeed, if any harm should befall Diana in the future, I would go to the ends of the earth to hunt down the perpetrators."

Venus gave a delicate shudder at his expression, and looked sober and distracted when Thorne changed the subject.

He presented Venus with the final payment for Kitty's services in saving his ward, saying that Reginald Kneighly had been kept so well occupied, he hadn't approached Amy in weeks—with the result that Amy had declared their budding affair at an end. Thorne was satisfied that the girl's infatuation with her fortune-hunter was now over. But he was also satisfied, at least the moment, to have put Venus on notice.

e next called on Macky, whom he roused from When he repeated the tale of the carriage holdup and his suspicions that Venus's bruisers might have been the culprits, Macky confided that he hadn't seen either hulking brute at the club last night. Thorne ordered Macky to keep an eye out for them both, and then he took his leave.

His final call of the morning was on a different madam. The previous night Diana had shyly expressed her worry about the unintended consequences of their lovemaking, and Thorne had promised to see to the matter. If he managed to get her with child, it would only serve his purpose, for Diana would be forced to wed him then or face being banished from society for good. But he wasn't prepared to be quite so devious, and knew Mme Fouchet would discreetly provide him with what he sought.

From her sin club, he went directly to Diana's house, where he found her working in her studio as expected.

The soft smile she gave him when he entered made Thorne's heartbeat quicken and his loins harden.

He took her in his arms and kissed her deeply— until she gave a laughing protest and pushed him away. "Stop that! We have work to do. Now take off your shirt, if you please."

"I would be more than happy to undress completely," Thorne offered with a wicked grin.

"Thank you, but no. It would be too distracting."

They had agreed she would paint his portrait to excuse his frequent visits to her studio over the next few weeks, and she had decided to finish the paintin she'd begun on board the schooner during their vc age to England.

As he removed his jacket and cravat and waistc Thorne glanced at the canvas, which rested o easel. She had only begun the basics—sketched his face and form and blocked out shapes and lines and shadows. But he had no doubt the end result would be extraordinary as usual.

It didn't matter, though, how spectacular the completed portrait was, since he would never permit it to be seen by anyone else. This would be strictly a private endeavor, just between the two of them. And he intended to use the opportunity to chip away at Diana's defenses.

For now, Thorne obediently removed his shirt and stood where Diana posed him, leaning against a sturdy wood frame fashioned like a ship's bulkhead, which she had put into position so that the angles of light were ideal.

Thorne allowed her to work uninterrupted for nearly an hour before asking permission to stretch. When she gave it, he gently flexed his injured ankle to ease the stiffness, then went into the adjacent storeroom to fetch a sable cloak he'd seen earlier among the props and costumes. Returning to the studio, he spread the luxurious fur on the floor before the hearth and added a log to the flagging fire. Next he retrieved a silk pouch from his jacket pocket and tossed it on the fur.

He noted Diana's raised eyebrows but gave her no explanation as he crossed the studio to lock the door. When finally he came back to her, he set aside her brush and palette and pretended to view the developing portrait.

"I don't think you have captured my mouth precisely," he said lazily. "You need a closer study of m and texture."

rawing her against him, he kissed her again, his e dancing with hers, making her feel his urgent desire. He thought she might protest, but she gave a sweet sigh and surrendered to him willingly.

When he eventually allowed her up for air, Diana gazed at him with dreamy-eyed exasperation. "You seem determined to distract me from working on your portrait."

"My portrait can wait. For now I intend to make love to you before the fire."

"You are perfectly wicked, you know."

"And you have too many inhibitions, my love. I mean to set you free of the strictures that have kept you chained for so long."

Diana's expression turned uncertain. "In broad daylight?"

"There is no better time. You still have a great deal to learn about passion. I want to show you how to feel pleasure and how to give pleasure in return. Now let's begin by undressing you."

Reaching behind her to untie the sashes at her waist and neck, he removed the paint-smeared smock that protected her gown. "I've dreamed about peeling you out of this for weeks, since the very first time I saw you in it."

Next came her gown and slippers and stockings. And finally her corset and chemise. As he bared her breasts to his hot gaze, Thorne bent to lightly kiss her peaked nipples, making Diana inhale sharply. Yet when she stood completely naked before him, except for the bandage at her shoulder, she wrapped her arms around herself as if embarrassed by his intense scrutiny.

Her sudden shyness was endearing, Thorne thought tenderly as he held her arms away.

"I cannot boast the charms of your opera dancers

and Cyprians such as Venus," Diana said, a flush coloring her cheeks.

"I think by now it should be obvious how enchanting I find you. You are by far the most intriguing woman I have ever met. And your body is perfect," he assured her.

And it was. Her lithe, curved body was the idol of erotic male fantasies. Just looking at her made him hungry.

He wanted her badly, wanted her passionate, wanted her arching beneath him, but he forced himself to go slowly, taking the time to remove the pins from her dark, shining hair.

"God, that beautiful hair," Thorne said huskily. "You don't know how many times I've pictured it down, how much I've wanted to feel it running over my skin."

He stole another taste of her lips before stepping back to shed his own clothing.

Diana watched, feeling her pulse quicken. It was not only with her artist's eye that she admired the graceful strength of his lean, muscular body, the tanned golden skin, the narrow hips and powerful thighs. It was with her woman's senses, as well.

As she viewed Thorne's beautiful nude body, her gaze unconsciously locked on his loins, on the thick column of flesh that sprang so boldly from between his thighs; already he was heavy and aroused.

A smile played across his lips as he noted her rapt focus. "As you see, your attractions fascinate me."

His attractions fascinated *her*, Diana thought, recalling last night's sensual memory of his hot, hard flesh filling her.

Stepping closer then, he covered her bare breasts with his hands. Even with his palm bandaged, his touch sent a pulse of pure pleasure shafting through her loins.

Seeing her reaction, he gave her a smile of breathtaking charm. "You are absolutely perfect for me," he assured her. "And I intend to show you how perfect." He managed to invest so much sensual promise in his declaration that her breath faltered.

She felt dazed with anticipation when he led her to the fur and laid her down, spreading her hair across the rich sable before sinking back on his heels to study her.

"You're an incredibly beautiful woman, Diana. If you could see yourself as I see you, you would have no doubts about how vibrant and sensual you are. How desirable I find you."

Diana stirred restlessly at the now familiar quickening between her legs. The mere feel of Thorne's heated eyes on her naked body made her quiver with sensation.

Yet he didn't lie beside her as she'd expected. Instead he emptied the silk pouch onto the fur, showing her the contents: several small sponges with strings attached, as well as a vial of amber liquid.

"A sponge soaked in vinegar or brandy," Thorne explained with his customary disarming frankness, "is the best way to keep my seed from taking root. I'll have to place it deep inside your body."

He wet a sponge and set the vial aside. When his hand splayed over her belly, her skin burned like a fever. Then his caress moved lower, his fingers encountering her thatch of fleecy curls, making her tense. He teased her cleft for a moment before finally inserting the sponge as he'd warned he would.

The chill made Diana shiver, but any shyness she might have felt was erased by the profound tenderness of Thorne's expression. Holding her gaze with those astonishingly warm eyes, he pushed the sponge deep inside her. A stray lock of amber-gold hair fell over his forehead as he bent to his task, and she found herself yearning to reach up and smooth it back into place.

When he was done, he stretched out beside her, pressing his naked body against hers, letting her feel his arousal.

"Do you find my anatomy as fascinating as I find yours?" he asked in a low, provocative tone.

"You know I do."

"Then show me."

"But I don't know what to do."

"Use your instincts, my sweet. Start by touching me."

When Thorne guided her hand to his broad chest, Diana willingly complied . . . caressing his finely muscled body, feeling the potent heat of him, marveling at his earthiness and obvious maleness.

Her fingers trailed lower, lingering on his hard, flat belly, but she hesitated to be even bolder. "You said you would teach me how to give you pleasure."

"I would be delighted to." His eyes shone with a heated brightness. "Touch me where I am most sensitive."

"Where?" Diana asked curiously.

"My sacs. My cock."

When she cupped the soft, velvety pouch of his loins, his body tensed. Then her fingers curled around his hard shaft, and the thick length surged in her hand.

"Is this the way?" she asked, lightly fondling the rigid, straining arousal.

"Yes," Thorne replied, his voice suddenly hoarse. "Stroke me with your hand."

When he rolled onto his back, Diana rose up on her knees, the better to minister to him. She could feel herself growing warm and liquid as she stared at Thorne's masculine beauty. When brazenly she began to stroke his swollen flesh, it quivered in her hand. In response, something deep within her body shivered in purely sensual reaction.

She glanced up to see that Thorne had shut his eyes, obviously enjoying her caresses.

"What else?" she inquired.

"Take me in your mouth." The huskiness of his command hinted at the need that was spiking through his body, just as it was through hers.

She bent closer to the long, dark phallus that jutted from the curling hair at his groin. Trying to restrain her eagerness, Diana lowered her lips, tasting the rounded head of his shaft. His entire body clenched.

"Is that pleasurable?"

"Oh, yes . . ." His sound of bliss was half-sigh, half-groan.

She let her lips close over him fully then.

His flesh was smooth and hot, and she took great joy in exploring the hardness and detail of him, her tongue caressing every virile male inch of him. She wanted to make Thorne tremble and lose control the way he'd made her.

When she drew him farther into her mouth, sucking harder, she dredged another groan from his throat.

She drew back in dismay. "Does that hurt?"

"It's pure torment."

"Do you want me to stop?"

Thorne's strangled laughter clearly expressed his

opinion, even before his hand reached behind Diana's head to draw her back down to him. "Sweet mercy, no. I don't want you to stop."

Diana was glad for his reply, for she didn't want to stop. Her body was beginning to throb and come alive with hunger, her erotic attentions arousing herself as much as him.

Thorne seemed to understand what was happening to her, for in a few more moments, he suddenly grasped her arms and drew her up to straddle his loins.

Diana knew an instant of surprise when she realized what he wanted from her. But when he positioned her cleft directly over his erection, her body was aching so shamelessly for him that she sank down eagerly upon him, almost impaling herself.

"Easy now," Thorne murmured at her startled gasp. "You are still new to this."

Yet in another few heartbeats Diana's shock faded, and the intense pleasure returned. And Thorne was clearly determined to rouse her even further.

His heated gaze holding hers enthralled, he filled his hands with her breasts, plucking the nipples with his fingers, while his hips rose rhythmically to push his shaft more deeply into her.

Diana moaned to feel his rigid fullness inside her.

"See how perfectly you fit me?" Thorne asked. His voice was warm and devastatingly sensual, making her soft flesh clamor for release. "See how lusciously you flow around me?"

Then he surprised her again by gently rolling over with her, so that Diana lay beneath him.

"Wrap your legs around me," he ordered. "I want your thighs hugging me."

At the same time his body began driving in a slow, maddening undulation above her.

Diana moaned in ecstasy while her hips surged against his.

"That's right, let me feel you move," Thorne rasped. "Grasp my buttocks as I'm thrusting into you. . . ."

She was only vaguely aware of his erotic words in her ear. He was telling her how lovely she was, how much he wanted her, urging on her passionate response. But then she could no longer hear him over the keening cry of her shattering climax.

She went wild in his arms. And as wave after wave of rapture racked her quivering body, Thorne lost control himself and sought his own blinding, tumultuous release.

In the aftermath, they lay sprawled in a tangle of pleasure, their breaths coming in harsh pants.

Dazed, Diana kept her eyes shut, relishing the feel of Thorne's warm, nude, male body covering hers. She could feel the smooth, shifting pattern of muscle in his back where her fingers still clung to him, could smell the hot musk of arousal between them.

Finally he eased away from her and drew her weary body against his. "See what heights you can reach," he said hoarsely, "if you will only let yourself be a little wanton?"

She did indeed see, Diana reflected. The searing pleasure of their second joining had been even more remarkable than the first, intoxicating her beyond anything she'd ever known.

"Is lovemaking always this . . . shattering?"

"It should be. I intend to make certain of it." He pressed his lips against her damp temple. "You still have a great deal to learn. And I need to work on mastering my savage urges. I have difficulty containing myself when I'm inside your sweet body, I still want you so badly. But I promise we will go more slowly next time, make it last longer. Give me a few moments to recover, and I'll show you."

Unable to repress a languid smile, Diana buried her face in Thorne's bare shoulder. "I should have more mastery of myself. In fact, I should banish you from my studio before you end up making me as wicked as you are."

He gave a soft chuckle. "That is precisely my intent, love, so you had best resign yourself."

Thorne visited her studio frequently after that, using his consummate skill to introduce Diana to a stunning world of sensuality.

Continuing their lessons in pleasure, he taught her to enjoy the passionate fire between a man and a woman. And as promised, he liberated her from the careful strictures that had ruled her actions for much of her life. It was as if she became someone else when he touched her, someone without shame or inhibitions.

Diana refused to think about her wanton behavior, however, or about right or wrong. Nor would she contemplate the future, or probe Thorne's motives too deeply.

Instinctively she understood why he was so set on pursuing her. Clearly part of him loved the challenge of overcoming her resistance; the rest of him wanted her. But he was an expert seducer, and for now she was determined simply to enjoy the moment.

Her career also took some startling new twists over the next few days. Diana was amazed when her notoriety resulted in several, totally unexpected, positive events.

The first was when a stranger called at her studio, wanting to purchase her artwork. The card he sent up proclaimed him to be a Mr. James Attree, Merchant, and when Diana agreed to receive him in the drawing room with one of Thorne's footmen standing protectively by, she was greeted by a balding, large-girthed, elderly man whose accent proclaimed him to be of the lower classes.

After shaking her hand, Mr. Attree lowered his large bulk onto the settee at Diana's invitation.

"I am known for me plain-speaking, Miss Sheridan, so I will come straight to the point. Madam Venus's splendid portrait—I must 'ave it."

Diana felt surprise widen her eyes. Her allegorical portrait of Venus had been hung at the British Academy's newly opened spring exhibit only two afternoons ago, along with several of her landscapes, a more stately historical painting, and a simple genre scene. She still owned the last three, but not the first.

"I would like to accommodate you, Mr. Attree," Diana replied politely, "but the portrait is not mine to sell. Once the exhibit has ended, it will belong to Madam Venus."

Attree frowned. "I'm a nabob, Miss Sheridan. Made me fortune with the East India Company and will make no bones about the price. Just name a figure."

"I am sorry, but I really can't help you, sir."

"Ah, then, I suppose I'll 'ave to negotiate with Venus. No doubt she'll drive a 'ard bargain. So what other pieces do you 'ave for sale?"

"Other pieces?" Diana repeated.

"I know quality when I see it, Miss Sheridan, and I

want yer work. I have me own private collection of paintings and am planning me own exhibit shortly."

When Diana hesitated, he went on. "Sure, you'll think me pretensions odd—a Cit with no breeding buying respectability. Call me a mushroom if you like. But I fancy good art, and I like to promote it. Me dearly departed wife was a painter 'erself. And I'm making a name for meself in the field."

Clearly Mr. Attree was of the opinion that the acquisition and display of fine art lent an air of culture to the owner, yet Diana was immediately suspicious of his offer to purchase her work. She gave the merchant a cool smile. "By any chance, did Lord Thorne put you up to this?"

"Eh? Lord Thorne? No, no, never met 'is lordship, though I've 'eard many a tale about 'im. No, this is just a'tween you and me. I'll offer you a pretty price, I promise you. Can I see your paintings now? Or I could return at another time, if it's more convenient for you. I'm quite determined to 'ave your work, Miss Sheridan."

"Well, if you will give me a moment to display my inventory in my studio, I will be happy to show you what pieces I have for sale."

Thus it was in short order that Diana found herself selling Mr. James Attree, Merchant, four of her best paintings—two landscapes, a portrait, and a domestic scene. He did have an excellent eye for quality, as well as a generous nature. He wrote her out a bank draft on the spot for a hundred pounds more than her asking price, saying he would send a footman to wrap and fetch them that very afternoon.

Still a little dazed by her strange good fortune, Diana confronted Thorne the moment he arrived at her studio, demanding to know if he'd coerced the merchant into making a purchase.

Thorne looked offended and pleased all at once. "I swear, sweeting, I had nothing whatsoever to do with his interest. But I commend your Mr. Attree for his superb good taste. Now come here, and we'll make love to celebrate."

Diana actually believed Thorne's protestations of innocence, since she didn't think he would lie that baldly to her. And so she gave herself up to his fervent embrace, all the while feeling a measure of pride that she had sold several of her paintings without his aid.

It was two days after that when Thorne strolled into her dining room while she was breakfasting, smiling smugly as he set a newspaper on the table before her.

"Did you happen to see the *Morning Chronicle* yet? I had nothing to do with this, either, I'll have you know."

On the front page, Diana saw, taking up a full third of the sheet, was a column by England's major art critic of the day, Lord Howell, regarding the current exhibit at the British Academy for the Fine Arts.

Thorne settled at the table uninvited and helped himself to coffee while she swiftly read.

Her stomach knotted when her name leapt out at her, but Lord Howell seemed to have muted his usual vitriolic pen in favor of lauding her talent.

Miss Sheridan is the freshest artist to come along in a decade. . . . Her use of luminosity and color to create atmosphere is nothing short of remarkable. . . . The fact that she is female is frankly even more remarkable, given the restrictions under which she must work. Miss Sheridan has recently been permitted to enroll in classes at the British Academy for the Fine Arts, but it is this columnist's opinion that she is skilled enough to teach expression, perspective, and composition at this very moment, and that it would be a great pity if she allowed her professors to stymie her obvious genius. . . .

The entire column was unabashed praise of her work from a prime arbiter of artistic taste in Britain, and Diana was stunned.

Thorne chuckled at her overwhelmed look. "Howell prides himself on his own genius, and his approval could not have been bought for any sum, even had I tried. This is solely the result of your own talent and dedication to your craft. I predict you'll be in great demand now, so you had best keep your appointment book handy."

Thorne's prediction proved to be utterly correct. Before Diana had even finished breakfasting, her footman announced that she had a visitor awaiting her in the drawing room.

When she went to investigate, a tall, silver-haired matron with a haughty expression greeted her. "I am Lady Ranworth, Miss Sheridan. You will recall we met at Lady Hennessy's recent ball. I am an intimate of Judith's, and she gave me the direction of your studio. Pray forgive me for calling at this early hour, but after that most admiring article in the *Chronicle* this morning, I thought I had best act to secure your time before anyone else does. I wish to offer you a commission to paint my portrait."

After an addled moment, Diana managed a smile. "I would be pleased to paint you, Lady Ranworth. When would you like to arrange your first sitting?"

"As soon as possible. I expect any number of my friends will wish to have their portraits painted by you, and I want to be first."

Diana hoped that was the case. One of the few successful female portraitists of the last century, Angelica Kauffman, had earned a very good living by developing a secure circle of patrons among well-born British ladies.

"Would tomorrow morning suit you?"

"That would be most excellent."

They set the time for the appointment and agreed on a price—four times the sum that Diana's portraits had fetched in the country.

After showing Lady Ranworth out, Diana returned to the dining room, still marveling at her sudden change of fortune.

Thorne was still there, reading the morning papers. "Good news?" he asked as Diana sank distractedly into her chair.

"*Amazing* news. I have just been offered my first commission since coming to London." Lifting her gaze to Thorne's, she shook her head. "I think I must be dreaming. If I pinch myself, I will awaken."

Thorne merely grinned. "I won't be so trite as to say I told you so, but only warn you not to accept too many commissions just now. Until you finish my portrait, I have first claim on your time, and I mean to hold you to it." His voice dropped to a husky murmur. "Besides, I have yet to pose fully nude for you, and you require practice painting nudes."

Diana felt her cheeks warm at the wicked, heated look Thorne was giving her. Then casually he returned to perusing the papers, leaving her body tingling with anticipation of their next sitting, just as the rogue had obviously intended.

Sixteen

Thorne did indeed insist on posing nude for their next sitting, but Diana willingly agreed, rationalizing that this could be her best and perhaps only opportunity to study the male form.

Rather than complete his nearly finished shipboard portrait, she used the time to make detailed sketches of his body, particularly his chest but also the forbidden area of his loins. But as usual, Thorne made concentration difficult.

He lay reclining at ease on the chaise longue, lean, lithe, and naked, while she sat in an adjacent chair with her sketch pad. All too often Diana found her focus straying from her task to marvel at her subject. Thorne was a beautiful god of a man, and intensely sexual, with his loins fully aroused.

After a quarter hour or so, he arched his back and stretched, as if to purposely call attention to the part of his body that could give her such wild pleasure.

Diana managed to ignore him until he complained of the chill. The spring weather had turned exceedingly fine of late, enough to forgo a fire in her studio, and the sunlight streaming in the long windows had further raised the temperature, so that his grievance only made her suspect a ploy.

"If you like," she offered wryly, "I will fetch you a blanket to cover your bare limbs."

"I would rather have *you* covering me, sweeting. I think you should come here and warm me."

She shot Thorne an exasperated look. "Can you not control your lust for a mere hour?"

"I can, certainly, but why the devil would I wish to?"

His irreverent charm made her want to laugh, and when he gave her the full effect of his lazy smile, Diana felt a flush warm her entire body.

"I don't know how much longer I can last," Thorne drawled. "I had no trouble becoming aroused with you studying me so intently. But if you want my manhood to remain erect for much longer, you need to offer me some incentive, such as taking off your clothes."

"Your manhood needn't remain erect for my sake. Your mere nudity is adequate for my purposes."

Holding her gaze, he reached down to cup his swollen member. "Wouldn't you like to feel this inside you?" he asked, his voice now maddeningly sensuous.

Remembering that heat and hardness filling her, Diana felt her mouth go dry. Thorne was uncompromisingly masculine, thoroughly shameless, and entirely too irresistible.

"Half an hour more," she replied, summoning all her willpower.

He lay back with a smug smile. "Very well, but you are deceiving yourself if you think you can hold out that long against me."

*　　*　　*

Thorne proved to be right that time; Diana lasted a mere twenty minutes longer, despite her vows to resist his wicked blandishments. But it was his next lesson in pleasure that was truly wicked—when he made *her* pose nude for *him* and then painted her body instead of a canvas.

Until then Diana had never known her profession could be so erotic.

He started by undressing her and lightly kissing the now-healed bullet scar on her shoulder. Next, he shed his own clothing, leaving his beautiful body entirely naked, since his own injuries no longer required bandages. Then, laying her down on the chaise, Thorne knelt beside her and made use of the sponges. Finally he opened the basket he had brought with him.

Lifting out two wooden bowls—one of lush, ripe strawberries, one of clotted cream—he bit into a juicy berry and ran the sweet pulp over Diana's lips before allowing her to eat it. All the while he made no effort to disguise his blatant appraisal of her body.

His sensual scrutiny made her loins throb; she could feel his glance heat her skin, just as if he was caressing her with his lips, with his warm breath. The next strawberry he bit into, he rubbed on her nipples, then bent to suck off the juice, making Diana inhale a breath and arch involuntarily.

"Hungry?" he asked tauntingly as he fed her the berry. "I certainly am, but not for food. And for what I have in mind, I want you just so. . . ."

He arranged her limbs to his satisfaction: her left arm draped over the back of the chaise, the other resting beside her bare hip, her left leg upraised slightly, knee bent, while her right fell over the edge of the seat, her foot touching the floor.

"I like the flagrant display," he said thoughtfully,

those devilish eyes moving over her with raking leisure. "But I want you hot and wanton, all wet and hungry for me."

His hands reaching for her, he slid his thumbs upward to brush the underside of her breasts, shooting sparks through Diana.

When he pinched one nipple into an obedient pout, she clenched her teeth. "Do you mean to torment me?"

His slow smile was part wolfish, wholly enticing. "Oh, yes. But mainly I intend to play the artist today." He dipped a forefinger in the thick cream. "I've always appreciated art. It excites the senses and stimulates the intellectual faculties. . . ."

Lazily his slick finger coated the engorged tips of her breasts, his erotic attentions instantly making her ache with pleasure.

"And I've always admired your skills. . . ."

Dipping into the cream once more, he used careful brushstrokes to first paint the dusky triangle of curls between her thighs and then the lips of her sex, daubing until Diana was whimpering with need.

"But today," Thorne said wickedly before bending his golden head, "I mean to show you just how artistically talented *I* can be."

He *was* artistically talented, Diana discovered to her incredible delight. Amazingly so.

That sensual afternoon, however, was the last time she allowed herself the luxury of indulging in Thorne's lessons in pleasure, since in a matter of days, the *Chronicle* article had made her art the latest rage of the ton. Half the noble ladies in London, it seemed, suddenly wanted Diana to paint them, and her portraits were in such high demand that she had difficult making time in her schedule for all her new commissions. She was even required to turn down several of them.

The following day when Thorne came to collect Diana for a five-o'clock drive in the park, she was completing the final stage of her very first commission, adding the draperies to Lady Ranworth's portrait.

When she begged off their drive, Thorne sympathetically agreed, but before taking his leave, he paused to study the nearly finished work on her easel.

"I don't recall Lady Ranworth looking this striking," he observed. "You have more than done her justice."

Diana smiled a bit sardonically as she added a dab of vermillion to the canvas. "I believe I mentioned the importance of flattery. I learned long ago that for a portraitist to sell, it is wise to improve the features of the sitter and to play down the worst flaws. Subjects are more willing to pay high prices for pleasing portraits than for ugly ones."

Thorne walked over to inspect her finished portrait of him onboard ship, which was leaning against the far studio wall, in the final stage of drying.

"So you purposely embellished my attractions in my portrait? How lowering."

At his pained tone, Diana uttered a wry laugh. "Doubtless you are fishing for compliments, your lordship. But at the risk of puffing up your self-esteem any higher than it is, I admit that your attractions didn't require the least bit of embellishing."

Just then she heard a commotion beyond the open studio door—rapid footsteps mounting the stairs, accompanied by her cousin's voice angrily calling her name. Amy had been to the house once before, Diana recalled, and no doubt knew the way to the studio.

An instant later the girl burst into the room, her gaze searching wildly, her body stiffening when she spied Diana. "How could you!" she exclaimed in a hoarse voice. "How could you betray me that way?"

Diana's brows drew together in bewilderment. "I beg your pardon?"

A flustered John Yates limped into the studio directly behind Amy, looking red-faced and out of breath, as if he had rushed to keep up with her. "Miss Lunsford, you should not hold your cousin to blame."

Thorne stepped forward, frowning. "Hold her to blame for what?"

"Yes, for what?" Diana echoed. "Perhaps you had best sit down, Amy, and explain."

"I don't wish to sit down!" she cried, her eyes filling with tears. "You have ruined my life!"

Diana carefully put down her brush and palette. "If I have, then I am sorry, but truly, my dear, I haven't the faintest idea what you are talking about. How did I betray you?"

"You hired that doxy to turn Reggie against me. You dare not deny it!"

Diana felt her face flush with guilt. They had indeed hired Venus's employee to seduce Reginald Kneighly away from Amy. But evidently Amy had somehow just learned of their conspiracy.

"Do sit down, Miss Lunsford," Yates implored. Taking the girl's elbow, he tried to guide her toward the sitting area near the hearth. But Amy pulled her arm from his grasp and stared at Diana, her lower lip trembling, her tears spilling over. "I cannot believe you capable of such treachery."

Thorne's jaw tightened. "You'll keep a civil tongue

when you address your cousin, brat. Diana was not responsible for your suitor's defection."

But Amy was too distraught to heed anyone but herself. "Why do you hate me so much, Diana? *Why?* Is it that you want me to be as miserable as you are?"

Dismayed, Diana moved toward her young cousin. "Dearest, you know I don't hate you, and I certainly don't want you to be miserable. Why don't you tell me what happened?"

Fiercely Amy drew a gloved hand across her damp eyes. "I was shopping this afternoon on Bond Street—Mr. Yates was kind enough to escort me—when what do I see? Reggie embracing a lightskirt right there on the street! My suitor who vowed to love me forever! I would have challenged him at once, but he drove away in his curricle before I could. So I confronted that . . . Kitty person. I threatened to report her to Bow Street and have her thrown in prison for thievery if she didn't keep away from Reggie, but she said she had been legitimately employed, paid a generous sum to divert Reggie's attention from me! It had to be you, Diana."

"No, it didn't," Thorne interrupted. "In fact, I hired Kitty. As your guardian, I felt it my responsibility to protect you from a libertine who was only after your fortune."

"It was *you?*" Amy gave Thorne a furious glare. "Then you are a horrid, horrid devil. You have ruined my life!"

"I seriously doubt that," Thorne returned mildly. "And if you could manage to contain your overwrought sensibilities for a moment, you would see that if Kneighly truly loved you, he could never have been seduced away from you."

Amy recoiled as if Thorne had struck her. For a moment she stared at him, obviously grappling with the truth of his blunt pronouncement. Unable to maintain the eye contact any longer, she glanced blindly beyond him, her gaze coming to rest on his portrait that was leaning against the wall.

Then suddenly covering her face with her hands, Amy burst into tears and turned to run from the studio.

John Yates gave Diana an apologetic, pleading glance. "It is only her pride that is wounded. She doesn't love that rackety fellow. I will try to console her, Miss Sheridan, to make her see that you and Thorne only wanted what was best for her. She might listen once she is a bit calmer."

Giving Diana a swift bow, he turned and hurried after Amy.

Diana took a step forward instinctively, as if she, too, might follow her cousin, but Thorne put a hand up to stop her.

"I suggest we allow the tempest to die down for a few days. Yates is right. Amy needs time to come to her senses."

"I trust you are right," Diana said dubiously, raising a hand to her throbbing temple. "But it would have been less painful for Amy if she'd never learned about Kitty. I wish I could have spared her that."

Hearing her own words, Diana felt another stab of guilt. Since moving into her studio house three weeks ago, she'd barely even seen her cousin. She'd neglected Amy purposely, believing the girl would be better off without her presence. But perhaps her strategy had been a mistake. If she'd been with Amy this morning, she could have prevented her from confronting Kitty.

Crossing the studio, Thorne took both Diana's

hands and firmly kissed her on the lips. "Stop fretting. Amy will recover eventually. And Yates will make her see reason once she calms down."

Diana shook her head, not reassured. It was a moment longer before she registered Thorne's last comment.

She cast him a puzzled frown. "Since when did John Yates rank so high in Amy's opinion? She has always treated him so wretchedly."

"Since she decided to use him to salve her wounded pride at her suitor's desertion. Yates has called on her frequently the past several weeks. I suspect he sees it as an opportunity to court her."

"To *court* her?" Diana asked, her tone one of amazement.

Thorne sent her a wry grin. "I know. The course of young love is frequently incomprehensible. But whatever Yates sees in Amy is *beyond* baffling."

Seventeen

The very next evening Diana was given another illustration of the incomprehensible course of love when she attended Drury Lane Theatre with Thorne. Seated in the box directly across from theirs was none other than her former intended, Francis, Lord Ackland, along with his plump, stiff-necked baroness, Lady Ackland.

For an emotional moment, the sight of Francis's handsome features and gleaming fair hair gave Diana a pang of bitter memory, but she managed to shrug it off and focus her attention on the other nobles and gentry in the glittering crowd. Since encountering Francis at Amy's comeout ball, Diana had heard bits and pieces of gossip about his marriage to the wealthy baroness, most notably that he had sired four children and that his wife kept him on a tight leash. And clearly Lady Ackland did not approve of Diana.

It startled her, therefore, when during the first intermission Francis sought her out. Thorne had left the box to speak to friends and to bring her some refreshment, and Francis entered immediately afterward, as if he had been waiting to catch her alone.

He bowed over her hand, and when Diana did not invite him to be seated, stood staring down at her wistfully.

Diana forced a polite smile, aware of the countless pairs of eyes that were trained on her, knowing the crowd anticipated a spectacle.

"Lord Ackland," she said, finally finding her voice. "What brings you here?"

"I wished to congratulate you on your success, Diana. I saw your work at the British Academy exhibit. It is quite superb. But then I always knew you would go far. You must be pleased to have the career you always dreamed of."

"I have been extremely fortunate," she replied agreeably.

"I no longer paint." Francis gave her a sad grimace. "My wife considers artistic endeavors beneath a gentleman of birth and breeding. That is the prime disadvantage of wedding out of necessity—whoever controls the purse strings has the final say."

Diana frowned, wondering if he had come here seeking her sympathy. "I am sorry," she said, attempting to sound sincere. "Your art meant a great deal to you, I know."

His voice dropped to a whisper. "I also wished to say . . . to tell you how much I regret hurting you, Diana. If I had had any choice—"

"You did have a choice, Francis," Diana reminded him quietly.

Yet his anguished expression was so full of regret that she took pity on him.

"But all that is long past," she added brightly. "Truly, I no longer think of it at all."

"Think of what, darling?" Thorne's cool voice interrupted. He had returned to the box, carrying two cups of punch, one of which he handed to Diana. A hard smile touched his lips as he eyed the baron. "Ackland, I believe your wife is glaring daggers at you. You had best return to her side before she calls the Watch to bring you to heel."

With a glower and a curt bow, Francis took his leave, and Thorne resumed his seat beside Diana.

Holding her gaze, he took her gloved hand and brought it to his lips in a loverlike gesture—for the benefit of the watching audience, she suspected. His hazel eyes were sparking with anger, though, despite his tender display.

Diana felt her cheeks flush as she firmly withdrew her hand and sipped her punch. "There was no need for such rudeness. Francis was merely congratulating me on my recent success."

"When he jilted you, that bastard renounced any right even to speak to you," Thorne retorted in a silken tone. "And if he dares accost you again, I will call him out."

Diana refrained from replying and was glad when the play eventually resumed with the second act, but her thoughts remained distracted.

It soothed her pride that Thorne seemed jealous of her former suitor, yet he had no reason to be. She'd spoken the truth when she told Francis she never thought of the past between them anymore.

He was still as stunningly handsome as ever, but his visage no longer had any power to move her. She felt no attraction at all any longer—not even a heart flutter—and not one ounce of envy for his wealthy wife.

Indeed, Diana realized, the only emotion Franc roused in her now was disdain. She was profound glad she had escaped marriage to him, even if it me enduring the scandal of their aborted elopement all these years. She never would have been happy wed to a man of so weak a character.

The unexpected realization left Diana aware of an unmistakable feeling of liberation. There was nothing left of the green, naïve girl who had given her heart so joyously and so recklessly. Now she could finally write *finis* to a painful chapter of her life that she should have been done with long ago.

What future chapters would hold, however, was another question entirely.

She glanced at Thorne, admiring his striking profile, his golden hair gleaming in the light of the theater's massive chandelier.

It struck her that this man was just as beautiful as Francis, perhaps more so. But there the similarities ended. Thorne had a great deal more depth to him than her first betrothed, and far more character. Rather than jilting her for the promise of greater wealth, Thorne had championed her and protected her at every turn, defending her against the world, putting her interests even above his own.

He was also, Diana readily admitted, the most exciting, sensual, fascinating, provocative man she had ever met. Unquestionably he had changed her life. He had drawn her out of her colorless existence, making her feel alive again, letting her experience joy and hope and exhilaration once more.

Thorne filled her life with pleasure. Not merely carnal bliss, but something more profound: an unburdening of the spirit that allowed her to soar unfettered.

She owed him so much. And yet the tenderness she'd begun to feel for him was more than simple gratitude—

Diana drew a sharp breath, aware of the shocking sentiment she'd just acknowledged. The grave mistake she had made. For the past several weeks she had purposely—indeed, stubbornly—ignored the danger signs. She had forgotten all her ardent vows and self-warnings not to allow herself to become too vulnerable to him.

Diana bit her lower lip hard, a troubled frown darkening her brow. Was that what Thorne had intended all along? To dismantle her defenses, bit by bit?

But no matter his intentions, she couldn't afford to let their affair continue. She needed to draw back now, before she became too addicted to Thorne's searing passion. Before she became too dependent on his support and protection.

Regrettably, she couldn't break their betrothal just yet. At some point, she would be able to end their sham engagement, but for now, Nathaniel's death was still a gaping ambiguity, and Amy's future was yet to be settled.

Even so, Diana reminded herself sternly as she forced her attention back to the play, she needed to quell the perilous feelings of tenderness she'd so unwisely allowed Thorne to awaken in her.

And for that she would have to wean herself away from him and the passionate intimacies they had shared.

Much to Diana's dismay, her new resolve lasted barely a few hours. For the remainder of the play, she treated Thorne with a distant coolness, but he evidently was so attuned to her moods, he sensed the change in her at once.

She had no difficulty perceiving his darkening tem

per, either, even though he waited to comment until they were settled in his town coach and driving through the dark streets of Mayfair.

"You are very quiet tonight, sweeting. Are you by chance musing about that bastard?"

Seeing his grim expression in the dim glow from the exterior carriage lamps, Diana affected an indifferent smile. "Actually, I was reflecting how my ardor all those years ago was merely a girlish infatuation."

"Good," Thorne said tersely. "I'm pleased you have finally come to your senses."

She raised an eyebrow, determined to remain cool. "I never would have suspected you to be the kind of man to fall prone to jealousy."

"Well, you can revise your suppositions. You are mine, love, and I have no intention of sharing you, even if it's merely in your thoughts."

His show of possessiveness was flattering but misplaced, Diana thought, regarding him narrowly. "I am *not* yours, Thorne. We have a pretend betrothal, nothing more."

"We have a great deal more."

Sliding an arm around her shoulders, he drew her close against his side.

Diana stiffened, yet desire flared inside her, fanned to instant life at his touch, even before Thorne bent to kiss her. Clamping her head between his hands, he slanted his mouth over hers and took her lips in a searing assault.

The very rawness of his male hunger caught her off guard. But when his tongue danced, dueling with hers, plundering, she found herself surrendering helplessly to the fierce, sensual caress.

His eyes were hard and bright when he drew back. Before she could even take a breath, he clasped her hand and guided it to his groin, making her feel the hard bulge beneath the fabric of his satin breeches.

Her mouth went dry.

He opened the front placket so that his swollen arousal sprang free. Then grasping the skirts of her evening gown, he pulled them up to bare her naked thighs. His quick, hard breathing feathered her face as his hand slipped between her legs, pressing against her feminine cleft.

"Thorne . . ."

"Be quiet," he ordered.

He spread his fingers against the quivering softness of her sex, feeling the heat and dampness and need of her. She was wet silk between her legs, and his caressing fingers made her flow even hotter, more wanton, teasing a moan from deep in her throat. Her hips arched in desperation as she rubbed herself against his hand in time with the rhythmic rocking of the coach.

Thorne felt a surge of triumph. She was trembling now, making no protest as he pulled her astride him. One thrust, he knew, and she would be writhing in his arms.

His hands gripped her yielding buttocks and ground her against the hard ridge of his manhood. He thought he would explode without her moist heat around him.

Lifting her up, he entered her swiftly, feeling the delicious clasping and gripping of her inner muscles around him. She gloved him so hotly, so tightly, that he knew he could finish before he gave her any pleasure.

Thorne gritted his teeth, fighting the shudder of stark heat that sizzled through him. But when Diana bucked against him, he gave a growl that was raw and primitive and kissed her again fiercely.

A taut, savage need was blazing between them now. Want had become craving, and his own rough excitement was matching Diana's frenzy. She welcomed the hard thrusting of his body as he took her, his tongue plunging in the same demanding rhythm as he filled her again and again.

In the next instant a low, rough groan burst from his throat. His control snapped, shattered, while she ignited with fiery urgency. His lips drinking in her wild moans, they came together in a firestorm of pleasure.

When at last it was over, Diana collapsed weakly against him, their breaths rasping in harsh gasps.

Dazed, Thorne sprawled on the carriage seat beneath her, trying to make sense of their primitive, reckless coupling. From the moment he'd entered the carriage behind Diana, he'd fought the savage heat of his body. And the instant he touched his mouth to hers, he'd been wild to get inside her, to claim her for his own.

He hadn't meant to take her like that, with such raw, unbridled need. But he couldn't regret making love to her.

He suspected Diana regretted it, however, for she suddenly pushed herself off him and retreated to the opposite seat, smoothing down the skirts of her gown with tight, jerking movements.

"I cannot believe I let that happen," she muttered to herself, not even looking at Thorne.

"Why not?" he asked sardonically as he rebuttoned his breeches.

"Because I had just vowed to myself—" Diana cut

off the answer she'd begun. "Every time you touch me, I turn into a perfect wanton."

"I fail to see the problem."

"*Thorne* . . ." She gritted the word in frustration, before taking a deep breath. "For one thing, I don't dare risk bearing a child out of wedlock."

"If that should come to pass, we'll be married at once."

Her body stiffened, her chin rising stubbornly. "No, we will *not*, Thorne. This has to end. We cannot continue this way."

Just then, the coach began slowing. Frantically straightening her bodice and hair, Diana clenched her jaw, yet Thorne suspected she was even angrier at herself than at him.

When the coach rolled to a halt, however, she lifted her gaze to meet his sternly. "Please do not call on me tomorrow—or any time in the near future. We need a respite from each other."

Before he could reply, a footman opened the carriage door and let down the step. Diana alighted and fled, running up the entrance stairs to her house before disappearing inside.

Thorne sat there unmoving, jolted by her abrupt dismissal—and even more disturbed by how badly he had lost control of himself. His savage jealousy had driven him to treat Diana like the veriest doxy, taking her in a *carriage,* for Christ's sake. He'd been determined to claim her and make her forget that damned Ackland, who had dominated her thoughts all evening.

Wincing as her front door slammed shut, Thorne wondered if he should go after her. Perhaps if he exercised his most valiant charm, he might be able to soothe her obviously distraught temper.

Then again, perhaps it *was* a good idea for them to have a brief respite from each other. They'd been together in each other's company nearly every day for weeks now, until just recently many of those hours engaged in fervent passion, satisfying their every lustful desire.

His own response to their carnal interludes, Thorne acknowledged, was totally unexpected. He'd been certain that once he made love to Diana a score or so times, his desire for her would diminish to a manageable level. Yet his sexual attraction had swelled to almost frantic intensity.

He had never been so hungry for a woman before, so hot. He couldn't get enough of her. He spent the hours away from Diana craving the feel of her, the touch and taste and smell of her. And when he was with her, all he could think of was making love to her again. Even when he'd been deep inside her body just now, feeling every ripple of pleasure from their explosive climax fade, he'd wanted her again.

No, Thorne thought, setting his jaw. He wouldn't follow her and try to apologize. A respite was just what they needed. Time for his burgeoning obsession for Diana to cool.

Perhaps then he could regain command of himself and quell the ruthless craving that had grown nearly beyond control.

Thorne was still telling himself that two nights later when he visited Venus's sin club. Instead of diminishing his craving, however, the enforced time apart from Diana had only increased his frustration. By the time he arrived, his restlessness had grown so strong, he was ready to lash out at anyone at the least provocation.

He could have eased his sexual needs with one of Venus's doves, of course, but the thought of bedding any woman but Diana was frankly distasteful.

He was also supremely frustrated by the lack of progress at exposing Nathaniel's murderer. Yates had received letters from several retired Guardians, but none of them recalled any Forresters or knew of any mission twenty years ago that might have provoked the Forrester children's enmity.

Thorne himself had revisited the Foreign Office and made certain every old case involving French spies had been reexamined, but the name Forrester was never mentioned in any file.

The only positive evidence that they were on the right track had come to light yesterday. The larger of Venus's two bruisers had gone missing since the coach incident a fortnight earlier, but returned to work last night. Macky had reported that Sam Birkin was favoring his left shoulder, an injury that could have been caused by a bullet wound from Thorne's pistol. It seemed highly probable that Birkin was indeed the highwayman he'd shot. Regardless, both bruisers were being closely watched by Macky and two more of Thorne's men, who'd been employed at the club as servants.

Thorne had hoped to relieve some of his frustration by joining a game of faro with his friends, but the moment he entered the club's glittering gaming room, he discovered a new concern that soon had his blood boiling. A significant number of the company had eschewed cards and were standing around discussing *him*.

"If it isn't the famous buck with the bare chest," Lord Hastings drawled, welcoming Thorne into their group.

"How does it feel to be immortalized half-naked on canvas, Thorne?" Lord Boothe added.

"Yes, my lord, do allow me to commend you on your fine figure," a third gentleman commented with an amused smirk.

Having no trouble pretending puzzlement, Thorne raised a quizzical eyebrow. "I beg your pardon? What in Hades are you all talking about?"

Hastings answered the question for him. "The portrait hanging at Attree's exhibit. Boothe saw it there this afternoon and dragged the rest of us to view it. I must say I was impressed."

Thorne frowned, recalling that James Attree was the wealthy Cit with a passion for art who had recently purchased several of Diana's paintings.

"Indeed, you lucky devil," Boothe said, laughing. "Every woman in London will want you once they get a glimpse of that painting."

It took some questioning, but Thorne eventually deduced that the shipboard portrait of him had somehow wound up in James Attree's private collection and put on exhibit, but how it had gotten there, Thorne couldn't begin to guess. He didn't believe Diana would have sold it for public display. . . . Unless she had been so irate at his boorish behavior the other night that she'd acted out of vindictiveness.

The thought was barely formed when Venus came up to him and offered him a snifter of brandy, then took his arm to draw him away from his still-snickering friends.

"My darling Venus, you have my undying gratitude," Thorne remarked sincerely. "How did you know I needed rescuing?"

"I could see you were being roasted unmercifully."

A frown shadowed her beautiful face. "This cannot be good for Diana's reputation, I shouldn't think."

"Have you seen the painting?"

"Yes, at Attree's place this afternoon. When I heard of it, I felt I had to see for myself. It is a stunning piece. Very sensual and alluring. She captured you to perfection—your virility and the wicked devilry in your eyes."

"Is it so obvious Diana painted it?" Thorne asked with a sinking heart.

"The canvas is unsigned, but it wasn't difficult for me to guess the artist, since I have seen her other work. I'm certain the world will suspect her, even if it can't be proved."

Thorne ground his teeth even as he feigned a smile for the benefit of his watching audience. It was irritating to find himself the subject of so much amused gossip, but he was incensed that the painting had been made public when it should have been something intimate and private between him and Diana. And very likely, this new titillating incident would once more make Diana the center of scandal.

It required a strong effort to refrain from storming out of the club and marching over to Attree's mansion to quiz him about how the portrait had come to be in his possession, but Thorne remained at the club until late that evening, preferring not to give the appearance of being overly concerned.

He was up early the next morning, however, intent on seeing the exhibition for himself. John Yates was already in the breakfast room when he entered, enjoying eggs and kippers and reading the *Morning Post*.

Thorne had just taken his first drink of coffee when Yates nearly choked on a mouthful of egg. Unable to speak for coughing, he handed Thorne the newspaper, which was folded back to the third page.

A cartoon leapt out at him—a lifelike caricature of himself as a ship's masthead, his hair blowing in the wind, his bare chest puffed out, and a lecherous grin on his face. The wicked drawing was by Thomas Rowlandson, England's most popular cartoonist.

Thorne clenched his jaw and rose without a word, not waiting to eat before calling for his carriage.

He interrupted Mr. Attree at the breakfast table, but the merchant was eager to receive so illustrious a caller as Viscount Thorne.

"A pleasure indeed, milord," Attree exclaimed. "To what do I owe this honor?"

"Surely you can guess why I am here, sir."

"The portrait?" The florid-faced man looked rather uncomfortable, almost guilty, in fact.

"Precisely. I am curious as to how my portrait came to be in your possession."

"Why, I paid a pretty sum for it, to be sure. 'Twas for sale in a public gallery on Bond Street. The proprietor always informs me when a good piece shows up in 'is shop. I recognized Miss Sheridan's style at once and wanted it for me private collection."

"May I see it?"

"But of course, milord. The exhibit is not open to the public until ten, but I will escort you meself."

Mr. Attree preceded Thorne to a separate wing of his house—a wide, well-lit hall that had been devoted to art. Unlike the Royal Academy exhibitions, whose walls were crammed edge to edge with paintings, Attree's collection was displayed with taste and care. Thorne's portrait hung near the center of the hall, surrounded by four other signed works of Diana's, which the merchant owned. Her exquisite artistic style was indeed readily recognizable, and so unmistakably distinct that the unsigned portrait of Thorne fairly shouted the artist's name.

When Thorne stood staring grimly at the grouping, Attree grimaced. "I take it you ain't 'appy to be on public display like this, milord?"

Thorne forcibly summoned his most charming smile. "Becoming fodder for the cartoonists is hardly pleasant. It is not, however, my injured pride that concerns me, but rather Miss Sheridan's reputation. Having so risqué a piece brandished in such a prominent exhibit as yours, my good sir, will have the tongues of every gossipmonger in town wagging about her. She never intended it for sale. It was to be her wedding gift to me."

"Then 'ow did I find it in that gallery?"

"I expect it must have been stolen from her studio."

"Stolen! But who would do such a cavey thing?"

Thorne had his suspicions, but refrained from sharing them. "I wish to buy the portrait back from you, Mr. Attree. I assure you, I will make it worth your while."

The merchant clasped his hands together, as if in dismay, yet a cunning gleam entered his eyes. "I would be 'appy to oblige, milord, but you ken my reluctance to give over such a stunning work—"

"Just name your price."

"Perhaps Miss Sheridan could be persuaded to exchange it for a different piece of equal value?"

"Two works of your choice. Will that suffice?"

"Done!" Attree agreed with glee.

"Perhaps you'll be so kind as to have it wrapped so that I may return it to Miss Sheridan."

"*Now,* milord?"

"I would prefer to get it out of the public eye immediately—I'm certain you understand. I give you my word, sir, that you will have your replacements before the day is through."

When Thorne arrived at Diana's house a short while later, he found her pacing her studio, too distraught to work. She felt cold, sick inside, knowing that the cartoon could ruin her for good this time, destroying everything she had worked for.

The sight of Thorne's dark expression, however, penetrated her despair, for she suddenly realized the theft of her painting would hurt him, as well.

"I am truly sorry about that dreadful cartoon, Thorne," Diana began. "I have no notion how it came about, but your portrait is missing. I have searched the entire house twice—"

"Don't worry. I have the portrait in my possession now, where I intend to keep it."

Her eyes widened with bewilderment. "Wherever did you find it?"

"I purchased it this morning from your ardent admirer, Mr. Attree. And *he* purchased it yesterday from a gallery on Bond Street. I assured him that it must have been stolen, since you never meant it for public consumption."

"Of course not! I would never sell so brazen a work. I only just now realized it was missing from my studio. I've been too busy even to notice until I saw that wretched cartoon. I can't imagine how it disappeared—"

"I can," Thorne said tersely. "Has Amy visited here since our confrontation about bribing her fortune-hunter?"

"Actually . . ." Diana frowned, trying to remember.

"She called the day afterward, when I was out." Diana gave Thorne a troubled look. "I know Amy was furious, but surely she wouldn't be so devious as to steal your portrait and sell it?"

"Oh, I have no doubt she is devious enough. And she'll be fortunate if I don't throttle her. Go fetch your bonnet," Thorne said in a tone that made Diana shiver. "I think a visit to my ward is in order."

His seething anger did not bode well for Amy in the least, Diana knew. But during the drive to Berkeley Square, she tried to come to terms with her own anger, and to determine the best course to take with her aggravating young cousin.

When they arrived, they were informed that Miss Lunsford could be found in the drawing room, as could Mr. John Yates, who had come to call.

When Thorne strode into the room, followed closely by Diana, Lady Hennessy was there, too, no doubt acting as chaperone.

Upon spying her glowering guardian, Amy leapt up from the sofa, all color draining from her face. She stood staring, the picture of guilt, while Thorne pointed an accusing finger at her.

"What do you have to say for yourself, brat? You stole my portrait and sold it, didn't you?"

Amy's hands twisted nervously, but her chin rose with belligerence. "Yes, I stole it! I wanted to repay you for driving Reggie away from me. It was no more than you deserve!"

A muscle in Thorne's jaw worked visibly. When he took another step toward his ward, however, as if he might truly do her violence, Diana placed a restraining hand on his arm. "Thorne, please, you cannot strangle her—"

"Why not?" He pinned Amy with a fulminating glare, while his tone took on a lethal softness. "I don't give a damn that you made me into a laughingstock for the ton, but you hurt your cousin far worse. She has struggled for years to gain the respect of London's art authorities, not to mention acceptance by the arbiters of society. This incident will only savage her reputation and give her critics and detractors ammunition to shun her as scandalous. After this, she'll be fortunate not to be drummed out of town."

Amy's expression suddenly turned stricken. "Oh, my God . . . I didn't think about Diana—"

"Obviously not," Thorne said scathingly.

Her gaze flew to Diana, before returning to Thorne. "I didn't mean to hurt her," Amy insisted hoarsely. "I only wanted to get back at you. You ruined my life."

"So your revenge is to ruin Diana's life? Do you have any inkling of the sacrifices she has made for you, you spoiled, selfish little brat?"

Though staring white-faced, Amy remained mute.

John Yates, who had been watching the entire interchange, stepped slowly forward then, a dark scowl knotting his brow as he regarded Amy. "It is true, isn't it? You actually stole a painting of Thorne from your cousin. *You* were the cause of that despicable cartoon."

She held out her hands pleadingly. "John, I can explain!"

He stiffened, his shoulders drawing back, ramrod straight, the bearing of the cavalry officer he'd once been. "I do not believe you *can* explain, Miss Lunsford. Nothing you say can excuse such dishonorable acts as you have perpetrated."

Amy's dismayed expression showed how sharply

his harsh accusation had pierced her. But Yates was not yet finished, it seemed.

"I have made allowances for your tender age, Miss Lunsford. I hoped you would grow up someday. But I see now how foolish I have been. This is beyond childish. This is *criminal*. Thorne is right—you are nothing but a spoiled, selfish child. And I am through catering to you."

Turning abruptly, Yates gave a curt bow to Lady Hennessy and then to Diana. "You will forgive me, ladies, if I refrain from calling here in future."

Amy watched, stunned, as Yates's rigid, uneven gait carried him out the door. Then she promptly burst into tears and, after another moment, ran blindly from the drawing room.

Lady Hennessy had wisely kept silent all this time, but now she rose wearily and gave a disgusted sigh. "I suppose I had best try to stem that wretched child's histrionics before she makes herself ill."

"No, I'll go," Diana said abruptly. "I have a few words of my own that I intend for her to hear."

Upon going upstairs, she found Amy in her bedchamber, sprawled facedown on her bed, sobbing her heart out into her pillow.

Ruthlessly Diana crushed the urge to console the girl, and instead, settled grimly in a chair to wait while Amy lay there weeping passionately.

Eventually she must have realized her dramatics would get no sympathy, for her sobs finally quieted a measure. She hugged her pillow, gulping great tearful gasps of air and shuddering. When at last she pushed herself up to face Diana, her face was mottled red and still streaming with tears.

"You needn't scold me any further. I am miserable enough as is."

"You know very well that you've brought this misery on yourself."

Amy looked away, the picture of bleakness. "I do know. I behaved wretchedly, Diana. I can't imagine how you will ever forgive me. Or John either."

"It will doubtless be difficult for him," Diana replied, suspecting the girl was just now realizing how much she cared for John Yates.

Amy flung herself back down on the bed, burying her face in her soaked pillow. "My life truly is ruined now," she declared in a muffled wail. "I have driven him away. He is the only man I have really ever cared for."

"Is he indeed?" Diana said sardonically. "What of Reginald Kneighly?"

"That snake? I cannot believe what I ever saw in him! John is ten times the man Reggie is."

"He is indeed," Diana agreed, wishing to encourage this line of thinking. "But Mr. Yates is hurt and disappointed in you, with good reason."

Amy turned her head and sniffed. "I know you are hurt and disappointed in me, too."

Diana sent her cousin a chill smile. "Well, yes. Not to mention furious."

"I swear I did not mean to hurt you, Diana. I only wanted to get back at Thorne."

"Well, that should be a lesson to you. Such puerile behavior not only wounds others, but can also hurt you yourself, since it can drive away the people you care about."

Wiping her eyes, Amy sat up again. "Have I driven you away?" she asked in a small voice, her lower lip trembling. "Please tell me you will forgive me."

Diana pressed her lips together, refusing to give in

too easily. "I don't know, Amy. If I thought you were truly remorseful—"

"But I am—*truly*!"

"Well, we shall see." She rose then and turned away.

"Diana!" Amy cried. "You *must* forgive me!"

"Actually, I needn't, dearest. Until you prove yourself worthy of forgiveness, I intend to withhold judgment."

At her cousin's fresh sob, Diana walked out of the room, leaving the girl to stew in her own despairing reflections.

Eighteen

Diana's day was *not* going well.

First she'd awakened to find that dreadful cartoon in the morning paper, which rudely alerted her to the latest brewing scandal. Next she'd discovered Thorne's portrait missing. Then the furor with Amy.

Then, when Thorne had driven her home from Berkeley Square, he'd announced his intentions of procuring a special license to marry without delay, insisting that an immediate wedding was the only possible way to salvage what was left of her reputation. Diana had firmly refused, declaring she was determined to weather the tempest. She had no intention of forcing Thorne into marriage in order to save her.

Additionally, upon arriving home three hours ago, she'd discovered that her current client had canceled her afternoon appointment for a sitting without a word of explanation. The defection was no doubt due to her newest disgrace, Diana knew, since when she'd finished her first commission two days before, Lady Ranworth had been so delighted with her portrait that she'd vowed to tell all her friends of Miss Sheridan's "magnificent talent." Diana had the sinking suspicion this cancellation was only the beginning of her downward slide in popularity.

And now her footman had just informed her that the Duke of Redcliffe was waiting below in her parlor, requesting a word with her.

Diana wasn't certain what had brought Thorne's father to her doorstep, but she had a good notion. With trepidation, she went downstairs to meet the duke.

He stood, tall and elegant, at the parlor window, staring out at the street, but he turned at her entrance, a grave frown upon his brow.

"I presume you are here because of this morning's cartoon," Diana said guardedly once polite greetings had been exchanged.

A humorless smile twisted the corner of Redcliffe's handsome mouth. "Certainly I am not pleased that my son is the object of notoriety once more. I have a severe dislike of imbroglios that reflect poorly on my family name. For shame, Miss Sheridan. I had not thought you would abet Christopher in his rebel tendencies."

Diana clasped her hands together, wondering what she could say in her own defense without seeming the coward. "I assure you, your grace, I did not set out to embroil your son in scandal, and I regret it enormously, even more than you yourself do, I expect."

The duke gave an elegant shrug. "I do not lay the blame entirely upon you, of course. Scandal follows my son around like a shadow. I had hoped your betrothal would be the making of him, perhaps cure him of his wild ways, but. . . ." Redcliffe hesitated, pinning her with his gaze. "If I may be candid, it is not this new stir that troubles me. Christopher has survived far worse. I am not so certain, however, that his heart will emerge unscathed this time."

Diana raised an eyebrow in puzzlement. "I'm afraid I don't understand, your grace."

"I wish to ask you a highly personal question, Miss Sheridan. One that is more normally the purview of a father harboring concerns for a daughter. What are your intentions toward my son? Are they honorable?"

"I beg your pardon?"

"Do you love him, Miss Sheridan?"

"Well . . . yes, of course," Diana stammered, determined to uphold their pretense of a love match—although she was no longer certain it was wholly pretense on her part. She winced inwardly at the thought. "Why do you ask?"

"I fear my son is headed for a serious fall. Simply put, I think you could very well break his heart."

Diana stared, surprise and denial warring within her. "Whatever leads you to that conclusion?"

"In part because Christopher overcame his aversion to marriage enough to propose to you. He has always adamantly refused my choices, claiming he would never wed any of the milksop brides I threw at his head. So if he wants you for his wife, you must be very special indeed."

"I think you give me too much credit, your grace."

"I doubt it. You are vastly different from any woman he has ever pursued, and therein lies the danger."

"I would never deliberately hurt him, I promise you," Diana vowed truthfully.

"I pray that you don't," Redcliffe said, his tone grave. "Take my word for it, Miss Sheridan. My son has extremely strong feelings for you. To my utter amazement, he paid me a visit a short while ago regarding the exposure of his portrait. He was quite angry and disturbed in your behalf—enough to ask my assistance in controlling the damage to your reputation. If you wonder at my shock, it is because this is the first time since he was a boy that Christopher has ever willingly sought my help."

Even so, Diana thought frowning, that proved little about the nature of Thorne's feelings toward her. It was not so remarkable that he'd enlisted his father's aid, since he felt largely responsible for this new scrape about his portrait.

Yet before she could respond, the duke continued. "Of course I will do whatever I can. I believe you know I am a patron of the Royal Academy. I intend to rally some of their chief artists to your defense, starting with Lawrence. He is already an admirer of your work, and I shall make certain he makes his opinion quite public."

Diana felt her jaw go slack in amazement of her own. Sir Thomas Lawrence was the premier portraitist in England, and the favorite of the Prince Regent. His support would go a long way toward restoring her withering prestige.

"Th-thank you, your grace," she heard herself stammer.

"I am sure you know that if the talk cannot be stemmed at once, you are liable to lose many of your clients."

"Yes, I know all too well. And I am grateful for your support, truly."

"You are to be my daughter-in-marriage soon. It is the least I can do. As I mentioned, your fame—or infamy, either one—reflects on my family name. But for my son's sake, as well as your own, I would rather it be fame."

With a courteous bow then, the duke took his leave of her, but his visit had jolted Diana and given her new reflections to stew over.

She could not put much credence in his concern. It seemed clear that Redcliffe truly loved his son and wanted to see him happy, but she couldn't believe Thorne was all that vulnerable to her.

In the first place, the duke didn't realize their betrothal had begun as a pretense and was only temporary. Thorne was only insisting on marriage now out of honor and a wish to protect her.

But more important, a man like Thorne was unlikely ever to give his heart.

He is far more likely to break my *heart,* Diana thought with despair and a growing fury at herself for allowing her emotions to become so involved.

Clenching her fists, Diana moved over to a chair and sank down weakly. She was grateful for the duke's warning, though. How *could* she have been so witless? She had let her relationship with Thorne go much too far.

It had been criminally easy to relax her guard with him these past two months. She'd never been so fiercely attracted to any man as she was to Thorne. He had filled her life with passion and laughter and beauty. But she was in grave danger of falling in love with him.

And this time if she lost her heart, it would be a thousand times worse than the last.

Diana squeezed her eyes shut. She was furious at herself for being so incredibly foolish again, yet it was not too late to act. She had to break off their betrothal without delay.

Thorne was prepared to disregard his aversion to matrimony in order to give her the protection of his name. But she couldn't let him make such a sacrifice. He had already done so much for her. It was her turn to protect him.

She had to end their engagement; she had to set Thorne free of any obligation he felt toward her.

And then, somehow, she would have to carry on with her life and try to fill the gaping hole that his absence would assuredly leave.

Thorne had no difficulty procuring a special marriage license that very afternoon, although he knew persuading Diana to make use of it would be another problem altogether. Rather than press her, he resolved to spend his time trying to undo the damage that making public his scandalous portrait had wrought.

Enlisting his father's aid had gone sorely against the grain, but Thorne would willingly humble himself before his noble sire if it meant salvaging Diana's reputation. And if anyone could influence the outcome of the battle, it would likely be Redcliffe.

When Thorne returned home late that afternoon, however, with a special license burning a hole in his pocket, he had a visitor who drove any thought of impending nuptials or familial feuds from his mind.

John Yates met him in the entrance hall, a grave look on his face. "We finally have word about the elder Forresters," Yates said. "And it's much as you suspected."

"One of our retired agents responded to your inquiries?" Thorne asked, knowing it was still too soon to have received any reply from Sir Gawain on Cyrene.

"Yes. Mr. Richard Ruddock. He came all the way from Yorkshire and is waiting in your study to speak to you."

Thorne immediately followed Yates to his study, where an elderly man rose to greet him. Thorne recognized Ruddock as a fellow Guardian who had given up the excitement and danger of the order in favor of a quieter existence in his old age.

"I would have responded to Mr. Yates's letter much sooner, my lord," Ruddock apologized, "but regrettably I was visiting my granddaughter for her lying-in."

"I thank you for coming now, sir," Thorne said sincerely. "Yates tells me you have knowledge of the Forresters."

"Indeed I do, my lord."

Ruddock had already been offered wine, so Thorne settled himself in an armchair to hear the elder man's story.

"Your letter said you wished to know if anyone recognized the name of Forrester, and so I did. Josiah Forrester was a traitor to the Crown and came to a tragic end. It was during a mission in August nearly twenty years ago."

"What was his crime?" Thorne asked.

"He was a country gentleman who ran a profitable smuggling ring with the deadly habit of murdering the King's Revenuers. For years the local authorities had no success against their perfidy, so the Guardians were called in—charged with crushing the band of smugglers and stopping the murders."

"Did Sir Gawain have any responsibilities for this mission?"

"To be sure. Sir Gawain was our designated leader. We apprehended several of the killers, and meant to arrest Forrester and bring him to London to stand trial. His estate was near Eastbourne in Sussex. We went there with a handful of troops to serve a warrant, but from the first moment, we ran into difficulties. When Forrester spied us coming, he shot one of our men and barricaded himself inside the manor house, using his own family as hostages. He vowed he would kill them rather than be taken alive."

"He had two children?" Yates interjected.

Ruddock nodded. "A boy and a girl. For nearly two days we were at a standoff, but then Forrester's wife tried to escape and he killed her. We managed to shoot him and save the children."

"How old were the children then?" Thorne asked.

"I couldn't say exactly. The boy was perhaps twelve. The girl was several years younger, possibly seven or eight. The boy's name was Thomas. I remember vividly because he was covered in his parents' blood. He not only held us to blame, he was like a rabid animal in his hatred for us—sobbing and snarling and calling us murderers while trying to claw our faces. It took three soldiers to restrain him."

Thorne could picture the violent scene that the two young children had witnessed. *Thomas and Venus*.

"I also remember," Ruddock added grimly, "because Sir Gawain himself was wounded—shot in the leg by that vengeful boy."

It was Thorne's turn to nod. The baronet still walked with a limp twenty years later. It must have been after that disastrous incident that Sir Gawain had retired from active missions and returned to Cyrene to take over leadership of the Guardians. The timing seemed to fit.

"So what happened then?" he asked Ruddock.

"All of Forrester's properties were confiscated by the Crown, but we saw to it that his children were sent to respectable work homes."

"And they never forgave you for it," Thorne murmured to himself.

For a moment, he fell silent. An eight-year-old girl was possibly too young to understand exactly what had happened, but the boy had evidently put his own construction on events: The Guardians were murderers, while his treacherous father was elevated to sainthood. Yet both children had suffered the trauma of losing their parents and their privileged life at the same stroke. It would be no wonder if they held the Guardians—and Sir Gawain specifically—to blame for the collapse of their entire world. No wonder if they were set on vengeance even after all this time.

Thorne now had little doubt that Venus wanted revenge against the Guardians. Not only were they responsible for her parents' deaths, but afterward, she had been separated from her brother and sent to an orphanage, and then ended up earning her living as a lady of the evening.

It was no stretch to imagine that she'd purposefully seduced Nathaniel as part of her plan for revenge. Either Venus or her brother might have killed Nathaniel because he'd suspected them of working with French spies.

Yates interrupted his dark thoughts. "So how do we proceed? We need more evidence against Madam Venus, do we not?"

"That we do." Thorne felt his mouth set in a grim line. "I think a return visit to Sussex is in order."

Despite his frustration at having to abandon Diana at this crucial juncture, Thorne penned a note to her, expressing regret that business required him to be away from town for a few days. Then he and Yates set out for Sussex early the next morning.

Thorne's first intent was to visit the estate that had once belonged to Josiah Forrester, where the attempted arrest of a traitor by the Guardians had ended in violence and tragedy. The second was to call on the magistrate of the district to discover any further knowledge about Josiah Forrester's orphaned children and their possible relationship to the local smugglers. If Thomas and Venus-Madeline had indeed been involved with French spies last spring, there might somehow be a connection to their Sussex past.

To Thorne's gratification, both visits yielded enlightenment. And both his hunches proved right.

Upon arriving in Eastbourne, he and Yates booked rooms at the largest inn and immediately began making inquiries, starting with the parish church, where land deeds were recorded. There was no need to examine church records, however, for the young vicar was somewhat familiar with the transactions, even though they had occurred before his time.

After confiscation by the Crown, the Forrester estate had been sold to a neighboring gentleman. But then approximately ten years ago, Thomas Forrester had returned to Eastbourne and purchased his childhood home for himself and his sister Madeline. The property now belonged to Madeline Forrester, after her brother's sad demise in a London fire last fall.

When Thorne and Yates drove out to the estate, they found the manor house in good repair but with only a small staff of servants. The butler, however, readily answered their questions, saying that his mistress rarely visited but paid them well to oversee its upkeep.

They were required to wait until the next morning before the local magistrate, Squire Whickers, was available to receive them, but the squire proved a font of information.

He clearly remembered the violent death of Josiah Forrester twenty years ago and could fill in numerous details about his treachery—how his deadly band of Freetraders had murdered several British revenue officers, and how he'd killed his own wife and threatened to kill his innocent children rather than be arrested.

Whickers also knew the location of the workhouse where young Thomas Forrester had been sent: nearby Lewes. It was Thomas's more recent intrigues that most interested Thorne, and the squire also had some damning information about those.

"Last fall," he recounted, "I aided the Home Office in exposing a spy ring that had long been suspected of selling secrets to the French. Two of the spies we captured claimed to have been given documents by Thomas Forrester, which resulted in a warrant for his arrest. It was shortly afterward—in October—that Thomas perished in a fire. I always wondered if he killed himself to avoid paying for his crimes, but it seemed ironic that his fate was so similar to his father's brutal end."

Thorne frowned thoughtfully. This was the most promising lead yet that Nathaniel had had valid reason to investigate Thomas Forrester last spring—and why Thomas and perhaps Venus, as well, would have wanted Nathaniel dead. It also explained why the Foreign Office had no knowledge of Thomas Forrester: because the Home Office had been the one to crush the ring of spies.

"Is there anyone hereabouts," Thorne asked, "who could connect Thomas directly to these spies? Anyone he might have employed to aid him?"

"Aye, there are a handful of Freetraders who hired

out their services to him. They were duped into carrying letters to France, transporting agents and such, but their roles weren't serious enough to get them hanged. I expect they could be persuaded to tell you what they know about Thomas, especially if you were to offer a reward. Now that the fellow is dead, there is no longer any reason to keep his secrets, I'd say. Even less so, since he was likely a traitor. If you wish, my lord, I could arrange for you to interview them, although it may take a day or two to contrive."

"That would be very helpful, squire."

The magistrate suddenly frowned thoughtfully. "Come to think of it . . . I find it odd that you're the second person to come here with inquiries about Thomas Forrester. A gentleman was here last spring asking the same kind of questions."

Thorne felt his heart begin to thud. "Oh? Can you recall this gentleman's name?"

"Yes indeed, my lord. His name was Lunsford. Nathaniel Lunsford."

Nineteen

Although Diana had resolved to break off her betrothal with Thorne, she had no chance to act before receiving his message that he would be away from town for a few days. Yet she wasn't sure whether his absence left her more frustrated or relieved.

In the interim, the duke's strategy to salvage her artistic reputation seemed to be working. Sir Thomas Lawrence was quoted as saying, "Miss Sheridan brings the best qualities of style and grace to her art." Additionally, it was rumored that the Royal Academy judges were considering the remarkable step of extending her an invitation to join the summer exhibition when it officially opened this week, even though the entrants had been determined several weeks before that.

And both affirmations of her talent helped to stop the hemorrhaging of her clientele.

Thus, Diana was in her studio one afternoon completing a sitting when her housekeeper apologetically interrupted her, saying there was a "young woman" below who begged to speak with Miss Sheridan on a matter of great urgency. The visitor, whose name was Kitty Wathen, would *not* go away.

Kitty, Diana recollected, was the Cyprian in Venus's employ who had captivated Amy's fortune-hunter.

Highly puzzled—and a bit disquieted that her cousin might have provoked some further mischief as she'd done by stealing Thorne's portrait—Diana called an early end to the sitting and saw her client away, then stepped into the parlor, where Kitty Wathen awaited her.

The blond woman was quite a beauty, petite and fair, with the kind of sweet, helpless air that made gentlemen want to play rescuer. But Diana could see at once from Kitty's expression that her current distress was no calculated act.

"I beg your pardon for coming here like this, Miss Sheridan," she said at once, "but I didn't know where else to turn. Lord Thorne has not been at home for the past several days, and his butler refuses to tell me how I could reach him. I thought someone should warn his lordship. I fear . . . I think he might be in grave danger."

Diana tried to quell the stab of alarm Kitty's pronouncement stirred in her. "Won't you please be seated and tell me why you think so?"

Kitty perched on the sofa and clasped her hands in agitation. "I'm not sure where to begin. Perhaps the conversation I recently overheard. . . . Two bruisers at our club talking about how they meant to do away with Lord Thorne. Kill him, I mean."

"*Kill* him?" Diana exclaimed, her heart jolting in her chest.

"I fear so. Billy Finch and Sam Birkin work at the club as bruisers."

Those must be the same two men Thorne suspected of attempted murder during the holdup, Diana remembered. *Dear God.*

"I heard them arguing with Madam Venus," Kitty went on. "Or rather, Venus was arguing with them. She told them they couldn't kill Lord Thorne or there would be the devil to pay. She was very angry."

With effort, Diana kept the panic from her voice. "You think Venus asked them to kill Lord Thorne?"

"No, just the opposite. I figured someone else gave Billy and Sam orders, but Venus told them they worked for *her,* not Thomas, whoever that is. And it wasn't my place to interfere. But now Madam Venus is missing, and I am dreadfully worried. No one has seen her since the night I heard her arguing . . . last Thursday."

Five days ago. Diana swallowed convulsively as her mind raced ahead. Thorne had sent her a message on Friday saying he would be out of town on business for a few days, yet his note had seemed calm enough. Surely nothing had happened to him. Surely her heart would have sensed it if he had been injured or worse.

"I thought Lord Thorne should be warned," Kitty said. "I went to his house twice and was turned away. The second time I left a note, but I didn't feel that was enough."

"I will go at once," Diana responded. "His servants will listen to me."

"Maybe something has already happened to him. And to Madam Venus, as well."

Diana took a deep breath and shook her head, refusing to consider that dreadful possibility. "There is likely a simple explanation. Lord Thorne did indeed leave town for a few days. In fact, I wonder if Venus might have accompanied him."

"But why would she not have told us she would be away? She has never been gone this long before."

Hearing the fear in Kitty's voice, Diana tried to remain calm and to marshal her scattered thoughts. "But she has disappeared before this?"

"Sometimes she visits a . . . certain house in London, but never for more than a night."

Diana raised a hand to her temple, trying feverishly to think. If she could find Venus and question her, she could perhaps discover why the two bruisers wanted Thorne dead and could ward off the danger. "Do you have any notion where Venus might have gone? Perhaps this house you spoke of?"

"I suppose it's possible. I was afraid to look for her there, in case Sam and Billy were to see me and think I was meddling. They aren't blokes you want to cross. And it's doubtful Venus wants anyone knowing where she goes. I suspect she has a lover there. I only know about the house because I ran an errand for her there once."

"Can you take me to this house?"

Kitty's face grew pale. "Oh, Miss Sheridan, I daren't go. If I was to rat on Sam and Billy, they would likely kill me, too. I can give you the direction, though. It's near the theater district, not too far from the club. Parker Street, Number Twelve. Venus has been a good mistress, and I would hate it if something bad were to happen to her."

"So would I. And she could be ill or possibly injured. I think I should visit the house without delay, to see if she is there—"

"Oh, would you, Miss Sheridan? It would be best if you went, since Sam and Billy aren't likely to do you harm."

Diana wasn't so certain about that, but there was

no need to discuss her fears with her caller. Before she
went anywhere in search of Venus, she would take
adequate precautions. "I will visit the house as soon
as I speak to Thorne's servants, unless you know
where else I should look for her."

"No place I can think of. Thank you, Miss Sheridan." Kitty grimaced. "I know you don't want the
likes of me calling on you, but I didn't know what else
to do."

"No, you did very well to come to me, Kitty. I will
make certain Lord Thorne hears your warning. And I
will do my best to find Venus, I promise you."

As soon as she changed her gown, Diana called for
her carriage and had her coachman drive her to
Thorne's house in Cavendish Square. She was accompanied by the three strapping footmen Thorne had established in her house for her protection, and she
carried the loaded brace of pistols he'd insisted she
take. If she intended to search unfamiliar districts of
London, she wanted to be well prepared.

As she feared, Thorne was not at home—traveling
in Sussex, according to his butler—but she took the
time to write him a long note of explanation, telling
him the basic details of Kitty's disturbing tale and
warning him to take care.

Diana had descended the front steps of his grand
mansion and was debating whether to go to Parker
Street and look for Venus just then when, to her
startlement, she saw Thorne's traveling chaise approaching.

Relief overwhelmed her when he stepped down a
few moments later, while her heart leapt deplorably at
the sight of his handsome face—and not simply be-

cause he was unharmed. Thorne had been absent only four days, but she had missed him dreadfully.

A wretched sign, Diana thought, wincing. If her feelings were so pitifully agitated after so short a time, how could she bear to end their relationship altogether? But this was no time to be missish, she scolded herself.

When he gave her a quizzical frown, she cast an apologetic glance at John Yates and drew Thorne away from the crowd of carriages and servants, out of earshot.

"What's amiss?" he demanded in a low voice, studying her expression.

"Kitty Wathen just came to see me." Diana quickly explained about the Cyprian's visit, including her warning that Thorne might be a target for murder and the fact that Venus had been missing for days. "Do you know where she might have gone?" Diana asked at the conclusion. "She has not been with you?"

"No, I haven't seen her."

"Then I think we should try to find her. She could be in trouble. At the very least, she can tell us why her two brutes want to kill you. In fact, I was just on my way to search for her."

"I'll go," Thorne said curtly. "It's time I confronted Venus, in any case. Where is this house on Parker Street?"

"Number Twelve."

He started to turn, but Diana laid a restraining hand on his arm. "Thorne, is it at all possible we were wrong about Venus? I know it is only instinct, but . . . I don't want to believe she could brutally order your murder, or that she could have killed Nathaniel in cold blood. Do you truly think her capable of such horrible acts?"

With a grim smile, Thorne took Diana's gloved hand and brought it to his lips. "Of course you don't want to believe her capable of murder, but I've learned never to underestimate the enemy."

"But Venus may not be the enemy—"

"If so, then she will have to prove it," he said darkly. "Now we are wasting time." Turning, he strode toward the carriages.

"I am coming with you," Diana announced as she hurried after him, which made Thorne halt abruptly. "If she is guilty," Diana added as his lips formed the word *no,* "then I want to see her punished. But if she is in trouble, I want to help her."

"You have my word, I won't condemn Venus unjustly."

"Even so, you are not going alone. I worry you might encounter something dangerous. What if those two brigands are waiting for you? I don't want you to be killed."

Thorne flashed her a scowl. "And you meant to go searching for Venus there on your own?"

"I came prepared." Briefly Diana told him about the footmen and the pistols she'd brought with her. "You cannot stop me, Thorne. If you won't let me come, I will simply follow you."

He gave her a long look that was three parts annoyance, one part resignation. "Very well, but you'll stay in the carriage while Yates and I investigate."

Diana bit back a protest, knowing she had to be satisfied with that small victory.

Number Twelve was a modest two-story house halfway down a quiet lane, Thorne saw as Diana's carriage drew to a halt. He and Yates had ridden with her in her vehicle, while his traveling chaise carrying several armed footmen followed a discreet distance behind. Uncertain what to expect, Thorne had decided it wiser to bring solid reinforcements.

Unlike Diana, he had little doubt that Venus was guilty of ordering her bruisers to kill him during the holdup of his coach. And her complicity in Nathaniel's murder was even more likely.

Venus's disappearance, however, admittedly disturbed him.

He'd planned to confront her with the mounting evidence he'd collected against her brother and, if necessary, incarcerate her until she confessed her complicity. But given this puzzling turn of events, he would have to improvise.

He made certain Diana had a pistol that was primed and loaded, and told her to wait in her carriage while he and Yates called at the house. Then he ordered two of his men around back to block any escape routes, and a third to accompany him to the front door.

When he rapped briskly, there was no response at first, so he knocked again. It was a long moment before the door swung open.

The uglier of Venus's two bruisers stood there, a bleary-eyed scowl on his face, as if he'd just awakened from a drunken stupor. Upon glimpsing Thorne, Billy Finch opened his eyes wide in shock. "Devil save me," Finch swore under his breath.

"I wouldn't count on it," Thorne returned mildly.

Finch turned and bolted, giving a shout as he raced toward the back of the house.

Thorne went after him. The bruiser had almost reached the end of the hall when Thorne lunged for his legs and tackled him to the wooden floor.

Finch came down hard, grunting, but immediately

scrambled onto his back and began flailing at Thorne's face with his fists.

Thorne saw a painful burst of hot stars as one powerful blow connected with his cheekbone. In one section of his mind, he was aware of a commotion behind him—the thud of boot steps on wooden stairs—and suspected the bruiser's cohort was attempting to flee the house, but he was too busy trying to subdue Finch to react, and had to trust that Yates could stop their quarry.

His hope faltered when a sideways glance let him see the larger of Venus's bruisers barrel into Yates first and then into the third footman. Both men gave grunting curses and went crashing to the floor along with their pistols. The second weapon discharged harmlessly into a wall, the shot reverberating as Sam Birkin fled out the front door.

Another blow claimed Thorne's full attention then. Pinning the struggling Finch with his weight, Thorne managed to pull his knife from his pocket and hold the blade to his opponent's throat.

Finch instantly went still, although both of them were breathing hard after their bout.

Thorne glanced down the hall, seeing that the footman was on his feet again and moving quickly toward the door in pursuit of Birkin. Yates, hampered by his wooden leg, was rising more slowly.

Just then the brawny figure of Sam Birkin backed through the doorway, his hands held high over his head in surrender.

Diana was holding the man at gunpoint, Thorne realized, a chill squeezing his ribs.

He wanted to curse her for putting herself in danger when he'd specifically ordered her to remain out of it, but he couldn't help it; he felt himself grin. The sight of the elegant lady facing down a much larger brute was highly entertaining and roused his sense of pride at the same time.

She kept her pistol trained on Birkin, while her glance searched the hall. When it came to rest on Thorne, he saw the relief in her eyes and knew she had been worried for him.

But she merely raised her pistol a slight degree and asked coolly, "Now what am I supposed to do with him?"

Thorne gave a bark of laughter and climbed to his feet, hauling Billy Finch up after him.

When Finch looked hard at the front door, as if judging whether he could get away, Thorne grinned again. "You are welcome to try. I'm just looking for an excuse to perforate your spleen."

He clamped a hand over Finch's shoulder and turned him toward the rear of the hall. "Mr. Yates, let us escort our friends to a more suitable room. We need to have a little chat. And Ned," he added, addressing the footman, "take Miss Sheridan's pistol and search the house to see if there are any other bloodthirsty culprits lurking about."

"Aye, m'lord."

By this time Yates had recovered his own pistol from where it had fallen, so he took control of the prisoner from Diana and brandished his weapon at Birkin.

They escorted their captives to the kitchen and made them sit on the floor while they proceeded to bind their hands and feet with twine.

Diana, noticing that Thorne's cheek was bleeding from a cut, found a dry dishcloth and silently pressed it to his wound. With a slight smile, he took the cloth from her, then settled a hip on the long wooden table and proceeded to interrogate the prisoners.

Initially both bruisers remained sullenly mute, until Thorne commanded Yates to check Birkin's chest for bullet wounds. Yates was none too gentle when he ripped open the burly man's shirt and exposed a healing scar in his left shoulder, most likely from a lead ball.

"I shot you, didn't I?" Thorne prodded.

Birkin sent him a look of savage dislike.

"It's all the same to me, but you'll hang for highway robbery unless you convince me to show you leniency. Who gave you your orders to kill me? Your mistress, Venus?"

Billy Finch answered for his cohort. "Nay, it warn't her."

"Who, then?"

"It was 'er brother Thomas."

Thorne went very still. So, it *was* true—Kitty had been speaking of Thomas Forrester. "How is that possible? I was under the impression Thomas Forrester died in a fire seven months ago."

" 'E didn't die."

"Shut yer trap," Birkin snapped.

Finch scowled back. "I ain't dancing on the gibbet for the likes of you."

"Ye're just as guilty as me—"

Thorne gave a weary sigh. "My good sirs, I'll thank you to spare your breaths unless it's to answer my questions. Let's start at the beginning. You say that Thomas Forrester is actually alive?"

Billy Finch nodded reluctantly. " 'E was wanted for treason, so 'e burned down 'is lodgings to make it look like 'e was dead and killed a bloke so there would be a body."

Thorne tried to hide his frown. If Forrester had fabricated his own death last fall, then it possibly put a different slant on the events of the past weeks and months, including his own suspicions of Venus.

"Is this Madam Venus's house?" Thorne asked, sweeping an arm around the kitchen. "I was told she came here occasionally to visit her lover, but that wasn't the case, was it? She came here to see her brother."

"Aye," Sam Birkin growled.

"And Forrester was the one who ordered you to kill me? Not Venus?"

Birkin gave a terse nod. "Our orders came from Forrester. 'E wanted you dead."

"Why?"

There was a brief pause. "Ye're a Guardian, ain't you? Seems like Mr. Forrester 'ates all Guardians."

Thorne saw Diana's frown of puzzlement, but she held her tongue as he quickly changed the subject and asked a different question. "What about Nathaniel Lunsford? Who killed him last spring? The two of you?"

"Nay, 'twas Forrester that knifed 'im, I swear it."

"Did Madam Venus have a hand in it?"

Birkin shook his head. "She grieved when she learned of it."

"Where is Venus now?"

"I don't ken," Birkin answered. "We 'aven't laid eyes on 'er since last week. She told us we couldn't kill you, and if we tried, she would 'ave our skins. She wasn't 'appy, I can tell you that. Mayhap she went to give 'er brother a piece of 'er mind."

"Then where has Forrester gone?" Thorne pressed.

The two bruisers glanced at each other.

"We can't say," Birkin muttered.

"You can't, or you won't?"

"Can't. Forrester ain't even in the country, as far as we know. 'E planned to set sail last week."

Thorne felt his heart lurch. "What was his destination?" he forced himself to ask casually.

"Some island, 'e said. On the other side of Spain."

This time Thorne felt his blood go cold. Thomas Forrester was likely sailing for Cyrene, no doubt to carry out his plans for revenge against Sir Gawain Olwen and the Guardians. But had Venus sailed with him? That would explain her disappearance five days ago. The two of them likely intended to avenge their parents' deaths by killing Sir Gawain.

Narrowing his eyes, Thorne met Sam Birkin's gaze. "Tell me, when exactly was the last time you saw Forrester?"

"Thursday. 'Twas afternoon sometime."

Then he had no time to lose. Forrester likely had sailed Thursday night and so had five days' head start already.

Thorne stood up, thinking furiously. He first had to see to Birkin and Finch, to arrange their incarceration in prison until he could deal with them. And if at all feasible, he wanted to confirm Forrester's destination by examining the rosters of all the shipping agents in London. He had to alert his crew and order his schooner made ready to sail as soon as possible, which likely would not be until tomorrow evening. He would have to send Diana home—

Remembering her presence, he looked up to meet Diana's troubled eyes. Out of all his tasks, he suspected this last would prove the most difficult, for she was watching him intently. He would have to offer her some sort of explanation, Thorne knew, for why he had to follow Forrester to Cyrene, but he wasn't looking forward to answering the questions she was certain to ask.

Diana made no protest when Thorne escorted her to her carriage so that she could be driven home, since he promised to call on her as soon as he was able. But as he started to hand her inside, she directed her coachman to take her to Lord Thorne's house instead.

"I intend to wait for you there," Diana said sweetly to Thorne, ignoring his scowl of exasperation. Until now she had been patient and meekly obliging, but it was time he stopped fobbing her off with concerns for her safety and told her what was happening.

The wait, however, proved surprisingly difficult for Diana. Thorne's majordomo and household staff welcomed her and made her comfortable in the drawing room, but her agitation wouldn't leave her.

For one thing, her nerves were still unsettled from the fear and tumult of the day, particularly their brief brush with danger.

Upon hearing shouts and gunfire coming from inside the house, she'd left her carriage against Thorne's orders and approached the front steps just as that huge brute Birkin came racing out the door. He was too wild-eyed and frantic to see her at first, so reacting instinctively, she had stepped into his path and put out her foot, tripping him and watching him land with a satisfying thud, then raising her pistol when he tried to struggle to his feet. He obviously believed her threat to shoot him, for all the fight suddenly seemed to drain out of him.

But it was her concern for Thorne that had unnerved her more. She couldn't help remembering the alarming scene that had met her eyes when she'd followed her prisoner into the house: Thorne locked in a savage struggle, then holding a knife to his opponent's throat, his own face bloodied and bruised.

She knew he was capable of violence, but seeing him risk his life again like that had set her emotions in turmoil. Her relief that he'd emerged relatively unscathed barely outweighed her fear for him, knowing those men and others—including Venus's brother, apparently—were determined to kill him.

A final source of agitation was her frustration at being kept in the dark. Her distress over Venus's evident culpability was only compounded by her ignorance regarding the murderous machinations of this Thomas Forrester.

There was far more to the tale than Thorne had revealed thus far, Diana realized, and she wanted answers.

She also knew that her own personal wishes would have to be put on hold for now. She'd had every intention of ending her betrothal to Thorne the next time she saw him, but the need to keep him safe from a murderer certainly took precedence over her desire to keep him safe from an obligatory marriage to her.

It was nearly ten o'clock before Thorne joined her in the drawing room, looking tired and grim. He went straight to the brandy decanter and poured himself a full measure of the amber liquid before settling in an armchair across from her.

Diana set down the book she'd been attempting to read and waited.

Thorne took a long swallow of brandy and then met her gaze. "So where do you want me to begin?" he asked simply.

Relieved that he understood her need and that she wouldn't have to fight to drag the information out of him, Diana smiled faintly. "I suppose you should start with the unknown element in this mystery. Who is Thomas Forrester, and why does he want you dead?"

"He's Venus's older brother. I first learned of his existence from the administrator of the girl's orphanage in Rye. As for his motives, I presume he dislikes the fact that I've been investigating his possible treason. Our government has long suspected him of collaborating with the French."

"Nathaniel suspected him also? He mentioned French spies in his letter to you."

Thorne grimaced. "Yes, there's no question now. Nathaniel was on Thomas Forrester's trail last spring. I spent the past four days in Sussex confirming it— and tracing Forrester's footsteps. Last fall he was nearly arrested for treason, but then he reportedly perished in a fire when his lodging house burned down. Today was the first inkling I've had that he was still alive. I now realize why."

Diana was silent for a long moment while she searched Thorne's face. "Do you mean to tell me about the Guardians?"

Thorne's body went very still as he eyed her warily. "I swore an oath of secrecy, Diana."

"I presumed as much. It's long been clear to me that you're hiding a deeper secret than merely the motive for Nathaniel's murder. You are intent on foiling some sort of wider intrigue, aren't you? Was Nathaniel a Guardian? I think I deserve to know," she added softly when he remained mute.

Roughly Thorne ran a hand through his hair and finally exhaled a sigh. Diana did deserve to know why Nathaniel had been killed, and why he himself was in danger now. Not only had she proved herself, but he'd come to trust and respect her abilities and judgment. Yet he still had to preserve his oath to the order.

"I cannot tell you much. There are too many lives at risk. Once we're wed, it will be a different matter."

She hesitated at that. "What *can* you tell me? You don't just work for the Foreign Office, do you?"

"No. We're a centuries-old order, established to fight tyranny and evil. A society of protectors, if you will, charged with upholding a noble cause. We keep our existence clandestine, since revealing our activities could destroy our effectiveness and imperil not only our members but those we aid. That's really all I can say about it."

Although Diana frowned, she seemed prepared to accept his explanation. "Does your Aunt Hennessy know about the Guardians?"

"No, she knows nothing of it. She thinks I perform a few commissions now and then for the Foreign Office and for Sir Gawain Olwen, but she has no notion that I'm one of Sir Gawain's chief representatives in London."

"What about your father?"

Thorne's mouth quirked in a wry smile. "Oh, yes, my father knows I joined the order. In fact, he's the one who sent me to Sir Gawain in the first place, because he thought I needed redeeming."

A flicker of amusement crossed Diana's features as she scrutinized him. "And were you redeemed?"

"For the most part. As an outsider, my father isn't privy to our secrets, but he does realize that what I do is often dangerous—which is the prime reason he's so set on me marrying and siring an heir." His smile fading, Thorne leaned forward, his own gaze intense. "I believe in our cause, Diana. I would die for it. But I can't share any more details."

The troubled look she gave him suggested she wanted to press him, but she refrained. "So what do you intend to do now?"

Silently blessing her, Thorne leaned back in his chair. "There is a strong likelihood that Forrester means to kill Sir Gawain, and I must stop him."

"Kill Sir Gawain?" Diana asked in alarm.

Thorne nodded. "I'm certain he will attempt it at some point. Forrester has long wanted revenge against the Guardians, and I expect he considers this his last chance."

"But how can you stop him?"

"By reaching Cyrene before he does. I've ordered my ship made ready to sail tomorrow night with the tide. My schooner is undoubtedly faster than anything Forrester could command, but he will have nearly a week's head start. And it would be helpful to confirm that's where he is headed. At the moment, Yates is scouring London shipping agents, trying to discover if Forrester booked passage on any packets destined for the Mediterranean or perhaps hired his own vessel. We haven't time to check any other ports such as Falmouth or Southhampton."

"Then you are leaving tomorrow evening?"

Thorne heard the dismay in her voice and felt his heart warm. "That's the soonest my crew can be assembled. I only hope I reach Cyrene before Forrester does. Sir Gawain has been like a father to me—more so than my own illustrious sire, in fact. I could never forgive myself if I allowed his murder."

"Of course not," Diana murmured. Her gaze turned even more troubled as another thought apparently occurred to her. "I suppose Venus sailed with her brother? That is why she hasn't been seen for days?"

"That's my best guess, yes. Like Thomas, she blames the Guardians for killing her parents. You remember how bitter she was even after all these years. She may be just as guilty as her brother. In fact, it's probable they were working together to lure Nathaniel to his death."

"But she didn't want you to be killed, her bruisers said so."

"Perhaps she bears a fondness for me—or more likely, for you. But I doubt her affection extends to Sir Gawain."

To his surprise, Diana rose slowly and moved to stand before him, looking down at him with dark intensity. "I want to go with you, Thorne."

His eyebrow shot up. "To Cyrene?"

"Yes. I am involved in this, whether you like it or not. Nathaniel was my cousin, and Venus my friend. And you are—" She broke off, pressing her lips together.

"I am what?" he prodded, wondering if her unfinished sentence was, *You are my lover.*

Diana shrugged. "I just don't like to think of you facing a murderer alone."

"I will hardly be alone. Yates will be with me, and so will my crew. And I have always been able to take care of myself."

"Even so, I would go mad waiting here, not knowing what might be befalling you."

Setting down his brandy, Thorne got to his feet and studied Diana's expression. She was worried for him—that much was clear—and wanted to protect him. "What about your art? You're just now starting to make a name for yourself. And you're to begin classes at the Academy next week, not to mention that you'll disappoint all your new patrons. If you leave now, your career is bound to suffer."

"I expect so, but this is far more important. I can try to resurrect my career when I return."

For a moment Thorne stood there debating. He didn't want Diana exposed to any more danger, certainly. But merely letting her sail with him was no grave risk. Once they reached the island, he would make certain she remained safe and out of harm's way.

And the prospect of being without her for at least a month while he traveled to Cyrene and back was damned unappealing. He also didn't like the thought of her remaining here and facing the ton's wolves alone. Moreover, he couldn't be certain that she would be willing to honor their betrothal by the time he returned.

A more seductive thought occurred to him: he could use the time together to convince Diana to wed him for real. Two weeks together onboard a ship would give him the chance to put his most persuasive talents to the test.

In fact, he could begin right now, Thorne realized. Just now he wanted nothing more than to kiss her, to taste her sweet lips and claim her body and reassure himself that she was still his.

He reached up and touched her cheek. "Very well, you may come with me on one condition."

"What condition?"

"That you stay here with me tonight."

Her gaze sharpened, and she looked as if she might refuse. But Thorne slipped his hand behind her nape, determined not to take no for an answer.

"I intend to make love to you tonight, Diana. I haven't seen you in days, and I've been burning for you the entire time."

"Thorne—" she began, before he cut her off with a brief, feather-soft kiss.

The fire that leapt between them told him more than words how much she wanted him.

Raising his head, Thorne surveyed the indecision on her beautiful face. "Can you honestly say you don't want to stay with me tonight?"

"No, I can't say that," she whispered, raising her lips to his with a sigh of reluctant surrender.

Twenty

He took her hand and led her upstairs to his darkened bedchamber. The moment Thorne shut the door behind him, Diana was in his arms, as eager as he.

The intensity of her passion didn't surprise him. Physical danger was an aphrodisiac, and the emotional turmoil of their discoveries this afternoon had sparked a harsh reminder of just how precious life was. Moreover, the time they'd spent apart had only heightened their need for each other.

Just as passionately, Thorne captured Diana's mouth in a fierce kiss. His thrusting tongue met hers hungrily, but he knew he wouldn't stop until he was plunging deep and tight inside her body. His own body flared with raw desire. He wanted Diana so intensely, the pain was a raw ache inside him.

Forcibly he tried to slow his ravenous hunger as he drew back in order to undress her. They removed each other's clothing impatiently and then came together again on the high bed.

"I need to feel you," he whispered hoarsely, reaching his hands up to cup her bare breasts.

The ripe flesh overflowed in his palms as he dipped

his head to suckle one taut nipple. Diana responded with a sharp moan, writhing against him with an urgency that couldn't be denied.

"Have you missed this as much as I have?" Thorne muttered, already knowing the answer even before she drew him back up to her for another feverish kiss.

It was the only invitation Thorne required. An agony of longing swept over him. He wanted to drive himself into her until they were both mindless with intolerable pleasure. Wanted to impale her till he drowned in her.

Shifting his weight to cover her, he eased between her spread thighs. Then he sank in hard, filling her to the brink. With a sob, Diana arched her back to draw him in even more completely, her hips moving in a rhythm that was ancient and mindless.

A score of frantic heartbeats later, their world crumbled apart in flaming pieces. As Diana cried out beneath him, Thorne convulsed around her, claiming and conquering and worshiping her all at once.

Afterward he lay heavy and spent upon her, gasping for breath.

When finally the flames cooled, Thorne wearily rolled away, taking Diana with him so that she curled against him. Not knowing whether to curse or laugh, he stared unseeing at the dark canopy overhead, bewildered by his inexplicable loss of control.

He'd been as much at the mercy of his body as Diana had been of hers. More so, probably. He'd deliberately given no thought to sponges or anything else in his desperate need to have her. Or perhaps he'd simply wanted to bind her to him any way he could.

Thorne squeezed his eyes shut. What the devil happened to him every time he took her? What made him feel this fierce want, this intense craving to bury himself so deeply inside her that he could never pull free?

Only with her had he ever experienced this fervent, overwhelming desire, so rich, so potent that it took control of his senses, his body . . . his heart.

Sweet hell—was that what ailed him? Had he become smitten with Diana?

The possibility dismayed Thorne, in part because it was so damned unexpected.

How had he allowed her to slip past all his defenses? He thought of his past lovers, their seductive charms, the endless ways they'd tried to please him, but not one of them had ever succeeded in arousing such a stark hunger in him without even trying, the way Diana did. Not one of them had ever made him feel this ravenous and obsessed.

His fingers clenched involuntarily around a silken tress of her hair as he contemplated the hitherto inconceivable mortality of his bachelorhood.

Was it possible that he had met his match in Diana?

She was remarkable, certainly; he'd known that from the very first. He could think of few other women who would have confronted Venus's brute of a henchman at gunpoint. Fewer still who would have insisted on accompanying him to follow the trail of a killer and try to prevent another possible murder.

And none that he truly wanted for his bride, the way he wanted Diana.

Whenever his father had pressed marriage on him, he'd always claimed he was waiting for the right woman. Someone worthy of being a Guardian's mate. Someone who would face danger at his side.

Diana was that kind of woman.

Even so, he'd never thought anyone could make him actually *want* to give up his freedom. In all the years of eluding the marriage traps set for him, he'd never been the least susceptible to love.

But tonight had shown him his own frightening vulnerability to her. He'd wanted to claim her, to make her his own, to lose himself in her, fully, without reservations, and to keep her with him always.

Thorne swore again silently, stunned by the realization. The damnable truth was, he'd become possessed by a woman who might never be able to love him in return. Diana had been so hurt and betrayed by her first love years ago that she'd vowed never to surrender to any other man.

Even without that impediment, Thorne acknowledged grimly, he had to question his ability to win her. What had he ever done to make Diana want to give him her heart? She thought him a rake, a reckless rebel, interested only in his own pleasure.

But what would it take to earn her respect, to prove himself worthy of her love? And what if he couldn't manage it?

A feeling oddly like panic swept over Thorne.

Ruthlessly stifling it, he tilted Diana's face up to his and bent his head, seeking her lips. He refused to consider defeat.

For now he would concentrate on deliberately rousing her hunger, trying to make Diana as savagely obsessed as he himself was.

The following day was a whirlwind for Diana, yet she was grateful for the activity, since it kept her from dwelling on her decision to accompany Thorne to Cyrene.

Doubtless it was mad to risk being in such close proximity to him for so long when her heart was so vulnerable. But the deplorable truth was, she couldn't bear to give him up just yet.

If he were to sail without her, she would find it impossible to endure the uncertainty of waiting, never knowing what danger he might be in or when he might return, worrying that he would do something wild and reckless if she was not beside him. An absurd notion, perhaps, but she felt the vague conviction that if she was with him, she could somehow watch over him.

She had other strong reasons for going, as well. She earnestly wanted justice for her cousin Nathaniel. And she wanted to do everything in her power to prevent Sir Gawain from being harmed or even killed. Although Thorne hadn't been able to tell her much about the Guardians, the idea of a secret society of protectors championing a noble cause had caught fire in her imagination. It also explained a great deal about Nathaniel's death and strangely made his loss easier to bear, knowing he'd been performing a laudable duty for his country.

Her new discovery increased her admiration for Thorne, as well, but despite the risks to her heart, Diana had no intention of changing her mind.

She distracted herself by keeping busy the entire day—canceling her sittings for the next month and composing an apology to Sir George Enderly of the British Academy, pleading urgent business that required her absence from town. Next, she arranged for her servants to care for her house and paintings, and packed her trunks with clothing and art supplies for the voyage.

When that was completed, she called on Amy, needing to say farewell in person.

Amy was out shopping when Diana arrived, however, so she took her leave of Lady Hennessy, explaining that she was returning to Cyrene with Thorne and John Yates to settle a lingering problem with her late cousin Nathaniel's affairs.

After an hour of restless waiting, Diana finally penned a note for Amy, keenly regretting that she'd missed seeing her cousin. Then Diana hurried home to change. They would board Thorne's schooner before sunset, since the tide was expected to go out shortly afterward, and she couldn't chance being late.

In her absence, Thorne had sent a dray to take her trunks to the ship. Diana was ready and waiting by six o'clock when he arrived in his town coach to escort her to the London docks.

His expression was grim, Diana saw at once, but she waited until Thorne had handed her inside and the carriage moved off before asking if he'd had any success learning more about Thomas Forrester's intentions.

"Unfortunately, yes," Thorne replied. "Yates was able to confirm that Forrester hired a brigantine and crew and set sail last Thursday night, bound for the Mediterranean. I suspect it was no small feat for Forrester to find a seaworthy vessel, considering how many ships our government has employed for transporting troops to Europe."

Diana nodded somberly in comprehension. In the past month, she'd read numerous accounts in the papers regarding the latest developments in Napoleon Bonaparte's return to power. When the Corsican Monster had mustered another vast army with the aim of conquering Belgium, the Allies had joined forces in hopes of crushing him again, sending troops and munitions to Europe under the commands of General Lord Wellington and Prussia's Marshal Blucher. Thorne was convinced there would be a war soon, one that could likely be as bloody as any battles that had gone before.

But Diana's fear over a possible war that she had no power to prevent was less immediate than her dread at the danger Forrester presented.

"So you think Forrester means to kill Sir Gawain if he can?"

"I have little doubt of it now," Thorne said tersely.

"But will we reach Cyrene before Forrester does?"

"Possibly. My schooner was designed for speed and can make the voyage in two weeks, while his should take three or more. So barring storms, we may very well catch him."

The thought barely comforted Diana, for Thorne's grim tone seemed to suggest there was as good a chance they would be too late.

She was glad for the distraction when they arrived at the London docks, which were a scene of bustling activity. John Yates was already onboard the schooner waiting, she saw as they made their way up the gangplank. His expression grave, he supervised the loading of their baggage and her art trunks.

Diana spent the next few minutes settling into her cabin, then returned above deck and found a spot at the railing, out of the way of the scurrying crew as they dealt with sails and lines and cargo while preparing to depart.

After perhaps another quarter hour, they were about to disengage the gangway when Diana saw a heavily laden carriage barrelling along the docks below at an unsafe speed. A familiar blond head hung out the window—a girl obviously searching all the ships at anchor.

It was her cousin Amy, Diana realized with a sense of shock.

Amy let out a shriek when she spied Diana onboard the schooner, and abruptly the carriage came to a rollicking halt. Instantly the girl sprang out, waving the bonnet clutched in her hand.

"Wait! You must wait for me!" she cried, hurrying forward.

She bounded awkwardly onto the gangway, nearly bowling over a seaman in her haste to board, and ran the length of the plank till she could leap down onto the deck.

"I am going with you!" Amy panted, attempting to catch her breath.

Halfway across the ship, John Yates moved toward her, a look of astonishment on his face.

Thorne, too, strode across the deck and reached the girl at the same time Diana did. Yet Amy only had eyes for Yates.

"What are you doing here?" the former cavalry officer demanded, scowling suspiciously now. "We are about to set sail."

"I know, Diana's note told me so," Amy answered. "But I want to accompany you."

"That is out of the question. We have dangerous business to attend to."

"John, please . . . You were right, I was a wretched brat, I know. But I can be better, I promise. If you will only forgive me."

When he only eyed Amy warily, she turned a pleading gaze to Thorne. "Please, I swear to you, I've come to my senses. You see, I've realized that I love John. And I can't bear to live without him."

Diana's eyes widened at her cousin's declaration, while one of Thorne's eyebrows shot up.

"What about your Season?" Thorne asked skeptically. "What of all the other beaux you've kept dancing to your tune?"

"The devil take my Season," Amy declared emphatically. "I don't care a fig for London society or any of my other suitors. I care only for John. All I want is to be his wife and live with him on Cyrene—if he can ever forgive me for treating him and everyone else so abominably."

Thorne suddenly looked amused. "Was that a proposal of marriage you just made him, brat?"

"Yes. If he will have me."

Amy turned back to Yates, who was staring at her now, dumbfounded. "It doesn't matter if you don't love me yet, John. I am willing to wait. I will *make* you love me." When he didn't reply, she cast a worried glance up at her guardian. "*Please,* Thorne, may I go with you to Cyrene?"

"If Yates will take full responsibility for you, then yes, I suppose you may come."

Amy gave a glad little shriek and looked hopefully at her true love.

Diana, despite her surprise, smiled to see John Yates's expression. The wonder and joy on his face suggested he would ultimately surrender, if he hadn't already. But it was clear Amy would always lead him on a merry chase.

"Well?" the girl demanded when he still remained mute. "Will you marry me or not?"

John cleared his throat. "Yes," he said hoarsely. "You know very well that I love you, that I've been besotted with you since we first met. And I could ask for nothing more than to have you for my wife."

"Hurry then," Thorne ordered Amy, "and see to your baggage. We have to sail with the tide."

Amy, however, paid him no attention, for she was too occupied with flinging herself into John's arms and kissing him madly in front of the entire crew and highly diverted audience.

Twenty-one

Unlike her first voyage to Cyrene, this one filled Diana with a sense of urgency and danger that left her tense and restless. But her trepidation was briefly tempered two nights later when Amy and John were married by the schooner's captain.

Helping her cousin dress before the ceremony, Diana experienced a swell of maternal pride when the girl stood garbed in a jonquil crepe gown, her blond curls laced with ribbons and pearls.

"You look beautiful," Diana pronounced, eyeing Amy's glowing face and feeling a lump form in her throat at this bittersweet moment. Amy was her only family, but that responsibility was now coming to an end. John Yates would care for her from this point forward.

Even so, Diana felt she had to ask. "You are certain this marriage is what you want, Amy? You will be living on Cyrene and are bound to miss England and home."

The girl nodded emphatically. "I know I will miss home. And I will miss you more than anything, Diana. But John says we can return to England yearly.

And I know with absolute certainty that I would be miserable living without him." Amy wrinkled her pert nose. "I can't imagine what I ever saw in Reginald Kneighly. John is ten times the man Reggie is, even if he *is* missing a leg. Thank heavens I finally came to my senses."

Diana couldn't help but smile at yet one more indication that Amy was growing up. But still the girl was very young.

"Amy, about the marriage bed . . . You have no mother to advise you, so if you have questions . . . I could attempt to answer them."

Unexpectedly shy, Amy ducked her head, hiding her blushing cheeks. "I am sure John will show me whatever I need to know. I have every faith in him. But I thank you, Diana, for your concern and for everything else you have done for me." Closing the distance, she took Diana's hands. "Can you ever forgive me? I was so horrid to you. It was criminal of me, stealing that painting of Thorne."

"I told you it's forgiven and forgotten," Diana replied lightly, accepting Amy's humble apology for the fourth time since they had set sail. "And I hope you realize now that I had only your best interests at heart. I only want you to be happy, dearest."

"I will be, I have no doubt. And I hope that when you marry Thorne, you will be as happy with him as I am with John."

Diana felt her heart twist. Now that her cousin's future was settled, there was no longer any reason to continue her betrothal to Thorne.

And she would have to tell him so without delay, Diana sternly admonished herself. Perhaps tonight, directly after the wedding. The sooner she set Thorne free, the sooner she could attempt to heal the pain in her aching heart and try to embrace a new future without him.

A future that was looking bleaker by the moment.

The simple marriage ceremony was over quickly, and afterward, the wedding party shared an excellent dinner in the captain's quarters and drank numerous toasts to the young couple's future happiness.

The wine helped bolster Diana's courage, yet by the end of the evening, her nerves had grown taut. Then the captain proposed a final dismaying toast—to Lord Thorne's happiness in his impending nuptials. When she felt Thorne's gaze settle on her, she knew she had to act.

As the company dispersed to retire to their respective cabins, Diana waylaid Thorne and asked to speak to him in private. Knowing better than to allow him into her cabin, she chose to go above deck and brave a blustery sea wind in order to deliver her pronouncement. When she moved to stand at the port railing, he joined her.

Diana took a deep breath to steel her emotions and launched into her prepared speech. Although she could see Thorne's face in the glimmer of moonlight, she couldn't tell from his impassive expression what he was thinking when she explained that since Amy was now safely wed, there was no longer any reason for their charade and that she considered their betrothal at an end.

Thorne remained silent for a long moment before murmuring his reply. "I agree. With Amy's future settled, there is no longer any reason for our charade."

Diana's fingers clenched involuntarily on the railing. She had expected—even hoped for?—a great deal more resistance from him. "Did you hear me? I am terminating our betrothal."

"Yes, I heard you. You are jilting me."

At his congenial tone, a tightness constricted her throat. Absurdly she had wanted Thorne to argue, to refuse to allow her to end their engagement.

Swallowing forcibly, Diana strove to keep her own response light. "I am *not* jilting you. I am simply ending this foolish masquerade. I should think you would be grateful to be let off the hook. You never wanted to wed anyone. And you certainly don't want to be forced into matrimony simply because you feel you compromised my reputation."

"Perhaps," Thorne replied. "Although I was becoming rather accustomed to the notion of having you for my wife."

"You will quickly become unaccustomed, no doubt," Diana murmured. "Without me for an encumbrance, you can freely return to your former licentious life. I am absolving you of all responsibility for me, Thorne."

A muscle flexed in his jaw, but otherwise, he merely caught her hand and raised her fingers to his lips, giving Diana a careless smile. "You are right, there is nothing whatever forcing us to wed."

His ready capitulation flooded Diana with a feeling of misery, leaving a fierce ache in her chest. "Very well, then . . . good night," she managed to say without faltering.

Cursing her foolish heart then, she turned abruptly and made her way to her cabin, aware that Thorne's gaze was following her all the while.

Although she was confident she had made the wisest choice, the remainder of the voyage proved difficult for Diana. Her proximity to Thorne was a prime reason. Despite the severance of their betrothal, he acted no differently from his usual charming, captivating self, and she found it a continual struggle to resist his tantalizing allure.

She had to keep forcibly reminding herself why she'd been right to end their engagement. Being tied together in a marriage where the attachment was only one-sided would be unbearable for them both. For Thorne, it would likely lead to resentment and perhaps even disdain. For her, it would be a sure path to devastating heartbreak, to be hopelessly in love with her husband when her affections weren't returned.

Yet even though Diana knew she should feel relief at ending their relationship, she couldn't prevent a dark melancholy from settling over her during the rest of their two-week journey, a feeling almost of despair. Nor could she forget that this voyage would be her last time with Thorne.

It didn't help, either, that she was constantly aware of their purpose for being on the ship, and that she felt a constant nagging dread—both at the possibility of failure and at the danger Thorne might face when they arrived.

Her apprehension only grew as they sailed through the Strait of Gibraltar and the choppy gray waters of the Atlantic gave way to the warmer, calmer blue Mediterranean. Even if Thorne's schooner was much faster than a normal ship, the Forresters had still had nearly a week's head start. Diana attempted to keep busy with her painting, but her heart had never been less engaged in her work.

And then they sighted their quarry.

They were barely a day out from Cyrene, according to the captain, when a shout from the lookout posted in the rigging spotted a ship ahead. It was another half day before the captain could tell with a spyglass that they were trailing a brigantine.

When she heard the news, Diana felt her stomach lurch. "Is that Forrester's ship?" she asked Thorne anxiously as they stood watching at the prow railing.

"I'd lay odds it is. At this rate, he should make Cyrene's harbor tomorrow morning."

"Will we catch him?"

Thorne's jaw tightened. "It will be damned close."

A coldness seized Diana, despite her best efforts to quell it, and filled her with a dark foreboding about what the morrow would bring.

She went to Thorne that night. She couldn't stay away. Once they reached Cyrene, she knew anything might happen, and the potential peril left her unnerved. She needed Thorne's magical touch to soothe her dread.

Even more, Diana admitted to herself, she felt an aching need to store up just one more memory of him to last her all the lonely days ahead.

When Thorne answered her knock on his cabin door, he showed no surprise to see her standing there. Silently he moved aside to let her enter, and then shut the door softly behind her.

"I couldn't sleep," Diana whispered.

"Nor could I."

He was still fully clothed and had been reading, she realized. A lamp next to the bunk cast a warm glow over the small cabin and showed the bedcovers were still drawn up.

He didn't question her explanation but merely drew her into his arms for a devastating kiss, instantly stirring the fires of arousal to life.

Still wordlessly, he undressed her and shed his own clothing before joining her on the narrow bunk. As their naked flesh met, a fierce heat and desperate longing to cherish him spread throughout Diana's body. Her limbs clinging, she took him inside her, straining to become even closer.

Thorne fed her fire with the flames of his own desire, and passion converged into burning enchantment. Soon the ecstasy became more than she could bear, and she climaxed with a wild, sobbing cry.

When she shattered, Thorne felt each tremor burn through him with an exquisite torture. Heart racing, blood pounding, he thrust more urgently, delving into her body, trying to satisfy the hunger that went so deep, he didn't think it would ever be satisfied.

How will I ever get enough of you? The question thundered in his mind as rapture screamed through his body.

When finally she lay quietly in his arms, their limbs entangled, his hands stroking down her silken back, he pondered the answer.

The simple truth was that he could never get enough of Diana.

When she'd broken off their betrothal early in their voyage, he had panicked for a brief moment. But then he'd forcibly recovered, reminding himself that her withdrawal was only a temporary setback. He'd pretended to accept her rationale, but there wasn't a chance in hell he would let Diana go. He would fight tooth and claw to claim her for his own.

Nothing would stop him. In the end, he would have her for his wife. And he would win her love, just as she had won his. . . .

Thorne's breath caught abruptly as he acknowledged the profound feeling wrenching at his chest.

Love. It was the only possible word to describe the fierce, overwhelming tenderness that had wrapped around his heart. The powerful, stunning emotion he hadn't even known he possessed.

Without a doubt, he loved Diana.

He lay there stunned, holding her and marveling at the realization.

How had it happened? When he'd proposed their sham betrothal, he'd had his course all planned out. Their pretense would shelter him from his father's machinations and the unwanted attentions of countless scheming mamas and their nubile daughters.

He'd never once expected to be ensnared by love.

Yet it had been a serious mistake to think he could be intimate with Diana and remain immune to her. He should have known from the very first. What happened each time he touched her was beyond his experience, and beyond his ability to prevent.

Against all odds, he'd lost his heart to her. Because of Diana herself.

He'd been waiting his whole life for her, although he hadn't realized it. His burning need for her had always been about so much more than physical passion. She had taken hold of him in a way that was far beyond desire, in a way he could no longer control.

She satisfied his soul-deep hunger. She filled the emptiness inside him and made him feel whole.

He wanted Diana in his life—needed her in his life—forever. And he was willing to do whatever it took to make her feel the same way. He would be truly terrified if he thought she could never love him in return, but he wouldn't allow it—

The tension in his body must have communicated itself to her, for just then he felt her shudder. Turning her head slightly, Diana buried her face against the bare skin of his chest.

The tender, anxious gesture tightened his chest even more, yet Thorne took a steadying breath, willing himself to be calm. "What's wrong, love?"

Her quiet admission was a long time in coming. "I am afraid of what could happen tomorrow, Thorne. I'm afraid for *you*."

"Why would you be afraid for me?"

Pushing herself up on one elbow, Diana gazed down at him, her expression grave and troubled. "If we do catch Thomas Forrester, what then? He wants you dead."

Thorne's lips curved. "Well, he isn't going to get his wish, I assure you."

"Even so . . . it frightens me to think of the danger you might face. I know you are fearless, but please, Thorne, will you promise to be careful? I don't want you to risk being killed like Nathaniel was."

Reaching up, he brushed a dark tendril back from her forehead. "Danger is an inherent part of my job, love. It can't be avoided. But I promise I won't take any unnecessary risks. Trust me, I'm not eager for an untimely demise. Never more so than now. I want to live to a ripe old age."

It was true, Thorne thought, more than a little amazed. In the past he had never shied away from physical risk; indeed, he'd actually *sought* it. He never felt more alive than when he was challenging fate and facing perils that would make normal men quake.

Yet for the first time he could remember, he no longer wanted to court danger simply for the thrill of it. Life had suddenly become quite precious to him. Possibly because he now had something else to live for besides the satisfaction of triumphing over evil: Diana.

He had every intention of staying alive. Not only didn't he want to die, but he'd sworn he would never betray her. If he allowed himself to be killed, it would be much the same as jilting her. He would leave Diana alone and forsaken, and that would be unforgivable.

Slipping a hand behind the rich curtain of her hair, Thorne drew her face down to his and pressed a tender kiss against her lips. "You are not about to lose me," he vowed solemnly.

Yet when he wrapped his arms about her tightly, he felt Diana shudder again and knew he hadn't totally reassured her.

Diana returned to her own cabin just after midnight, somewhat calmer, but she was up early the next morning, anxious to discover the results of their chase. When she went up on deck, Thorne was already there at the prow, holding a spyglass to his eye, watching the brigantine ahead.

During the night they had closed the distance between the two ships, and Diana could clearly see the outline of the brigantine's three masts. An hour later she could even make out figures of the crew scurrying over the decks and in the rigging. The brigantine apparently had raised every square yard of sail to achieve maximum speed.

The schooner's captain had done the same, and they were gaining slowly but surely. Yet Thorne still doubted they would catch their quarry before it made harbor—a pronouncement that brought Diana's trepidation rushing back full measure.

An hour after that, the Isle of Cyrene was sighted. From a distance, Diana could see the silhouette of

Cyrene's two forested mountain peaks to the north, dominating the rugged, picturesque coastline.

The island still possessed an unmistakable enchantment, shimmering in the golden Mediterranean sun, surrounded by the jeweled colors of a dazzling sea—sapphire and turquoise and aquamarine. Yet every inch was protected by natural or man-made defenses: jagged, soaring cliffs, rocky reefs, numerous fortresses and watchtowers, all significant deterrents to invasion.

By the time they neared the island's southern point, Yates had joined them, as had Amy, her face grave. Amy had been told the basic situation—that Thomas Forrester and his sister Venus were set on harming Sir Gawain—and she seemed as anxious as Diana to arrive.

"Sir Gawain lives there," Yates said, pointing to the massive castle stronghold on the bluffs to their left. "Olwen Castle has been in his family for centuries."

"Will he know we are coming?" Diana asked quietly.

Thorne answered her question. "There will be lookouts posted in several towers around the island, watching for arriving ships. But the brigantine is flying a British flag, so they won't expect treachery from that quarter. Sir Gawain won't know to beware of Forrester. We're sending a message by heliostat as we speak—that's an instrument using sunlight and mirrors to flash a code—but it's possible the sentry at Olwen Castle may not see it."

"We won't make it in time, will we?" Amy observed in a small voice.

Thorne replied grimly. "No. We're at least an hour behind."

The brigantine was no longer in sight.

with a sinking heart. It had already rounded the southernmost tip.

"What is our plan, my lord?" Yates asked calmly, exhibiting every faith in Thorne's leadership.

"I'll pursue Forrester as soon as we arrive," Thorne answered, "and try to catch him before he reaches the castle."

"We may still have a chance," Yates declared. "Surely Forrester isn't familiar with the island. He will need time to arrange for transportation—a ferry from the ship to the docks and horses to take them into the interior. And he will have to inquire about the location of Sir Gawain's castle and then gain entrance."

Thorne shook his head. "The brigantine's captain or crew may have been to Cyrene before. And we must assume Forrester came prepared. Remember, he's had more than a year to plan his assault. He likely has maps and details about his destination. As for gaining entrance, couriers arrive regularly to bring Sir Gawain information. If I were Forrester, I would simply claim I'm on an urgent mission for Sir Gawain."

Yates frowned in comprehension. "And Forrester is aware of the need for speed. He knows we are directly behind him."

"Precisely. It would be miraculous if we found him still onboard the brigantine. But we'll know more once reach the harbor. I want to wait until then iding our exact plan."

nsion returned at his pronouncement, ed as they rounded the island and approx rt, which was also well defended. lue waters gave way to shallower green flecked with white, indicating more treacherous reefs.

To access the small harbor, the schooner had to navigate a narrow strait formed by two jutting rock promontories, while overhead guarding the entrance stood a massive fortress fortified with cannon.

It was not all ruggedness, however. The bustling town perched precariously on the hillside held an enchanting charm characteristic of the Mediterranean, its whitewashed houses colorfully accented by splashes of blue trim and roofs of red tile, shaded by tall palms and draped with bougainvillea. A steep cobblestone lane zigzagged down the hill face to the water, where gulls and terns swooped among the bare masts of countless fishing vessels moored at the docks.

The much larger brigantine was lying at anchor some distance from shore, Diana could see as they sailed into the harbor. But Thorne's attention was riveted on the quay.

He brought the spyglass to his eye for a moment, then silently handed the instrument to Yates.

"I see a party of men climbing the hill," Yates murmured. "Most likely Forrester and some of his crew."

Following his gaze, Diana could make out at least a dozen figures scurrying up the steep lane, toward the gleaming white walls of the town.

"I don't see any women," Yates added thoughtfully.

"Venus may have remained on the brigantine," Thorne replied. "You'll need to board and check while I follow Forrester."

"As you wish," the younger man said, before ca[s]t-ing a swift glance at his pretty new wife. "W[hat of] Amy and Diana?"

Thorne answered without hesitation. "They will stay here where it's safe."

Just then the schooner's captain barked out orders for the crew to begin lowering sails. Diana waited till the shouts had died down before placing a hand on Thorne's arm. "I would like to go with John. If Venus is there, I may be able to persuade her to confide in me, once she knows the game is up."

Thorne's gaze flickered over Diana, and she could see him mentally debating.

"Please," she implored. "I want to help."

"Very well," Thorne agreed. "Yates, you'll take Diana and suitable reinforcements. And you'll go armed to the teeth. I expect you to keep her safe."

"Certainly, my lord. And if we find Madam Venus onboard?"

"You'll arrest her and the captain, as well. I don't want that ship trying to escape," Thorne said as their own ship began slowing. "Once you deal with them, you can follow me. Meanwhile I'll take some men and find Verra so he can accompany me to the castle. And we'll raise an alarm and send for reinforcements to meet us there."

Diana bit her lower lip. She would rather Yates go with Thorne than her, to keep *him* safe. But with only one leg, the younger man might be more of an impediment than an asset. And the need for haste was imperative. Forrester's party—if it was Forrester—had already disappeared over the crest of the hill.

"What about me?" Amy interrupted. "May I

grinned at her. "I applaud your courage,
you'll stay right here and behave your-
to have to worry about you, too."

sion on her face, Amy started to

bristle, but her husband gave her a soft smile, and immediately the girl melted.

"Very well, Thorne, I will follow your orders. And I promise to behave."

Yates offered Amy his hand. "Come, my dear, quickly. I will help you get settled, and then I must make preparations."

When he had led her away, Diana turned to Thorne. "Who is Verra?"

"Santos Verra? He's a Spaniard, a former smuggler who owns a tavern in town."

"Is he one of your colleagues?"

Thorne's expression softened. "Yes. And I would trust him with my life. In fact I have, many times."

Feeling her fear for Thorne welling anew, Diana wanted to plead again with him to be careful. Yet she quelled the urge, knowing he didn't need the distraction.

He apparently saw the struggle on her face, though, for he brought her hand to his lips for a lingering kiss. "If you will try not to worry for me, I'll try to do the same for you. I'm allowing you to go with Yates because I understand your need to be involved, and because I think you could truly help. But every protective instinct I own is screaming in protest. Venus could be highly dangerous."

Realizing the concessions Thorne was making, Diana managed a smile. "Very well, I will try my best not to worry overmuch about you."

"Good. Now kiss me for luck, sweeting, before I go."

Not allowing her to resist, Thorne drew her close and covered her lips with his. Diana returned his fervent kiss with all the despairing passion roiling her.

When he finally released her, Thorne let out a ragged breath and swore. After searching her face one last time, he turned on his heel and strode away.

Numbly Diana watched him cross the deck to speak to the captain. Shortly, several of the crew members had circled around Thorne, evidently to receive their orders, and then dispersed to gather weapons and other gear.

The instant the schooner dropped anchor, they were ready. They first lowered a small rowboat from the deck to the water, then threw a rope ladder over the railing.

Her heart in her throat, Diana watched as Thorne dropped agilely over the side and negotiated the ladder, stepping into the boat. Five men climbed in after him, and in moments they were rowing powerfully toward the quay.

Just then, Yates spoke behind her. "Are you ready, Diana?"

Dragging her gaze from the rowboat, Diana turned to find John offering her a pistol.

She took a steadying breath and nodded. "As ready as I will ever be," she said, accepting the weapon and bolstering her courage for battle.

Twenty-two

$\mathcal{T}$*he moment* Thorne strode into the tavern at the top of the hill, he spied Santos Verra.

Immediately the swarthy Spaniard slipped away from his few customers and came forward, showing surprise but not questioning when he was ordered to alert the Guardians on the island and have them ride at once to Olwen Castle.

"I know Caro and Max are in Belgium," Thorne said urgently, "but who else is here?"

"Hawk is away on a mission," Verra replied, "but Ryder and Trey Deverill are present."

"Dev?" Thorne raised an eyebrow at learning the adventurer had returned after a long absence, but only added, "Send for Deverill and Ryder, then fetch some pistols and meet me at the stables."

Upon reaching the stables down the street with his five crew members, Thorne learned that an English gentleman had just hired nearly a dozen horses and paid in gold. Thorne quickly arranged for mounts for his own men, so that by the time Verra appea— few minutes later, bristling with weapons, th ready to set off.

As they rode swiftly from the town, heading toward the island's southern interior, Thorne explained the situation to Verra over the pounding sound of hoofbeats.

Grave concern furrowed the Spaniard's brow, his usual high humor missing as he observed, "Doubtless they are prepared to kill."

Nodding grimly, Thorne bent low over his mount's neck and spurred it to greater speed, while Verra did the same.

Their galloping horses passed countless groves of olive and citrus trees and acres of vineyards basking in the sun, and very shortly they reached the road to Olwen Castle. Both experienced horsemen, Thorne and Verra easily outpaced the seamen, and were a quarter mile ahead when they sighted the imposing stronghold in the distance. Bathed in sunlight, the massive castle glowed with golden warmth, an illusion that made it seem almost ethereal.

There was nothing ethereal, however, about the screeching, grinding sound Thorne heard. His stomach muscles clenched when he realized the ancient drawbridge was being raised.

"*Forrester!*" Thorne spat the word like an expletive.

"*Sí!*" Verra shouted, obviously coming to the same conclusion: Forrester was raising the heavy wooden bridge to foil any pursuit and to prevent anyone from entering the castle after them. They must have taken con___ of the gatehouse, probably by duping and ___owering the guard in the watchtower. The ___ants would have been unprepared for

___ his efforts, racing onward in the ___ the drawbridge in time to fling himself at the rising edge, but of course he was far too late. By the time he and Verra brought their sweating, panting horses to a sliding halt at the rim of the wide moat, the drawbridge had come to rest in a vertical position.

At the same instant the oak-grille portcullis of the gatehouse began falling to block the sole entrance to the castle—or to close off escape from within, Thorne suspected darkly.

He met Verra's gaze, thinking furiously. Even if they managed to swim the slime-filled moat, the walls were completely unscalable, and from the battlements overhead, their enemy could bring numerous weapons to bear upon them.

Just then the erratic sound of gunfire erupted from beyond the castle walls, followed by shouts and the agonized cries of men in pain.

Thorne gritted his teeth as he imagined what was happening. Sir Gawain's staff would have responded the moment they heard the unexpected screech of the drawbridge. But if they'd run unarmed into the bailey—the large courtyard between the castle walls and the main keep where the inhabitants lived—they would have made easy targets for Forrester's murderous attack.

And *he* was sitting out here helplessly—

A bullet zinged past his head, and Thorne ducked instinctively, realizing someone was shooting at him from the nearest tower. Cursing, he backed his horse away, signaling for Verra to do the same. Even the most advanced rifle couldn't fire accurately much more than a hundred yards.

The sound of galloping hooves behind him him that his five men had arrived—yet to n

"Keep back!" he shouted to the s

guard the drawbridge if it should be lowered. Don't let anyone escape."

Abruptly Thorne wheeled his horse to the left, motioning for Verra to follow. The castle had no sally ports, no entrance other than the main gate, so they had only one hope. Hidden in the rocky cliff face at the rear of the castle was a crevice that led to a secret passageway, which no one but the Guardians knew of and which was used only in dire need. Now obviously was that moment.

He rode swiftly alongside the moat with Verra hard on his heels. When they reached the southeast corner of the castle wall, the land ended in an almost sheer drop to the turquoise sea below.

Leaping off his horse, Thorne peered over the rocky ledge. "Can you make it?" he asked Verra.

The Spaniard's teeth flashed white in his swarthy face. "*Sí.* You needn't fear for me."

"What I fear is arriving too damned late to save Sir Gawain."

Dropping to his knees, Thorne studied the wall of the cliff, searching for footholds. He had been in the cramped tunnel only once, and knew the difficulty would be not only to avoid falling from the perilous cliff, but also to find the narrow opening in the rock.

Yet time was an even greater enemy. It would take precious time, perhaps a half hour or more, to climb down, locate the entrance, and negotiate the passageway that ended in the castle dungeons.

  the castle defenders could hold off For-
        and protect the baronet long enough
            side. If not . . .

            quelled a shudder as he carefully
            the rock ledge.

If not, then Sir Gawain could be long dead by the time they finally reached the castle keep.

Boarding the brigantine proved simple for Yates and his party, for the skeleton crew offered no resistance when he demanded their surrender in the name of the Crown and ensured compliance with an armed force. Diana's greatest difficulty, actually, was climbing from the small skiff and ascending the rope ladder encumbered by skirts.

Once onboard, they arrested the crew and searched the deck and then went below. As expected, they found no sign of Thomas Forrester. His sister, however, was in the last cabin, lying on the narrow bunk.

To Diana's shock and surprise, Venus had been bound and gagged.

Venus's astonishment was even more apparent at seeing Diana and Yates—or perhaps it was due more to the pistols they both had trained on her. The madam's eyes widened first in alarm, then relief as she struggled to sit up.

"May I remove her gag?" Diana asked Yates as he followed her into the cabin and shut the door behind them.

"Yes, but not her bindings. And be cautious. This may be some sort of trick."

Handing her pistol to Yates, Diana moved over to the bunk and used both hands to unknot the gag at the back of Venus's vivid red head.

"Thank God!" Venus exclaimed in a rasping voice.

"What sort of game are you playing, madam?" Yates demanded.

"It is no game." After clearing her throat, Venus worked her mouth, the corners of which had turned raw from the rag. "As you can see, I am not here by choice."

"Why *are* you here?" Diana asked.

Venus met her gaze unflinchingly. "Because I intervened where I wasn't wanted."

Her cryptic reply made Yates snap with impatience. "Pray explain yourself!"

She shot him a glare of defiance, but Diana could detect more than a trace of bitterness in her tone when she answered. "When I learned what my brother meant to do, I went down to the docks to try to stop him. He took me prisoner."

"Why would he do that?" Yates asked.

"Because he feared I would warn Lord Thorne about his intentions. Thomas didn't dare leave me free, so he locked me in a cabin and forced me to accompany him here to Cyrene. But you must have drawn your own conclusions or you wouldn't be here. You know Sir Gawain Olwen is in grave danger."

Yates looked a question at Diana, as if wondering whether to believe the madam's story. But the pleading emotion in Venus's green eyes was very convincing.

"I think she is telling the truth," Diana said quietly.

"I am prepared to hear her story," Yates conceded. "Well, madam?"

Venus responded with a question instead. "Is Lord Thorne with you? Did he . . . survive?"

Yates's jaw tightened. "Yes, he survived. Did you arrange for his murder?"

"No, of course not. It was Thomas who ordered my footmen to kill Lord Thorne. And he means to kill Sir Gawain now."

"We know."

"Then you have to stop him."

"Your brother is being dealt with at this very moment, madam. We are more interested in why he is so intent on assassinating Sir Gawain. And why he murdered Nathaniel Lunsford."

Her eyes lowering to her bound hands, Venus ran her tongue over her dry lips. "May I have a sip of water?"

"Of course," Diana said. Without waiting for Yates's approval, she went to the small desk and poured a cup of water from the pitcher there. Then she sat on the bunk and held the cup to Venus's chapped lips while she drank.

The madam flashed her a grateful smile. "I swear I didn't know my brother meant to kill Nathaniel. He did it completely without my knowledge. And later he tried to kill Thorne."

"But you are not entirely innocent, are you, madam?" Yates insisted in a hard voice. "You wanted the Guardians destroyed to avenge your parents' deaths."

"Yes." Her reply was merely a raw whisper. "But our plan was to let French agents perform whatever acts were required. Then Nathaniel Lunsford died. . . ." She faltered for a moment. "I couldn't stomach killing Lord Thorne in cold blood, or Sir Gawain either. I spent much of the voyage futilely trying to persuade my brother to abandon his violent plan."

Her imploring glance turned to Diana. "Please, you have to save Sir Gawain. He is in deadly danger. I know Thomas won't rest until he kills Sir Gawain, or he himself is dead."

And Thorne is dead, as well, Diana added silently, feeling a resurgence of the fear that had never left her.

She turned to Yates. "John . . . we have accomplished our task here. I want to go to Olwen Castle."

"Very well." He sent Venus a sharp look. "You will remain here, madam, until we return."

Venus offered him a bitter smile. "Certainly, sir. Trussed as I am, I am hardly in a position to do otherwise."

Climbing down the cliff face proved easier for Thorne and Verra than moving sideways, since to reach the hidden passage, they had to traverse a crumbling stretch of rock that was almost vertical.

Thorne inched his way along, clinging to scraggly clumps of bracken and rosemary that grew there haphazardly, searching for cracks large enough to allow purchase for his feet and wishing he'd thought to remove his boots before beginning the treacherous jaunt. The leather soles slipped more than once, forcing him to pause and regain his balance. And by the sounds of Verra's muttered curses, the Spaniard was not faring any better.

When finally they reached the safety of a narrow ledge, Thorne let out his breath and flexed his cramped fingers, before bending to claw at a formation of piled rocks that concealed the opening to the secret passage.

Removing the pile revealed the entrance—a crevice barely large enough for a man to crawl through. With a nod at Verra, Thorne squeezed inside first, on his hands and knees.

He found himself in a narrow, craggy tunnel. The ceiling was low and jagged, as were the walls, although the wet rock floor had been worn somewhat smooth by centuries of seepage.

The air smelled damp and musty, and by the time

he had crawled a half dozen yards, the temperature had dropped significantly and the light had completely disappeared, turning the tunnel pitch black.

It was like being buried in a cold, dark tomb. With no torches, Thorne had to trust his instincts, feeling blindly along the rock. After another twenty yards, by his count, he was suffering from aching knees, scraped palms, and a gash on his forehead where he'd banged into a sharp protrusion. Yet he forged onward.

In the blackness, the journey seemed endless, the minutes stretching like hours. The increasing tension knotting Thorne's muscles was only exacerbated by the uncertainty of not knowing what they would find when they finally reached the castle. And every passing moment merely heightened his awareness that Sir Gawain's time on earth was likely ticking away.

Thorne estimated they had been in the tunnel perhaps a quarter of an hour when he felt a surge of air on his face. He quickened his pace, and then regretted it when his head collided with a rock wall, sending a lance of pain spearing through him.

"Bloody hell," he swore roundly, realizing they had finally come to the end of the secret passage.

Behind him, Verra gave a low chuckle. "Surely you can be more inventive in your curses, my lord. Try this. . . ."

A string of foul expletives in Spanish followed, some obscene enough to blister the chill air of the tunnel.

Despite himself, Thorne found himself grinning as his fingers searched for the opening that had to be there. He found it low on the wall. A stone slab had been positioned to block the entrance to the tunnel, but when he shoved hard, the slab gave way.

Pushing again, Thorne made the opening wider and wormed through, into what he knew was a small cave.

It was just as black here, but if memory served, rag torches and a flintbox had been staged a few yards to his right. Fumbling, he found what he was seeking and managed to light a torch in only two tries.

The brilliant flames were temporarily blinding, but showed they were in a low, jagged cavern—secreted deep in the castle dungeons, Thorne knew.

Verra was already standing and offering him a hand. Clasping it, Thorne climbed to his feet and bent to cross the cavern.

With light, the going was much easier and more rapid. On the far wall, they found a miniature wooden door but had to spend several more precious moments searching crannies for the key to unlock it. The door opened into the dungeons proper—vast, cold stone chambers that boasted a score of iron-barred cells for holding prisoners forgotten by civilization, as well as rooms filled with medieval armor and chain mail and even instruments of torture.

Ascending a narrow stone stairway, Thorne found another hidden key and unlocked a heavier door. This one spilled into the castle storerooms and cellars below the keep, and they quickly moved through the warren to another steep flight of steps and yet another door, which was unlocked, since it provided direct access to the kitchens.

After hanging the torch in a wall holder, Thorne drew both pistols from his belt, as did Verra. Then Thorne furtively pushed open the door.

He was unsurprised to find the vast kitchen chamber empty. All the servants—cook and scullery maids and pot boys—would have immediately gone to the castle's defense. A cauldron still bubbled in the massive hearth, while a haunch of beef had been left charring on a spit, suggesting the room had been abandoned in haste.

"We should split up," Thorne murmured. "Double our chances of finding Sir Gawain."

"*Sí,*" Verra agreed.

"I'll take the great hall first, then head outside to the bailey. You start with the rest of this floor, then make your way upstairs."

Nodding, Verra turned around and silently melted away.

Thorne crossed the kitchens and slipped through the open door. He heard no gunfire as he advanced along the stone corridors. The castle was eerily quiet. But when he came to a narrow window, he risked glancing out and saw a seaman armed with a long rifle manning the walls. Forrester's brigands continued to be in control of the bailey, Thorne concluded with a sinking heart.

As he came closer to the great hall, he heard the angry hum of voices. Pausing, he felt his pulse jump with relief when he recognized the familiar deep voice of the Guardians' leader.

Sir Gawain was still alive for the moment, at least.

Thorne crept forward silently. The great hall—the center of activity of any castle—had several entrances, and he was coming from the rear. When he finally reached the arched doorway and eased inside, he crouched in the shadow of a massive column to take stock of the situation.

To come to this pass, the delay he'd prayed for during his time in the tunnels must have occurred . . . a temporary standoff between Forrester's men and the castle defenders. But Forrester had obviously managed to gain the great hall with three of his ruffians.

Halfway down the cavernous hall, a tall man with dark red hair stood training a pistol on Sir Gawain. The baronet had his back to the wall, which was hung with weapons and armaments as well as ancient tapestries.

The elderly Guardian was speaking with great eloquence, evidently playing for time. Yet from the aggressive responses, Forrester's frustration and anger were growing with every moment.

Inhaling a short, steadying breath, Thorne burst into the hall, shouting at Forrester as he ran, intent on attracting attention to himself.

His unexpected action had the desired effect, making Forrester turn instinctively toward the threat and aim his pistol at Thorne.

Instantly Sir Gawain spun and reached up to grasp a knight's shield, yanking it down from the wall. By the time Forrester comprehended enough to shift his focus back to the baronet and fire his pistol, Sir Gawain had brought the shield up in front of his chest. The exploding bullet lodged harmlessly in the polished steel.

Cursing, Forrester pulled a second pistol from his belt, but Sir Gawain threw the shield at him with enough force to send him staggering backward, so that the gun slipped from his grasp to discharge loudly on the stone floor, while the shield skidded, clanging, in Thorne's direction.

Undeterred, Forrester lunged for the wall, grabbing the hilt of a heavy broadsword and tugging it free.

Thorne registered the events in only one corner of his mind as he raced toward the attackers, for he was forced to deal with Forrester's cohorts. One of the ruffians leapt into Thorne's path and received a bullet in the shoulder for his pains.

A second man shot at Thorne and barely missed.

Lowering his shoulder, Thorne threw himself at the brawny seaman, his forward momentum carrying them both crashing to the floor. Thorne ended on top, but unluckily, his remaining pistol skittered away. Raising himself slightly, he drew back his fist and delivered a fierce blow to the jaw of the man beneath him, rendering him unconscious.

Regretting the delay, Thorne looked up in time to see Forrester charge the baronet. Snarling in deadly rage, Forrester raised the broadsword and, aiming for Sir Gawain's head, brought the wicked blade down in a whooshing arc. The aging Guardian barely leapt away in time.

"Forrester!" Thorne shouted again.

Swiveling, Forrester shifted his full attention to Thorne this time, possibly because he considered the younger Guardian a more immediate threat. Raising the broadsword in a savage grip, Forrester rushed his new target.

Unarmed, Thorne rolled to one side and managed to grasp the shield and heft it up to protect his head as he rose to one knee. When the blade struck the polished metal surface, the impact shuddered all the way along his arm and shoulder to his chest.

Forrester pressed his advantage, hammering at the shield in violent fury.

"Thorne!" Sir Gawain suddenly shouted. He had pulled another sword off the wall, although this one was not so broad or heavy. Swiftly he tossed it to Thorne, who caught the hilt deftly and surged to his feet.

"Give over, Forrester!" Thorne advised. "You're finished here."

"Never! I'll have your heart on a spit first. Just as I had that damned Lunsford's. And then I'll kill this whore's get, Olwen."

Rage surged through Thorne at the reminder of Nathaniel's senseless death, while Forrester's taunting tone made him see flaming red. When he heard the clatter of boot heels as Verra ran into the great hall, Thorne jerked up an imperative hand.

"Stay back!" he ordered. "This bastard is *mine*."

Verra complied, merely training his pistols on the one remaining ruffian, who immediately threw up his hands in surrender.

Tossing the shield aside, Thorne lifted his weapon, preparing to do battle. Instantly Forrester engaged swords, the steel clashing with a loud clang.

From the first blows, Thorne could tell his opponent was a skilled swordsman, since no doubt he'd spent years training to enact his revenge. It was also an uneven match because Forrester's blade was significantly heavier. And from the bloodlust shining in his eyes, he wouldn't stop from killing with his bare hands if necessary.

But Thorne was just as determined. He stood his ground, blocking the powerful blows and nimbly fending off the attack.

Suddenly changing tacks, Forrester made a quick feint and lunged, nearly slipping through Thorne's guard; he would have been skewered had he not parried at the last instant.

Disengaging, the two men circled each other. Then Forrester charged again, his eyes fiery and blazing, his sword swinging.

When their blades came together again, sparks flew from the clashing steel.

They fought for what seemed an eternity, with neither man able to achieve the advantage. After perhaps six or seven minutes, Thorne's sword arm had begun to ache, but he could tell Forrester was tiring also, and the sneer on his face was not so obvious.

It was a few moments later when Forrester stumbled.

Thorne pressed the attack, advancing with a flurry of two-handed blows that kept the man off balance and finally sent him sprawling.

Forrester scrambled to right himself, turning onto his back, only to find Thorne standing over him, pressing a deadly sword tip into his throat.

"Surrender or forfeit your life," Thorne hissed.

"You can rot in hell," Forrester spat back.

Evidently prepared to die, he let out a shrieking cry and swung his blade wildly at Thorne's head.

When Thorne jerked back to save himself from decapitation, Forrester leapt to his feet. Rather than continue the battle, however, he turned to flee, sprinting toward the rear of the great hall.

Thorne immediately gave chase. There was nowhere for the traitor to run, but there were countless weapons strewn all over the castle, including the armory and gallery where the Guardians frequently held fencing practice.

Thorne followed closely, yet surprisingly, instead of heading toward the depths of the keep, Forrester suddenly changed course and took the stone stairway that led to the upper reaches of the castle.

Thorne was right behind him. By the time he'd raced up four flights, he was breathing hard and could hear Forrester's ragged breaths, as well.

Staying hard on his quarry's heels, Thorne burst through the door at the top of the stairs and found himself on the wall walk of the keep.

The golden sunlight was overly bright after the cool dimness of the great hall, and it made him blink as he quickly scanned his surroundings. The crenellated parapet to his right was perhaps waist high. Squinting, Thorne looked down, eyeing the long drop to the bailey below. They were directly above the stone courtyard of the stables, he realized.

Beyond the castle walls, he spied the men he'd left to guard the drawbridge, plus a dozen others who were likely the reinforcements Verra had summoned. Just then another fleet group of riders rode up to join them. *Diana,* was Thorne's first thought, before he wisely returned his attention to his opponent.

Forrester had turned to face him, looking crazed, his broadsword raised high. He wasn't entirely cornered yet, but he had to know there was no escape.

Just then Forrester threw down his sword with a clang. Bending low, he gave another wild, shrieking cry and ran full tilt at Thorne.

He hit with the impact of a battering ram, his red head striking the center of Thorne's chest and sending him reeling against the parapet wall behind him.

Thorne crashed into the wall, the air knocked from his lungs, then tumbled backward as Forrester's maniacal dive carried them both over the edge.

Twenty-three

Horror closing off her throat, Diana stared up at the castle battlements as she watched Thorne fall backward over the parapet.

Yet somehow his downward plunge was checked, even as Forrester flew past him, keening the unearthly wail of a man plummeting to his death.

Diana clamped her hand over her mouth to mute the scream welling in her own throat. Thorne had jolted to a halt, his head smashing against the wall at his back. Now he hung suspended upside down, one leg hooked precariously over the edge.

Needles of fear stabbed through her as she watched, afraid to move, afraid even to breathe. For the past hour she had imagined Thorne locked in a deadly battle with Thomas Forrester, but nothing she'd envisioned was as terrifying as this.

Thorne remained there for an endless moment, while Diana wondered frantically why he was waiting so long to try to right himself.

"He must be attempting to regain his bearings," Yates said beside her. "Striking the wall like that no doubt knocked him half senseless and drove the breath from him, as well. And now he's trying to summon his strength."

That must have been the case, Diana realized, for Thorne finally began to move. Reaching up slowly with one hand, he clutched at the stone parapet and managed to wrap his fingers over one of the crenellations.

Then he seemed to take a deep breath and stretched up his other arm, grasping the edge.

Paralyzed, her fists clenched, Diana watched his struggle. She could almost feel his muscles straining as he strove desperately to pull himself up.

"Please, God . . ." Every prayer she could think of clamored in her mind; every nerve and sinew in her body willed him to succeed.

An eternity later, he managed to hook one arm around the crenellation.

He held on for a long moment. Then with a final, fierce effort, he hauled his torso up and heaved himself over the wall.

A sob of relief choking her, Diana squeezed her eyes shut and swayed in the saddle. Her vision was swimming from all the blood rushing to her head, for her heart had suddenly starting beating again.

Through a daze she heard Yates's whispered prayer of gratitude. "Thank God."

"Yes," she rasped so weakly that Yates turned to give her a sharp glance.

He apparently noticed she was shaking, for alarm etched his countenance. "You are quite pale, Diana. Do you want to dismount and lie down?"

She managed a wan smile. "No . . . I am fine . . . really. But that was so terrifying."

"Indeed. But Thorne has had countless close calls

before this, and he always manages to survive. You really shouldn't worry for him."

She bit back a helpless laugh. It would be impossible for her not to worry about Thorne. Now, however, she just needed to see him, to assure herself that he was safe and alive and unharmed.

With Yates, she waited anxiously to gain access to the castle. She was aware that a score of other riders milled about behind her—no doubt islanders summoned to the castle's defense—and she heard Yates speak to several of them. But she paid them little mind. When the drawbridge was lowered a few moments later, Diana was the first one across.

Upon reaching the bailey, she abruptly halted her horse, searching wildly for Thorne. All the fighting seemed to be over. A number of people crowded the courtyard, some of whom were obviously prisoners—Forrester's brigands, of course—and others who must be the castle inhabitants.

To her right, some distance away, she saw a group of men in earnest consultation, and her heart leapt when she recognized Thorne's golden head a moment before he turned and spied her. She spurred her horse toward him, while he broke away at once, moving to intercept her.

When they met, he grasped her mount's bridle to steady her, then reached up to haul Diana from her saddle, into his embrace. She wrapped her arms tightly around his neck as Thorne kissed her fiercely. She was half-laughing, half-sobbing, wholly rejoicing that he was alive as his hot mouth wordlessly gave her the reassurance she so desperately needed.

Even so, she was still trembling when he finally drew back, and she felt another stab of fear upon realizing his forehead was matted with blood.

Thorne's mouth curved ruefully at her gasp. "It's merely a scratch from an encounter with a rock," he assured her. "Otherwise I'm uninjured."

He was doubtless stretching the truth, she could tell from his poor bruised face. But he gave her no time to question him before grasping her elbow and guiding her away from the group of men behind him. "You don't want to see this."

"See what?" Diana asked, reflexively looking over her shoulder.

He had been standing over a prone figure—the body of Thomas Forrester, Diana realized, her stomach lurching. Of course a fall from that tremendous height would have rendered any features beyond recognition. And that could so easily have been Thorne lying there. . . .

She reeled dizzily, clutching his arm, and was grateful for the bracing effect when he planted another firm kiss on her lips.

Just then a silver-haired man came forward, a welcoming smile on his lips. Distractedly, Diana recognized Sir Gawain from her previous visit to the island several months ago.

Graciously he took her gloved hand. "I understand I owe you a major debt, Miss Sheridan. Permit Yates to make you comfortable in the drawing room while we deal with matters here. I will join you as soon as may be, to offer you my gratitude in a more civilized fashion."

"Yes, go with Yates," Thorne seconded. "I mean to return to the harbor to fetch Venus."

"If you will come with me, Diana," Yates said, taking her elbow.

Reluctantly she yielded, accompanying Yates into the castle. But she halted when they reached the great hall, preferring, she explained to her escort, to remain here where she could see what was happening.

Yates was not overjoyed to disregard his superior's orders, but he didn't press her. Instead he led her to an out-of-the-way corner and let her watch.

More people had congregated in the vast hall—some prisoners, some wounded, and some dead, Diana saw with a shudder. There were weapons strewn on the floor and furniture overturned, as if a battle had taken place here.

She could sense the subdued mood that had fallen over the castle, and in the succeeding interval, she learned why: Thorne might have triumphed in killing his foe, and the remainder of Forrester's men had surrendered without a fight, but two of Sir Gawain's servants had been killed defending the castle, and several more were wounded.

During the next hour, the island doctor was sent for to care for the wounded, arrangements were made to bury the dead, and the disposition of the prisoners was decided. And Thorne reportedly returned to the harbor to escort Venus under guard to the castle, since Sir Gawain wanted to interview the madam personally.

The meeting was to be held in the baronet's private study, and Diana was permitted to attend, to her surprise.

Sir Gawain himself escorted her there and settled her in a comfortable sitting area with a glass of wine, along with John Yates and Santos Verra, the jovial Spaniard whom Thorne had said was a former smuggler.

She was barely seated when a striking, dark-haired man sauntered in—an Englishman by the name of Alex Ryder, whom she had met during her first visit to

Cyrene. With his black-eyed gaze and smoldering intensity, Mr. Ryder looked so dangerous that Diana now suspected he was also a Guardian like Thorne.

A few moments later, they were joined by another virile, even taller gentleman, who was introduced to her as Mr. Trey Deverill. Diana was immediately struck by his powerful build, bold gaze, and strong, sun-bronzed features.

Both Ryder and Deverill would make excellent subjects for a portrait, Diana found herself thinking.

Sir Gawain must have been waiting for the newcomer, for he commented immediately, "Excellent timing, Deverill. I have asked Miss Sheridan to give an account of all her dealings with Madam Venus, and I wish you to hear it."

Diana complied readily, telling them everything she could remember about the conversations during their portrait sittings and the pertinent events afterward: Venus's confessions about being an orphan, the nearly lethal coach holdup by the club's two bruisers, Venus's subsequent disappearance from London, Kitty's eavesdropping, capturing the two bruisers who'd admitted Thomas Forrester's intent to kill Thorne and his earlier murder of her cousin Nathaniel.

Sir Gawain's gentle, probing questions showed a keen mind as he drew details from Diana that she forgot she even knew. And he listened carefully to her opinions about how seriously Venus had been involved in her brother Thomas's conspiracy.

When the baronet praised Diana's courage, however, and thanked her for her efforts in behalf of the Guardians, she demurred, saying that anyone would have done the same.

Alex Ryder's crooked smile was amused. "If you think that, Miss Sheridan, you greatly overestimate human nature. I would say Thorne is extremely lucky to have you."

"I am indeed lucky," Thorne drawled in agreement as he entered the study.

Her head lifting abruptly, Diana drank in the sight of him. He still looked the worse for wear, and she found herself upset by the languid, careless smile he gave her. The wine had fortified her, so that her nerves were calmer now, but she shuddered to remember how narrowly he'd escaped death—and here he was, acting as if he'd performed no more strenuous a feat than a stroll in Hyde Park.

Her attention shifted a moment later, though, when Venus was led in by two guards.

Diana surveyed the beautiful madam with sadness, noticing for the first time that her gown was stained and torn; but then Venus would have had nothing else to wear during the long voyage to Cyrene, if she had indeed been forced to accompany Thomas against her will. Additionally, her wrists were raw from her bonds, Diana saw, wincing.

Dismissing the guards, Thorne brought Venus forward and made her known to the baronet and then to the other gentlemen in the room besides Yates— Ryder, Deverill, and Señor Verra.

Sir Gawain was extremely polite to her, offering her wine and waiting until she was settled beside Diana before speaking.

"My condolences on the death of your brother, Miss Forrester."

Dismay flashed in her green eyes, but she met Sir Gawain's gaze steadily. "You may address me as Venus, or madam. Miss Forrester died a long time ago."

"Very well, madam. I am certain you comprehend

our need to investigate the events leading to today's tragedy."

Venus glanced briefly at Thorne, who had remained standing. "Lord Thorne suggested as much. You want a full confession."

"The truth would be preferable. We lost two good men today, with several more injured, one critically."

For the first time she lowered her gaze. "I am truly sorry for that. I did not want it to happen."

"Perhaps you will be so kind as to explain why your brother was so set on achieving my demise."

Absently Venus rubbed her ravaged wrists with her thumbs. "I believe you know why, Sir Gawain. Thomas has always wanted revenge."

"I should like to hear your perspective."

She looked up again to regard him levelly. "It is simple. We hated you. We hated the Guardians, but you most of all, Sir Gawain. We were mere children when you killed our parents. We were sent to toil in work homes, under brutal conditions. You cost us everything: our family, our future, our innocence."

The elderly man gave a soft sigh. "I regret the death of your parents, Madam Venus, but you are laboring under a severe misconception about what actually happened."

A humorless smile twisted her lush mouth. "So Lord Thorne tells me. Apparently my father was the one who killed my mother after taking us all hostage. He refused to surrender and be hanged for treason." She shook her head briefly. "You must forgive me if I have difficulty accepting that account. For twenty years I have believed otherwise."

"Nevertheless, it is the truth. You were a mere child at the time, however, so I can understand how you might have misconstrued events. But pray continue.

You were explaining how your brother was driven by hatred of me, and that you shared his hatred."

"Thomas was all the family I had. When he rescued me from a life of toil and poverty, I was more than willing to follow him."

"How did he become set on destroying the Guardians?"

"His entire life he sought to discover your identities. But it was only four years ago, when you visited London, that he recognized you as the man who led the raid that resulted in our parents' deaths. Then another of your enemies, a Frenchman, identified you as a Guardian. It was then that Thomas hired French agents to learn all he could about you and your fellow Guardians, where you lived, how you functioned, what your vulnerabilities might be."

Observing Venus, Sir Gawain steepled his fingers and pressed them to his lips in grave contemplation. "Tell me about these French agents. I presume they were Bonapartists?"

"Yes. Some of Napoleon's chief delegates. They were nearly as eager for your destruction as my brother was, since the Guardians were responsible for thwarting their goals on numerous occasions. Together with Thomas they hatched a plot to achieve your downfall. Killing you would not only satisfy my brother's need for vengeance, but decapitate the head of your order and cripple its effectiveness, as well."

"But they failed, did they not?"

"Because Napoleon was unexpectedly defeated. After the emperor's abdication last April, Thomas could no longer rely on the French to aid him. And your isolation here on Cyrene made it difficult to gain access to your secrets."

"So last fall he hired two informants to infiltrate

our island society to discover our identities? Danielle and Peter Newham."

Venus nodded. "They were charged with developing a roster of your membership. But Thomas's ultimate goal always was to kill you, Sir Gawain."

"How did Nathaniel Lunsford become involved?"

Venus looked down at her hands once more. "By chance he saw Thomas in the company of a French agent and so began watching for other signs. Nathaniel soon realized my brother was colluding with the French and set about gathering proof for an arrest."

"Which is why your brother killed him?"

"Yes." Her voice was a mere whisper.

"And what role did you play, madam?"

"Yes, tell him," Thorne interrupted. He had propped a shoulder casually against the wall, but his voice was hard. "Tell Sir Gawain what you confided to me a short while ago during our ride here."

Venus gave a faint shudder, but then squared her shoulders, as if steeling herself to admit her guilt. "It was my task to seduce Nathaniel. To learn any secrets I could about the Guardians. We suspected he was one of you because he had traveled to Cyrene before on several occasions." Venus paused. "I regret to say that I played on Nathaniel's tender feelings for me."

"And what secrets did you learn?" the baronet queried softly.

Raising her gaze, she met Sir Gawain's with courage. "I persuaded him to tell me about Cyrene, about his work for the Foreign Office. He thought it was safe to share such confidences, since he had no idea Thomas was my brother. Then Thomas made the mistake of visiting my club twice in one week, and Nathaniel began to fear that we were lovers, that I was in league with Thomas and selling secrets to the

French. The next time Nathaniel shared my bed, he demanded to know what I knew about Thomas and warned me to keep away from him."

"He was attempting to protect you," Thorne interjected.

"I believe so. He wouldn't accuse me without proof. But then he followed Thomas to Sussex and discovered that my brother was hip-deep in treason. Two days after Nathaniel's return to London, Thomas lured him to a rendezvous and murdered him."

Her voice wavered. "His death was a tragedy, and I bear some of the blame. I should have known how Thomas would act when cornered." She turned to look sadly at Diana. "I am so very sorry. Nathaniel had great affection for you and spoke fondly of you."

Diana's throat constricted at this reminder of her dear cousin, but before she could reply, Thorne broke in.

"You never suspected your brother would kill Nathaniel?"

"No," Venus answered. "Thomas lied to me, pretending he only wanted to use Nathaniel to bring down Sir Gawain. I would have tried to stop him had I known."

"But he recently ordered your footmen to kill me. And nearly got Diana killed in the process."

Venus winced. "I know. I regret that terribly. But I had no sway over my brother by then. His hatred had blinded him to all rational thought." She turned to the baronet. "I make no excuses, Sir Gawain. I sought your downfall. But in the end I couldn't continue."

"So what caused your change of heart?" the baronet asked gently.

"I realized that enough blood had been shed. And I

couldn't bear the thought of anyone else dying as Nathaniel Lunsford had."

"You are aware that you committed treason, madam? Some would say you should hang."

"No!" Diana exclaimed without thinking. She bit her lip when she saw the entire company eyeing her. "Forgive me, Sir Gawain, but I have come to know Venus over the past months. She is not evil, certainly nothing like her brother. I don't believe she deserves to hang. I would even venture to say that under similar circumstances, you would have acted as she did. You would have sided with your brother against the very people who killed your parents. Please . . . don't you think she has suffered enough?"

At her impassioned plea, Sir Gawain looked thoughtful. "The question is," he asked Venus slowly, "can you be trusted in future?"

"I *can*," she answered emphatically. "I swear it. If you give me the chance, I will prove it to you."

"There are alternatives to hanging, of course. I could send you to live on a remote island, where you would remain under the Guardians' watchful eye."

"Or she could return to London," Thorne volunteered, "and work in our behalf."

Sir Gawain's faint smile was dry. "You are suggesting that I recruit her to work for the Foreign Office?"

"Precisely. She already knows a great deal about us. And with her gaming club in the heart of London, she has significant opportunities to interact with our enemies. Even more to the point, I have rarely met a more clever adversary than Madam Venus. We would do well to have her on our side."

"Mr. Yates, what is your opinion? Would we be foolish to take such a risk when Madam Venus played a part in Nathaniel's murder and the attempts on Thorne's life?"

John Yates answered with grave reluctance. "I believe the risk would be worthwhile. She did, after all, try to stop her brother this last time."

Sir Gawain glanced at each of the other three men— all of whom offered brief comments of approval— before he returned his attention to Venus. "Could you stomach entering my employment, working for the same man you have despised for so long?"

Venus looked a little taken aback by the proposal, but after a moment, she replied quietly. "I no longer despise you as I once did, Sir Gawain."

Thorne made one other point. "I would be willing to keep a close eye on her in London. If she strays, you can always deal with her then."

Sir Gawain's blue eyes shimmered with humor. "It seems you have a number of advocates, Madam Venus. And I confess, I do feel somewhat responsible for the difficult course your life took. I suspect perhaps we can come to some mutually beneficial arrangement. You will be my guest here until I make my decision." The baronet rose then. "If you will accompany Yates, he will have someone escort you to your chamber . . . and find some appropriate clothing for you, as well."

"Thank you, Sir Gawain," Venus said humbly. There was vast relief in her tone, and when she met Diana's gaze, her green eyes were filled with gratitude. In response, Diana squeezed her hand, offering silent encouragement.

The other gentlemen stood when Venus and Diana did, and they watched as the madam was ushered from the room by Yates.

Thorne waited until the door had shut before eyeing

Sir Gawain. "You have already made your decision, haven't you, sir?"

"Yes." The baronet gave a faint smile. "I am persuaded she deserves the chance to redeem herself in service to the Guardians. But I intend to proceed with caution."

He looked at Alex Ryder. "Mr. Ryder, I wish you to escort Madam Venus to London, where you will keep a close watch on her. More important, you will find several commissions for her to perform."

"With the intent of testing her resolve?" Ryder asked.

"Precisely. I trust you will be able to resist the lovely madam's formidable charms?"

Ryder laughed softly. "I will endeavor to restrain myself."

Sir Gawain's attention then shifted to the tallest gentleman. "Mr. Deverill, if I recall, you have personal business that takes you to London soon?"

"Yes. I thought to sail next week."

"Will you do me the kindness of transporting the lovely madam in your ship?"

"Of course, Sir Gawain."

"Excellent. When you return to Cyrene, we can discuss your next duties. Mr. Deverill," Sir Gawain explained to Diana, "has spent the past year in foreign waters, ridding the seas of pirates. But we are eager for him to rejoin us."

Thus addressed, Diana took the opportunity to express her gratitude. "Sir Gawain, please allow me to thank you for showing Venus such leniency."

"I assure you, the obligation is all mine, Miss Sheridan. You have done us an immense service. Now, I pray you will forgive me. There are several other important matters requiring my attention. And I am certain you and Lord Thorne have your own matters to discuss."

With a gentle smile, he bowed deeply over her hand, then turned away.

Just as Sir Gawain left the study, however, John Yates returned.

Ryder flashed the younger man an amused grin. "I hear you are now leg-shackled to Miss Sheridan's cousin. My condolences."

Yates returned a sheepish smile. "Condolences are not in order in this case. I consider myself extremely fortunate. I thought my suit had utterly failed, but then Miss Lunsford decided she couldn't live without me."

"I wish you happy," Deverill said, his tone somewhat dubious.

"So, Thorne," Ryder interjected wickedly, "when is your wedding to be?"

Thorne's gaze locked with Diana's, the look in his eyes enigmatic. "That is for Miss Sheridan to decide."

He was leaving it to her to break the news that their betrothal was over, Diana realized, feeling a sudden depression at the reminder. But now was not the time to announce their broken engagement.

Yates seemed to agree, for he bowed to her before addressing his friends. "If you will excuse me, I need to return to the ship and fetch my bride. If I know Amy, she will be wild with impatience, wanting to learn how events unfolded."

"Yes," Ryder added, "I must also take my leave and return to interrogating our prisoners. It was a pleasure to meet you, Miss Sheridan. You must be a very special lady to have snared"—he clapped Thorne on the back—"this reckless makebate. I trust you will keep him in line."

"It is certainly a pleasure, Miss Sheridan," Deverill seconded. "If I can help in any way, you need only ask."

"And I, as well, señorita," Verra added.

Diana managed a faint smile of appreciation, but when she turned toward the door, Thorne held up a hand to forestall her. "Wait here for me, will you, love? I need to confer with these three a moment."

Before she could reply, he had followed his colleagues from the study.

Left with little choice, Diana sank down on the settee to await him. It was only a few moments before she suddenly felt a great weariness settle over her.

The worry and uncertainty of the past days, the terror of seeing Thorne nearly die, had left her emotions in shreds, her spirits enervated. But it was the thought of what was to come that filled her with a terrible despondency. Simply put, she faced a bleak, empty future without Thorne.

Feeling the sting of threatening tears, Diana dragged a hand furiously over her eyes. Now that she knew he was safe, she should begin thinking about her next steps, begin making plans to return to London. But the future yawned like a dark, wide chasm before her, and she didn't know if she could bear it.

When Thorne returned a moment later, Diana straightened and set her jaw, trying to swallow the ache in her throat. She didn't want him to see her cry.

To her dismay, he sat beside her on the settee and took her hand in his, sending an unexpected jolt of warmth surging through her. Perhaps he meant to comfort her, but her entire body stiffened at the contact, for his mere touch was pure agony.

"I mean to get you settled," Thorne began, "but we have a few issues to discuss first. Chiefly the matter of where you will stay tonight. Amy will go home with her new husband, of course, and it would be highly improper for you to live alone with me at my villa. I don't intend to offer the gossips any more fodder for scandal."

The knot in Diana's stomach coiled more tightly. Was Thorne saying good-bye to her? Telling her it was time for them to part?

No, her heart cried silently. *I can't.*

Leaving him would be like cutting out her heart.

Taking a deep breath, Diana raised her gaze to his. "I don't care anything about the scandal, Thorne. I want to stay with you."

She felt him go still, felt his searching eyes examining her face.

"As your lover, not your wife," she added in a small voice. "I know you want nothing to do with marriage. And even though you were nobly prepared to sacrifice your freedom out of honor, I can't allow that. But I am willing to stay with you as your mistress."

The sudden silence in the room was palpable. Diana could hear her heart thudding as she waited for his answer.

Thorne's gaze narrowed on her. "There is only one problem," he said mildly. "I could never be content with only an affair."

Feeling a sob well up in her chest, Diana averted her face while she strove for control. She was willing to plead with him, to beg if need be, but she couldn't manage to speak just now without succumbing to tears, and weeping helplessly would only give Thorne a disgust of her.

His fingers tightened around her hand. "Look at me, Diana."

He waited, but she gave a sharp shake of her head, unable to comply.

"I think," he said finally, "I gave you a mistaken impression of my feelings about matrimony. I'm not averse to marriage. I have only been waiting for the right woman. One who could prove my match. You're my match in every way, sweeting. I've known it for some time—since the night we nearly died together in that coach." He paused, his voice dropping to a low murmur. "Until you, I never found a woman I wanted for my wife, one who would face danger at my side. But it took me a while to admit to myself how much I love you."

Not certain she had heard him correctly, Diana turned to stare at him. "You . . . love me?"

"More than I ever thought possible." His mouth curling in a wry smile, he glanced down at their entwined fingers. "It shocked the devil out of me, to tell the truth. I never expected to fall madly in love with anyone, the way I fell madly for you." He brought her hand to his chest, directly over his heart. "I've never felt this yearning ache inside. I've never felt anything so profound."

Speechless, Diana stared at Thorne with amazement and disbelief and a wild, burgeoning joy. She had never let herself imagine such a possibility.

"I must be dreaming," she whispered, feeling tears spill from her eyes. "I never dared hope you could come to love me."

Muttering a low curse, Thorne captured her face in his hands, brushing the wetness away with his thumbs. "You aren't dreaming, sweetheart. My love for you is very, very real. Diana . . ."

He hesitated, his gaze searching her face earnestly. "I only hope to God I can prove myself worthy of you. You were hurt by your first love, but I swear, I will never do the same to you, if you'll only give me the chance. If you can trust your heart to me, I vow on my life, I will never betray you."

Diana felt her own heart wrench at his intensity. The vulnerable look in his eyes, the plea she saw there, told her more than words how utterly sincere his confession was.

Recognizing the fervent feelings that shimmered in the hazel depths, she made a sound that was part sob, part laughter. She wanted Thorne desperately, but the yearning ache inside her, the fierce need that suffused her entire being, was far, far more than desire.

"You already have my heart, Thorne," she whispered. "You have for a long time. It was only when I thought you might die that I realized how badly I've lied to myself. I tried futilely not to love you, but it was impossible."

He squeezed his eyes shut and drew her against him, breathing a soft prayer. "Thank God."

His restraint lasted barely a moment, though. The next instant Thorne wrapped his arms around her tightly and captured her mouth beneath his with a fierceness that stole her breath.

Diana melted in his embrace, clutching the hard muscles of his forearms as he pressed her back on the settee.

He kissed her until she was whimpering with need, his tongue thrusting deep, claiming her, but she returned his passionate caresses with all the tender yearning that was in her heart.

After several breathless, panting moments, Thorne finally tore his mouth away and raised his head to gaze down at her.

"Then you'll marry me for real?" he demanded hoarsely.

It took several heartbeats for Diana to marshal her scattered wits, and his fingers tightened impatiently on her shoulders at the delay.

"*Will* you?"

"Yes," she replied, her own voice husky with desire and need.

A slow, brilliantly devastating smile crept across his lips, and he bent to nibble at hers. "Good, because you won't be leaving this island unless it's as my bride."

When the import of his declaration registered, Diana raised an amused eyebrow at his arrogance. "Is that so? And just how did you plan to stop me?"

"By force, if necessary. I intended to hold you captive and employ all my considerable powers of seduction until you agreed." His grin widened. "But I hoped it wouldn't come to that."

It was Diana's turn to search his face. "Are you truly certain marriage is what you want, Thorne?"

Instantly his expression sobered. "Absolutely, utterly certain, sweeting." A new gleam entered his eyes. "For once my ward was smarter than I. Amy declared she couldn't live without her John, and I don't want to live my life without you. I can't imagine trying."

Diana smiled in misty pleasure. "You truly love me?"

"With every breath I take." He cradled her face in his hands. "You fill the emptiness inside, Diana. You make me complete. You are the other half of me, and I want you for my life's mate . . . for all time, till death do us part."

At his impassioned words, Diana gave an involuntary shudder, unable to help remembering how close she had come to losing him. Her throat tightening as she gazed up at him, she gingerly touched his battered face, tracing the gash on his forehead with her fingertips. "Oh, Thorne, if you had died, I could never have borne it."

He narrowed his gaze, frowning at her with feigned displeasure. "You won't lose me, love. I told you, I want to live to a ripe old age with you and our children."

His declaration gave her pause. "Our . . . children? You want children?"

Thorne's expression softened. "Yes, a whole brood of them, as long as you're their mother. Do you?"

"Yes, very much. I always have. But I never imagined you would want a family."

"Well, you can imagine all you like now. I want a family with you, Diana. I want daughters as incredibly beautiful and talented and special as you are. And I want sons with a bit of the devil in them, who can make me proud." The light of laughter filled his hazel eyes. "Besides, it's time I gave my father the heir he so badly craves."

His amusement faded. "Diana . . . I can't give up the Guardians, but I promise you, I intend to become more cautious in my work. I have no interest in ever risking my life so recklessly again."

Holding his gaze, she ran her fingers over his lips. "I would never ask you to give up the Guardians. I can see it's your life's calling."

It was true, she thought solemnly. The Guardians were in Thorne's blood. They were part of him, and part of what made her love him so deeply.

He couldn't give them up, she knew, any more than she could abandon her passion for her art. And she instinctively understood his need for excitement, for danger, for the challenge of matching wits with the enemy. "I realize how important the Guardians are to you. And I know how you thrive on danger."

His lips pressed together in a mild grimace. "Perhaps so—in my past. But it's no longer enough. I must have *you*, Diana. Loving you makes me feel more alive than any amount of danger ever did."

"Oh, Thorne . . ." With a sigh, she lifted her mouth for his kiss. Life with Thorne would never be calm and peaceful, she knew. Rather it would be exciting and dangerous and filled with challenge. But she was prepared to risk it.

She was ready to risk her heart again, as well. She had no doubt that Thorne would keep it safe. Her arms trailed up his back, holding him now with a desperate strength. She wanted his love, wanted a true marriage with him. He gave her unalloyed sensual joy, but far more than that, he gave her heart joy.

For a long moment Thorne responded to her fervent passion. Then abruptly, he gave a groan and drew back, putting a judicious distance between them on the settee.

"I could take you here and now," he told her gruffly, "but I've sworn to restrain myself until we're wed. I would like the ceremony to be tomorrow morning, but out of respect, we'll have to delay a few days to bury those who died today. I'll arrange for the island vicar to marry us by week's end, though. We'll make use of the special license I obtained in London, so we don't have to wait to call the banns. I mean for us to say our vows before you can change your mind."

With a wry smile, Diana sat up, straightening her gown and her disheveled hair. "You needn't worry. I have no intention of changing my mind. I just hope you are certain—"

Her words were abruptly cut off as, unable to resist, Thorne pulled her back into his arms for another devastating kiss.

He was damned certain he wanted Diana for his wife. She was the woman he'd wanted all his life, the only one he would ever want.

She challenged him—his mind, his senses, his heart. She filled his waking thoughts as she filled his dreams.

And he knew he would spend every day of his life thanking the Fates that he had found her.

Epilogue

THE ISLE OF CYRENE
JUNE 1815

This evening's crimson-gold sky would make another magnificent landscape, Diana reflected with delight, leaning back against her new husband's strong chest. She stood with Thorne on the bluffs behind his villa, his arms wrapped lightly around her shoulders, her heart full.

Since their marriage nearly two weeks ago, it had become a nightly ritual to watch the day fade to dusk over the azure sea.

In the whole of her life, Diana had never known such sensual enchantment; the whisper of waves breaking on the rocky shore below; the cooling sea breeze caressing her face, swaying the boughs of the nearby carob tree; the press of Thorne's lips against her hair; the steady cadence of his heartbeat resonating through her, matching her own.

They were lovers in paradise, and she had cherished every moment.

They'd spent much of the past two weeks exploring

the island's splendor, riding across golden valleys and up wooded mountain slopes, ambling barefoot along narrow, silken beaches and bathing in secluded coves. But mainly, they'd simply enjoyed the intimate pleasures of learning each other as man and wife. Earlier tonight they'd dined in the courtyard of Thorne's villa, serenaded by the trickling fountain of Cyrene and her lion, before walking hand in hand out to the bluffs overlooking the sea.

When the moon rose on the horizon, turning the vast Mediterranean to a shimmering expanse of dark silver, Diana sighed with contentment. The serene vista was utterly spellbinding.

"It is so incredibly beautiful here," she said finally.

"Not as beautiful as my lovely bride," Thorne responded.

Hearing the sensuality lacing his voice, Diana shivered in anticipation. In a short while, she knew, Thorne would sweep her away to a world of searing passion, as he had every night since they'd consummated their marriage.

Until their nuptials, Diana had stayed with Lady Isabella Wilde, an elegant, high-spirited Spanish noblewoman with a delightful lust for life and a penchant for creating scandals of her own.

After the church ceremony, Sir Gawain had held a large wedding breakfast and ball at Olwen Castle, with a great number of Cyrene's gentry in attendance, since Thorne was eager to show off his bride to island society.

Venus had been permitted to join the wedding festivities before sailing for London the following day, escorted by the dangerous-looking Alex Ryder and the bold, intriguing adventurer, Trey Deverill.

Diana had danced with both men at the ball. She'd

also been partnered by the Earl of Hawkhurst, a nobleman with a brooding hint of mystery in his piercing eyes, who owned a magnificent breeding stable on Cyrene. Upon witnessing their camaraderie with her new husband, Diana had been struck by how similar the Guardians were—all extraordinary, vital men dedicated to a noble cause.

A few of their members were women, however. In fact, Thorne had delayed their own return to London so Diana could meet two of his closest friends—Caro and Max Leighton—who were currently in Belgium. A former cavalry officer, Max had rejoined the army this past April in hopes of vanquishing Napoleon Bonaparte once and for all. A skilled healer, Caro had gone with her husband to be at his side and to nurse those wounded in the expected confrontation.

Two days ago, a courier had reached Cyrene with word of the Allied victory. Finally, after decades of war, the conflict had culminated in a terrible battle in a field near the village of Waterloo, but Caro and Max had made it safely through.

The whole island had rejoiced, including Diana, although she'd found herself wishing her cousin Nathaniel could have been present to share the celebrations.

"What are you thinking?" Thorne murmured in her ear, so attuned to her that he could sense her mood.

"I was remembering the memorial service yesterday. How special it was. How much it meant to me."

"It meant a great deal to me, also," Thorne admitted softly.

They'd held a memorial observance for Nathaniel yesterday in the terrace gardens, dedicating a new fountain to him. Two dozen people had attended, several of whom Diana knew were Guardians.

Reaching down to clasp Thorne's hand, she let her head fall back to rest against his shoulder. She would miss her cousin always, but Thorne had vowed to name their firstborn son after Nathaniel.

"I never realized Nathaniel was secretly a Guardian," Diana remarked, "although I suppose I should have. I always admired him immensely. He was my childhood champion, my gallant knight. I adored him as much as I could have any brother."

"Well, you can adore me now," Thorne said, brushing his lips against her nape.

"I already do."

She did adore him, Diana thought with a smile. And her admiration for him had only risen since she'd learned more about the Guardians of the Sword. The tale of how the order had been formed by the outcast followers of an ancient, legendary leader awed her.

Turning in Thorne's arms, she planted a light kiss on his lips. "You know very well that I am mad with love for you."

"I like the sound of that, wife. But I think I need a more personal demonstration. It has been far too long since last night."

Taking her hand with sudden urgency, Thorne headed toward the villa, tugging Diana along behind him. Laughing at his impatience, she willingly followed him through the lush terrace gardens and climbed the outer stairs leading to the gallery.

Pausing outside the master bedchamber, Thorne suddenly bent and scooped Diana up in his arms, making her gasp with more laughter. Unrepentant, he carried her inside and gave her a long, lingering kiss as he lowered her feet to the floor.

"So," he asked huskily against her lips, "how may I be of service tonight, love? Shall I paint you?"

Diana's reply was just as husky. "Not tonight, I think."

"But you must admit I am becoming quite a proficient artist."

"That you are," she agreed, loving the teasing light in his hazel eyes.

Last week when Thorne demanded a private sitting in the studio he'd created for her use, he'd used a sable brush to paint her body with four kinds of berry juice and then licked off every delicious drop. She would never again pick up a brush without thinking of him—which was precisely what the rogue intended, she knew.

"For tonight," Diana murmured, reaching up to remove his elegant cravat, "your proficiency as a lover will more than suffice."

They undressed each other slowly by the glow of candlelight, lingering to taste and touch. The fierce craving was still there, but the urgency had muted with the knowledge that they had all the time in the world.

When they were both nude, Thorne led Diana to the high bed and laid her down on the pale sheets.

"This has been my fantasy forever," he said, stretching out beside her. "Seducing you to my bed where I can ravish you to my heart's content."

Amused, Diana raised her arms to loop around his neck. "If I remember, you didn't have to work very hard to seduce me."

"The devil I didn't. You led me on a frustrating chase for months. And when I thought you still loved that bastard . . . I wanted to slay him with my bare hands."

Shaking her head, she met her husband's gaze steadily. "My other love died a long time ago, Thorne. And even then it was more girlish infatuation than true love. It was nothing like what I feel for you."

"Perhaps so, but to reassure me, you'll need to declare your undying love for me every day for the rest of our lives."

Diana smiled. "I think I could manage that."

His hand moved to cover her breast, his warm palm stroking. But then he suddenly paused, shutting his eyes and shuddering, as if remembering something dire. "To think how close we came to never finding each other. Thank God for your uncle. I'll always be eternally grateful to him for ending your elopement."

"So will I."

He gave her a soul-stopping smile, before his mouth turned wry. "And I suppose I owe my father a debt of thanks as well, damn his infernal interfering. Had he not been so adamant about seeing me wed, I would still be searching for you." Thorne's expression turned fervent as he bent to kiss her. "I've been waiting half my lifetime for you, Diana."

She had been waiting her entire life for him, she thought dreamily as she surrendered to the hungry plundering of his mouth. Thorne was every wonderful thing she had ever wanted—protector, lover, husband. . . .

Fierce joy blazed through her as he settled his strong, virile body over hers. She loved him so much, she trembled with it. When he filled his hands with her breasts and spread her thighs with his own, she opened fully to him, welcoming him with all the yearning inside her.

Their bodies joined, he surged heavily into her,

moving in an exquisite, relentless cadence, letting her know the pounding rhythm of his heartbeat.

Passion and pleasure, need and desire, all merged into one, the lines between giving and receiving blurring and melding, their powerful feelings of love as unbreakable as the marriage vows that now bound them together for life.

She shattered with him stroking deeply inside her, and then he came in his own fierce explosion, filling her with his seed as she wept soft, mindless cries of rapture.

Afterward Thorne lay with Diana in his arms, her cheek pressed over his heart, her dark hair spilling like a mantle over his skin. He felt utterly sated and content. Every time he made love to her, he felt as if he splintered in a thousand pieces, but then each and every time, she made him whole again.

Completeness. That was what he had missed all his life. He'd enjoyed a full, challenging existence before Diana, but loving her had brought brand-new meaning to the word *living*. To the word *fulfillment*. She was indeed his match, body and heart and soul.

She brought him more joy and contentment than he'd ever known, and he wanted it to last forever.

Tenderly Thorne pressed his lips against her hair and shut his eyes with a sigh. "My lovely wife . . ." he murmured, savoring the sweetness of it.

He must have dozed, but some subconscious part of him missed her warmth, for he gradually became aware that Diana was no longer lying in his arms.

When he opened his eyes, it was to find her sitting up in bed, her hair swirling around her bare breasts, candlelight glowing over her pale skin. Her vibrant loveliness not only made him ache, but instantly aroused him again.

Shifting his gaze lower, Thorne realized that she held a sketch pad in her lap and a pencil in her hand. Her teeth were worrying her lower lip while she frowned in concentration as she drew.

When her attention remained wholly focused on her art, he reached out to touch her bare hip. "What are you doing, love?"

Her frown disappearing, she turned her head to gaze down at him. "A preliminary sketch for a new portrait of you. I want to capture the look."

"What look?"

"Here, see for yourself."

Diana passed the pad to him.

Thorne pushed himself up on one elbow to study it. The sketch showed him fully nude, his hair wind-blown like many of her others. But his expression was different this time. She had caught a look of love and passion and joy in his eyes.

He nodded slowly in approval. "You've captured exactly how I feel about our marriage."

"It's how I feel, as well."

"I know," he said, his lips curving in a very male smile. "This is the same expression I see on your face every time you look at me."

"Is it?" Diana asked curiously.

"Exactly." Studying the sketch again, he frowned. "But there is one major problem."

"What problem?"

"This rendering is solely of me. I look lonely there all by myself. You should be in this sketch with me."

Her mouth quirked with laughter as she held out her hand. "Very well, let me have it."

"Later, love." Thorne tossed the pad on the floor and drew Diana down to him for another passionate kiss. "Your art can wait, but I cannot."

Please read on for a sneak peek at
Trey Deverill's story, the next breathtaking volume in
Nicole Jordan's Paradise series.
Coming in Summer 2005.

LONDON
APRIL 1811

Her first sight of the wicked, dashing adventurer Trey Deverill startled Antonia Maitland immensely, for he was unmistakably, breathtakingly nude.

Seeing his unclothed body was purely accidental, of course.

Glad to be home from her select boarding academy for a spring holiday, Antonia handed her bonnet and gloves over to the waiting butler and turned toward the map room, where her father oversaw his vast shipping empire. She was eager to see him for the first time in over a month.

"I believe you will find Mr. Maitland upstairs, Miss Maitland," the butler intoned. "Possibly in the gallery."

"Thank you," she replied, knowing her father must be communing with the portrait of his beloved late wife.

Antonia ran up the wide, sweeping staircase and hurried along the elegant east wing of the mansion. Ten years ago, shortly before her mother's unexpected death in childbirth, Samuel Maitland had spared no expense to build the grand residence in a newly fashionable district of London just south of Mayfair. But his favorite room was the portrait gallery, where he kept his wife's memory alive.

Antonia's current favorite room was the luxurious, newfangled bathing chamber, located at the far end of the corridor. When she saw her father's valet exit the room and disappear around the corner, she almost sighed in anticipation of a hot bath. Upon reaching the corridor's end, she saw that the door had been left partway open. But when absently she glanced inside, she stopped short.

A man had just stepped from the large oval copper tub.

A sleekly muscular, powerfully built man.

A shockingly nude man.

She could see the side of his tall form—his bronzed back and taut buttocks, his lean hips and long sinewed legs, all streaming with water. Suddenly breathless, she stood riveted at the sight of his body: hard muscled, vital, beautiful, except for the disfiguring scars on his torso. . . .

As if sensing her presence, he lifted his head alertly and swung toward her, giving her a fuller view of his loins.

"Oh, my . . ." Antonia murmured, startled and fascinated at the same time.

Swiftly she jerked her eyes away from that forbidden masculine territory, only to have her gaze roam helplessly back up his body. In all of her sixteen years she had never seen anything so stunning as this man. Or magnificent. Nor had she experienced such a purely, primal feminine reaction.

Heat flooded her skin, and she felt a sudden, shocking warmth between her thighs.

When she managed to drag her gaze higher, she realized that his face was as sinfully handsome as the rest of him. But it was more his striking, sea-green eyes beneath slashing brows that gave him such a bold and wicked appeal.

When those clear green eyes locked with hers, Antonia felt fresh heat sear along all her nerve endings.

He reached for a towel to cover himself and draped the linen around his lean hips. "I beg your pardon."

Realizing she had been staring witlessly, she blushed to the roots of her dark red hair and stammered a reply. "No— It was entirely my fault— I should not be here. . . ."

"Miss Maitland, I presume?"

"Yes. . . . Who are you?"

At her bluntness, a crooked smile flashed across his mouth. "Trey Deverill," he replied to her question, watching her expression for a reaction.

She gave him one; her eyebrows shot up as she recognized the name. She'd heard tales of the notorious Trey Deverill over the years—from various shipping merchants and sea captains, and from her father as well. Deverill was an adventurer and explorer, renowned in particular for battling pirates on the high seas.

She had often imagined what he was like, but given his celebrated reputation, he was younger than she'd expected. And in the flesh, he was far more . . . *vital* than her fantasies.

Deploring the direction her mind was taking, Antonia cleared her throat to compose herself and spoke, hoping to sound more mature than a green schoolgirl. "Forgive me for my rudeness, Mr. Deverill. It was merely a shock to find you . . . like this. I am not normally so easily flustered."

"Understandable under the circumstances," he observed, amusement glinting in his remarkable eyes.

He, on the other hand, seemed not the least embarrassed, she noted. Or inhibited. No doubt he was fully aware of the effect he had on females. On *her*. He stood at his ease, his head cocked to one side, contemplating her.

Or perhaps he was merely waiting politely for her to cease gawking and leave.

"Would you oblige me by shutting the door?" he finally said.

"Yes ... certainly." Coming to her senses at last, Antonia reached forward for the door handle.

"Oh, and Miss Maitland?"

She tensed, wondering what he meant to say. "Yes?"

"I don't think we should mention this unfortunate encounter to your father. He would skin me alive for compromising you."

Her blush only heightened, if that was possible. "Believe me, sir, I have no intention of mentioning this to *anyone*, most especially my father."

Firmly shutting the door, Antonia hurried away to resume her interrupted search for her father, determined to try to forget the decidedly scandalous encounter with the exciting adventurer.

Yet as she fled, Antonia knew without a doubt that the wicked, breathtaking image of Trey Deverill's body would be indelibly etched in her memory forever.

LONDON
JUNE 1815

With a start, Antonia awakened from a dream, her skin burning, her body shivering with longing. In the dim light of early morning, she lay in bed, tangled in her sheets, aching for the elusive fulfillment that had once again drifted just out of reach.

Giving a sigh of frustration, Antonia rolled onto her back to stare up at the canopy overhead. The dream always ended the same way—with a disappointing emptiness that left her aching and unfulfilled.

As a girl she'd had lovely dreams of a dashing pirate who carried her off on a glorious adventure. Then she'd met Deverill and tasted his stunning kiss. From that point on, he had become the sole focus of her dreams. For four years now she'd imagined him making love to her, sweeping her to a world of dark desire and searing pleasure.

Yet she was only tormenting herself by dwelling on him this way. And now that Deverill had returned to London in the flesh, it was imperative that she quell her wanton imaginings, or she would never be able to again look him in the eye.

With another sigh, this one of self-disgust, Antonia threw off the covers and rose to dress for her usual morning ride.

She was still feeling restless and out of sorts by the time she left the house, although the bright, sunny summer morning raised her spirits a little as she descended the front steps of the elegant mansion. Her horse and groom awaited her in the drive, but her thoughts were distracted enough that she noticed nothing else until she came face-to-face with the very object of her wicked fantasies.

Antonia halted abruptly, her eyes widening. With complete nonchalance, Trey Deverill leaned against the stone-and-ironwork livery post, watching her, his arms folded over his broad chest, one highly polished boot crossed over the other. He was dressed for riding in a tailored, bottle-green coat that reflected the green in his eyes, and he wore a tall beaver hat over his thick, unruly hair that seemed to tame his rakish good looks the slightest degree.

For a moment, Antonia simply stared at his strong, rugged features. It was disconcerting to find him on her doorstep, and even more disconcerting to remember how thoroughly he had occupied her thoughts only a short time ago. Could he tell that she'd been entertaining erotic visions of him all morning long? That vivid dreams of him had haunted her sleep last night and so many other nights?

Closing the final distance between them, she forced herself to offer him a calm greeting. "Were you waiting for me, Mr. Deverill?"

"No, I thought I would call on the milkmaid," he replied, a lazy, amused charm in his sea-green eyes. "Of course I was waiting for you, sweeting."

Beyond him, Antonia saw, her groom stood holding the bridles of her skittish bay mare along with his own hack, while a strapping chestnut stood patiently nearby, chewing the bit—evidently Deverill's mount, she deduced.

"How did you know to expect me? I suppose Mrs. Peeke told you I usually enjoy a daily ride in the park?"

Deverill shrugged. "It wasn't difficult to determine your routine." He glanced at her solitary groom. "Your betrothed isn't accompanying you, I see."

"He doesn't care to rise so early," Antonia answered truthfully. "Nor is he as fond of riding as I am."

"Good. I prefer to enjoy your company uninterrupted."

Antonia arched an eyebrow. "I don't recall inviting you, Mr. Deverill."

His smile was innocent and devilish at the same time. "You didn't. But I have a business matter to discuss with you that wasn't appropriate to introduce at the ball last night."

Antonia didn't know whether to believe him, but she made no further protest. A morning ride in Hyde Park with Deverill, chaperoned by her groom, was unexceptional, and since he wasn't the kind of man to give up, she suspected she would do better to give in gracefully now and get any conversation over with.

She hadn't counted on Deverill touching her, though. When she went to mount, he ignored her groom and took hold of her waist. Antonia drew a sharp breath, her spine tensing as her body eagerly responded to the memory his touch evoked. For a moment their eyes locked, and she felt certain Deverill understood exactly how he affected her. Then, with an ease that betrayed immense physical strength, he lifted her onto her sidesaddle.

A desperate wedding.
A night of passion.
A love that could last forever. . . .

The Passion
A Novel
by Nicole Jordan

To escape marriage to a despised man twice her age, Lady Aurora Demming makes a scandalous arrangement with Nicholas Sabine, a dangerously hand-some American facing execution for murder and piracy. She agrees to become his wife for one day...and one glorious, intoxicating night. Widowed, Aurora returns to London society with Nicholas's orphaned sister at her side to face a lifetime without love—until her "dead" husband returns, insisting that she honor their vows and haunting her dreams with promises of forbidden desire....

Published by Ivy Books
Available wherever books are sold